PERFECT RUIN

THE PERFECT SERIES

PERFECT ILLUSION
PERFECT ADDICTION
PERFECT RUIN
PERFECT REDEMPTION
SUMMER 2024

Claudia Tan

PERFECT RUIN

The PERFECT *Series*

CLAUDIA TAN

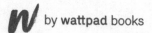

by **wattpad** books

An imprint of Wattpad WEBTOON Book Group

Copyright© 2023 Claudia Tan
All rights reserved.

36 Wellington Street E., Suite 200, Toronto, ON, M5E 1C7, Canada

www.wattpad.com

First W by Wattpad Books edition: March 2023

ISBN 978-1-99025-963-0 (Trade Paperback original)
ISBN 978-1-99025-964-7 (eBook edition)

Names, characters, places, and incidents featured in this publication are either the product of the author's imagination or are used fictitiously. Any resemblance to actual persons (living or dead), events, institutions, or locales, without satiric intent, is coincidental.

Library and Archives Canada Cataloguing in Publication information is available upon request.

Printed and bound in Canada

1 3 5 7 9 10 8 6 4 2

Cover design by Mumtaz Mustafa
Images © Arthurstudio-10 via Shutterstock
Author Photo by Louise Chan

Dedicated to every girl who's never felt enough for a man.

Men have a tendency to call women crazy.
Who do they think made them this way?

PROLOGUE

I'm certain I'm not the only girl in the world who was told I'd have to kiss a lot of frogs to get to The One. Capital *O*.

Aka my other half.

Aka the great love of my life.

I didn't believe there was someone like that out there for me. But there was, cheesy as it sounds. I wouldn't call him my soulmate in the way that a Disney princess talks about meeting Prince Charming in a predestined, stars-are-aligned kind of way. But he's perfect for me.

Kayden is every bit mine, as I am his. We fell deeply in love, and we fight hard for our relationship every day. It can get ugly at times, but we always learn from our mistakes, pick ourselves up, and do better. We swore by it. There was no way we were going to let a love like this go. We harbor both great passion and mutual respect, and our souls align so perfectly sometimes I think it'd be impossible to find a more suited match than ours. I have found the perfect ending to my story. That is done and dusted, and I'm satisfied with how we achieved it.

But unfortunately for you, this isn't that story.

This is the story of the one *before* The One.

The all-consuming one. The passionate and fiery one. The one I couldn't seem to let go of for years, no matter how much I cried over him, how much of my soul was corrupted by his sins. Every part, every flaw, every ounce of his darkness, I embraced like it was my own.

That was Jax to me for almost three years.

I loved him.

I hated him.

I hated that I loved him, because he sure as hell didn't deserve my love.

Every time I tried to fix him, he broke me.

Every time I kept him warm, he set me on fire.

But it wasn't that simple for us. I couldn't just leave. There were times when I wanted to, of course, but there was always a more powerful reason for me not to.

And it wasn't like the blame was all on him; there were times I went too far too. Did things I'm not proud of.

Like they say, love makes you do ugly things.

And together, we were the ugliest we ever were.

But I was convinced that the beautiful came with the ugly. That it was just a common side effect of romance. A small symptom of reality.

But now, looking back, it was much more than that.

It was a whole malignant tumor that neither of us even felt until years later.

So if being with Jax Deneris taught me a very valuable lesson, it's this:

If it ruins you,

it probably isn't love.

PART ONE
The Beginning of the End

ONE

Two and a Half Years Ago

It smells like shit in here.

A combination of sweat, alcohol, and smoke billows around in a thick, cloudy haze. Harsh spotlights glare down on us, startling our sight as we weave through the mass of sweaty, vibrant bodies.

Trying to get my vision back, I blink a couple of times as Dakota tugs me forward. Since the three of us are holding hands, my sister, Beth, gets pulled along as well. We're desperate to stick together. This isn't exactly our scene, and I'm not sure what we'd do if we got separated tonight. It feels dangerous in here. Lethal.

"We're almost there!" Dakota screams. Even though we're only a few feet away from each other, the crowd's earsplitting screams make it so I can barely hear what she says. But I nod along anyway, because she seems like she knows where she's going, and I'd be a fool to veer down my own path.

Cheers and hollers echo from the crowd and grow louder in anticipation of the looming fight.

Considering it's housing an illegal sport, I'm surprised at how huge the warehouse is. After we received a sketchy text message, it took us forty minutes to get to the abandoned warehouse outside the city. And even then, there was still a rather long line to get inside. The sheer commitment it takes just to watch blood spill in the ring is truly astounding.

I'm also surprised by the turnout. There're at least a hundred people milling about in the warehouse tonight. And I'm fairly certain I saw some cops cheering along with the crowd.

Guess I don't have to worry about getting arrested tonight.

A sense of discomfort coils around my spine as we push through the energetic crowd. I never thought I'd be spending my first weekend of college attending an underground fight. Ever since Dakota escaped to college with me and Trevor, she's been obsessed with the scene. When she found out that they were resuming the fights after the summer break, she knew she had to cross this off her college bucket list.

I, on the other hand, have never expressed much interest in the underground. There's something about watching men beat each other to near unconsciousness in a sketchy, greasy basement somewhere that makes my stomach churn. So when Dakota asked if we wanted to join her as spectators, I wasn't exactly jumping with joy.

"Trust me, you really don't want to miss this fight, ladies," Dakota said with a waggle of her eyebrows while she signed us up for tonight. Clearly I was the only one in the group who didn't get the memo because the second Dakota said those words, Beth let out the most excited squeal that I've ever heard from her.

When I asked Dakota what she meant, she told me, in a tone that made it sound obvious, "Jax is on the roster, silly."

As if that meant anything to me.

After some prodding, I did eventually manage to squeeze out some information from her and Beth. Apparently, a few weeks ago, word got around campus that a newbie named Jax had delivered the first KO of the year, knocking out Perez Mills. That was a big deal because Mills is the undefeated champion of the underground, winning the title for four years straight before Jax knocked him out in a one-off fight, sealing Perez's fate with a spinning heel kick to his face.

The shock that reverberated through the crowd was apparently cataclysmic.

I tried to imagine what a spinning heel kick would look like on the way over here, since I've never witnessed an actual fight in my life, and the only thing I could picture was someone's leg flying around like an out-of-control fidget spinner.

Despite my lack of knowledge about the fighting world, I do know that if Jax can make the undefeated champion tap out like that, he must be a damn good fighter. Revolutionary, even.

"Dee!" I scream. Dakota's pulling at my wrist so hard that it hurts. I cut through a couple making out in front of me and mumble a quick apology for interrupting them.

Just when I think I'll never know what normal air cycling through my lungs feels like again, Dakota jerks me forward, hard, and I stumble into an open area. When I peer over the rails, I expect to see a kickboxing ring, but instead it's an octagonal cage, which means that this might not be just regular *Rocky* shit. The crowd has surged in volume now. The fight is about to start.

"You all right?" Dakota asks me, her long dark hair whipping at my face as she turns around to inspect me. "Sorry."

"It's fine," I say, wrapping my arms around myself.

Behind me, Beth makes a disgusted face and pinches her nose with her fingers. "It smells so bad in here."

"You get used to it." Dakota shrugs. "Besides, it's totally worth it. We have such a good view of the cage! And you know what that means: direct view of the hotties."

"Dude, you have a boyfriend," I say with a laugh.

"We're in a healthy open relationship," she explains matter-of-factly. "Trevor will understand if I ogle hot dudes. Hell, he'd probably be okay if I hooked up with one of them tonight."

I smile, hoping that she's right about that. An open relationship isn't for me, but if it works for them, then who am I to judge?

"I wish we could come here every weekend," Beth gushes, her chubby cheeks pink. "I bet they get hotter and hotter every week, especially when they have to train all the time now to prepare for the titles."

"You're so right. Might just nab me one of them after the fight tonight." Dakota winks at my sister.

Beth laughs, and they lean into each other to discuss which underground fighters they'd like to approach.

I wish I could share their brazen intentions toward some of these men. Most of the time, I'm up for it too. But the only thing I can seem to focus on right now is the discomfort slithering up my spine as more people shove their way into the warehouse. The girl with the pink shaved head beside me offers me what looks like a blunt, but I politely decline. Not a good idea for me to get high for the first time here. Danger feels like it's sneaking around every corner, and I should try to stay alert to keep me, Beth, and Dakota safe.

As more familiar faces poke up from the crowd—a couple of high school friends I haven't seen since I graduated in the summer, a few boys from a freshman party I had the displeasure of attending a couple of days ago—I'm surprised by how much of an open secret the underground is in Boston. Dakota explains to me that it's because Breaking Point, the gym that hosts the tournament, has an unspoken agreement with the Boston Police Department, and many officers from the force participate in these fights. Breaking Point allows them to get a good kick out of illegally beating up dudes, and in return the BPD turns a blind eye to the gym's affairs.

Corruption at its finest.

I look over my shoulder to see several men busy making bets with the bookie about who's going to win tonight. And from what I overhear from a couple of spectators standing behind me, a lot of them have bet big money on that Jax guy.

"I can't wait to see Jax," I hear Beth gush. She tugs on my arm excitedly, her blue eyes shining bright with glee. "I saw him once in Caffeinated, but I was too shy to ask him for a picture."

Beth is obsessed with Jax. I don't know what her deal is, but she's been crazy for him ever since she started getting into all of this underground madness with Dakota. She'll jump at any chance to see him.

Personally, I don't get the hype. Is he really that hot? Beth has showed me pictures of him on his social media before. He's all right looking. Certainly not unattractive, but he's no early-'90s Brad Pitt either.

"Hey, if you want, I can bring you backstage later to meet him!" Dakota tells Beth, and she squeals even more. The sound feels like spikes driving into my ears.

"You can do that?" my sister asks, her expression glimmering with hope.

"Sure I can. My brother's fighting tonight. I should be able to get back there." Dakota winks at her.

Her older brother, Zach, dubbed himself The Sledgehammer in the cage. There's not a lot of talk about him tonight since it's his first fight, but I hope he does well.

"You betting tonight?" I ask Dakota.

"Hell, yeah, I am," Dakota says, wriggling her eyebrows at me. "I've got five hundred bucks on Jax."

"What?" I don't think I heard that correctly. "That's a lot of money."

"Money that I'll double if he wins!" she exclaims.

I stifle a laugh. I'm amazed at just how confident Dakota is that she's going to earn bank tonight. I don't know any fighter well enough to bet on them; perhaps if I end up coming back, I just might.

"You're betting on Zach too, right?" I ask Dakota.

She merely laughs. "God, no. I ain't investing a single penny in him," she tells me flippantly. "I've seen him fight before. He's gonna get beat up so bad. I already told Mom to be on standby in case he gets hospitalized tonight."

Christ.

Before I can say anything else, the crowd explodes as the announcer steps into the ring. He has long, stringy hair, and he's wearing a rhinestone-encrusted suit, which makes me wonder how much he earns doing this. He's no low-wage earner, that's for sure. Banking all that blood money, I suppose.

"Welcome to the vortex, fuckers!" the guy screams into the megaphone. "The only rule that exists here is that there are *no* rules! So let's. Get. Real. Toniiiiiiggghtt!"

More cheers and leg stomping flare from the crowd. Beside me, Beth and Dakota join in, screaming their hearts out. I cross my arms and close my eyes, immediately regretting my decision to come here in the first place.

"All right, all right! Now, the fight you've all been waiting for tonight! On your right, we've got your favorite prince of ghouls, our season regular, Damien 'The Beast' Wells!"

A few cheers erupt but are drowned out by boos when Damien emerges from the right side in a dark-gray robe. He's a stocky figure with Viking tattoos splattered across his chest and crawling up the shaved sides of his head. His expressions are animated—he's growling and huffing like he's the Big Bad Wolf of the cage.

The guy with the megaphone lets out a low whistle. "Man! He's going to have to give everything he's got tonight because he's going to be taking on *a legend*! Yeah, that's right, ladies and gentlemen! Over to your left, we have the guy who took down our reigning king, Perez, a few weeks ago, the *it* guy to watch out for this season, Jax 'Deadbeat' Denerisssssss!"

The warehouse explodes. Everyone's yelling and screaming his name. Girls are throwing their panties at the ring. I turn to Beth and shoot her a warning glare, telling her not to be an idiot. Everyone's beating their chests and hollering, "Dead-beat! Dead-beat! Dead-beat! Dead-beat!" in unison. Beth and

Dakota join in, drumming their chests and yelling along with the cultlike chant.

Finally, a shadow emerges from the left side of the cage. My jaw nearly drops to the ground and shatters when I spot him.

A black satin robe drapes over Jax's body, and it fits him so well it looks almost like a second skin. His untamed mass of golden hair rests on his sexy, chiseled face, with some strands falling past his striking brown eyes. I wish he wasn't hiding them because they're the best part of him. As if he hears my frustration, Jax pushes his hair back with one slick move before lifting his arms up to acknowledge his fans. The entire warehouse detonates with cheers. A smug grin stretches along his face.

Damn, the pictures that I've seen of Jax don't do him justice. His eyes are startling, beaming at me with a dark hue across his irises. A myriad of emotions dance across his viper-like eyes—but not one hint of nervousness. He strides toward the stage, his robe like a cape, his body language oozing menacing superiority.

I don't realize I'm holding my breath until Beth links her fingers with mine and gives an excited squeal. A few girls in our vicinity look like they want to faint from merely basking in his presence.

Jax sizes up his opponent, scanning him from head to toe, and when he's done, he scoffs and turns away.

I hold my breath again when Jax effortlessly shrugs his robe off. It pools on the floor, revealing more of those hard muscles spanning his huge shoulders and back. Holy shit. He's massively built—a broad, rippled chest, an abdomen packed tight with muscle, and arms so huge that they could destroy concrete. I think. I don't really know how much muscle you need to be packing to destroy concrete, but I'm sure it's something close to what Jax has.

But damn, he's gorgeous. Cut like a diamond. All hard edges and glistening skin and raw masculinity.

I'm surprised at the sight of his near-nakedness, which causes a deep arousal to erupt in my body.

I have to force myself to look away.

Beth and Dakota are jumping up and down, trying to get him to notice them. They're not the only ones doing it. At this point, most of the girls in the warehouse are screaming and hollering at him, attempting to get his attention.

When his eyes land on our area, Dakota and Beth go nuts. His eyes suddenly stop on me. I hold his stare because I don't know what else to do. I don't want to look away because, well, I don't want to.

Instead, I keep my head up, shoulders straight, and look challengingly at him.

Pleased with my response, a grin greets his lips.

His smile is perfect. Absolutely perfect. It's so beautiful that it speeds up my already erratic pulse.

"Oh my God!" Beth screams. She's pulling on my arm so much I'm sure it's going to detach itself from my body. "Sienna! Did you see that? He's smiling at me!"

I'm not going to admit that he was actually smiling at me, so I stay silent. I know it would break her heart if she knew the reality of the situation. Instead, I squeeze her arm and smile back, nodding along in agreement.

When I turn my attention back to the cage, Jax's back is

now facing me as he clashes his knuckles together, getting ready for the fight. The muscles in his upper body ripple as he leans forward. Damien eases into his stance as well. But his fists have a slight tremble to them, already predicting his fate.

"I want a clean fight, got it?" the guy with the megaphone says to them. Jax laughs.

"No promises," he snarls.

And as the bell rings, he pounces.

***

Jax wins the fight, of course.

When the bell rang, Jax darted forward, fist coming in hard, smashing into his opponent. Every hit caused me to flinch, punch after punch; the savagery on display was something I'd never imagined. Jax was crass, shouting expletives at Damien whenever he got the chance, edging and goading him forward into yet another kick or tackle. There wasn't a single ounce of polite sportsmanship displayed in the cage, especially by him. But he was ethereal, dancing circles around Damien.

At one point, he even turned to the crowd, pumping his hands up in the air, as Damien struggled to catch his breath after a particularly brutal encounter. This amplified the sound of cheers and encouraged an already semihysterical Beth. In the end, Jax had Damien tap out in under a minute by putting him in some kind of hold then beating him into submission. I barely had time to blink before the referee said the fight was over and the announcer declared Jax the winner.

The rest of the fights after Jax's paled in comparison. The

fighters weren't conniving or skilled like him. They kicked and threw and punched only because they were struggling to survive, not because they could actually plan. Jax's arrogance in that cage is not misplaced: every hit that he lands is calculated, falling into an intricate master plan that reduces his opponent to a panic-stricken, blubbering mess. And I love it. I love how much power he exerts—power that is rightfully *earned*.

No, I have to stop thinking about him. I don't even know him.

I force all thoughts of him out of my mind and instead return my focus to the fight at hand, but it's like he's already made permanent camp in my head.

"You all right, Sienna?" Dakota notices my distraught expression.

"Yeah." I nod back absentmindedly. "Just a little tired, that's all."

She looks like she wants to say more, but the sound of the horn blaring jerks her attention back to the cage.

Now that the last fight has come to a predictable close, people are beginning to move toward the exits. We're squeezing our way through, trying to get to the other side of the warehouse where all the fighters are. Despite the exhaustion visible on her face, Beth is still determined to say hello to Jax.

"Come on, Sienna!" Beth yells. "If we don't move fast enough, he's going to leave!"

"I'm coming!" I mutter. Dakota sends me an apologetic look. She knows that the only reason I came here in the first place was because Beth begged me to tag along.

After about twenty minutes, we finally make it backstage. It's even more crowded than the outside. Fighters loom over us; most of them are the ones who made it out of that cage victorious. Their opponents, on the other hand, are either too weak to move or are getting their faces fixed by poorly equipped medics.

"I'm going to find Zach!" Dakota yells at me. She points in the other direction and tells Beth, "Jax should be around here."

"Okay." Beth nods. When Dakota disappears, my sister turns to me and exhales softly. "Sienna, I'm nervous."

"You'll be fine. Just don't take too long, all right? And make sure he keeps his hands to himself," I tell her, my hands sliding over her shoulders. I squeeze them for reassurance. "If you need help, call me. I'll be right here by the washrooms."

"All right," Beth says cheerfully. "I'll see you soon."

"Good luck." I nudge her toward the hallway, and she smiles at me again before getting swallowed by the crowd.

I lean against the wall beside the washroom, trying to look inconspicuous by swiping on my phone. It's dangerously low on battery when I decide to send a quick text to Mom and Dad telling them that Beth and I are sleeping over at Dakota's tonight, conveniently leaving out the part about currently being outside the city watching an illegal sport.

As long as we're with Dakota, Mom and Dad know they don't need to worry about us. They're more preoccupied with each other—the screaming matches between them have gotten worse, and I don't think I can even be in the same room as them for more than ten minutes without them yelling at each other over the most mundane things. I'm just hoping it's a phase they can get over.

Around me, fighters run back and forth, some looking pleased and others looking pissed as fuck. The guy from the first fight, Damien Wells, stands in the corner with his friends, flailing his arms around angrily as he recalls what happened in the cage with Jax.

I wince when I catch a glimpse of his face. It's a rather gruesome sight—two of his teeth are chipped, and his nose is bloodied and bent out of shape. It's a miracle he's still talking right now.

"Fuck, I swear I almost had him," he snaps, his body trembling with forceful anger. He smashes his index finger and thumb together. "*This* close! Did you see the uppercut I gave him? The one to the ribs? Yeah, I could have knocked him dead with that shit. Wouldn't even have to break a damn sweat..."

I look down at my phone and snort, perhaps a little too loudly. *What a loser.*

"Hey!" I hear Damien yell from across the hallway. I look up, and when my eyes meet his, fear clamps its spiky teeth into me. "Yeah, I'm talking to you, bitch," he snarls at me. All his friends snap their heads in my direction. "Something funny to you?"

Back down, Sienna. You cannot *get into a fight with this guy. He might have lost big-time in that cage, but he could still snap your damn neck if he wanted to.*

"Uh, yes?" I say and immediately want to slap myself for saying something. *What the fuck are you doing, Sienna? Do you want to die tonight?* "You said you almost had Jax. I thought that was funny." I shrug.

Damien's nostrils flare with rage. He's walking toward me now, his bulky form shadowing his friends. My heart is slamming wildly against my chest, telling me, *Abort mission, abort mission right now!*

"How the fuck is it funny?" His eyes narrow at me.

He's about two feet away from me now. His friends have me cornered.

"Uh . . ." My voice trails off. *Keep your fucking mouth shut, Sienna!* "Well, you're a liar. Because I saw what happened in that cage with you and Jax tonight," I say nonchalantly. "And unless anyone mistook the match for a friendly little visit from the tooth fairy, I think it's pretty clear what went down."

That comment captures some people's attention. They mingle in the hallway, looking at us curiously.

I retreat as Damien approaches, backing myself against the wall. *Shit.* I think I might get seriously beaten up. And it's all because my mouth doesn't want to listen to my common sense.

"What did you just say?" Damien fumes.

He clenches his fists and flexes his arms to scare me. And it does work. A little. I try to swallow down the fear festering in my chest in hopes of appearing unfazed. There's no way I'm giving him the satisfaction of knowing that he's successfully intimidated a woman.

"Come on, Damien. You might be halfway to being blind with that right hook that Jax gave to your eye, but I'm sure your ears are fine enough hear what I just said," I say with a bored stare. "Is that like a signature move of yours, by the way? Float like a butterfly, KO like a roach that got spritzed with insecticide?" That earns me a couple of laughs, even some from Damien's friends.

Unfortunately, Damien doesn't think it's very funny.

"I didn't KO," he snaps back at me weakly.

"Well, you might as well have because the way you're lying

your ass off right now is coming across as a little desperate and embarrassing," I say nonchalantly. "Might wanna grow a pair of balls to own up to your losses. At least if I couldn't take the heat in that cage, I'd be *honest* about it."

He lets out a low laugh. "You talk a lot of shit for someone who has probably never stepped foot into that cage. You think you can take the heat? In front of all these people? I dare you to give it a shot," he challenges, and I gulp nervously.

Just as I think he's about to slam his fist into my face, I hear a deep voice echo in the hallway.

"Didn't your mama ever tell you not to hit pretty girls, Wells?" Jax says, materializing from the shadows. All eyes pivot toward him, even Damien's. His anger seems to skyrocket in Jax's presence. Jax pushes through the crowd and into our corner, occupying the space between me and Damien, shielding me from him. "Or was she too preoccupied with fucking other dudes to give a shit about you?"

"Back off, Deadbeat," Damien warns Jax coldly. "This is none of your business."

"Ah, that's where you're wrong. *She*," he says, gesturing to me, "is my business." My eyes widen.

"Why? Is she your girl or something?" Damien scoffs.

"Yes. Is that a problem?" Jax says sharply. "Baby, come here." When the silence drags, his jaw clamps up in annoyance.

"I said, *come here, baby*," he orders me again, and this time I begrudgingly oblige him. Jax slips a casual arm around my waist and pulls me to him protectively. He reeks of sweat and alcohol. I swallow the stench down and breathe in through my mouth. "Don't touch what's mine. Otherwise, I won't hesitate to fuck you up like I did in that cage."

Damien looks like he's about to have another go at Jax. I don't blame him. I would hit Jax too, if I were him. But then again, I'm pretty sure we'd *both* get decked with the amount of shit we just uttered to Damien.

Damien unclenches his fist and lets it drop to his side. One of his friends pats him on the shoulder and tells him to scram. He stares at Jax for a couple more seconds, growling with the commanding presence of a cub.

"This isn't over," he says weakly.

"Yes, it is. Or do you want me to toss you around like a fucking pretzel again? Because I'm all for round two." Jax cracks his knuckles. "I might even let you hit me once before I beat the shit out of you. How about that?"

Damien spits on Jax's feet. His friends tell him to go, but he shrugs them off. "I'll be back for you, Deadbeat," he growls. "Watch out."

"Dude, let's *go*." One of Damien's friends hauls at his arm.

"That's right. Stay down or be put down, little dog," Jax coos sinisterly.

Damien hisses out a breath, veins popping in his neck, but his friend gives him a shove from the back, breaking Damien's eye contact with Jax. Damien shrugs off his friend and stalks away in the opposite direction.

I let go of the breath I've been holding, finally allowing my shoulders to relax.

When the crowd disperses, Jax takes the opportunity to turn to me. He cups my face with his hand.

"Hey." His voice softens. "You all right?"

I slap his hand away in annoyance. "Why the hell did you do that?"

He stares at me, blinking, shock entering his expression. "What?"

"You know what!" I hiss. "*That!* You calling me out! I totally had the situation under control."

"No, you didn't!" he hisses back. "If I hadn't saved you, he would have knocked you unconscious. And God knows what he was planning on doing to you after that."

"Did you really have to say I was yours?" I snap. "Like I was your damn property?"

"It was the only way I could get you out of that situation, fuck!" Now he's pissed off at me. Damn, I'm on a roll tonight, pissing off fighters I don't even know. He gives me an irritated look. "Seriously? You couldn't just say thank you? I just saved your life, and you can't even put your ego aside to say two words."

"Thank-yous are not programmed into my system, sorry." I shrug.

"Wow." He exhales. "And I thought I was a jerk."

"I don't really care what you think I am," I say and start walking away from him.

"Wait, where are you going?"

"I'm going to find better company than you," I snap.

He blinks at me dumbly.

"My sister," I say when I find the strength in my tone again. "I need to find my sister. Goodbye."

I start to walk away from Jax again when I hear him mutter a curse and run after me. He places a heavy hand on my shoulder to stop me in my tracks again.

"Wait," he tells me. "I can't let you go. Not while Damien and his gang are still out there."

I make an aggravated noise. "I don't need your help."

"Yeah, you do, actually," he tells me urgently. His eyes dart around the hallway, and he lets out a sharp breath. "Look, it's rough out there. There're gonna be guys lingering outside, drunk and high on adrenaline, looking for trouble. And trust me, Damien is the least of your problems. My guess is that you don't come here a lot, otherwise you wouldn't be stupid enough to rile up any of the fighters here. I can help you find your sister."

"Why do you want to help me?" I ask.

"Because I'm a decent human being?" He shrugs. "And you're hot, so that's an added bonus."

"You're disgusting."

"I take that as a compliment."

"Only a fucked-up person would take that as a compliment."

"I am a fucked-up person." He offers me a twisted smile. "They call me Deadbeat for a reason, you know. I have no soul."

I roll my eyes at the absurdity of his words. "Whatever, *Satan*."

"So are you going to just let me stand here like an idiot or are you gonna let me help you?" No matter how annoyed he is, there is a thread of fondness in Jax's voice that makes me hesitate for a moment.

I eye him warily, unable to shake the apprehension churning in my stomach. The feeling of danger slips under my skin again—a feeling I became well acquainted with as soon as I stepped foot into this warehouse—and something tells me I might have just found the source.

All my instincts are screaming at me to leave. I'm sure I can figure out a way to get out of here myself. But then again, if I bump into Damien, next time I might not be so lucky as to leave the confrontation unscathed. And I doubt Beth and Dakota will appreciate it if the next time they see me is in the ER on life support.

I suck in an unsteady breath. Perhaps it would be a better idea to stick with Jax. I mean, if his intentions with me weren't good, he wouldn't have saved me from the clutches of Damien. Which means he can't be all bad, right?

"Fine," I say after a while. "But no funny business, all right?"

A grin climbs onto Jax's smug face. "You got it."

"What are you waiting for, then? Lead the way."

Jax nods, extending his arm in an inviting gesture. "Of course. After you, princess."

TWO

"So how does a girl like you get tangled up with the likes of Damien?" Jax asks as we walk side by side, crossing another hallway leading to the back exit of the warehouse.

I debate on whether I should answer Jax because I don't wish to encourage conversation between us since I have little intention of being friends with him. But the aggravation gripping onto my chest after the Damien encounter hasn't yet eased, and it manifests in my next words.

"Since he didn't like being told the harsh truth," I mutter.

"And that is?" Jax prods.

"That he's a pathetic fucking loser."

A hearty laugh leaves him.

"Well, I'm not gonna argue with that." He shrugs. "Damien might, though."

"Of course he would," I say, noting Damien's incredibly fragile ego.

"Hey, I'm always down for another fight," Jax says, oozing

confidence. "But it's best to get you out of the way before we start throwing fists."

For some reason, him being protective over my safety makes my chest flutter.

"Unless he's some kind of big shot around here, I doubt a fight over something as trivial as what happened is going to be necessary," I say.

"Oh, he wishes he was a big shot." Jax snorts. "His only claim to not-so-great fame is that his mom deals. And sometimes those exchanges can be of . . . lucrative means."

I curl my lips inward. The comment Jax had made about his mom made more sense now.

We pass by a couple making out in the corner and sidestep a fighter passed out on the floor with a towel over his face. I'm hoping that Jax and I can continue to drag along this much-needed silence between us, but unfortunately, it doesn't last very long, because, as I'm starting to learn, Jax doesn't like to keep his mouth shut.

"So . . . since we're gonna be spending some time together, are you going to tell me your name?" Jax says, walking backward so he can face me.

I give him a cursory glance. "Do I really have to?"

"I just wanna know whose cute ass I just saved," he says innocently, his powerful shoulders falling into a nonchalant shrug. "If not, I guess I'm just gonna have to keep calling you princess."

I make my displeasure known in the form of a frown. "I'm not a princess."

"Well . . ." Jax shrugs, as if to say, *That's what you think.* "Don't take this the wrong way, but you act like one."

"*Excuse* me?" I stare at him, baffled that he would make such a critical comment despite talking to me for what, five minutes total?

"It's not a big deal. You're passionate, and you like being in charge," he clarifies, his eyes shining as he looks at me. "I can admire that."

"I'm stubborn. I can admit that. But that hardly warrants being called a princess."

"It's not an insult, I promise." Jax grins as he steps in front of me to push the exit door open. The cool autumn air tackles my body, and I yank my sweater tightly over my chest so I can dispel some of the cold.

Dakota insisted that wearing a coat would be useless since it was going to be stuffy inside the warehouse and Breaking Point didn't care enough to set up a coatroom. She was right about the coat check, and I thanked her then for sparing us the trouble, but dammit, I am paying the price for it now. I'm just relieved I'm not Jax right now in his flimsy satin robe and MMA shorts that barely cover his thighs. But the cold doesn't seem to bother him that much, which is weird. If anything, he seems to relish it, his shoulders relaxed as he allows the wind to comb through his sweaty blond hair for a good few seconds before he sweeps it to the side.

As we near the exit, my eyes narrow skeptically at our supposed escape route. The door leads to nowhere except for a small patch of dirt in front of a dilapidated barbed wire fence with a gaping hole in the middle, with loose wires sticking out from its sides. And the hole opens out toward a seemingly never-ending sea of trees disappearing into the night.

I cock my head to the side when I look at him, fishing for an explanation.

"It's a little sketchy, I know," Jax explains, scratching the back of his head sheepishly. "Most of the fighters are either tending to their fans or getting high in the smoking area. It's better to avoid them entirely just to be safe."

"So you think the better alternative is for me to be alone with a stranger in a forest that I don't know the way out of?"

"First off, I'm pretty sure we're at least friends."

"Well, you still don't know my name, do you? So I doubt that."

I half expect him to look wounded after my remark, but if anything, it makes him grin.

"For now, perhaps. But I assure you, you won't be a stranger for long," Jax says, his grin widening. He jerks his head toward the darkness swallowing up most of the forest's trees. "Let's go, princess."

"Oh, hell no." I plant my feet firmly on the dirt. "I'm not going anywhere with you unless I have an exit plan if things go south."

Jax scoffs, as if he's never had any girl doubt his intentions before. "I'm not going to hurt you, you know."

It's amusing that he thinks his words are going to automatically flip a switch of trust inside me. I happen to watch enough crime documentaries to know that the most conventionally attractive men hide the most sinister secrets.

"Well, I don't know that," I retort back. "You beat up guys in a cage for a living, so excuse me for not trusting you with my safety."

He cocks his head sideways and shrugs, as if to say *fair enough*. "Fine. What will make you feel safe?"

"Give me a second." I fish out my phone from my pocket and start tapping on the screen, only to realize that my phone has decided to shut down on me. And here I thought the universe would be on my side for once. "Crap, my phone's dead. Give me yours." I hold my palm out toward Jax.

He lets out a laugh. "Yeah, no. That's the oldest trick in the book."

"What is?"

"Using my phone to send a text to yours in a desperate attempt to get my number?" He makes a tsk sound by rolling the back of his tongue. "And here I thought you were classier than that."

"You're right. Any classy girl wouldn't even dream of entertaining you." When he hesitates to give me his phone again, I almost laugh. "Look, I just want your phone so I have a way to call the cops on you if you try anything stupid. Trust me, the last thing I want right now is to get into your pants." Not true at all. I've already pictured what it would be like to see what's packing inside those pants. But there's no way I'm going to admit that to him. "Besides, I'm sure you have plenty of other women to . . . satisfy those needs."

Jax looks at me, amused. "Is that what you think I do during my spare time?"

"I don't need to look through your phone to know I'll find an essay's worth of dirty texts you send to your fling of the week."

"Essays?" He chokes on a laugh. "I assure you, I don't need that many words to get a woman into bed. They're usually just as eager to fuck me as I am them."

Something about the way the crude word rolls off his

tongue makes my cheeks go hot. Now all I can imagine is his huge hands gripping some girl around her waist like his life depends on it, leaning over to whisper his crude words in her ear to send her right over the edge.

I wonder if he'd be a selfish lover. His swaggering attitude would make most people assume so, but I don't know. If anything, I think it might be a misdirection. I think pleasuring women would feed his power. He seems like the type to get off once his partner does because his ego would be too massive for him to let a woman leave without an orgasm specially delivered by him.

Jax catches sight of the pink flush on my face and arches a brow. "You're thinking about it, aren't you? What it would be like to be one of them?"

"No," I croak out, trying to act composed.

"Right." He looks me up and down and smiles. "I'm sure you aren't usually the type of woman to be . . . flung."

I feel my cheeks burning, and I force myself to look away. Is my inexperience really that obvious? I thought I hid it pretty well.

Jax unlocks his smartphone with his face ID, then slaps it onto my palm with a grin. "Here you go."

I blink dumbly at his phone in my palm. For a moment, I've completely forgotten what I set out to do with it.

"You said you wanted to use it to make you feel safe," Jax fills in for me, looking amused.

"Right," I mumble, my brain coming back online. I punch 911 on the keypad, my finger hovering over the call button. "Okay, now we can go."

"Come on," he says, placing a hand on my back and

guiding me toward the fence. He gestures for me to climb through. "Ladies first," he says.

I push past him and loop a leg through, careful not to have any wires poke me as I cross over. He follows behind me once I'm through to the other side, the loose wires bouncing back into place once he's across.

My sneakers crunch heavily against the rocky dirt as we continue walking, Jax taking the lead. I struggle to catch up with his steps. It's difficult given his immense size and stride.

This doesn't look like a typical route that anyone would use to navigate the area, and it does nothing to dismiss my nerves. The forest is thick with trees and dense with shrubbery, with the occasional smattering of car lights as they cruise down the highway located about a mile from here. Despite the darkness, Jax seems to know where he's going.

We turn a corner, veering onto an even narrower pathway bound by the trees. Aside from the twigs crunching beneath my sneakers, the occasional sound of birds flying overhead and the faint billowing of leaves are the only sounds accompanying us during our walk. I welcome the noises because the more silence there is between me and Jax, the more my mind starts to wonder about him, and not in a particularly innocent way.

The sash of Jax's robe loosens as the wind continues to tug and tussle with it, so he unravels the knot and tightens it over his waist again. I stare at the robe for a little longer than I should, wondering if there's any significance to it, since I've seen some fighters wearing them, and some without. And Jax seems to wear his like it's some kind of status symbol.

"You look like you want to ask me something," Jax inserts.

"I'm not gonna bite, you know. Just ask me whatever's on your mind."

"Fine," I say, adjusting myself. I guess it wouldn't hurt to pry some information about the underground from him. "Is the robe a special thing for you? Cuz I've only seen a handful of fighters wearing them."

Jax smiles, welcoming my question.

"Robes aren't really a thing in real MMA. But in the underground, they're kind of a status symbol. This robe," Jax explains, pinching the satin fabric draped over his shoulder, "represents the blood and sweat I've spilled in that cage. It symbolizes my power. My reign. My freedom. Some fighters don't wear it because they feel like they're not deserving of it yet. And they would be right."

I bite my lip, parsing the words in my mind. It shouldn't surprise me that the underground has its own markers to establish hierarchy. Before seeing the underground, I was always under the impression that illegal fight clubs were just random guys duking it out in dodgy, run-down basements, looking to get rowdy and maybe earn a quick buck. But this—what Breaking Point is doing—is different. It's a rather well-organized establishment brewing in the underbelly of Boston, rife with shady connections and turning massive illegal profits. It makes me uneasy just thinking about it. I wonder if Jax has ever had any reservations about doing the whole underground fight thing. From the looks of it, he embraces it wholly—in fact, a little too much, if I dare say.

"When did you start wearing the robe?" I ask.

"When I beat Perez," Jax says pridefully. "Been waiting a long time to fuck him up just so I could wear it."

Right. The guy who, up until Jax came along, had supposedly held on to his title with an iron fist. I spotted his face on one of the posters outside the warehouse when Dakota, Beth, and I were waiting in line to get in. He appeared much older than most of the men I saw fight tonight: in his early forties, from the looks of it. Not to mention the shaved head and bright red scar ripping across his face that forced me to suppress a cold shudder.

From what I remember Dakota saying, Perez took his loss against Jax hard. And based on his reputation, there's no way he would swallow down a crushing defeat from a cocky newbie like Jax. I have a feeling things will get ugly if they end up going head-to-head during the finals.

I force my distaste inward. Men and their grudges. I wonder if all underground fighters are the same, holding on to these vendettas simply because their insanely fragile egos can't take a beating.

"So, if you lose to Perez next time . . ." I start, following the line of logic. "You'll have to give up the robe?"

That earns a low laugh from Jax. "Princess, I never lose."

"Anyone who thinks they're invincible will always be toppled over one way or another," I say. "It's history, Jax."

"It doesn't apply to me."

"Now you're just being ridiculous."

"I just have way too much faith in myself," he declares.

"Overconfidence kills, you know," I state dryly.

"Overconfidence comes from being prepared," he corrects me. "And I always am. It's something I pride myself on."

I don't know whether to feel contempt for his conceit or admiration for his self-confidence because he's earned the right to it. Maybe a bit of both.

"You're very blunt," I observe.

"So are you."

"I'm blunt because I don't like to waste my time. You're blunt because you're arrogant."

"Like I said before, it's not a bad thing. You should know. Our egos match in size."

I choke on a laugh. "That's so not true."

He glances at me challengingly. "Okay. So you're telling me what happened with Damien earlier tonight wasn't an act of arrogance?"

I blink at him, wondering what he's trying to get at. "It wasn't. He came at me first, and I was trying to defend myself."

"Yeah, piling insults on him like that was a real case of charity." He snorts. When I don't answer, he presses on. "Come on. What happened with him wasn't some selfless act to take the bad guy down. You did it because you wanted a reaction out of him, and you got it. That's why you didn't like it when I intervened. Because if you'd had your way, you would've kept going."

I look away. "I don't know what you're talking about."

Jax laughs. "You can just embrace it, you know. The viciousness. It's less exhausting than the weight you carry from pretending to be someone you're not."

My mouth pops open, ready to volley back a defense about how I'm not pretending, but the words fizzle out when the realization swamps me like a crashing tide.

Shit, he's right.

I was well aware of what the risks were when I said the things I said to Damien. I was goading him. I didn't do it because I was trying to be righteous. Quite the opposite.

I did it because it felt good to put him in his place. And I wanted everyone to see it.

I've never admitted that to myself. I've never allowed myself to. That side of me . . . I've always kept it buried. Because it's easier for people to stomach who you are when they only see the good in you.

Which is what's so intriguing and refreshing about Jax. He doesn't seem to care what people think about him. He doesn't seem to care about people at all. Just himself. He's exactly who he presents himself to be: faulty and despicable and unlikable, which, ironically enough, makes him that much more likable.

"I guess I never thought about it like that," I mumble, wrapping my arms tightly around myself.

"Just some food for thought," Jax says ever so casually, like he didn't just single-handedly shatter my perception of myself in a conversation. We resume walking again. "Since you're asking questions about me, it's my turn to ask one about you," Jax continues on, injecting some much-needed lightness back into our conversation. He walks backward so he can look at me when I respond. "Why the underground tonight? This doesn't seem like your usual scene."

"How do you know tonight is my first night?"

"Because I would definitely remember you if it wasn't."

The heat crawls up my face.

"So, why the underground tonight? You heard about it somewhere and wanted a piece of the action?" he prods.

I don't want to tell him that it's because Dakota and Beth really wanted to see him in action, so instead I throw out another minor reason. "It's my friend's brother's first time fighting tonight, so we came for moral support." Technically not a lie, even though there wasn't much moral support on my end since I missed the match during a toilet break.

A curious lift of a brow. "Who's her brother?"

"Zach," I tell him. "He goes by, uh . . . something like Hammerhead."

"The Sledgehammer?" Jax gives me a pointed look, stopping in his tracks. "Well, shit. Saw him get wheeled off to the ER after he got into a postfight brawl. Maybe that's where your friend went."

I draw in a ragged, nervous breath, my hand clutching my chest. "You think my sister would have gone with her too?"

Panic begins to set in. If Beth has gone with Dakota, I need to find a phone charger ASAP so I can check my messages to see what the hell is going on. I can't afford to waste another second stalling in these woods.

Jax's face turns serious when he realizes how anxious I am. "We'll hurry. Come."

He gestures for me to pick up my pace, and I do, my breathing coming in short spurts. Jax's fit body puts me to shame. Man, I should really start working out again.

"Are you sure we're going the right way?" I ask softly, worry gripping my chest. All I see are endless rows of trees shrouded by more darkness.

"Yeah. Breaking Point often cycles through fights here when the cops are hot on their trail, so I'm familiar with the area. If you're scared or something, you can hold my hand."

Jax extends a hand toward me, and I'm so taken aback by the offer that I lean backward to avoid him touching me with it.

He groans, flipping his palm upward in annoyance. "It's just a hand, princess. Not a flesh-eating monster."

For a second, the prospect of tethering myself to his strong hand is tempting. *Really* tempting. But everything feels dangerous with him, a slippery slope that I feel like I'm already teetering on the edge of.

"I'm good," I say softly, tucking both my hands into my back pockets instead.

A frustrated sigh rumbles from his throat as he comes to a halt again. "Is it because you still think I have bad intentions toward you?"

I don't answer. I'd rather have him think that's the reason than the real one: I'm afraid that if I do hold his hand, I'll feel things that I don't want to feel for him. I need to keep him at arm's length. Aside from the fact that my sister has a major crush on him, guys like Jax are dangerous to fall for, and I'm not going to let myself do it. So, I let the silence speak for me, hoping he'll form a conclusion himself.

And naturally, Jax does because his jaw clamps hard, trying to contain annoyance. "Are you like this with all guys, or is it just me?"

"Just you," I say candidly. "You're probably the only guy that I've ever spent more than ten minutes alone with, so . . ."

He stops abruptly in his tracks and whips back around, disbelief manifesting in his expression. "You're joking."

"No, I'm not," I mumble, brushing the fallen strands of hair away from my face. "And I would appreciate it if you didn't rub it in my face."

"I wasn't going to, I swear." Jax walks over to me, and his face is suddenly so close that I can feel his breath tickling my lips. Fingers drag over my jaw, tilting my face up to pull my gaze toward his. "It's just that . . . I can't possibly understand why," he murmurs, sieving my wind-whipped hair through his hand. "You're so fucking beautiful."

His eyes meet mine in such an intense way that I'm tempted to look away. But they are as mesmerizing as they are overpowering, and I can't help but hold his gaze.

Shit. Shit, shit, shit.

Think about the risks of being with him. Think about Beth!

I pry Jax's hand from my hair, and he drops it to his side. "I bet you say that to a lot of women," I mumble. I feel stupid for dismissing his comment because my heart can't possibly own the compliment, even though that's all it's been craving.

"Well, not all of them," he replies smoothly. "I don't dish out compliments unless I really mean them."

"Yeah, right."

"Hey, come on. It's true," he insists. "Of everyone in that warehouse, my eyes landed on you. That's gotta mean something."

Suddenly I'm grateful for the darkness because at least he won't be able to see my cheeks turning into a pair of tomatoes.

"Must be fate then," I say sarcastically.

I expect to find humor in his expression, but he looks back at me with all seriousness. "Must be," he says.

Cupid's arrow lodges straight into my heart.

"Come on." He nudges me. "Let's keep moving."

This time, Jax slides a strong arm around my waist to guide me through the last section of the woods. My mind spins being so close to him. And when his thumb drifts down to feel the exposed skin at the side of my stomach where my top has ridden up, I can't think anymore. All the warning bells have been set on Mute, like my mind has grown tired of the noise, and in that quiet, I allow my body to surrender to him and lean into his touch.

"Are you okay?" he whispers. "Do you want me to stop?"

I should say yes, but my words have completely dried up. All I can think about is wanting his hands all over my skin, fingers rubbing the achy parts of my body where I'm already affected by just his words and a whisper of a touch.

No guy has ever touched me like this before. No guy has ever *wanted* to touch me before.

I shouldn't be this affected by one man, but fuck it, I am. Which makes me so tragically pathetic I could just cry.

When we're finally out of the forest, I spot the crowd in front of the entrance to the warehouse. When I click on Jax's phone, the flashing time reveals that it's been well over an hour since the last fight ended, yet people are still milling about. They're mostly girls wanting to get their hands on one of the fighters for the night.

I turn back to the woods, a little confused at how long we've been gone. Factoring in the time I sent the text to my parents before encountering Damien, which was about half an hour ago . . . how the hell did we end up walking for *thirty* minutes? The distance from the back of the warehouse to the front is certainly not that far.

"Did we get lost in the woods?" I ask Jax. "Why did we take so long to get here?"

"I took a detour."

"What? Why?"

He steps forward to tuck a stray hair behind my ear. "I wanted to spend time with you." The corners of his eyes crinkle sweetly at me.

Before I can find the words to respond, a familiar voice rings through the air.

"Sienna, oh my God!" Relief washes across my sister's face as she sprints over to me. She pulls me into a hug, winding her arms around me tightly. "Thank God you're okay. I tried calling you, but I think your phone's dead. Dakota needed to rush to the hospital with Zach, and I panicked, but I didn't want to leave you here alone—" Beth pulls back enough to register the massive presence looming beside me. When she realizes who it is, her mouth gapes open with surprise. "Oh my God, Jax?"

"Hey." Jax gives a curt nod of acknowledgment. "You're the sister, I gather."

"Elizabeth." She drops her hands to her sides awkwardly. "But everyone calls me Beth. Gosh, I'm your biggest fan."

"Thanks," he replies, like the comment is nothing new for him. His gaze darts between me and my sister. "You guys look nothing alike. Well, except for the"—he gestures to the top of his head—"blond hair."

"Yeah, we get that a lot," I say.

Growing up, everyone who knew my parents always made a habit of pointing out that I took after my mom's features, with my long face and high cheekbones, a stark contrast to Beth, who takes after my dad with her heart-shaped face and round, flushed cheeks. I never minded, preferring comparisons to my mom over my dad anyway.

Beth's gaze ping-pongs back and forth between me and Jax. "How do you . . . uh . . ." Beth fumbles with her words as she struggles to process the fact that I was the one who found him, not her. "How do you guys know each other?"

Jax rests a bent elbow over my shoulder and leans against me in such a friendly way that it causes Beth's brow to quirk. "I took the liberty of saving her when she nearly got herself beaten up after she provoked the shit out of Damien," he explains smoothly.

Beth's expression grows worried, jerking her attention back to me. "You almost got beaten up?"

"It's fine. He's being dramatic." I brush her off. "I had it handled."

Jax scoffs. "And by 'had it handled' she means she was actually going to take that beating if I hadn't swooped in."

I nudge his elbow from my shoulder. "Seriously? Can you not make it sound like you're my guardian angel or something? Because you're not."

"Sienna!" Beth scolds, flushing pink with embarrassment. "Why are you being so rude to him?"

"She likes to play hard to get with me," Jax muses. "Isn't that right, *Sienna*?"

My eyes squeeze shut briefly.

So much for trying to keep anonymous.

"Whatever. Thanks for helping me out tonight," I say, brushing him off. "But we gotta go."

"And here I thought thank-yous were not programmed into your system." Jax grins, folding his arms across his massive chest in a smug manner.

I clench my jaw tightly. Clearly I'm not good with keeping track of things—moral high horses included—when it comes to Jax.

Instead of trying to explain myself, I wave a hand at my

sister, gesturing for her to follow me. "Let's go. We should get a cab since Dee took off."

"Yeah, about that . . ." Beth purses her lips, rocking back and forth on the balls of her feet anxiously. "Everyone has been trying to get a cab for the past twenty minutes. We're gonna be stuck here for a while."

"Okay then, we'll wait. Preferably over there." I grasp her wrist and start tugging her toward the entrance, away from Jax.

Beth pulls back, unconvinced. "But once we leave . . . where do we go? Dee just texted saying she might be in the hospital all night, and her whole family is there. I don't know about you, but I feel weird intruding."

I drop Beth's hand. Dammit, she's right. And going home isn't an option either. The last thing I want is for Mom and Dad to find out that we lied about our whereabouts.

From behind us, Jax clears his throat, and I can already sense that I'm not going to like what he's about to say.

"You girls can stay with me tonight," he offers.

THREE

There are a thousand reasons why it is a bad idea to spend the night with Jax.

Apparently, none of them deter Beth in the slightest because as soon as we arrive at Jax's apartment, she is the first one through the door, gaping at the space like she's just found the gateway to heaven.

"*This* is where you live?" she gasps in wonderment.

I don't know why she continues to be surprised by Jax's wealth. We escaped the warehouse in a brand-new Cadillac—its fresh leather smell and plastic-wrapped visors a dead giveaway—into a eleven-story luxury apartment building with a concierge.

I step over the threshold last, hugging myself tightly as I let my gaze roam around the space. It's a neatly furnished apartment on the tenth floor with floor-to-ceiling windows, beautiful white countertops, hardwood floors, and masculine touches like leather seats, industrial fixtures, and gray accents.

An electric fireplace sits in front of an L-shaped leather couch, and in the corner, a black punching bag floats on a chain hanging from the ceiling. A small bar sits beside the couch, boasting a generous display of half-empty liquor bottles.

The space itself makes a big statement. It reminds me a little of the mansion that my family used to live in when I was younger, back when my dad still held his job and our finances were good. I wasn't a huge fan of that house; it was more of a status thing for my dad. It didn't feel like a home—more like a luxury hotel we'd one day be checking out of. Which, eventually, we did.

Looking around Jax's place, I wonder how he's managed to secure an apartment like this. He doesn't look much older than me—probably two years. Having a luxurious apartment at his age is an impressive feat.

"Yep. And it's all mine," Jax says, dropping his keys into a metal bowl on top of his shoe rack and shrugging off his coat. "Been saving up all year to move in."

Beth blinks dumbly. "And you got this with money you earned from the underground?"

Another flash of that prideful grin. "Pays to be a good fighter, right?"

"That's so cool." My sister smiles at him, her attention quickly diverted as she lets out a loud squeal. "Oh my God, look at the view!"

She skips toward the balcony in excitement, tightly gripping the railing as she stares down over the topography of the neighborhood, tucked behind a stunning view of the Charles River.

I shuffle toward the balcony, staying behind the window

separating the living room from the outdoor space. Outside, the dark sky is punctuated by the twinkling lights of the Boston skyline, offering brightness in the absence of stars. Jax joins me, hands deep in his pockets as he inhales the view. I wonder if he ever gets bored with it. I know if I lived in the city and had a place like this, I certainly wouldn't.

I watch as my sister snaps some pictures to post on Instagram, no doubt bragging about her current residence and its incredibly hot owner. My front teeth dig into my bottom lip with concern. Even if Jax did offer up his place from the goodness of his heart, it feels intrusive to be here, especially when I know that Beth probably won't be shutting up about it to anyone who'll listen to her when she returns to school on Monday. Discomfort churns in my stomach—the same feeling that was begrudgingly tossed aside to accept Jax's offer in the first place.

"Look, Jax, I appreciate you doing all this for us," I start off, turning toward him, "but we can't—"

"Stop. It's fine. I don't mind," he assures me. I frown, still contemplating biting the bullet and going home. He steps toward me so he can lower his voice, out of earshot of Beth. "Look, do you want to make both our lives miserable tonight?"

"Well . . ." I hesitate. "No."

"Then stop complaining. I offered my place out of goodwill. So use it," he tells me, chin jerking toward the direction of the bathroom. "Spare towels are in the cabinet under the sink. You girls can take my bed, and I'll sleep on the couch. If you need a change of clothes, grab anything you want from the closet."

The thought of sleeping in his bed and wearing his clothes both unsettles and excites me.

"You sure you don't mind?" I ask wearily.

"For the last time, no," he insists, flashing his trademark grin at me. "The pleasure's all mine, princess. And hopefully yours too."

I swallow hard, pushing my heart back down my throat.

When Beth emerges from the balcony, I waste no time linking my arm with hers and steering her away from Jax. "Come on. We'll take turns with the bathroom."

***

Half an hour later, I pop out of the bathroom in an oversize AC/DC shirt from Jax's closet and step into his bedroom to find Beth spread out on the king-size bed like she's making a snow angel. She looks so happy to be here. It's been a while since I've seen her like this.

"Great. You're ready for bed," I say as I towel off my damp hair and pick up my dirty clothes from the floor. "Let's get some rest. We're leaving first thing in the morning."

"What? Why?" Beth immediately straightens up, propping her elbows under her. When she notices I'm not going to budge on my decision, she makes a whiny sound. "Are you serious right now? This is Jax's apartment." She says it like we're on holy ground right now. "You don't know how lucky we are that we're here. We need to make the most of it." She drags herself to the edge of the bed, desperation pouring out of her eyes as she watches me collect my clothes from the bathroom and fold them. "Aren't you even a little curious about him?"

"No. And you shouldn't be either," I say, placing the clothes in a neat pile beside my phone that's now charging on Jax's empty nightstand.

"Ugh, you're such a buzzkill." She drops her head back onto the mattress, pouting at the ceiling again.

"I'm not trying to make your life miserable, Beth." I heave out a sigh, sitting by the corner of the bed as I stroke her hair. "Whether you like it or not, you're still sixteen. What would Mom and Dad say about you getting tangled up with a guy like Jax?"

"That I'm mature for dating someone older than me?" she asks sheepishly.

"Beth," I say in a warning tone.

"Sienna," she volleys back.

"I'm being serious. Besides, he's way too old for you."

She takes a moment to mull over my words. After a couple seconds, she lets out a loud, conceding groan. "Fine. I guess you're right. It probably wouldn't be a good idea."

"I'm glad you understand."

"I do, but that doesn't mean I'm okay with it."

I smile down at her. "Let's get some rest. I'm going to grab a glass of water from the kitchen. Want one?"

She shakes her head, turning over to the right side of the bed, getting under the covers, and pulling out her phone.

I scuttle toward the kitchen, swiping a glass from the top cabinet and flipping the tap on to fill it up. It's a big sink—but then again, so is this kitchen and this place—and it makes me wonder how depressing it must be, surrounded by all these luxuries and not having anyone to enjoy them with.

It's none of your business, Si. What, like you *could be the girl to fill the empty void of this place?*

I banish the internal taunt. When my eyes find the living room, a familiar pair of golden-brown eyes returns my curious gaze.

"Looks like I was right," Jax drawls, lying lazily on the couch with one arm propped over the armrest as his gaze sweeps over me casually. He's no longer in his robe; he's all freshened up, half naked in a pair of black shorts. The sight of him like this arouses a desire in me that I quickly push back down.

"What?" I sound confused.

"I was right," he repeats again, his gaze blanketing me. "I made a bet with myself about whether you'd look good in my clothes. And you do."

"How do you even make a bet with yourself?"

"Easy. I just do. In my head."

"But betting with yourself isn't exactly fair competition."

"It is. Every time I lose, I also win. And I like those odds."

My God, this man.

"I also made another bet about two minutes ago," Jax tells me.

"Oh yeah? What was it?"

He drops his gaze to the glass of water in my hand. "That you'd use any excuse to come out to the living room to see me."

I roll my eyes. "I was thirsty."

"For my company."

"For water," I retort with annoyance.

"Whatever you say, princess."

I wince. The nickname is starting to get on my nerves. "Listen, since you know my name now, would you mind dropping the nickname?"

"Nah, I've decided that *princess* suits you more," Jax declares. He doesn't seem to register my frustration because he pats the available space next to him in invitation. "Come. Sit."

I shake my head, the glass of water heavy in my hand despite only being half full. "I should get back."

"Just stay for a bit. I'm lonely and cold."

"Now, *that's* a line if I've ever heard one."

He flashes me a captivating grin. "Please . . . Sienna."

It should annoy me that Jax is so brazen with his intentions. And yet my body refuses to acknowledge any resistance. It's like I'm on autopilot around him. Every time I try to assert control, there he is steering me right back to him.

"Fine." I sigh, crossing the dining area and plopping the glass onto the coffee table next to his. I make sure to put a respectable amount of space between us by sitting on the far edge of the couch. That doesn't stop his leg from brushing against mine, though. My body jolts when it makes contact with his cold skin.

"Damn, you weren't kidding," I gasp, moving my leg away and readjusting myself so my legs are folded beneath me. "You're freezing."

"I took an ice bath," Jax explains, taking a sip of his drink. As he swirls the liquid in his hand, the large, clear ice cube clanging against the glass, I realize it isn't water but most likely a gin he's nursing. "Helps with muscle recovery."

I nod in acknowledgment. It shouldn't surprise me to know that no matter how well you perform in that cage, your body is still going to feel the effects of it later. I remember back when I first started ballet, I'd come home feeling like I'd been to war and back.

As Jax readjusts his position on the couch—now sitting cross-legged to face me—I wonder if every part of him is sore. If so, he doesn't give it away; an emotionless mask is propped over his face.

As I continue staring at him, rather shamelessly, I'm unable to stop a burning question from slipping out. "Why do you live alone, Jax?"

His lips flatten with displeasure.

"I'd rather not say."

"Huh." I try to seem casual. "And here I thought you prided yourself on being honest."

"Withholding information does not count as a lie."

"Does it not? Really?"

His mouth twitches. "My family and I are not in a great place. That's all you need to know."

I purse my lips into a frown. That doesn't sound good. I want to press him further about it, but I hold back, reminding myself that he has every right not to share those details with me right now.

Jax flicks his thumb over my chin in assurance. "Ask me anything else."

"Okay," I say, propping myself on the couch the same way as him, folding both my legs in front of me. "How old are you?"

"Twenty," Jax says, scooting closer to my side of the couch. "You?"

"Eighteen," I answer, feeling embarrassed at how young and inexperienced I must seem to him. I quickly change the subject. "Are you in college?"

"I did a two-year degree," he explains. "Graduated in the summer."

That explains how he's able to fight in the underground full-time and afford this place.

"I just started my freshman year at BU," I say.

Curiosity sparks in Jax's eyes as he leans in toward me. His closeness starts a wild stammering of my heart against my rib cage, and I hope he can't hear it. My eyes fall to my lap; I'm too shy to even share a glance with him.

"What are you studying?" he asks, scooting closer. Invading my territory, my safe space. And yet I don't say anything about it.

"Business and marketing."

Jax gives a disappointed headshake. "That's boring for someone like you."

"Someone like me?"

"Someone who's meant for astronomical things."

My heartbeat momentarily screeches to a stop.

I hate that he has a straight path to my heart with his sweet words.

"You don't really think that," I mumble, not wanting to feel exhilarated about his comment.

"I do. I also know that this," he says, making a circling gesture with his hand in front of me, "is all a front. You have a lot of fire inside of you. What happened with Damien was just a tiny spark of it."

I lean back against the couch, gulping hard. My propensity to hurl myself straight into trouble has been a recurring argument with my dad, which is why I've always tried hard not to fall out of line. College meant that I could start fresh. No more detention for decking a jock in the face after he tried to cop a feel of my ass. Gone were the verbal scuffles with ballet girls trying to get me kicked out of the studio because I refused to partake in their cocaine binges.

So far, I've suppressed those instincts well.

Except for tonight.

Sweat prickles along my neck as Jax leans in, eager to close the last fraction of distance between us. And shit, *shit*, I want him to. The scent of his aftershave is intoxicating, his presence overpowering, and I can't seem to force my body to leave his orbit. My heartbeat is a constant roar in my ears as he traces my skin with his fingers, gliding down my cheek and gently twisting my hair. His smug grin is gone; he's serious now, and my breath hitches with his touch—like he knows just one whisper of contact sends all my nerve endings into overdrive. When his gaze wanders down to my mouth, I find my lips parting open in yearning.

For a second, I think about what it would be like to end my agony and lean in. Squash the deep, compounding ache inside me and catch Jax's lips with mine. I've never been kissed before, and I wonder if it would be as explosive as I think it would be to kiss him.

I want to. Desperately.

But . . . I can't.

Not when it comes to the inevitability of hurting someone I love.

"I . . . I can't do this." It takes every bit of effort I have to pull myself away from him. I bury my face in my hands. "My sister . . . she has a crush on you, and she's literally in the next room. I just can't do that to her."

"Do what, baby?" Jax pries my trembling hands from my face and hauls me over to him, turning me to press my back against his chest. His hands cup my hands, and his next words arrive as a soothing elixir to ease the guilt gripping me by my neck. "Sit here on the couch to keep me company? I would hardly think that's anything for Beth to get mad about."

"Jax . . ." I say uncertainly. He reads the indecision in my voice and knows I'm caving because I don't want to leave.

"Feel this," he whispers, responding to my unspoken desire. He adjusts me on his lap so the apex of my thighs makes contact with his bulging erection. "Feel what you're doing to me."

Holy shit.

In a daring move, Jax pinches the collar of his shirt that I'm wearing and slides it to the side. It's so big I could wear it as an off-the-shoulder top. He even manages to push it past my shoulder blade and smooth his lips over the sensitive skin of my neck. *Oh God.* As if he anticipates the loud moan coming out of me, he clamps a hand over my mouth to muffle the sound.

"You need to be quiet for me, baby," he orders. "Or we're both going to be in trouble. Can you do that?"

The only response I manage is a small nod.

"Good girl," he whispers.

Hot air scorches my lungs.

"Would you like me to go lower?" Jax asks, his voice rough and needy as he lays another kiss along my collarbone. It's like he knows how sensitive that area of my neck is. I wonder if that is his experience with other women talking or if it's because he reads me so well.

"How about lower . . . here?" Meanwhile, his fingers sift through mine, and he guides my other hand down my lap, teasing the flimsy fabric of the shirt. I mentally slap myself for not wearing pants over my underwear because then at least access to the most sensitive part of my body would require a two-factor authentication.

Now the security is just in shambles.

I nod again.

My body burns with yearning as he drags my hand to my thigh, fingering the edge of my panties. The sensation of the fabric brushing against my fingertips sends a bolt of anticipation running down my body. He hasn't touched me there yet, and I'm already soaked with need.

"I want you to touch yourself for me." Jax breathes hard against the hollow of my ear.

"I—I can't." I shake my head, feeling too embarrassed. Usually when I need to take care of myself, I do it quickly in the bathroom. I've never touched myself in front of anyone before.

"Let me help you, then," he says, husky voice sliding into my ear, guiding my hand under the waistband of my panties, allowing my fingers to brush over my clit. He helps me apply pressure to it, circling my index and middle fingers over the sensitive bud.

I moan into the hand still clamped around my mouth as my fingers move faster. My hips are following the movements of my hands, chasing the euphoria as it continues to build between my thighs, my moans becoming more desperate for release.

"Oh, Jax, please."

"*Fuck*, I love when you beg for it like that, baby." His voice is warm and rough in my ear as he guides an index finger inside me.

Desire explodes in my stomach and escapes me in the form of a loud, throaty cry, thankfully muffled by his hand. He rocks his hips to my movements, his teeth digging into my shoulder blade, plunging his fingers deep into me with his own, dictating the pace. I clench my inner walls together, hoping I can elicit some kind of reaction from him, and my body quivers with purpose when Jax lets out a low groan in response.

And then he increases the speed of my fingers.

I want to moan. Or cry. Or both. Because touching myself has never felt so good before. It's hard to get off when there aren't many mental images or people that turn you on in the first place. But tonight . . . just the memory of Jax, rock-hard against me while he helps me touch myself, is going to be my favorite to put on Replay after tonight.

I can feel Jax's erection poking against my lower back, and God, I want to pull down the waistband of his boxers and take it in my mouth. I would be lying if the thought of it didn't make me nervous, but I want it. I want him. Even if it's for a fleeting moment.

Our hands are pushing against my clit, finding a perfect rhythm on that sweet spot, and I'm soaring higher and higher—

"Good night, princess," he says as he frees his hand from my underwear and lays a gentle kiss on my forehead.

What the fuck?

What. The. Actual. *Fuck?!*

"Excuse me?" I spin back toward him, frustration flooding my body. "What the hell was that?"

Jax pulls the fabric of my shirt back down. "Something to remember me by until you return."

"Are you serious?" I push to my feet. My legs wobble when I shoot up, desire still coursing through me. I can already feel my cheeks burning. Whether with rage or embarrassment, I'm not quite sure.

"Yes. I am," he says point-blank. "Because you and I both know this isn't going to be the last time we see each other."

I choke on a dry laugh. "After what just happened, do you really think I would ever let that happen?"

He shrugs and lies back on the couch nonchalantly, looking like the past fifteen minutes haven't affected him in the same way they did me, the only remnant the erection still tenting his shorts.

"Look, you want me, princess. I know that you do. But I'm not going to do anything else unless you want *me* to want you." He says it like it's stated fact. "And I'm gonna want all of you. In every fucking way I can get you."

The declaration travels all the way through my body. I push away the feeling of excitement, too clouded by my anger at being left high and dry like this.

"You barely know me." I huff out a laugh.

"You barely know *me*. And yet, here we are," Jax says.

His idleness about the situation stokes my anger. I should stop pretending that what happened between us was anything but a typical Saturday night for Jax, despite it being the most special thing that's ever happened to me. I will not keep letting him draw me in like this. He doesn't deserve to revel in my submission, especially when he's hell-bent on being a massive fucking dick afterward.

"You know what? Fuck you," I spit out at him, spinning around so I don't have to listen to any more of his bullshit.

I hear Jax rising to his feet from the couch. "You're kidding yourself, Sienna. You don't want to hate me. I know that." I can almost picture the overconfident grin on his face as he says it. "And when you finally realize it, I'll be waiting."

I laugh hoarsely, loathing the way his arrogance manages to insert itself into every conversation we have. "Go choke on your own ego, Deadbeat."

"Mmm, I'm sure it'll taste as delicious as you." And he has the audacity to stick his two fingers in his mouth and lick them. A slow smile spreads across his mouth when his tongue sweeps over his fingers like he's savoring every drop of me.

I make a disgusted sound. Snatching the half-empty glass of water from the coffee table, I storm back into the bedroom.

FOUR

"Good morning, princess," Jax greets me as I shuffle into the kitchen.

He appears to have been up and cooking breakfast for quite some time, in a black tank top and a pair of athletic shorts, muscles in his arm flexing as he pushes the bacon around with his spatula. I manage to slide past him to get to the sink with my now-empty glass from last night.

"How'd you sleep? You look a little tired. Did something keep you up last night?" he asks not-so-innocently.

I drop the glass into the sink and shoot him the dirtiest look I can muster.

He shrugs, turning toward the stove and scooping out the fried bacon from the pan onto three plates, already piled high with scrambled eggs and sausages. "Well, I see you're still angry at me, so here's a peace offering." He swipes the nearest plate from the stove and hands it to me.

I shake my head. "I'm good."

"You're not." He offers the plate again. "Eat. It'll make you feel better."

I'm about to say no a second time when my stomach betrays me by letting out a loud rumble.

Jax gives me a look, the kind that says, *You really want to keep fighting me about this?* I snatch the plate away from his grasp, begrudgingly parking myself on the other side of the kitchen counter to dig in. Jax doesn't join me yet, preferring to clean up the kitchen first before attacking his breakfast. I notice that he has a small blender filled with some kind of protein shake and a black duffel bag resting by the side of the refrigerator. Embroidered in big white letters on the bag and written on the bottle sitting inside it is "UFG."

I eye the bottle, then the bag, then him. "You've got another fight today?"

Jax shuts the refrigerator door. "I have training."

"You don't need to rest?"

"Champions don't rest."

"But athletes do."

"I appreciate the concern. It's sincere." Jax grins as he grabs his breakfast plate and drags a chair over to sit right in front of me. "If it means that much to you, I'll take it easy today."

"I'm not concerned. If anything, I hope you break a rib and end up in the hospital."

His face falls. "That's mean."

"But also sincere." I grin, forking another bite into my mouth.

He whistles low. "Looks like someone's a little worked up today because she didn't get to come last night, huh?"

"Oh my God—" I duck my head down like I'm in a death

match and am about to get ripped to shreds. "Lower your voice, will you?"

"Why? Afraid of what your sister will say when she finds out we hooked up?" Jax teases.

"We didn't hook up."

"Yes. We did."

"We didn't even kiss," I insist. "It was barely even a hookup. Just the world's worst jerk-off session."

"You are agitated." He states the obvious.

"That's because you are making *me* agitated."

"You know, I've got the perfect remedy for you to work out some of those feelings . . ." He dangles a strip of bacon in his mouth, smiling at me devilishly as he does.

He's not serious.

He's going to offer sex to me now? After he turned me down so coldly last night?

I'm about to get riled up again when he shakes his head, disputing my angry thoughts. "Relax. I'm not talking about that. I'm talking about MMA."

Oh.

"Still not interested," I say flatly.

"Really? After what you witnessed last night, are you not even the least bit curious about the sport? It could help unload some of that anger you seem to be clinging to." He stuffs a hand down a pocket in his shorts and takes out his wallet. He sifts through the wad of cash tucked in between the folds and picks out a very faded business card. He slides it across the counter. I notice that it's not his business card; it's for some guy named Julian James. "I train at Universal Fight Gym, in Brookline. You should drop by."

I slide the business card back over to him. "I doubt I will."

"Take it anyway. It'll be an easy way for you to find me."

"*Find* you?" I choke on a laugh. "What makes you think I'd even want to see you again?"

"Call it intuition," he says smoothly. He takes out his phone and snaps a picture of the business card, then taps away on his phone. Two seconds later, I feel my phone vibrate in my pocket. I glance up at him, questioning. He tucks his phone away, smiling. "AirDropped it to your phone, along with my phone number. You'll thank me later."

I roll my eyes and stab the leftover bacon on my plate with my fork a little too hard.

"Morning, guys. What did I miss?" Beth's chirpy voice floats into the kitchen. She's already dressed in last night's clothes—a deep-neck cropped tank and shorts. The tube top shelf in the tank has been removed for maximum cleavage.

"Nothing," I say, snatching my now-empty plate and dunking it into the sink. "I'm gonna go get my things together so we can leave."

Beth eyes me warily when I pass her. She cuts a look at Jax. "What's with her today?"

"No idea." Jax's expression remains eerily nonchalant.

***

Monday arrives, and I spend the whole day swatting away unwanted thoughts about Jax. It's annoying as hell how much space he already consumes in my head in the little time I've known him.

Screw him and his stupidly talented fingers and his stupidly smug face.

It's all I can think about as I try to enjoy my chicken salad sandwich in the college cafeteria. I'm having a staring contest with the contact he AirDropped to my phone.

If I let him rattle me again or do the things I let him do to me, I'm not sure my heart will be able to handle the hurt that comes along with it.

My finger has been hovering over the Delete button for ten minutes now. It's supposed to be so simple. Delete him and move on. Find a nice guy to settle down with. I'm a freshman, for fuck's sake. The world's my goddamned oyster. I'm sure there's someone here for me who isn't going to bring me what I'm already convinced will be a lifetime of trouble.

I look at the number again. Then back at the Delete button. Then the number again. I stare so hard at the digits that I'm certain I have them memorized by this point. Deleting his contact wouldn't even matter anymore. The irony.

This is so fucking stupid.

I click my phone off, stuff the last of my sandwich into my mouth, and force myself to get moving. I'm already late to run lines with Dakota, and she won't appreciate me blowing her off because I'm distracted over a guy I'm not even dating.

It's my first time in the rehearsal building, and I'm surprised by the number of practice spaces and the array of creatives here. From the corner of my eye, I see students in leotards flit up the stairs for their movement class. When I reach Dakota's practice room, I notice a couple of musicians with their huge instrument cases waiting for their turn to use the room beside ours.

I poke my head through the door and find Dakota already inside, getting started on some vocal warm-ups. She's wearing her "Live, Laugh, Theater" shirt again. She claims she wears it ironically, but I believe otherwise. Today, she's wearing the shirt as a crop top, bunching the extra fabric at the back and tying it into a knot. Her long dark hair is slicked into a high ponytail. When she wears her hair up like that, she usually means business.

Sometimes I wish I was artistic like Dakota. Even when I met her, at sixteen, she knew she wanted to do theater. When she's not yelling at underground fighters to shed more blood, she has an amazing, unique voice that could rival anyone on Broadway's right now. And when she belts, that's when the musical side of her voice really shines.

Meanwhile, her boyfriend, Trevor, matches her talent in equal measure. He's set to become one of the best pastry chefs in his culinary arts program. I could live on the double-nut baklava he makes. In high school, he liked to use me and Dee as guinea pigs for his creations. Back then, he had more misses than hits—I remember him nearly poisoning us at one point with vinegar that he'd mistaken for corn syrup in his chocolate chip cookies—but now, thankfully, he's found his stride and is thriving in his program.

I purse my lips into a frown, envying the talent of my friends. No hobby has ever really stuck with me, which is probably why I settled on a business major. There's nothing else I seem to be good at. It makes what Jax said about me being meant for astronomical things all the more perplexing. It's clear the only future waiting for me is a boring nine-to-five desk job, where I'll spend every waking moment climbing up the corporate ladder until I'm so burned-out from all the overtime and a lack of a social life that I descend into a depressive hole and stay there until I finally die.

It's not an ambitious plan, but at least it's *a* plan.

"Hey." I wave to Dakota as I stroll into the practice room, swinging my bag around to pull out a script and placing it on a music stand.

"Thank God you're here." A subtle relief washes over Dakota's face when she sees me. "I thought I was going have to get Trevor to be Petruchio today."

"Well, he'd probably get the voice down better than I can."

"True, but you're a natural drama queen. Which is exactly what good ol' Pet is," she says with a smirk.

"So does that means Trevor's not joining us?" I ask, remembering that it wasn't going to be just me and Dakota today.

"He's covering a shift at the doughnut shop. He should be done in the evening, though. And then he's all mine," she says excitedly, all while wriggling her eyebrows.

"Date night?"

"More like dicked-down night," she corrects me.

My shock manifests into a sharp laugh. "Ma'am, your inner hoe is showing."

"So sue me. It's been a while since we hooked up." She swipes a coffee cup from the stool behind her and hands it to me. "Here. You're gonna need this today."

"Thanks," I say, taking a sip of the dirty matcha latte. It's run cold, but it doesn't matter. Caffeine is caffeine.

I rest the coffee cup on a stool, drop my bag onto the floor, and flip through the pages of the script to find the one I dog-eared when we stopped on Friday. It's the scene where the two lead characters, Petruchio and Katherine, are fighting over getting married. I lean against the table and smooth the pages out over the music stand.

The play in question, *The Taming of the Shrew*, has always rubbed me the wrong way—ever since I had to perform part of it for literature class during my senior year. While the classic rom-com it inspired, *10 Things I Hate About You*, is one of my favorites ever, it barely resembles the original material that I read in class. The film version turns what was supposed to be a toxic relationship into a rather cheesy high school romance. While supercute, it lacks depth.

The reality of the play is that this poor woman, Katherine, who was defiant and candid and powerful, had her power taken away by Petruchio under the guise of love. It's a tragedy, really. There's nothing romantic about it.

Dakota catches me daydreaming and snaps me back to reality. "Can we please focus? I'm really nervous, and I could use your full attention."

"Well, I don't see why you should be. You're essentially playing yourself."

"Ha-ha," she deadpans. "Dakota is the shrew that needs taming. Real original, Si."

"Yeah, that was bad. I'm just a little distracted," I say, pushing myself off the edge of the table.

Dakota walks over and props an arm over my music stand, her cheek resting on her hand as she peers up at me with a pout. Her ponytail falls over my script, strands pooling in thick squiggles. "Okay, since you're begging for me to ask: Is this about Jax?"

"No."

"Really?" Her luscious eyebrows perk up with interest. "Cuz I heard you bumped into him after the fight."

"Yeah, I did. But . . . that was it."

Dakota makes a face. "Well, that's not what I heard. Didn't Beth say that you had the time of your life at his apartment? Or was she lying about that?"

My body immediately clamps up with fear.

How does she know about me and Jax? Did Beth happen to see us on the couch? She never mentioned anything to me when we came back—

"Don't play dumb. Beth couldn't stop tweeting about sleeping in his bed this weekend. I heard the Egyptian cotton sheets made the both of you sleep like babies."

"Oh yeah. Right," I breathe.

"Guess my brother ending up in the ER worked in your guys' favor. Thanks for checking up on him, by the way."

"Shit, I'm so sorry, Dee," I say sympathetically. I'd been too consumed with Jax for my own good. "How is he?" I'm worried that it might not be the good news everyone was hoping for.

"He's fine. Just resting at home for the week. Lucky bastard." She sighs, straightening herself up and shuffling over to the other side of the practice room. She yanks another music stand by the neck and drags it over opposite me so we're face-to-face, then slaps her script on top of the stand. "Meanwhile, I'm stuck here practicing lines for a character that I'm probably not even going to get."

"Hey, you wanted to audition," I remind her.

"I know, I know, it's my own fault." She frowns, flicking the page stoppers over the script to keep it in place. "But I just keep thinking about what we said when we found out we both got accepted to BU."

I nod. Vividly, I recall Dakota and I promising each other that the next chapter of our lives was going to be filled with spontaneous, awesome memories that we'd never, ever forget.

"We said we were always going to put ourselves out there," I say.

"Because we only regret the chances we don't take," she finishes.

"You got this." I nod in reassurance. "I have a good feeling about it."

"You think?" She glances at me, her eyes hopeful.

"Yeah, I do."

Dakota smiles back. I'm happy she's going after what she loves. I want nothing more than for my best friend to shine on that stage. She rarely got big roles in our high school plays, so I know she's eager to leave that bad streak behind.

But I guess it's always going to be bittersweet when I think about my friends and the big things that they're doing out there—the things that make their lives glow with purpose. It just reminds me of what my life sorely lacks.

I'm just happy they're happy and thriving. If I can't be someone for myself, it's a consolation that I can support my friends and their dreams.

"You wanna start from the top again?" I offer.

Dakota nods enthusiastically. She launches the scene.

"Fie, fie!" Dakota cries. "Unknit that threat'ning unkind brow . . . . and, and dart not scornful glances from those eyes. To would—"

"To wound," I correct her softly.

"To wound thy lord, thy king, thy governor," she recites

dramatically. "It blots thy beauty as frosts do bite the meads . . . confounds thy fame as whirlwinds shake their fair buds and in no sense is meet or amiable." She stops midway and looks at me. "God, I'm dreadful, aren't I?"

"I think your reading is too tragic for this comedy. We may have to arrange you literally breaking a leg before going up."

"Fuck." She does a slow pace around the room, anxiety creeping into her body and showing on her worried face. She comes to a halt in front of me and gives me a dead-serious look. "You think I should just sleep with the director?"

"Dee!"

"It's not like it'd be my first rodeo," she mutters.

"What?" I blast out. "Who?"

"Mr. Mangioni," she admits, and I make a gagging sound, disgusted over her spilled-out confession about having sex with our eleventh-grade drama teacher. "What? Don't look at me like that."

"I will *absolutely* look at you like that because that's horrifying."

"Not even in a girl boss kinda way?" Dakota squeaks out.

"*Dee*," I warn, continuing to glare at her. "He's almost forty with two *kids*."

"Fie, fie!" my best friend says amusedly. "Unknit that threat'ning unkind brow. Dart not scornful glances from those eyes, thy judgmental bitch—"

I fling my script at her, and she narrowly evades my throw.

She crumbles to the ground in laughter.

***

I wish I lived on campus.

When we graduated high school, Dakota asked if I wanted to be her roommate. She was planning on living in the dorms, since she didn't feel like she and Trevor were serious enough to get a place together yet. I considered her offer. It made sense for us to move in together; it would've been a more convenient solution than having to commute between the city and the suburbs. And for once in my life, I'd be away from my family. I could go to parties and hang out with my friends all night, experiment with boys, and do whatever other rites of passage eighteen-year-olds enjoy when they're freshly moved out.

But then again, I'd be away from my family. And more importantly, I'd be away from *Mom*. I can't do that to her. She's already sacrificed so much for us. Moving away feels like I'd be betraying her somehow. Plus, money is tight enough as it is. If I didn't have a full tuition scholarship to BU, I'd probably have to drop out. And I'm not about to let crippling student debt plague me for the rest of my life. Deciding to give up on living on my own was a small sacrifice, but it's one I didn't mind making at the time.

The forty-five-minute commute home is a surefire way of making me second-guess my decision.

When I step foot back in Norwood after another grueling train ride from the city, it's almost five in the evening. I make sure to swing by Beth's high school to walk her home. We do this whenever my schedule allows it. Today, I'm so late she's the only one left. When I find her, she's sitting alone outside by the curb of the parking lot, pecking away on her phone. I texted her before I left, telling her to go on without me, but she insisted on waiting.

Usually she's more than glad to be on her merry way if it means she can get home early, so it's weird that today she'd wait. And about five minutes into our walk home, I find out why.

"I need you to cover for me this Friday," Beth gushes out after we've stopped at a red light.

"Why?"

"Kinley's throwing a party at her place because her parents are going to Portland for the weekend, and I don't wanna miss it," she tells me. "You know I rarely get invited to anything, so this is a big deal for me."

"But you hate parties," I remark.

"It's my junior year. And . . . I don't know . . ." Her voice trails off, and her gaze drops to her shoes as she kicks her heels together nervously. "I hate feeling left out."

My lips drag into a frown. Sometimes I feel bad for Beth. I know it's hard for her to connect with people. Her nerves usually get the better of her whenever she tries to strike up a conversation with someone, so people see her as awkward and timid. When I was still in school, I always made sure to invite her along to hang out with me, Dakota, and Trevor. The four of us formed a little group that stayed tight until the three of us graduated.

Beth was devastated when we left for college. I think, in a way, she felt like we were all moving on from her. I'm glad that this year, she's trying to grab as many opportunities as possible to make high school less miserable than it already is.

I mull over Kinley's party until the light turns green and we make it all the way to the other end of the road. There, we take a hard left, and the sprawling bungalows begin morphing into modest homes.

"This is the third time I'm covering for you," I remind her.

"Does that mean you'll do it?" She perks up, and I nod. She clenches her fist in victory.

"At least Kinley's party will be safer than that underground fight." I shrug.

"Well, we made it out of that one fine, didn't we? More than fine," she says, her features becoming dreamy, and I know she's thinking about Jax. Guilt prickles my skin. She still doesn't know about what happened between us. I don't know if I can ever bring myself to tell her.

"You think we'll ever see him again?" Beth asks, her eyes shining with hope as she whips her gaze back to me.

"I don't know, Beth," I say, another frown pulling on my mouth at the thought of seeing Jax again. "I don't think you should seek him out. He's not safe to be around—and he's too old for you. Maybe you'll meet someone cute at Kinley's party."

"I'll try," she says. Her teeth dig into her bottom lip before she adds, "Oh, and one last thing. The party's BYOB and . . . I'm kinda low on my allowance."

I narrow my eyes. "How low?"

"Like . . . zero."

"Seriously?"

"Yeah, I know. I'm sorry," she says with a pout. Before I can suggest that she ask our mom, she beats me to it. "I don't wanna ask Mom for more. She's been so stressed out lately with Dad, and I'm afraid I'll just add to it."

I tighten my hand around the strap of my bag at the thought of it. It's hard not to walk on eggshells around Mom. She's the main provider of our household, and my dad is making things more difficult for her. I wish we could afford a therapist for her because she's in desperate need. But every time I try to get a part-time job on the side to help her make ends meet, she forces me to quit because she says it's her responsibility, not mine, and she wants me to focus on school. "Enjoy your youth. You only get to experience it once," is her typical response.

But that doesn't mean I don't try. I spent my senior year in high school doing whatever odd jobs I could find on the weekends—walking dogs, tutoring kids, doing a thousand online surveys—just so Beth and I would have some extra spending money.

"Here," I say, digging into my bag to grab my wallet. I hand her a fifty-dollar bill, the last of my cash. "This will cover a six-pack and your ride home, plus give you some extra for the week."

"Si, are you sure?" She halts on the sidewalk, staring at the cash. "You've got enough to survive the next few days?"

"Yeah. Don't worry about it."

She doesn't look convinced. "I don't know . . . this is a lot."

"It's okay," I say, nudging the cash toward her. "Just take it."

We've just turned the corner to our street. Beth catches me up on some high school gossip and fills me in on how she's been doing in her classes. She tells me she's going to try out for cheer soon.

"Really? That's amazing." I gape at her.

"Yeah. I figure I've only got two years left in this hellhole, I might as well try to make the most of it." Beth tries to sound confident, but there's an anxiousness in her voice that suggests she's dreading the tryouts. Still, there's no mistaking the excited sparkle in her eyes. I wonder if Dakota has been nudging her with all her *carpe diem* shit. Whatever the case, it seems that everyone is moving on to bigger things.

"Seriously, Beth. I'm happy for you," I say as we arrive in front of our house. The curtains are closed, but there's soft light filtering through, which means my parents are home. My hand slips into my back pocket to produce the key. "You need to tell Mom and Dad about it."

Beth's cheeks flush with embarrassment. "Let's not jump the gun. I haven't even made the team yet."

"Why? They might just stop arguing with each other for five seconds to celebrate with you."

"But there's nothing to celebrate yet."

"Who cares? Finally putting yourself out there is reason enough." I grin, unlocking the front door and removing my coat and scarf to hang them on the coatrack. Beth follows suit. "Hey, guys, Beth's got some news to share," I yell out. My ears perk up, waiting for an enthusiastic response from my parents, but it doesn't arrive. "Mom? Dad?" I drop my bag at the foot of the staircase and shuffle down the hallway.

"We're in the living room," my dad says in a clipped voice.

I step into the room carefully, given his tone. I expect the usual sight to greet me—my dad settled in front of the TV, scrolling through the sports channels, while my mom's seated in front of her laptop at the dining table, typing out work emails. Instead, they sit side by side on the sofa, silent as they watch me walk in. Like they've been waiting for us for a while. Dad looks uncomfortable. Mom is sullen. Dad is tapping his feet nervously on the carpet. Mom looks like she's been crying, if the half dozen or so tissues scattered across the side table are any indication.

A sinking feeling settles itself into the pit of my stomach.

"What's going on?" I whisper.

Dad rises out of his seat once Beth has also entered.

"We need to talk," he says.

FIVE

My parents were high school sweethearts.

Everyone who knew them would gush about how romantic it was that they'd been in love with each other since the ninth grade. They balanced each other well. Mom was confident and ambitious, the kind of woman who could certainly take care of herself. She was brought up in a single-parent household after her dad died of a sudden heart attack, so she had to be self-sufficient if she wanted a proper future for herself.

But that never stomped out her inner romantic, the part that craved being adored and looked after. Enter my dad, who seemed to check all of my mom's boxes. He was a noble, up-front, and overall stand-up guy. Solid in the way you knew you could depend on him. My mom sure did. They went to the same college, graduated, and started a life together. Held equally distinguished jobs. Twenty years and two kids later, they looked like they had the perfect marriage.

Then, tiny cracks started to show.

It started five years ago, when my dad was laid off from his job—a senior position at a marketing firm. It was a huge blow for him. Jobs in the area were scarce to begin with, and even when he managed to land an interview for something in his field, nobody wanted to hire someone who didn't know their way around the digital landscape into a senior position. He was an old-school fellow; it was all he'd known. He didn't know how to leave all that training behind and start over, so he held on with desperate hope that there was something out there that would suit his skills. But he kept coming up short, and six months later, he just . . . stopped.

We all thought he was just taking a break, so we went easy on him. He stopped helping around the house. Could no longer be bothered with the upkeep, so he pushed it all on Mom or Beth and me. His favorite pastime became sitting in front of the TV. It was annoying, but we figured he'd snap out of it eventually. *He's just going through it*, my mom assured us. *It'll pass.*

It didn't.

Then came the excessive amount of liquor that Dad persuaded us was "just casual drinking." But the alcohol allowed him to slip further and further into idleness. He spent the next four years living off the money he and Mom had saved for our college tuition. By that point, he'd completely let himself go. And he didn't seem to care in the least. Maybe it was an ego thing for him—he just couldn't cope with being beaten down by life like that. Or perhaps it was seeing my mom effortlessly pick up the pieces of his negligence to provide for the family, knowing all too well that if he disappeared tomorrow, the house would still function fine without him.

I hated that Mom always cleaned up his messes. Every. Single. Time. Picking up after him, helping him get sober, she did it all. And he just let her. Like it was her responsibility in the first place. Because what was his purpose in life now if not to let his beautiful, much more successful partner take care of everything for him?

I can remember only a handful of times when he felt like a normal dad. He rarely cared about what I was doing unless it contributed to how we were perceived by others. He had a reputation to uphold in our neighborhood, so he became obsessed with how people saw us. That was the only time I ever saw him put any effort into himself. He didn't want people to think that he was a bum now, so he'd just flat-out lie about his life. I couldn't even count on both hands how many jobs he's supposedly held. A hedge fund manager, a stockbroker, a senior partner at a law firm . . . any executive position that held any amount of respect, he claimed he'd done it. He'd embellish other parts of our lives too. I apparently still did ballet despite quitting years ago. Beth was a straight-A student even though she barely passed her science classes every semester. And the main reason we'd been living in shoddy rentals, according to Dad, was because we were waiting for renovations on our new, much bigger home to be completed.

People bought the stories for a while. Which was why no one ever knew how far gone he was. And Mom kept quiet about it too. As Dad dug the hole deeper, she became too embarrassed to own the truth.

Eventually, the lies did catch up to him. People started digging, and Dad couldn't handle it, so we moved away to this modest house where Beth and I now share a bedroom. In

Dad's eyes, it was a downgrade from what we had before, but Mom, Beth, and I didn't care. We made it work. And as far as I knew, Mom and Dad were trying to do the same with their marriage.

***

For a moment, nobody speaks as my dad's statement rings in the air. The only sounds are the soft whirring of the heater, a shocked breath hissing out of Beth, and my mom's discreet sniffles as she wipes another tissue over her nose.

My dad glances at me, waiting for me to say something. My mom does too. So far, I'm the only one who hasn't reacted to the news.

I don't like the silence stretching on for this long. I should probably say something, but it feels like my whole body has shut down as it registers the shock, the muscles in my throat clamping up tight.

I suppose, in a way, I should've known this was coming. I should've prepared my heart for the inevitable: all their arguments, never coming to any resolution—this was clearly the next, unavoidable step.

But I never wanted to think about the next step. Because that meant that all the work my mom put into this marriage to keep it intact was for nothing.

I'm frustrated and brokenhearted at the decision, but I understand it needed to happen. But if I'm being honest with myself, the divorce itself isn't the reason why I'm frustrated. It's *who* most likely instigated it that's running circles in my mind.

"When was . . . uh . . . when was this decided?" Beth

shuffles forward, her eyes filled with tears as they dart back and forth between Mom and Dad.

"We signed the papers today." My dad's voice is constrained and hoarse when he answers. "I'm sorry, girls. But please know that this is no one's fault. Neither of you did anything wrong."

Oh, trust me, we're not blaming ourselves for this, I think sourly to myself.

"And I'm not going anywhere, at least not for a long while." My dad leans forward, cupping my mom's hand in his. My mom relaxes against his touch, inhaling deeply. It's been a while since he's shown any kind of affection toward her. His gaze zigzags between me and Beth with renewed determination. "We're both going to do whatever we can to make sure that you guys are settling into this new . . . arrangement as smoothly as possible. We want you girls to be comfortable with what's happening before we make any big changes."

An unexpected, hysterical laugh bursts out of me. Of course, he's acting like this now. Playing the role of the rational parent by breaking the news to us in a mature way. Pretending that it was him all along that was putting in all the work in the marriage.

My heart rate picks up, just as my anger does.

I should take the moral high road. I should want to react to this news with mild regret and acceptance, because that's what my mom deserves. But I've never been the type to let things go, especially when the person who's been burned happens to be the woman I've looked up to my entire life.

Fuck. This. Shit.

The muscles in my throat relax, and I finally manage to find my voice.

"Who filed?"

My mom shifts in discomfort, crossing one leg over the other. She looks the other way, careful not to meet my gaze. The tension in my dad's jaw builds as he looks at me in warning.

Instead of giving me a direct answer, he deflects. "Let's, uh . . . let's not play the blame game here."

My gaze flickers between my parents. My mom's face is turned away, so I only see her side profile, but there is no mistaking the large, glassy tears filling her beautiful, somber blue eyes. They are tears of mourning, not defeat.

"Dad?" Beth says breathlessly, looking absolutely crushed as she waits for a response to my question.

Dad sighs, rubbing his chin with his thumb and index finger. "It was a mutual decision to end the marriage," he explains. "But yes, I was the one who filed. It doesn't matter."

"Of course it matters," I challenge him. I drop my chin and push away the hair from my face, gathering as much momentum as I can physically muster. "Look. I'm not happy about you and Mom getting a divorce, but I get it. We're not going to be one big loving family anymore. Fine. Big deal. We haven't been for a while now, so this isn't some new thing Beth and I need to adjust to. But you're gonna do this *now*? After you've taken everything from this woman—this fearless, selfless woman who stood by you while you fell apart?" I point to my sister, who's hugging herself tightly to keep from falling apart herself. "You gave up on me and Beth a long time ago. I've made my peace with that. But now you're giving up on Mom too?"

"I'm not giving up, Sienna." He shakes his head, his dark brows thunderous. "I tried hard with your mom."

"Oh, come on," I scoff. "You didn't do jack *shit*. Giving up is in your nature. It's what got us here in the first place."

"I made mistakes. I get it. And I'm sorry."

I shake my head in refusal, taking a step back from him. It's suffocating to be in his delusional bubble of lies.

"No. I don't accept your apology, *Dad*. You don't get to be sorry. Because you weren't the one who put in all the hard work to get this family back on track. *She* did." I gesture toward Mom. Dad's entire face turns a deep shade of red. "You know, I thought after all these years, you would have learned something by now. If you weren't going to take some goddamned responsibility for taking care of this family, I thought at least you'd stand by her side. Be her fucking support system while she's out there fighting the real fight. But I guess that's just too much responsibility for you. And now you're just gonna fuck off like nothing happened, like you weren't the one to take the pin out of the grenade and hurl it right in the heart of this family."

"Sienna, please stop." My mom exhales loudly, looking desperate and exhausted by the back-and-forth. "Your dad's been through enough."

"I don't get it. Why are you defending him?" I demand. "Am I the only person in this family who's angry about this? I mean, for fuck's sake, Mom, he used you for years. He's the cause of all your problems, all your hardships. And yet you're still putting up with it!" I stalk over to my dad, my throat tight with emotion. "And *you*. Do you see what you're doing to her? What you *continue* to do to her?"

Dad lets out a breath, his gaze lowered to the ground. His fingers are on his left temple, moving in small circles as he attempts to stay calm. "I'm sorry you're disappointed in me. But it's just . . . not that simple, Sienna. It's not . . . I couldn't—"

Mom rises from the couch, laying a hand on my dad's shoulder. "John . . . if you have to tell her about the—"

"I know. I know . . ." my dad whispers back. "But I think I have to."

"What?" I spin around, confused. "What's going to crush me that hasn't already?"

My dad looks up at me, wearing a colossally guilty look that means he had fucked up, bigger than any alcohol abuse or all the lies he's told about our family. That could only mean one thing . . .

"Did you . . ." I struggle to find the strength to throw such a huge accusation. "Did you have an affair?"

"Sienna," my mom whispers, warning me not to go there.

"What? We deserve to know," I say, my tone low and menacing. "Tell me I'm wrong, Dad. Tell us you didn't cheat on Mom, you *goddamned* asshole. *Tell us!*"

My dad swallows hard. I wait for him to tell me that I'm completely out of line to accuse him of something so horrid, to ground me for having the nerve to accuse him in the first place.

But he doesn't.

This is fucked up. This is so fucked up—

"Oh my God." Beth clamps a hand over her mouth, trying to contain her horror.

My dad begins to panic. "Wait," he pleads, shuffling over to the both of us. "Just . . . let me explain—"

I recoil from him, nauseated at the revelation. "God, I can't even look at you right now!"

"Sienna," Dad says, dropping his voice to a strangled whisper. *"Please."*

"How dare you?" I yell out. "How. Fucking. *Dare*. You!"

"I know it's difficult to understand the position that I'm in, but you have to know," he pleads, "you *have* to know, the last thing I wanted to do was to hurt your mom."

"But you did it anyway!" I bellow. I'm livid now. My cheeks burn from the heat of rage. My gaze shoots toward my mom, who's standing beside the couch, hands covering her cheeks as the tears streak down her face. I want to reach out to her, to hold her hand, to pull her into my arms because God knows she needs a hug right now. But I'm *so* angry. Not just at him but at her, for refusing to call him out for what he did, for standing by his side—like him fucking another woman doesn't mean anything to her.

"Mom, how can you just sit there and grieve over this man? How can you still be in the same *room* as him?" I turn my face to my dad, ready to curse him out, when he tries to reach for me again.

"Si—" my dad starts off.

"Don't touch me!" I scream it with every ounce of disgust I can muster in my body. I'm so pissed off that my shoulders are shaking when I cast out the last of my venom. "You don't deserve us," I growl at him. "You never have, and you never will. And one day, you're going to wake up and realize you'll never have anyone remotely as good as me, Beth, and Mom, and you're going to be so miserable, and I hope you'll *stay* miserable when you have to carry the weight of your mistakes for the rest of your life."

It takes everything for my dad not to bite back, even

though it's clear from his expression that that's what he wants to do. Behind the tears, my mom glances at my dad. The sadness disappears for a moment, and her lips curl upward a little at him, giving him a look of kindness after having endured my outburst.

He turns to her and nods, like he's telling her, *It's fine.*

I don't get anything that happens in this family anymore. Clearly, they have more secrets between them than either is willing to share.

"I . . . I gotta get out of here," I say, throwing my hands up in defeat before spinning toward the door.

"Sienna!" my dad yells. "Sienna!"

I ignore him, snatching my coat from the stand and punching my arms through the sleeves as quickly as I can. My hands are trembling. My body is shaking, brain spinning out of control like it's about to fall out of my head. With a hard grip, I wrench the front door open and bolt out of the house.

It's pouring outside. The rain smacks at my face and burrows into my coat, but I push on anyway because there's no way I'm going back inside, defeated by a little rain.

"Sienna! Wait!" I hear Beth yelling after me as I race down the steps of our front porch. "Where the hell are you *going*?"

I turn toward her. "I don't know!" I say, exasperated. She frowns at my tone, and I feel guilty for raising my voice at her. Surely she knows that my frustrations are not directed at her. I press my fingers to my temples and close my eyes for a moment. "I'm sorry. I can't stay there. Not with him in the house."

"I know," Beth says, following me down the steps. She stops a few feet away from me, her hands shoved into the pockets of her jeans. She's not wearing a coat, and the rain is already soaking through her clothes. "But you can't just run away."

I feel my eyes filling with frustrated tears. I don't even know what I'm angry about anymore. It feels like this feeling has no beginning or end, like it's always been there, except that now I'm feeling it full force.

"I don't get it," I say, my voice sharpening. "Why does it feel like I'm the only one that's pissed off about this situation?"

Beth lets out a long sigh. "I'm pissed too, Si, you have no idea. But there's nothing we can do about it. It's their lives. We don't get a say in it."

"And you're just going to go back into that house and pretend that everything's okay? Like we've been doing for the past five years?"

"No, of course not. But . . . one way or another, we're gonna have to put this behind us."

Why is she so rational about this? Why doesn't she want to punch a fist through the wall after Dad betrayed us yet again?

I shake my head, gritting my teeth in determination. "I'm not going to do it. I've forgiven Dad for many things, but I can't forgive him for this. I'll die before I ever let that happen."

Concern darkens her once bright, beautiful eyes as she pushes a hand through her damp hair. "Then what are you going to do? Where are you gonna *go*? It's pouring out there."

My mouth drops open, and I blink rapidly, trying to figure out how I'm going to answer her. I don't have a plan. All I know is that my head feels like it's a ticking time bomb, and if I don't leave in the next five seconds, it might explode and take the whole neighborhood down with it.

"I don't know," I say, a little more softly this time. "I just need some space right now."

Beth looks hesitant to let me go, but she nods, reluctant understanding in her eyes.

"Fine. Please . . . text me," she says.

I nod.

And then I turn back around and plunge into the rain.

***

The rain doesn't stop. It picks up strength, turning into a torrential downpour.

I scramble to find some form of shelter amidst the row of houses along the cul-de-sac; all I can do is take refuge under some trees. They do little to halt the sheets of rain coming down on my skin in hard, painful spatters. I wipe the droplets from my phone screen and hit Dakota's number. After a couple of rings, it goes straight to voicemail.

Right.

She and Trevor are doing date night tonight. How could I forget?

I scroll through my contacts list. It isn't long, just a couple of relatives and friends I'm not close enough with to unload all my family drama on. I reach the end of the list and sigh, scrolling back up again. What the hell do I do now? I don't want to go back, but I'm strapped for cash, and my options are bleak. The only two people who understand me are Dakota and Beth, and my sister would rather try to make peace with my parents than share my frustrations.

My finger stops scrolling when I spot Jax's number.

A heavy breath falls out of me.

Before I can backpedal, my finger slams on the Call button, and I lift the phone to my ear.

"Hey," I say. "Where are you?"

SIX

Jax Venmos me some cash to call an Uber. I tell him I have just enough in my bank account to walk to the train station and buy a ticket to the city, but he doesn't want me stranded out in the rain for another second. I don't like owing people debts but Jax insists that I keep the change and says that if I try to put up a fight about it, he'll Venmo me even *more* cash.

I type in the gym address from the card Jax gave me, and five minutes later, I've got a ride. The Uber drops me off at the corner in front of a long row of shops on Brookline Avenue. UFG is nestled among them. The rain has already dissipated to a light patter, and I'm grateful because I'm not sure if I can take being beaten down by it again. I push my damp hair aside and lift my head to stare at the minimalist black-and-white signboard above the storefront that reads UNIVERSAL FIGHTER'S GYM.

The exterior of the gym has probably seen better days, the white paint now oxidized to an icky beige color. Flyers are stuck on every available space of the storefront—everything from gym promotions and services to local business ads that someone has attempted to peel off with lackluster success. Even the black paint on the front doors is heavily chipped.

I startle when they suddenly swing open. A familiar golden-haired man emerges, whirling his head back and forth before spotting me and jogging down the steps to get me. I shouldn't feel this relieved to see his face.

"Hey." Jax's voice is a warm hearth that pulls me to shelter. His eyes light up with concern as he stares into the depths of my eyes. "Are you okay?"

"I—I don't know," I mutter, my heartbeat picking up—from anger or nerves, I'm still not sure.

"Well, you came to the right place." He guides me up the steps and pushes the door open for me. "Welcome to UFG, a sanctuary for misfits."

My heart lurches as soon as I enter the gym. An unexpected feeling descends upon me, settling on me like snow falling to the ground.

Home.

The gym is deceptively larger than it looks from the outside. Worn-out equipment crowds one corner, rows of kettlebells and weights displayed on metal racks. In another corner, two boxing rings stand erect on either side of an MMA cage. Above them lies a nearly empty half floor with a perfect view of the octagon. The cage is a sight to behold, and it's clear MMA is what the gym specializes in. A pair of guys are already going at it in the cage, throwing jabs at each other with determined huffs. Unlike the fight in the warehouse, they are both wearing gloves, and the sparring looks more controlled. More professional.

Meanwhile, the brick walls are spray-painted with graffiti-styled quotes from famous fighters, bringing color and character into the gym. There are quotes that are unfamiliar to me—some by Mike Tyson, Conor McGregor, Anderson Silva. As my gaze flits across each one, I feel my chest swelling with an odd feeling of pride—admiration, even. Like I crave my words being on that wall one day too.

Jax leads me across the gym, and I take in the row of punching bags circling the cage. Curious, I tighten my hand into a fist and press my knuckles against one of them, testing its density. I wonder if my hand would bruise if I knocked my fist against it with enough force.

We enter an office tucked behind all the equipment. There is a huge shelf filled with biographies of Ronda Rousey and Georges St-Pierre, as well as several massive gold belts and plaques awarded by the UFC and other big promotions. *Wow*, I instantly think to myself. *The guy who runs this place must be a legend.*

A tall, muscular man sits behind an immense desk in the middle of the office; he wipes a towel over his sweat-coated face. Tattoos slither up his huge arms, even running up the sides of his neck, stopping short of his shaved head. When he looks up at me, he drops the towel onto the table and his thick eyebrows draw low over his square face.

"This is Julian, my trainer." Jax introduces me to the stranger. "He also runs the gym."

So this is the guy on the business card. I stick my hand out awkwardly toward him. "Sienna."

Julian doesn't stand up or even shake my hand. Despite me hovering over him, his presence feels large and intimidating.

He looks me up and down, the intensity of his gaze burning into my face.

"Well?" he asks expectantly.

"Well, what?"

"What are you looking to do in my gym? Kickboxing? Muay Thai?" He presses on, tenting his hands together in front of him. He pauses, gaze darting to my messy, damp hair then to my drenched clothes. "Or are you just looking for a shower, because you reek right now."

I mash my lips together tightly. "Funny, because I was going to say the same about you," I say, noting the musky, sweaty scent coming from him. The greasiness of his hair and the sweat pooling on the front of his shirt tell me he just finished a session before tending to his work in the office.

Julian doesn't seem impressed with my reply.

"Do you have experience with any combat sport?" His tone is harsh as he continues to stare me down. I imagine he's picking my body apart in his mind—evaluative eyes roaming over my loosely defined waist, slender arms, and massive thighs, concluding that I'm far from being athletic.

"She's a friend of mine," Jax answers for me.

Julian laughs casually, swinging his gaze to his fighter. "You don't have female friends."

Jax grins. "She's a first."

"Something tells me that it wasn't up to you."

"Doesn't matter." Jax shrugs. "She's here to stay."

"She won't stay a friend, that's for sure," Julian ridicules.

"Can we stop talking like I'm not here?" I cut in.

"Then what do you want to talk about?" Julian rises from his chair, pressing all ten of his fingers against the table surface.

"Because I'm still not sure why you're here or what you're good for, other than to throw shitty comebacks."

"Well, I'm also good at putting men in their place when they're in my face," I sneer defiantly, lifting my head up bravely.

A bored stare is the only reply I get from Julian.

Jax notices the heavy tension building and steps in. "She's here because she's thinking of getting some lessons, and I want to show her the ropes. Anyone that walks through the door is good for business, right?"

Julian grunts. I wonder if he's always this surly or if I've just caught him in a bad mood.

"Fine," Julian snaps. "Go show her around."

Jax grabs a hold of my wrist and drags me out of the office.

"Is he always like that?" I ask when we're out of earshot.

"Yeah. He can be intense. He's trained a lot of people in the past, but many don't stick around long enough to take the sport seriously. And he needs good fighters to represent the gym."

"Okay," I say, stringing out the last syllable. "But why did you tell him I wanted lessons?"

"Because I don't want him to throw you out. I would bring you back to my place, but he's not gonna let me leave without finishing my session tonight." Concern floods back into Jax's eyes, and he jerks his head toward me, folding his arms across his chest. "So are you going to tell me what happened with you? Because you sounded desperate on the phone."

I purse my lips. When I was on the phone with Jax, I was quite vague about what had gone down, focusing instead on the urgency to get away. I wasn't sure if I wanted him to know about my dad, if I could trust him with the truth.

But there's something about his presence in this moment that pulls my guard down. I let out a breath, expelling the truth with it. "I . . . uh . . . I just found out my parents are getting divorced because my dad cheated on my mom."

It still feels surreal to say.

"I'm sorry." His face appears crestfallen. His fingers twitch as if he wants to touch me, perhaps draw me into a comforting embrace, but he stops short and settles for dropping his hands onto his hips. "How are you feeling?"

"I don't know. It's hard to explain," I say with a huge sigh, dropping onto the edge of the mat to bury my face in my hands. I don't know why I feel compelled to spill my inner turmoil to someone I only met two days ago. "I feel a lot of things. I feel hurt. I feel betrayed. And I'm angry. So fucking angry. And it's exhausting feeling like this. Like I won't be able to survive it all."

He shakes his head vehemently. "That's the stupidest thing I've heard you say, Sienna. You can survive it. You can survive anything if you put your mind to it."

He joins me on the mat, plopping down beside me. He leans in and strokes my face, tangles a finger in my drenched hair. I stare at the way he twirls it over his index finger, so painfully slow, then pulls to unravel the curl. Because it's wet, the curl stays in place. Jax's gaze is earnest when he tells me, "You think anger is your biggest weakness? No. Fear makes you weak. Anger gives you focus. Drives your ambitions. Tap into that and you'll finally know what real power feels like."

A drop of water emerges from the curl, but he catches it on his finger. The water droplet rests so perfectly on his skin. I stare at it, completely mesmerized by such a trivial sight. I emit a gasp when he squashes the droplet with his thumb and he turns to face me, his tone serious. "Listen to me: you're not just rain, Sienna. You're a fucking hurricane. You're a swirling, raging storm that's going to reset the whole damn world. You just need to know what you want to do about it."

A hurricane. What an odd thing to call someone.

My gaze falls onto my trembling, nervous hands resting on my lap.

"What *do* I want?" I mumble, unsure if I'm emotionally equipped to answer that question right now. I cup my hands together. No matter how much I want the trembling to stop, it doesn't.

I haven't felt this powerless in a long time. If I could fix everything wrong with my family, I would in a heartbeat. But maybe fixing it isn't the solution. Maybe things are meant to stay broken. My dad's affair wasn't the event that shattered this family. It only exposed what was already so dysfunctional about us. And knowing that there was absolutely nothing I could have done makes me feel so utterly useless.

"I want . . ." I let out an exhale, along with the rest of my words. "I want to feel in control again."

My response earns a big grin from Jax.

"Look around, princess." His beautiful eyes slide over mine. "The opportunity is everywhere."

I follow his gaze, roaming over the MMA cage and the rows of heavy bags.

"Oh . . ." I look down at my feet with uncertainty. "I don't know about that."

That isn't entirely true. I felt it in my bones the second I stepped foot in the gym—that this is where I belong. I had zero interest in anything related to MMA until I saw Jax in that cage. It lit something in me. And now, being in this gym, the possibility real . . .

Am I brave enough to take the leap?

"Come. You need a hot shower. You don't want to get hypothermia." Jax pulls me onto my feet. "There are fresh towels and some spare gym clothes in the locker room. You can meet me by the bags later when you're done."

"You want me to train with you right now?"

"What better time is there? Your emotions are still raw and burning. It's the best time to train. You can use it." He steps closer. "You want to do this. I know you do. You already made your decision when you walked in here."

"I came here because that's where you were," I argue back. "I came because you told me to."

"That's true. But you stayed because you wanted to."

My mouth hangs open, speechless.

Jax grins down at me, knowing there's nothing else I can say that'll help my case.

Instead, I sigh and drag myself into the locker room, loathing the fact that he's right about me.

***

When I emerge from the locker room, I'm dressed in gym attire—a UFG-branded black sports bra and matching leggings with shoes that are one size too big for me. The gym clothes feel new, but the shoes not so much. I try not to think about who this pair belongs to and what else we might share besides these greasy soles. My damp hair is pulled back into a high ponytail so it won't get in the way of what we might be doing today.

I find Jax waiting for me by the punching bags, doing a fierce combination of hits and jabs. Unlike the last underground fight, his fists are padded with a pair of black-and-gold boxing gloves as he strikes the bag forcefully, each hit causing it to swing back and forth like a pendulum. I'm fascinated whenever he lands a punch. He never loses momentum, meeting the bag with his fists with increasing strength and power each time he leans in.

When he spots me, he pushes a hand out to stop the bag from moving, and a satisfied smile spreads across his face when he sees me clad in all black.

Unstrapping the gloves from his wrists, he jogs over to the shelves propped by the wall and snatches a pair of boxing wraps along with some gloves.

"Palms up and spread your fingers for me," he orders when he walks over to me.

"Okay."

He puts the loop over my thumb and drags the wrap around my palm, going over and in between each finger before securing it around my wrist. Then he proceeds to do the same to the other hand before putting on the gloves.

"Whoa," I say, stretching both my hands after he's done with them. "Feels weird."

"You'll get used to it," Jax says, motioning me toward the punching bag. "So, quick overview of mixed martial arts: it's a full-contact combat sport blending elements of different disciplines like kickboxing, Muay Thai, Brazilian jujitsu, and wrestling. Now, there are three core components to MMA—striking, grappling, and submission. I'm not going to go into all the specifics because it'll get overwhelming. So for now, let's work on some basic boxing moves." He gets in front of the punching bag in demonstration. "Get into position, legs wide, but not too close to the bag. Ready your fists. You have to hit flush with the knuckles. You want to be landing palm down on the bag just like this. Jab—cross—" He pulls back his left arm and drives his fist forward, followed quickly by his right, sending the punching bag backward.

I gape at him, wondering if it's even possible for me to make that much impact with a punch.

"Now you try." Jax steps away, and I take my place in front of the punching bag. I lift up my arms exactly as he did, and my fist connects with the bag.

Hit.

A sharp pain attacks my fist.

"Ow!" My body recoils from the bag. I unstrap the boxing glove from my hand, shaking my wrist to get rid of the pain. It goes away after a couple of seconds.

"Don't loosen your wrist, or you're gonna sprain it. And don't sway your hips too much," Jax tells me, placing his large hands over my hips to keep me steady. My body is set aflame by his touch, my heart thundering in my chest. When he lets me go, I almost whine.

"Reset. Let's try again," he says, and I clench my fists. "Jab. Cross." *Hit. Hit.* "Come on. More power. Jab. Cross." *Hit. Hit. Hit.* My fists fly toward the punching bag with every order from Jax. They connect with the bag in loud thuds as I struggle to keep my body moving to the pacing of Jax's yelled jabs and crosses.

"Focus, Sienna," Jax barks at me.

I send him a glare. "I *am* focused."

"Not hard enough. *Again*. Jab. Cross." *Hit. Hit. Hit.* "Come on, *focus*! You're hitting it right. All you need is power. Tap into your emotions. Harness them. Dive deep into all those feelings that've been raging inside of you and *unleash*."

I blow out a frustrated breath along with the rest of my nerves. It's hard to focus when my mind is so clogged up. My brain refuses to turn off when my head and body feel so heavy with thoughts.

"Reset," Jax snaps. "Again."

I step back, keeping my eyes trained on the bag.

This time, my eyes flutter closed, and I inhale a long, deep breath as I sift through all the thoughts in my head. Instead of blocking them out, I land on a few and play them over in my mind, the anger and sadness and frustration coming to the surface. I allow all the pain of my thoughts to flow from my mind, past my shoulders, and into my arms, letting the pain turn into power. By the time I let my breath out, I'm a fueled rocket, ready to shred through the clouds and rip the entire sky apart. I close my fingers to tighten my fist, reel it back, and—

Hit.

I slam hard into the punching bag, the force and power of contact speeding through my veins as the bag connects with my knuckles. The punching bag swings back like a wild pendulum.

From the corner of my eye, I spot Julian getting up from his desk and striding toward the window looking out into the gym, eyes narrowing at me with curiosity.

"Better," Jax comments, hands behind his back as he

slowly circles me and the punching bag. "Again. Swim in that rage and wear it like it's your second fucking skin."

I'm tuned back into him again when he says the magic words.

"Jab. Cross. Jab. Cross."

Hit hit. Hit hit.

My breath is steady, and my mind clears like rain dissolving a fog. I tap into my memories—pictures blurring and swirling together. My dad's guilt-ridden face as he admits his infidelity. My beautiful, strong-willed, brokenhearted mom looking at him with empathy he doesn't deserve. My sister staring at me with disappointment like she thinks I'm being too emotional about everything.

"Jab-cross-jab. Jab-cross-jab. Jab-cross-jab-cross-jab-cross—"

Hit hit hit hit—

My fists are numb and my lungs are burning and I'm hell-bent on pushing on. I hit and hit and hit and—

Hit for every time my dad has failed me.

Hit for every time my mom chooses to be kind to him rather than turn him away.

Hit for every time I can't protect my sister from their marriage politics.

Hit for every time I've felt bad for being a loose cannon because I can't stop myself from giving people hell if they deserve it.

I ram into the punching bag so rapidly that it recoils and nearly collides with my body. I sidestep it at the last minute, determined not to let anything or anyone else brutalize me tonight.

I take a couple of steps back, feeling like my body has

expelled all remaining oxygen. It takes a while to get my breath back. Everything feels strange. My mind is floating. I feel suspended from my own body. Like someone else was punching for me for the past minute and a half.

Or what if this is the real me, and everything that has led to this moment wasn't?

A slow clap of hands reverberates through the gym.

"Told you you're a hurricane," Jax says, pleased. It makes me feel good to earn his praise. "Make sure to breathe in between punches. Don't let your arms fall, keep them tight and locked into your upper body," he instructs, and I nod. Resting his hands on his hips, he jerks his head toward the bag, all the while looking at me expectantly. "You look like you're just getting started. You wanna go again?"

There is no hesitation when I answer.

"Yes."

"Then what are you waiting for? Let's go."

My body is on autopilot as it gets into position again.

And then I do exactly what he says.

I *hit*.

SEVEN

When I peel my eyes open and shift to the side of my bed, the first thing that hits me is the soreness radiating from my arms, followed by an ache in my lower back. I groan, feeling embarrassed by how physically wrecked I feel despite how beginner-friendly yesterday's session was supposed to be.

Guess I'm not even in the decent shape I thought I was.

As I lay motionless in my bed, urging my body parts to move, I find that Beth is already up, getting ready for school. She's dressed in a funky crop top, an oversize denim jacket, and a patchwork miniskirt. I want to ask why she keeps torturing herself with these clothes when it's getting kind of cold out, but I've accepted that I'll never understand why girls suffer in the name of fashion.

She sits on the edge of her bed, kicking her heels together. Her blue eyes are on me when I haul myself into a sitting position. It's like she's been waiting for me to get up for a while now, which is weird. Usually, if I'm sleeping in, she'll head to school without me. I plant both of my feet on the floor and brace my hands on either side of me, sucking in a breath as I get used to the ache in my muscles.

"Morning, Beth," I say, my eyes still heavy with sleep.

Instead of keeping the conversation light, my sister gets straight into it.

"Where did you go last night?"

I force myself to look up at her and draw a long breath. Sure enough, the guilt sneaks up on me again—a familiar feeling now when it comes to my sister. I know I shouldn't feel bad because nothing romantic has happened with Jax, but perhaps visiting his gym wasn't the most productive move in that department either.

"Well?" she asks in a not-so-casual tone.

"It was nowhere special."

As soon as the words leave me, my body hammers with instant regret. I shouldn't be keeping this from Beth. There's really no reason to. It's not like Jax and I did anything last night.

"Okayyy." Beth drags the word out like she's still suspicious. "You promised you'd text, though. I was worried sick."

"I guess I lost track of time," I mumble. This time, not a lie. Last night's MMA session was the first time I felt fully immersed in something that gave me so much joy that I blocked out everything else like white noise.

Just then, my phone buzzes on my nightstand, stealing both Beth's and my attention. I snatch it with a quick hand before she can see who it's from. My heart jumps when I find that it's a message from Jax.

Good morning, princess. Ready for an afternoon session today at UFG?

I squint at the message, trying to remember when I agreed to another session with him.

I type a curt reply, hoping he will get the message.

I have class. I don't have time.

It's barely five seconds later when I get another text.

How bout afterward?

My thumbs hover over the keyboard.

"Seriously, who is that?" Beth cranes her neck, curious. "You're acting weird."

"Just Dee telling me she had a fight with Trevor." The lie slips out of my mouth before I can catch it. Her eyes are still stuck on me, like she's deciding whether or not to believe me. I don't look away because then she'll know I've been lying.

After a while, a sigh escapes her, and she rises to her feet, grabbing her backpack and looping it over one shoulder. "Okay. Whatever," Beth mutters, and my breath leaves me in a rushed exhale. "You gonna pick me up from school today? It's cheer tryouts. I'd love for you to come and see."

I click my phone shut and glance up at her. "What about Mom and Dad?"

She looks surprised that I would even suggest it. And then, like a heavy brick, it slams into me. Last night. My parents announcing their divorce. *My dad admitting he's a cheater.*

And here I was just starting to forget that it ever happened.

"No." Sadness catches Beth's tone. "I don't wanna see either of them right now. Just you."

There it is. The reminder that after last night, nothing about this family will ever be the same again.

"Sure," I say, forcing a smile. "I'll be there. I got your back, Beth. Always."

My phone vibrates in my hand again.

You'll cave, princess, Jax texts. *Just you wait.*

***

It's not until about five hours later that I do cave.

After sitting through an entire morning lecture not paying attention and streaming as many MMA fights I can find online, it becomes clear to me where I'd rather be spending the rest of my time right now.

In a cage. With a pair of gloves.

I want to fight again. I want to feel what I felt when I rammed that punching bag last night. And I want to do it with Jax. He brings out a ferocity in me that I didn't even know I had.

Which begs the question—what is Jax to me? Is he my friend? My *trainer*? I guess that last one would depend on whether I'll be stepping foot inside UFG again. I could train elsewhere if I wanted to. It would make it easier to do the right thing and keep him at arm's length to avoid hurting Beth.

Maybe I just have to set some stricter boundaries with him. If I keep some proper distance between us, it should be easy to stick to a professional relationship. I have to try. For my sister. It makes me sick to keep lying to her like this.

The gym is fairly empty at one in the afternoon—only a few casuals using the gym equipment to work out and two guys working the punching bags. The cage is empty, but the door to the octagon has been peeled open like it's anticipating a fighter.

"Took you long enough," Jax says, hopping onto the stairs of the cage when he sees me stepping into the gym. He's half naked, his magnificent form glistening with sweat under the harsh lights of the gym. Black shorts hang on his hips, and a pair of matching gloves hides his hands. Today's gloves are different, I realize. They're sleeker, with openings for your fingers to poke through.

Jax rests a hand on his hip while he waits for me to walk over. The movement of his arm has my gaze unwittingly drawn to the thick trail of hair traveling below the low waistband of his shorts. An unwelcome flicker of heat shoots down my body and settles deep in my core.

"Hey," I say, darting my gaze back up to his face, hoping he won't read on my face the thoughts I've been having about him. "You sure Julian won't mind that I'm here again without a pass?"

"It's fine. He's out with some investors," he tells me when I approach him. "I was going to train solo today . . . but I'm glad I don't have to." He smiles.

I drop my bag onto the bench at the foot of the cage and pull out a water bottle and a towel, slinging the towel over my neck. "So, what do you have in store for me today?"

He flicks a finger over my chin. "You just focus on getting good and getting strong."

"I'll try. Yesterday's session took a big toll on my body."

"It's recovering and building up tolerance. You'll be fine after a day or two."

Right. Pains and aches must be a constant for him.

"How do you deal with it?" I ask, curious. "You're breaking your body every like . . . what? Three to four days a week?"

"*Six* days a week. Four to five hours a day," he clarifies. "And it's not that bad. Your body will acclimate."

"I can't commit to those crazy hours. I've just started school," I say.

"We'll start slow. Any spare time you have, you can come here," Jax replies coolly.

I want to tell him that it's still a big commitment to make. Am I ready for something like this? And during my freshman year too?

We only regret the chances we don't take. Dakota's words sing back to me.

We promised each other we'd try. We *promised*.

"Here you go," Jax says as he slaps a pair of red MMA gloves into my palm.

I maneuver my hands into them. "I have a question: Why don't we use MMA gloves for boxing? Or boxing gloves for MMA?"

"When you're boxing, you're delivering hard-hitting punches, so you need more padding," he explains, strapping on a pair of his own gloves. "In MMA, you need gloves with holes for your fingers so you can grapple. As in, you know— grabbing and gripping to force a submission."

I immediately recognize the words he throws out from commentators at UFC fights.

"Right. So it looks like we're doing some ground fighting today, then?" I say, perking up with interest. The thought of learning grappling today has me all jittery and excited.

Jax looks impressed that I'm familiar with the terms now.

"Looks like you've been doing some homework."

I smile proudly. "I have."

"That's cute. But that's not what we're doing today," he tells me, helping me up the steps and into the octagon cage. "We're picking up where we left off yesterday. Working on your balance and technique. Now that you have your basic punches down, you need to know how to move around the cage. Get into your fighting stance. I'll show you."

The next half hour feels like an uphill battle as we repeat seemingly simple exercises to work on my stance and mobility. I move forward and backward repeatedly, focusing on throwing punches while moving strategically with quick feet. I realize it's quite similar to ballet in that it's a well-choreographed dance, focused on refining until you get precise movements.

"Make sure your hands are relaxed and open. Push and throw. Push and throw. That's it," Jax says when I push off my lead leg as I go backward, my fists darting toward him with every retreating movement. "Now forward. One-two. One-two. One-two. Now add a hook. One-two-three. One-two-three. Good." I do what Jax says, coming at him with quick hits as I keep pushing off my back leg.

I repeat the movements, going forward and backward as many times as he tells me. Then I begin weaving to the left and right to practice dodging blows from an imaginary opponent.

I pick up the drills so fast that after a while, I barely need any supervision from Jax, which gives him time to work on his own training beside me. He begins tackling a flurry of striking combinations with masterful purpose. I side-eye him with envy as he moves fluidly around the cage, starting with punches and setting up kicks along the way. My arms drop to my sides. I can't stop watching him. The way he strikes. Every move he makes is precise and distinct. It's obvious he's put in years to master them. Coupled with his aura of confidence, he's truly an unstoppable force in the cage.

I want that.

I want to be like that, in *and* out of the cage.

"Jax, I'm tired of this," I groan after about half an hour of repeating the same few motions, collapsing my stance. "When do we get to do the more advanced stuff? I want to do what you do."

He gives me a look, but he doesn't stop with his shadow-boxing. "When you've mastered all your basics, Sienna."

"Come on. I'm ready. I can do this," I say, shaking my arms in anticipation. "I've done my research."

"Research does not constitute real combat." He drops his stance. "You're still highly untrained."

"Well." I shrug, a cocky smile dangling on the corner of my lips. "Give me a chance to prove you wrong." Challenge extended.

He shakes his head. "You don't want to fight me."

"Maybe I do."

I go for a straight jab toward Jax's head, but he's faster and dodges me. Then he grabs a hold of my arm and throws his leg behind mine to collapse my knee, sending me straight to the ground. I land on my back with a loud thud, groaning. Jax climbs over me, one leg wedged in between mine, and makes his displeasure known.

"What did I say about you being a princess again?"

I lift my chin up defiantly. I decide that I like it when he's frustrated with me, and I want to poke the dragon a little more to see how far I can take it.

"That I'm cute and pretty and that you should worship the ground I walk on?" I tease.

Jax's head dips down, breath ghosting the shell of my ear.

"Or that you deserve to be punished for your careless sense of entitlement," he barks. His words are poisonous yet sugary sweet, with promises of a devilish side as his gaze scrapes against me like angry claws, like if he could sink them into my body and claim me, he would.

"I swear to God, Sienna," he growls, grazing his lips on my ear, "if you try to skip steps again, I *will* follow through with that promise. And the things I'd do to you . . ." He lets out a tortured breath. "Your body will never know anything like it. I'll *ruin* you for any man that'll dare take my place after."

Tingles sprout all along my skin. If it were any other guy, I would curse him out for being this blunt about his less-than-friendly intentions. But this is Jax, Goddammit. Every dirty syllable that rolls off his tongue is a rather tempting invitation to let him drag me down to hell with him.

Both of us are breathing hard, silent as our eyes bore into each other, desire sweeping our bodies. Jax's gaze dips past my face, down my breasts, all the way to the throbbing, aching area between my thighs. I'm so tempted to squeeze my legs shut to ease some of the ache, but it's as if he's read my thoughts, and Jax pushes his leg farther upward, intensifying the feeling by grazing his knee against the sweet spot. I squirm against him, the slight friction making me ache with longing.

He clenches his jaw and squeezes his eyes shut, looking like he's having an internal debate on whether he should lose all of his restraint and follow through with what he's just said to me. And honestly, I don't know if I would even stop him. The thought of Jax taking complete possession of my body, gripping tightly at my skin as he plunges into me like a frenzied animal, has my brain scrambled. I'd want him to be aggressive. Dominating. Testing the limits of how far he can take it with me.

Come on, I plead with my eyes. *Kiss me. Take the decision off my hands. At least I'll feel less guilty about it . . .*

"You drive me crazy, princess. Holy fuck," he swears. One large hand brushes over my shoulder and down my waist. He grabs a fistful of my shirt. Hard. Like he wants to rip it off me and save it as a keepsake after having his way with me.

Kiss me, I want to scream at him. *Kiss me, please. Come on.*

"Come on," he says instead, letting out a long-suffering sigh as he releases his grip on my shirt and pries himself off me. "Let's get back to work."

I blink up at him, dumbfounded.

It takes everything in me to not whimper in disappointment.

He pulls me off the ground, and I straighten myself out, pulling up my leggings, which have ridden below my waist. All the while, I feel Jax's intense gaze burning tiny fires all over my body, watching me as I do nothing to extinguish the flames.

***

We continue with the rest of the session like nothing happened.

This time, I'm careful not to cross the line, dutifully resuming the easy drills while Jax does his own training. He stops only occasionally to watch me and assess my progress. I make sure to avoid his gaze because I know that if I don't, I'll be reminded of the way his eyes prowl my body like he'll do anything to stake his claim on me.

"All right, we're done for now," Jax says, bending over to

pick his phone up from the ground as he checks the time. "Good work today."

"Thanks," I say.

"Here. Make sure you hydrate," he says, offering me his bottle of water. I can tell he's had it for a long time, with most of the black coating already chipped off the metal. I swipe the water bottle from him and twist off the cap, pouring the liquid into my mouth. I wish the water was cooler to provide me some relief from all this heat.

"You hungry?" Jax asks when I hand him back the bottle. "There's a burrito place nearby that's pretty good."

I purse my lips, considering his offer. I suppose it wouldn't hurt to grab an innocent burrito. As long as I make it back by the time Beth's cheerleading tryouts begin, I should be good.

"Sure." I nod. "I'm down for a meal."

Ten minutes later, we arrive at a modest Mexican restaurant near Coolidge Corner. The interior is mostly covered with glossy plywood, and there's a blackboard propped on top of the counter neatly detailing the menu and today's specials in chalk. Jax decides that we should do takeout and go to a nearby park to enjoy the food. I nod in agreement and let him place an order for me. When the waiter yells out our number, Jax picks up the burritos by the counter and loops a casual arm around me, letting the paper bag hang from his other hand.

I'm anxious to dig in, so he hands me my chicken burrito while we make our way to the park. The warm food is a soothing elixir to my soul as the autumn chill sneaks its way into my body. I don't let it get to me because I don't want to look like a coward in front of Jax, who walked right out of UFG in a flimsy gray shirt and the same pair of shorts from earlier. The wet pavement is littered with leaves, and I use the tip of my trainers to push them away so I won't slip.

A few minutes later, we arrive at Griggs Park. The swing set is empty at this time of the day, so I tackle one of the swings. Jax laughs as he strolls over to occupy the other one. It's a comical sight, him being so massive on a tiny little swing. Smiling, I rock myself back and forth on my feet steadily as I take another mouthful of my burrito.

"It's been a while since I've been to this park," I say.

He lifts a brow, angling his body toward me. The chains holding up the swing twist a little, and he has to plant his feet on the ground firmly to stop the chains from snapping back into position. "You come here a lot?"

"No. But we used to live close by," I tell him, swallowing my bite down and balancing the burrito on my lap. "I think I fell and broke my nose somewhere around here."

"No way."

"Yeah." I smile, remembering how stupid the circumstances were. "I think it was . . . there," I say as I twist myself around, remembering it was the other swing set that faces the mouth of the slide. "It was during the summer, so the park was always busy, and the swings were always occupied. But one day, one of the swings was available, so Beth and I took turns. I was pushing her for like half an hour straight. All I wanted was just five minutes on it, but she got impatient and pushed me off. I fell face-first, hard, and had to have surgery to fix it. That's how I got this—" I say, pointing to the now barely visible scar on the bridge of my nose. "Anyway, my dad wasn't too happy about the medical bill, so he grounded me for a month. We haven't come back since."

"Damn, that's cold," Jax remarks.

"Yeah. Don't get me wrong, most times, Beth is the nicest human being on earth, but she can get really vicious when she wants to."

"I'm sure she gets that from you."

"That's why I came back to UFG. To manage it," I say, pursing my lips. "How about you? Why do you fight?"

Jax lowers his burrito, giving me a contemplative look. "I do it to confront fear," he says. "Every time I'm in that cage, there's another guy on the other side whose entire purpose is to hurt me as much as possible. And I want to be fearless. Because to be fearless is to live without limits, and I don't ever want to feel like I'm scared of anything."

I hum in agreement. I like that his reasoning is to fight through the feeling of being afraid. Being vulnerable. And I see that he incorporates that mantra into his personal life too.

I don't know why, but I smile.

"Fuck fear," I say.

Jax grins back at me, almost in disbelief.

"Fuck fear," he echoes.

I don't think I'll ever get tired of that easygoing grin. Every time it appears, a flight of butterflies swirls in my belly. It likely doesn't bode well for me. But then again, after what happened in that cage today, training with Jax *period* doesn't bode well for me. It's a shame because in those intense moments when I've fought through the sexual attraction, I find myself enjoying his coaching techniques.

"You're a good trainer, you know that?" I say reluctantly, picking up the burrito from my lap and taking another bite.

"I know." Jax's teeth gleam when he stretches himself

out, an arm still holding his body steady on the swing. "I'm not exactly certified to be one, though. I'm just helping you out."

A perplexed brow. "Oh, why is that?"

"Because I'll use any excuse to get close to you."

My heart leaps in my chest.

This conversation is venturing into dangerous territory. It's hard to keep boundaries when he's being this flirty with me. At the same time, I can't deny how good it makes me feel. But good doesn't mean it's right.

"You have chipotle sauce all over you," Jax says.

"Oh my God. Where?"

"Wait. Let me."

Before I can stop him, he's off the swing, hovering over me like a giant. He tilts my chin up with a curved index finger, and his thumb grazes my skin, smoothing itself over my lip. A gentle touch from him is enough to get my heart pounding like a bass drum. "There."

"Sorry," I say, the heat of my cheeks causing me to pull away from him with a shyness that I've never felt before.

I keep apologizing to him. I don't apologize to anyone. He's wearing me down with every searing moment, and it's getting harder to hold on to my willpower.

"Don't be sorry. I like a woman who's sloppy with her food," Jax says with a rugged smile. He places himself on the ground beside me, his back against the pole of the swing set. "Most women I meet are too manicured. They care more about how they look eating than what they're actually eating."

"Ah, so this is some kind of test, then? To see if I meet with your approval?"

He grabs the chain of my swing and pulls me toward him with a hard tug. "Depends—are you looking for my approval?"

Smiling, I break his grip on the chain by kicking my feet off the ground to launch myself backward. "Good sir, have you ever thought about the fact that maybe you should be seeking *my* approval?"

"Pray tell, my lady. What are your preferences when seeking a man?"

I swing back toward him. "I'm looking for someone who doesn't tease me. Who doesn't leave me high and dry."

"*Dry?* Pretty certain I left you wetter than you've ever been. What else?"

I pause to think, swinging away and back again.

"I want someone who's kind. Selfless."

"I once bought twenty boxes of Thin Mints from a Girl Scout because I didn't want her to carry all those boxes around the whole day."

"But did you eat all the cookies?"

"Yeah."

"Oof. So close."

He rolls his eyes, feigning a smile. "Next?"

"Someone who doesn't patronize me by calling me a princess."

"It's not supposed to be patronizing. I told you, you only see being a princess as someone who's a spoiled brat. I see it as empowering."

"Okay, Mr. Feminist." I rub my heels on the ground to slow the swing down. "Your turn, then. What are *your* preferences, besides sloppy eaters?"

"Let me see," he says, stretching his arms and legs out on

the ground like he's warming up. "I like a woman who can hold her own ground," he says after a pause, thinking.

"It's too bad I'm a damsel then."

"But I also like being relied on," he adds.

"Too bad I'm a fiercely independent woman."

"She's gotta be blond. I'm a sucker for blonds."

"It's about time I tell you I'm a natural brunet."

Jax laughs hoarsely.

"You'll do anything to deny you like me, won't you?"

"I don't like you."

"Bullshit," he says, and with one sweeping move, he thrusts his hand out to grab the chain of my swing. The unexpected momentum forces the swing out of balance as I wobble around for a good few seconds. When it slows down, I steady myself, gripping the ground with my shoes. Jax is on his knees, and his face is right in front of mine when he says, "You like me. You like me so much that you keep trying to push me away because all you really want to do is pull me in."

"Jax." I say it like it's half warning, half submission.

"Tell me I'm wrong." He leans farther into me. I catch a whiff of his scent. The musty smell from the gym lingers, but for the most part, he smells fresh. Woody. Piney. Like he rubbed his neck against a tree before making his way over here. I suddenly find myself struggling to breathe.

"If you really think that, I'm sorry," I say, pushing myself off the swing and taking a couple of steps away from him. "We're . . . friends, Jax."

"Friends," Jax echoes, like it's the most hated word in his vocabulary. "Trust me, we're not friends."

I shake my head, hugging myself. "We can be. We *have* to be."

"Why?"

"You know why, Jax."

"Because of your sister?" he asks, slowly rising to his feet. "So she has a little crush. Who cares?"

"I do. I can't do that to her. My family is broken enough as it is."

A muscle in his jaw twitches when he looks away, his hands going to cup the back of his head. I hold my breath. When he turns back to me, he sounds vaguely aggrieved. "Aren't you sick of caring about what other people want? What do *you* want?"

"I want . . ." The tension between my brows grows as I struggle with my words. "I want . . ."

Jax doesn't wait for me to come up with an excuse. He leans toward me with such urgency that I'm caught off guard. "You want *me*, Sienna." He takes another small step forward, mere inches between us. I step backward. I feel my back hit a tree. He closes the gap between our bodies, laying a hand on either side of me. Caging me in. "Your body does not lie when it's near me," he mutters. "You might want to tell your heart to do the same."

There's something so chilling about his statement. I swallow down my nerves, but it's hard to make them go away with my heart beating so erratically.

He intensifies everything by pressing himself against me. The clash of his body against mine makes me emit a small gasp. He's barely touched me, and it already feels so erotic. So *wrong*.

"Jax, this is a public park," I whisper, acutely aware that

any minute now anyone might walk past us. "People can see us."

"So? Let them see what you're doing to me," he says, mouth so close to mine now. "How fucking *feral* I am for you."

Oh God.

My self-restraint is at a dangerously low level now. I feel like I'm in the deep end of the ocean, nose and mouth struggling to catch air. I can't think. I can't breathe. There's not enough oxygen in this world for my lungs to feel okay again. I can't function when he's so close to me like this. Touching me. Fingers drifting from my face down to my abdomen, fingering the waistband of my leggings like he wants to pull them down, shove me against the tree, and fuck me so hard I won't be able to walk tomorrow.

"Stop," I whisper desperately. "Please, Jax. You're confusing me."

Jax's eyes spark with annoyance.

He pulls back from me.

"Are you serious? You're confusing *me*." There is a sharp edge in his voice. He's so frustrated that he lets his arms drop to his sides. "You claimed you wanted nothing to do with me after that night at the warehouse and then next thing I know you're calling me and showing up at *my* gym, craving *my* comfort. And now here you are, responding to me like you've never wanted to be touched like this by anyone in your life. You're playing me, Sienna. You're playing me like a fiddle, and I'm just letting you."

I feel my breath fading from me.

"I'm not trying to make it confusing on purpose, Jax." I shake my head, my arms winding around myself tightly. This is getting too complicated. I let loose a long sigh. "If it's this hard to be around each other . . . maybe we shouldn't see each other again."

Jax tightens his mouth into a thin line as he takes a moment to think about it.

"Then give me one night to completely win you over," he tells me, gaze sliding back to mine. "You and me. Dinner on Friday, eight o'clock."

"What the hell does that solve?"

"That's the only solution. You want to end this? We end it for good. If you're not completely smitten with me by the end of dinner, you never have to see me again. And if I can make you fall for me, you'll have to give in, plummet all the way down."

I bite my lip, frowning. "Sounds painful."

"It's the price you have to pay. If you're willing to, that is."

I roll my eyes. "How poetic. To fall in love with you is to lose."

He backs away from me, a smirk pulling at the seam of his lips.

"I dare you to lose, Sienna," he murmurs. "I dare you to fall in love with me so hard you'll never recover from it."

"You're insane," I whisper.

"You're scared," he says challengingly. "But what is it you said earlier? 'Fuck fear'?"

I swallow down my nerves, but the signal doesn't make it to my stomach. The tightness sits lodged in my rib cage.

"Text me once you decide," he says with a slight tilt of his head before walking away. "I'll be waiting, princess."

EIGHT

By the time I finally make it to the school's gymnasium, only a few cheerleaders remain, their high-waisted cheer skirts swaying as they pack up their megaphones and pom-poms. I spot Beth sitting alone on the bleachers, arms resting over her knees, a faraway look in her eyes. Her blond hair is slicked back into a high ponytail, a bright red bow perched on top. It should be a good sign because I doubt students who don't make it onto the team would get a bow, but the devastation on Beth's face has me thinking otherwise. My shoes squeak underneath me as I pick up my pace, crossing the court to get to her.

"I'm so sorry I missed tryouts. You have no idea," I say in a rush, dropping my bag to the ground and occupying the spot beside my sister. She refuses to look at me, her eyes still glued to the court.

"I'm on the team," she mumbles eventually.

"Oh my God, that's great!" I'm relieved as I loop an arm

around her, giving her shoulder a tight squeeze. "I'm so proud of you—"

"But I got benched."

"Oh." My heart sinks. "That's still good though, right?"

"No, it's not." She pushes my arm away and shoots to her feet, resting her hands on her hips and tilting her head up to the ceiling, trying to contain the tears threatening to fall. "It means I'm only wanted if I'm convenient."

"Come on. Don't discredit your position like that," I console. "You're just as important as anyone else on the squad."

Beth huffs out a sharp breath. "Yeah, right. I bet if you were in my position, you would say the same thing." She drops her gaze to her feet, almost muttering to herself, "But then again, you would never be in my position."

My brows draw low in confusion.

"What's going on with you, Beth?" I say, looking up at her with concern. "Is this about more than just cheer?"

"What's going on with *you*?" She grips her hands tightly behind her, challenging my gaze with resolve. "Is it more than just what's happening with Mom and Dad?"

"What do you mean?"

"You've been distracted the last few days," she tells me observantly. "And I don't think it's because of the divorce and the cheating stuff. Where did you go last night, Si? Don't tell me you went to Dee's place because she called me just now asking where you were yesterday and said that she tried to call you back but your phone was on Silent the whole night. So if you weren't with them, where were you? Why did you lie to me? And why are you late today?"

The weight of all her questions settles in my stomach, pressing against the insides of my chest and palms.

"I don't want to talk about it," I say because I don't know what else to say. Okay, I do know what I should say, but I'm not sure if she can handle the truth. Certainly not now when her self-esteem is at its lowest.

"I'm worried about you." Beth's bottom lip quivers. "I don't know if you're in some kind of trouble . . ."

"I'm not in trouble," I assure her. Definitely not the kind of trouble she's thinking of.

She doesn't look convinced. "I know you're always looking out for me, looking out for the whole family, but who looks out for you?"

"You know I'm more than capable of looking out for myself."

She frowns, because she knows that's not always true.

"Fine. I'm sorry I was late today. And I know I've been distracted." A long, heavy breath drags itself out of me as I debate my next words. I decide that it's better to just come clean with her about what's been going on. "It's because I've been spending time with Jax."

Beth snaps her head at me, looking incredulous.

"What?" Her face is a mask of hurt and confusion.

"Yes." I suddenly feel shy about the revelation, even though there's nothing to feel embarrassed about. "He's, uh . . . he's been training me."

"In MMA?" She looks even more confused. "Since when were you interested in MMA?"

"I don't know. Since last weekend?"

"And so it's just a professional relationship, then?"

"Well . . ." This time, I'm the one looking down at my feet in uncertainty. "Beth, I'm not gonna lie. It's more complicated than that."

"Wait." She's trying hard to grasp the reality of what's happening between me and Jax. "You have *feelings* for him? And you didn't think to tell me about it?"

"At the time, I didn't know what it was," I explain to her, crossing and uncrossing my legs uncomfortably. "I still don't know what it is."

Beth squeezes her eyes shut as if to gather her thoughts. The entire gymnasium falls eerily quiet, the last cheerleader long gone, and the silence stretches out like a tight rubber band on the verge of snapping. When Beth's eyelids flutter open, her eyes brew a quiet, seething storm.

"So, all that talk about persuading me not to go for him last weekend, that was all just so you could date him instead?" she demands, her jaw clenched.

"No. Of course not." I push myself off the bleachers. "I know how it looks, but trust me when I say that I had *zero* intention of seeing him again after we stayed at his place," I say as I narrow the space between us with caution. "But that doesn't undermine what I said, Beth. You are still too young to get involved with someone like him."

"And *you* can just because you're like what, a barely legal adult?" she counters. I'm momentarily startled by the sharpness in her voice and the determined set of her shoulders as she steps toward me confrontationally. "Admit it: this is not about protecting me, and you know it. This is about you wanting to steal him away."

"Are you kidding me? That's the last thing I want to do!"

I say, exasperation clamping down on every word. "Do you think I *like* this? That I like having feelings for him? I've been a mess about it for the last few days because I don't want to hurt you."

"Then you should've ended it when you had the chance," she whispers. When I say nothing, she shakes her head, disappointed in me. "I can't believe you did this."

She looks so hurt. I want to pull her into my arms and console her like I always do when she's feeling anxious or down, but I can't. I did this to her. I have to accept that.

"So, what now?" Beth asks. "Are you going to keep seeing him?"

"I don't know. He asked me out to dinner. On Friday."

"And you're gonna go?"

"Like I said, I don't know."

"Well, it's not a no, is it?"

"Do you want me to say no?"

"Of course I want you to say no, Si. You know that's what I want." She sighs like it hurts her to admit it. "But if I tell you to do that, I'll never forgive myself for being in the way of your happiness. And if I tell you to go, I'll never forgive *you*."

"Fine," I say decidedly. "Then I won't go."

"But I know that's not really what you want!"

"Then what do you want me to say, Beth? *What do you want me to say?*" I blast out. "That you're delusional for spending months harboring a crush on a guy who never even knew you existed? Who never batted an eyelash at you once? That maybe I want to see what it's like to follow my heart without having to put my own happiness aside for other people? *Especially* for you?"

My words bounce off the walls of the court, echoing loudly. The shock and silence that follows is so palpable that my mouth hangs open, reeling from the magnitude of what I just uttered.

"I'm sorry," I say quickly. "That was so mean. I didn't mean it—"

Beth puts out a hand to stop me. She looks defeated.

"I need to get out of here," she whispers.

"Fine. Let's go home. Clear our heads. We'll continue this conversation later—"

"No, Si. I'm leaving without you." She snatches her bag up from the bleachers and swings it over one shoulder. When she turns her head back toward me, her eyes are brimming with tears. "*Don't* follow me."

She pushes past me and strides out of the gym.

Fuck. Fuck!

I sink back onto the bleachers, aggravated.

And then, I bury my face in my hands and scream into them, as loud as I possibly can.

***

When I finally pluck up the courage to go home, Beth isn't around. Her bag is on her bed, but there's no sign of her. When I check with Mom, she says that Beth has gone out with Dakota and Trevor. I don't know whether I should feel relieved or disappointed.

I must have looked like I was going to crumble under the weight of my own guilt when I approached Mom because ten minutes later, I find her by the door of our bedroom, looking at me like a wounded puppy.

Sometimes I have to remind myself that she's our mom and not my older sister because despite pushing forty, she's still rocking a great figure and youthful skin. Her long blond hair is tied up into one of those effortless, messy buns that I can never seem to imitate. The dark circles rimming her eyes make her look a little more tired than usual, but I chalk it up to the stress of the divorce.

"So, I know why your father and I aren't talking," my mom says, shuffling into the room and sinking onto the green beanbag lying in front of my bed. "Why aren't you and your sister?"

I look up at the ceiling. "That obvious, huh?"

"Beth couldn't get out of the house fast enough."

My eyes burn with hot tears of frustration when I pull myself into a sitting position on the bed, hugging my knees with my arms. "I really screwed up this time."

Mom's lip quivers as she leans forward. "Tell me what happened."

And I do. I spill every last detail, beginning with my first meeting with Jax up until the argument I had with Beth after her cheer tryouts. I make sure to leave out the part where we slept over at his house to avoid getting into an argument about that. My chest burns when I'm done, and Mom leans back against the beanbag, pursing her lips into a frown.

"I knew when I had two daughters, I had to prepare for a tricky scenario like this," she mumbles to herself.

"Look, I never set out to 'steal' Jax away from Beth. I never wanted any of this to happen," I say, resting my chin on my knees. "It's just that . . . it's hard to get him out of my head."

She offers me a sympathetic smile, getting up from the

beanbag and making herself comfortable beside me in bed. She pulls me into an embrace, smoothing my hair with a gentle hand. She doesn't need to say anything; her body language is enough for me to deduce that she wants me to think about what the right thing is to do here.

"I know what I should do," I say, leaning into her warmth. "I should probably stay away from him. Beth means more to me than some stupid guy."

"Except . . . he's not some stupid guy to you, is he?"

I lift my head, wrinkling my brows. "What do you mean?"

She pouts her lips. "I feel like if this were any other time, I would tell you to listen to what your father would tell you."

I nod wordlessly. Dad would probably get riled up at the thought of Beth being the slightest bit unhappy because of me.

"But you spent your whole life putting her needs above your own," my mom adds as she plants a light kiss on the top of my head. "Maybe it's time to put yourself first."

My eyes widen with surprise. Not what I expected her to say.

"Don't you think it's selfish for me to do that?" I ask.

Mom strokes a gentle, loving hand down my face. "Maybe sometimes being selfish is a good thing. But . . . at the end of the day, whatever you choose, I'll be here for you. Always."

I peer up at her to see her smiling down at me with so much sincerity that it's easy to believe she'll always be here. But I'm a realist, and I'm not going to entertain the whole "nothing big has to change after the divorce" narrative that my dad spewed to us yesterday. If there's one thing my dad's pattern of behavior has taught me, it is to never cling to hope.

"Okay," I say anyway.

My mom kisses me on the cheek. We move on to more exciting things, like the fact that I'm trying out MMA. She's happy for me, but a little worried about how I'm going to balance such a big hobby with school. I assure her I'll stay on top of my classes.

When my mom leaves my room to go to bed, I yank my phone from the charger and unlock my screen to dial Beth's number, but it goes straight to voicemail. All eight of my previous call attempts have gone unanswered, so I don't know why this time would be any different.

My face lands on my pillow with a groan. I know exactly what I should do to mend things with her, but I don't want to make that decision. Because that choice means I have to push aside what I want for what's good for everyone yet again.

And I'm so tired of it.

I think . . . it's finally time I listen to my mom.

It's time to be selfish.

Before I can think twice about it, my hand reaches for the phone again. My finger doesn't hover over Beth's contact.

It hovers over Jax's.

I'll see you Friday, I text.

Less than five seconds later, I receive a reply from Jax.

Looks like I'm your preference after all. ;)

NINE

The last time I went out with a guy, it was a blind date set up by Dakota.

She knew a lot of people in high school and was frustrated with my lack of dating experience, so she took it upon herself to find the ideal man for me. Turns out, her version of an ideal man was a way-too-full-of-himself jock whose first words to me—after arriving thirty-five minutes late to the diner—were *Thought you'd be skinnier.* He ordered three main courses for himself while I had an appetizer and a milkshake, and when it came time to pay for dinner, he asked if I could spot him just this once because he was saving up for a new spark plug for his truck. He later proceeded to ghost me for the rest of the school term.

I still haven't forgiven Dakota for that. She's paying me back by treating me to a coffee from Caffeinated whenever she can.

"So, is this a date or not?" Dakota inquires as she rummages through the closet to find me an outfit. Most of the closet is filled with Beth's clothes, while just a small corner holds my mostly black tops and jeans.

"Both," I say, staring at the mirror in the bathroom while I paint on some mascara with mediocre success. "And neither."

The rustling of clothes stops, and two seconds later, she peeks through the bathroom door. "What?"

"He didn't specify, Dee." I drop the mascara into my makeup bag and brush past Dakota as I rush out of the bathroom. I figure if it's not called a date, then, technically, I wouldn't be hurting Beth, right?

Jeez. Look at me trying to rationalize my own guilt.

"Let me see," Dakota prods. I heave a sigh, yanking my phone from its charger and throwing it at her. Dakota catches it easily, her fingers immediately going to work by scrolling through my messages with Jax. When she finally looks up from my phone, she cuts me a WTF look. "I don't get it, so this is all some kind of . . . ultimatum game?"

"Kinda?"

"You guys are so weird." Dakota makes a face, dropping the phone onto the bed and shuffling back to the closet. "I mean, the way you guys talk about it sounds like a date to me. Are you sure it's not?"

"Just going out to see if I like him or not."

"That's the literal definition of a date," she says, gasping when she pulls out the one thing I was hoping she wouldn't find. It's my satin cowl dress with a laced back—sleek, elegant, and refined. Dakota holds it out in front of me, her face gleaming with excitement. "Red is *so* your color."

I peel the hanger from her grasp and lay the dress on the

bed with no intention of getting into it. "Red is everyone's color."

"Not true." She clicks her tongue. "Jax can't pull off red. He looks too good in black anyway, he doesn't need it."

Black really does suit Jax well, especially when he pairs it with hints of gold, like the sunny, metallic hues of his hair.

My phone buzzes with an incoming message, and I scoop it up from my bed.

Pulling up in five minutes. Dress nice, princess.

A brown paper bag it is.

"Put this on." Dakota snatches the dress off the bed and thrusts it toward me. "He'll go nuts seeing you in this, I promise."

I clench my fist in hesitation. I'm scared that if I put on the dress, it'll make everything feel real.

"Has Beth texted you today?" I ask softly. "She's still not talking to me."

Dakota lowers the hanger, her expression dissolving into worry. "No. I don't think she's talking to anyone right now."

I gulp hard, hoping it'll ease the pressure building up in my chest. I think this is the worst thing I've ever done to Beth. She always has my back. And this is how I repay her? I'm despicable.

Dakota senses the inner turmoil punching my gut, and she reaches a hand forward to squeeze my shoulder. "For what it's worth, I don't think you're an ass for dating Jax. I think you're just finally listening to your heart."

I shake my head, snatching the dress from her and slipping back into the bathroom to change.

"It's not a date!" I announce.

Dakota blows out a frustrated breath. "Beth is gonna be mad at you either way, so you might as well just admit to yourself that it is."

"Nope," I say, emerging from the bathroom a minute later.

Dakota is right as usual; the dress is stunning. The cowl neck accentuates my chest, giving a sensual peek at my cleavage, while the rest of the fabric drapes past my now-slender waist and stops just above my ankles.

When my phone buzzes again, my heart buoys in my chest.

"He's almost here," I say after reading Jax's message. "I gotta go."

Dakota follows me around the room as I pick up a pair of black heels and a purse as well as a tan trench coat to complement the outfit. "So what do I do while you're out? Just wait here?" she asks.

"Call Beth, I don't know," I say after a pause. "Maybe you can tag along with her to Kinley's party tonight." And then I make sure to add, "And if you can get her to talk to me also, that'd be great."

She rolls her eyes. "You Lane sisters drive me insane."

I give her a quick hug and head out.

When I'm outside, I pull my coat tighter around me, feeling the nerves climb up my body. For a minute or two, there's no one in the driveway. Then a familiar sports car rumbles in the distance. It pulls over right beside my dad's beat-up Subaru. The door opens, and Jax steps out, looking devilishly handsome in a white button-down shirt and black trousers. A few buttons on his shirt are left open, and his sleeves are rolled up to show off his large, corded forearms. Every movement makes his muscles flex, which I'm sure is deliberate. I gulp hard, choosing to focus on his face instead. It's a fresh sight today, and his gelled-back golden hair allows me a direct view of his viciously smug eyes.

Yep, I unwillingly admit to myself, *this is definitely a date.*

A smile leaps onto my face when he walks over to open the passenger door. A minute later, Jax gets back in, resting his huge arms on the steering wheel. He looks at me and grins, his gaze lingering for an impossibly long time. I suddenly feel shy under the vulgar yet thrilling stare of this man. My skin is littered with goose bumps.

"You're staring." I state the obvious.

"I know. You just look too fucking beautiful."

I place an arm over the door handle, looking out, unable to prevent my smile from stretching wider. "Thanks, Jax."

My gratitude is in response to his compliment, but it feels like I'm thanking him for more. For *liberation*.

Jax doesn't waste another second before he flips on the ignition and speeds off.

***

Jax has pulled out all the stops on tonight's date.

We spend most of dinner traveling across the Charles River on a boat. On a *boat*. We have our own dedicated waiter serving us a five-course meal that includes seafood, foie gras, and an absurd amount of premium meat. The ambience is just as amazing as the menu, with lovely jazz music serenading us.

I expect conversation between us to be stilted and awkward, but much like the champagne being poured into our glasses, it flows endlessly. We talk about our favorite movies: mine is *Silence of the Lambs*; his is *Goodfellas*. I talk about college and my dilemma about sticking with my business and marketing degree, to which he laughingly responds, "Just quit college and you'll be much happier." I argue that my parents would probably never talk to me again if I did, plus I like being in college. It gives me the kind of stability that I can't find at home. My only problem is that I'm not crazy about my major. I steer the conversation back to him, and we talk about his ambitious plans for the underground.

"I'm looking to compete in the titles for the first time next year," he tells me, forking a piece of Wagyu beef into his mouth and chewing it. He swallows it and adds, "If I win, it'll be my first championship belt ever."

"Right. Do you think it'll be hard to win?"

"Shouldn't be. Most of the fighters looking to compete are highly unskilled."

I lift a brow. "Even Perez?"

A laugh shudders out. "I'm not worried about Perez."

"Why?"

"Perez is an old-school boxer," he explains, setting his fork down and dabbing the edges of his lips with a napkin. "He doesn't understand what it's like to fight someone from the next generation. The only way he can win is by a knockout. Which is what he's usually famous for. But relying on just boxing means less focus on grappling and takedowns. Control is harder, and submissions are more multifaceted now. All of which means I would pick him apart just as easily as I did when I first fought him in that cage."

I nod wordlessly, digesting everything he's telling me.

Every time I'm with him, I learn something new about MMA. It should overwhelm me, all of these different martial arts and their many strengths and weaknesses, but my curiosity about them only serves to pull me deeper into the sport.

When we're done with dessert, the boat plays a string quartet version of "Can't Take My Eyes Off You," and Jax starts singing the lyrics to me. I stifle a laugh with my hand as he gets more out of key. Gosh, he's so cute. It's clear that he doesn't usually show a side of him that isn't necessarily in his favor.

After we dock, I expect the date to be over. But instead of driving back to my house, he makes another stop within the city. When I finally realize what street we're on, I shoot Jax a confused look.

"Why are we here?" I ask when we pull into the empty parking lot behind UFG. "I'm not training in a dress and heels."

"While I would kill to see that, that's not what we're here for," he says with a knowing grin, helping me out of the car.

"Then what are we here for?"

"You'll see."

He laces his fingers through mine and walks me up the gym steps. At the top, he lets go and produces a key from his pocket to unlock the main doors. When I give him another look, he shrugs.

"Stole the keys from Jules," Jax tells me as he pushes the door open and holds it in place so I can saunter in first. "He'll be pissed off at me tomorrow, but it's worth it, trust me."

Once we enter, Jax takes the lead, weaving through all the gym equipment to get to the cage. That's when I see it—what was once a sweaty, grimy cage is now clean and sterilized. The roses lining the outer part of the cage infuse the air with a sweet fragrance. The lights in the gym have been dimmed to a smoky red color—sensual and passionate. Cozy blankets and pillows line the base of the cage, and in the middle lies an assortment of desserts that instantly has my mouth watering.

"H-how?" My mouth falls open in shock. "You did all this by yourself?"

"Don't act so surprised," Jax says, his hand on my back as he ushers me up the steps and into the cage. "Like I said, I'm pulling out all the stops." He smirks at me. "Are you impressed?"

I don't answer. My mind is still reeling from the surprise.

"I'll take that as a yes." He plops down onto a pillow, looking so pleased with himself. And as much as I don't want to fuel his smugness, I feel compelled to give this to him because the setup is breathtaking. "Sit," he says, opening a cooler. "You have to try the gelato."

I oblige, taking my place beside Jax and tucking my legs to the side. He feeds me a spoonful of pistachio gelato. I jam my lips together on the plastic spoon, smiling. And then I pluck it out of my mouth to lick it clean, tongue tracing the surface and catching every last drop.

Jax squeezes his eyes shut and groans like it's the sexiest thing he's ever seen.

We spend the next couple of minutes tasting the assortment of ice cream, cakes, and squares. I take my time with each of them while Jax attacks the chocolate ice cream and brownies. I know he's typically on a strict diet that excludes sugar and caffeine, so this must be a rare thing for him. It's nice to get glimpses of parts of him that he wouldn't show to anyone else.

"You know," I say, eyes gazing over at him, "you act like such a devil, but I don't think you're half as demented as you think you are. If you were, you wouldn't be doing all this for me."

His eyes burn like molten gold when he meets my gaze. "Bold claim, princess."

"I think it's the truth."

"I think you just haven't seen the darkest parts of me yet," he murmurs, a coy smile dancing on his lips as he tears a chunk off a brownie and pops it into his mouth. Without breaking eye contact with me, he gives his lips a slow and sultry lick, getting me back for earlier.

I fight the urge to readjust my sitting position.

"Are you curious about the monsters hiding in my closet?" He smirks.

My lips curl inward. "Maybe."

"You might wanna be careful. They're vicious creatures."

I wonder if this is another one of his tests.

"Fuck fear, right?" I reply.

"Fuck fear," he echoes, grinning.

I like how the motto sounds on his tongue. I decide that it's going to be the motto for the rest of my life.

I adjust myself again, leaning an elbow in front of me so I can be closer to Jax, my curiosity pulling me toward him. He's on his side now, facing me, an elbow propped over one of the pillows. I feel like the reason we're here, eating dessert in this cage, isn't because of some gimmick. He's showing me what really matters to him. This is his safe space. His real home.

"You really like it in here, don't you?" I ask softly.

He nods, eyes roaming over the fence. "It's the only place I feel like I'm completely in my own element."

I nod because I feel it as well.

He shrugs, trying to look nonchalant. "Plus, MMA's like, the ultimate form of competition between two people. And I am a *very* competitive person."

"I can tell."

"I have a feeling you are too."

"Nah." I wave him off. "I'm really not."

A brow quirks upward. "You mean you've never thought about what it'd be like to be in a real fight?"

"Not really."

"But that's what everyone who does MMA works toward. To fight in that cage."

"I don't know. To me, fighting competitively and training are two completely different things."

"You're right. One is definitely more entertaining than the other." He grins, and I fight the urge to roll my eyes.

Suddenly, Jax's eyes flicker wide as an idea forms in his head. He shoots up from the floor and gets to work, pushing the blankets, pillows, and food aside to make space for something. I jump to my feet, unsure what I should do.

"Uh, what's happening right now?"

When the center of the cage is clear of any food or pillows, he looks over at me, all serious and focused. "Stay right here and wait for my signal." Then he leaps toward the cage door. He jogs all the way up to the second floor of the gym, which is mostly bare except for some old equipment, cleaning supplies, and those big, chunky, manually operated spotlights. He goes over to one of the spotlights, flips a switch, and hauls it in my direction, blasting a harsh light onto me. "Introducing your favorite fighter, the one, the only, the princess of rage—Sienna 'Hurricane' Laaaaaaane!"

"Jax, oh my God." My hands immediately fly up to my cheeks in embarrassment. I can't believe he's doing this to me right now. "Stop that!"

"Pretend it's your first fight of the season!" he instructs me. I glare at him, not sure how to react. He drops his smile. "Come on, just entertain me a little! You need to learn how to loosen up," he shouts, then begins to imitate an audience. *"Ahhhhh! Wooooo! Wooooo!"* he yells unashamedly, mimicking their screams and hollers. Then he returns to his normal voice, encouraging me. "Lift your fists up, come on! Do a little dance!"

"Jax, I'm not doing it!" I whine.

"Why not?"

"Because it's *stupid*!"

He grabs his chest in mock pain, as if I shot him. "I'm insulted, princess. I do this twice a month."

"I'm not a real fighter," I say quietly.

"That's not true," he says, dead serious. "The second your fist hit that punching bag, you were a fighter. The second you fought back against your family, you were a fighter. And the second you get back up after being pushed down, you're a fucking *fighter*."

Regardless of his motivational words, my feet decide to stay put.

"Still not doing it," I huff out.

"What?" He lets loose a dramatic gasp, like an announcer who just witnessed something crazy happen during a fight. "Did she just say she's *tapping out*? Booooo! Booooo!"

"Jax, seriously!" I could just die of embarrassment right now.

"Booooo!" Jax slips into the role of the audience again. I

hate that he's having way too much fun with this. When I cut him a lethal glare, he acts like he doesn't know what I'm upset about, pretending to look around as if he's confused where the voices are coming from. "Sienna, I don't know what to tell you. I told them to stop, but they won't shut up," he says innocently, then switches back to being the audience again. *"Booooo! Come on, fight! Booooo!"*

Oh, for fuck's sake—

Groaning loudly, I roll my shoulder back and lift a fist up, exuding the same kind of punchy masculinity that I saw the male fighters give off during last weekend's fight. Jax throws me a look of disapproval, like he wants more or he's not going to stop, so I jog around the cage slowly like I'm greeting a few members of the crowd—seriously, just let me die *right now*—and Jax cheers, hauling the spotlight so it follows my every movement.

"Okay, I did it," I whine. "Can I please go now?"

"No!"

I groan.

"We want more! We want more!" Jax cries out.

Appeasing him, I force myself to jump around, do a few dramatic bows, and bang my fists together, showboating. I try to imagine what it's really like for anyone who steps into that cage to be greeted by the near eardrum-obliterating sounds of cheers. People murmur and nudge each other in awe. It must be nice, actually. To have people care about you like that. Rooting for you to win. It feels good to be adored unconditionally. I want that.

And now . . . I have it.

I pretend to bask in the glory of the moment, knowing

that I'm going to give them a fight that'll knock the breath out of them. And I do.

As the announcer lifts my hand in the air, signaling my victory, I smile to the adoring crowd with glee. A surreal rush of adrenaline is potent in my veins, and my confidence skyrockets with a win under my belt. My first one. The first of *many*.

The belt is heavy as it gets strapped around my waist, and when the audience roars again, another wave of pride bursts within my chest. Everything slows down as I try to capture it all and ingrain it into my brain as one of the greatest moments of my MMA career, one of the greatest moments of my *life* . . .

I feel someone sliding behind me. I've felt these hands before.

This isn't part of this moment.

This is real.

"Jax," I breathe, pulling myself out of my trance.

"Welcome back," he murmurs in my ear, pulling my front toward him so we're face-to-face.

"I can't believe you made me do that," I say, a disbelieving laugh floating from my mouth.

"You wanted to feel what it's like. I just gave you a little push."

Shivers float up my spine. The laugh dries up in my throat, the air around us growing more serious and tender. Jax's gaze drops to my mouth, which sparks the shimmering nerves in my belly.

It's then that I realize I no longer wish to participate in the tug-of-war my feelings have been playing with Jax. This isn't just a game to me anymore.

This is real.

And this could all be mine if I just let it happen. If I just *fuck fear—*

Ripping my self-restraint to tatters, I catch Jax's lips with mine.

The kiss is hungry, setting every inch of my body ablaze with hellfire. That's how hot everything feels right now; I've fallen all the way into the earth's core with him, molten lava scorching my bones. Jax buries a strong hand in my hair and, with a low growl, pulls me toward him, deepening the kiss like his entire life depends on it. And boy, does he deliver. He forces my mouth open with his tongue and sweeps it over mine with skillful greed.

I moan when the taste of him hits me—sinfully and overwhelmingly indulgent, like the desserts we just consumed. Except kissing Jax beats eating all of those delicious treats; it beats anything I've ever done in my entire eighteen years of existence.

The harsh spotlight continues to blare down at us, coating our bodies with warm sweat. I can feel my heart beating wildly as my hands roam the muscular planes of his back and up his neck, grasping him like some out-of-control animal. I never thought I was the kind of girl who'd be more than willing to give so much of myself to one person. But with Jax, I'd gladly bare everything to him. *Everything.*

Jax pulls away from my face long enough to stare down at me.

"Sienna . . ." His breathing is shallow. There's no mistaking the ache and arousal in his voice. "I . . ."

I can sense the *I told you so* coming, so I lean in again to whisper against his lips, "Just shut up for once, will you?"

Instead of fighting back, a grin stretches wide over his mouth. "You got it."

And he lets me reel him in for another worlds-colliding kiss.

TEN

My body is still floating from everything that happened on Friday.

Jax and I spent the rest of the night making out on the pillows like silly teenagers, sinking into each other's kisses. I knew kissing him was going to be good since he had an intimidating amount of experience, but when it finally came down to it, I was still woefully unprepared for how mind-scrambling it would be. The way he kissed me—daring and filthy and sinful—was like he was trying to light me on fire from the inside out. My entire body was buzzing with heat and ecstasy.

By the time we managed to pry ourselves off each other, it was nearly one in the morning. I didn't want Mom to get worried, so Jax helped me up from the cage floor, scooped me into his car, and drove me home.

And then we made out some more before I went back into the house.

I can't wait to kiss him again. If I could do nothing but swim in his kisses all day, I'd be living a very fulfilling life.

I wonder if he wants to see me again. We texted here and there throughout the weekend, but we haven't seen each other since Friday. Does he want to keep seeing me? God, I hope so. I hope I get to see him soon so we can talk about it.

But first, I have something more important to do.

Something that he's inspired me to do.

Usually, lectures are mentally draining for me, but this time, I'm squirming with nerves and anticipation. As my last class draws to a close, I'm the first to pack up my things and leave. I rush straight toward my faculty building, zipping up the stairs to get to the second-last office before its occupant leaves work for the day. The door rattles open when my fist knocks.

"Hi, Mrs. Colton?" I address my academic advisor, a little out of breath, as I grip the door. "Do you have a minute? I'd like some advice on changing my major."

***

Later on, I send out a couple of texts. One to Beth and Mom, explaining that I'm going to be staying in the city for a while, and another to Jax, telling him I'm on my way over to UFG. He hasn't replied to any of my texts so far, and it has me worried that he's ghosting me.

"You know, you've really got to start paying for a membership here, Sienna." Julian doesn't even lift his head to acknowledge me as I step into his office. His eyeglasses are perched on the crook of his nose as he sifts through some contracts laid on his table. "I don't care if you're Jax's guest."

"Fine. I will." I crane my neck to see if I can spot Jax training through the window. "Is he around?"

"He'll be here in a minute." This time, his gaze lifts to connect with mine. "But since you're here, let's talk."

"Um, okay."

Julian extends an inviting hand out toward the empty chair. I pull the seat out and plop down in front of him, resting my bag on my lap. He gathers the papers strewn across his desk into a neat pile and pushes the stack aside. When the surface is clear, he rests both his arms on the table and tents his fingers together, staring straight at me. "So, what do you really want to do here, Sienna?"

"I want to train."

"As a casual? Or are you looking to go pro here?"

"I don't know yet. I haven't figured it out. But I want to train like a pro," I say unhesitatingly. "I want to keep getting stronger, for now."

A frown touches Julian's mouth as soon as I make my ambitions known.

"I don't think you're serious."

I swallow the disappointment down.

"I am. I am passionate about this," I say determinedly.

Narrow lips pressed into a hard, formidable line.

"You don't have a goal. And that concerns me."

"I just started last week," I protest. "You can't expect me to have everything figured out."

"Well, figure it out soon. Because the training's gonna be tough," he outlines. "And I don't think you have what it takes."

Annoyance tightens my chest.

"Is it because I'm a woman that you think I won't be able to handle it?" I can't stop myself from asking. "Because I've handled Jax just fine."

Julian laughs like it's the funniest joke he's heard in a long time.

"Sienna, it's not because you're a woman that I have doubts. I'm the last person to judge a woman walking through those doors wanting to fight. It's more about *why* you want to fight."

"You can't possibly know why I want to fight."

"I'm good at reading people and their motivations. I don't want anyone to waste their time, and I certainly don't want to waste mine."

"Fine. Tell me what you learned from observing me, then."

Julian lets out a heavy sigh, losing steam.

"Fine. You know what I see? I see that you have a lot of anger in you, Sienna. And you aren't shy about it either. Anyone who looks at you can sense it. Stop treating MMA like it's a form of therapy. I don't care what Jax told you. I won't have that in my gym," he snaps, his voice terse. "You need help with your problem? You see a shrink for that. Not me or Jax."

"Fine," I snap back. "Done."

I definitely won't see a shrink, but I can learn to be more levelheaded when I train here. Besides, Jax already taught me that I don't need to be fixed.

Surprise momentarily registers on Julian's face. If I didn't know any better, I'd think he's a little impressed.

"Really? That easy?"

"Like I said, I may surprise you," I say, jerking my head at him. "What else?"

He gives a hard nod. "If you are doing this, you have to

stop training with Jax. He's a fighter, and he's gotta focus on his own fight. I don't want to give away too many details, but if he gets scouted, it'll bring a lot of credibility to this place," he says. Despite the fact that he always sounds angry when he talks, there's no mistaking the hope shining in those wise eyes. "Lord knows I need a decent, reputable fighter to represent this gym. And someone like Jax is difficult to come by."

I arch my brows in confusion. I was under the impression that Jax's sole focus was on the big fight against Perez. Is that not happening anymore? Or do I know something that Julian doesn't?

"If you want to train here, these are my rates," he says, dragging out a piece of paper from his top drawer and slapping it in front of me.

I lean forward to peer at the paper. *Yikes*. It's looking like I'll be skipping a lot of lunches this semester. Despite the panic setting in, my face remains neutral. I don't want Julian thinking I can barely afford this. I'll figure out a way, somehow. I always do.

Julian gives the paper a quick tap with his index finger. "Once you're good with that, you need to know the rules. And I've only got two. One: you do exactly as I say, and I mean *everything*, from diet to training times. And two: no underground business. It's a strict rule here. Ever since Point started doing that shit, I've got people calling in wanting to get in on that action. And I can't have anyone from my gym fighting in their cage, you got me? I'll kick you to the curb if you do."

My breath stalls in my throat.

Oh my God. Jax is living a double life.

Julian picks up on the internal conflict. "Are you okay?"

"Yeah, fine," I squeak out, my heart clenching at the realization that I clearly know something he doesn't. "Heard every word."

"Okay." His voice is cautious. "Well—"

"Thanks for this. I'll have a think about it." I snatch the paper and rush out.

The door swings open before I have the chance to open it myself, and I step aside to avoid getting hit.

"Hey, Jules." Jax saunters in casually, both hands tucked into the pockets of the gray joggers hanging low on his hips. "We doing conditioning today?"

"You know it," Julian says, his mood instantly perking up at Jax's presence. "Meet me at weights. I'll be out in five."

I follow Jax out of the office. When we're finally out of earshot, Jax tugs on my hand to pull me to the side. My heartbeat picks up, feeling like I'm back to being a schoolgirl who has a massive crush on the quarterback.

"Hey," I say breathlessly. I can't even look at him without looking at his mouth.

He doesn't say anything. He doesn't need to. Before I know it, his mouth is descending on mine, tenderly fusing our lips. Despite making out with him last Friday, I still can't get used to the contrast between the softness of his kisses and the roughness he displays in the cage.

"Been wanting to do that again since last week," he murmurs against my lips.

"Me too," I say with a hint of a smile. I'm so sucked in by him that I forget the gym is packed as hell this evening, as evidenced by the curious glances burning into my back.

Jax weaves his fingers through mine as we head toward the cage. I figure this is a good time to ask him what I've deduced from the conversation in Julian's office. "Before we talk about anything else, I need to ask you a question."

"Okay. Shoot."

I look around then drop my voice to a low whisper. "Julian doesn't know about you fighting in the underground."

Jax pauses midstep, looking at me like I'm stating the obvious. "That's not a question."

"I'm waiting for you to correct me." When he remains silent, I let loose a small gasp and pry my hand out of his. "Jax, how the hell does he not *know*?"

"He doesn't need to know." He resumes walking. "The underground is my own business, not his."

I catch up to him as fast as my legs can carry me. "He still thinks you're going for tryouts next year."

"I am."

"There's no way you can do both."

"It's cute that you think that, baby." He turns around and amusedly flicks my chin with his finger. I roll my eyes, nudging his shoulder for a straight answer. Eventually, he gives in, his expression turning dead serious. "Look, what I do in the underground I keep to myself. Jules is a good trainer, and I need him to keep me on track for this fight against Perez. And in exchange, if he wants me to get recruited, then I'll do just that."

"Do you have any intention of following through? Once you get recruited, you'll be too busy for the underground."

"I don't know about that yet. I'm just focusing on the championship. That's my priority right now." He lowers his head enough that his mouth is near my ear but far enough that our gazes are still locked. "So where does that leave you?"

My teeth dig into my bottom lip.

Perhaps it's none of my business. This is between Jax and Julian. I don't want to get involved. Besides, what Julian doesn't know won't hurt him . . . right? I'm here to focus on my own thing. And, well, to spend more time with Jax. Just as nothing will stand in the way of his championship, nothing will stand in the way of me being with him.

My decision is made as soon as I lean forward to plant a kiss on Jax's lips.

"I guess it leaves me here. With you," I breathe.

A pleased smile quirks Jax's mouth. "How about your sister?"

"I'm not going to let her be a problem anymore," I say with utter conviction.

It shouldn't matter how Beth feels about Jax. This sure as hell isn't her story.

It's mine and Jax's.

Nobody else matters.

"That's great," Jax drawls. "Fuck anyone who gets in the way of your happiness."

I nod in agreement. "Fuck 'em."

He lets out a breathy chuckle as he tugs me toward the cage. "I love that I've turned you into a monster, princess."

Yes, I think to myself. *Yes, you did.*

And the whole world is going to tremble under my two damn feet.

PART TWO
Cracks in Our Armor

ELEVEN

Six Months Later

Boom.

That's the sound of Jax's highly effective left kick as he blindsides his opponent, Wesley, and damages his torso.

It's the night of the semifinals in the underground, and Jax has been killing the game, predictably so. The audience goes insane with hollers and cheers as Jax lands another sickening crunch, severely weakening Wesley. Before this, Wesley's held his guard up the entire time, looking only to block punches. Noting his weak spots, Jax throws a jab-cross and then skillfully smashes him with a kick. A gnarly red splotch glows over the right side of Wesley's ribs—a visual reminder that anyone who dares to take Jax on won't leave the cage unscathed.

Even though it's Jax's first time participating in the underground competition, he has steamrolled everyone blocking his path to claiming his first title. Tonight, the cool spring air is heavy with the scent of blood and bones and savagery. Breaking Point claimed Wompatuck State Park in Hingham to host its first outdoor fight, and the abandoned location couldn't be more fitting for such a night. Its rotting, derelict World War II–era bunkers and wooden foundations have been a graffiti artist's wet dream, with artwork coating every available concrete slab.

Most spectators are packed tightly against the walls, and some have even managed to climb up and prop themselves over the edge for a better view. The fight tonight is taking place in the ammunition bunker. Rather than facing the logistical nightmare of setting up an octagon cage, Point opted for a simple raised platform, using the crowd as its perimeter.

Dakota, Trevor, and I are at the front. Dee wanted to hang back, too exhausted to fight through the crowd, but I insisted on being at the front of all the action. After all, what kind of girlfriend would it make me if I wasn't at the front line, cheering for my man?

"Yes!" I holler at Jax from the audience. "Aim for his head!"

Although it's nearly impossible for Jax to hear me given the loud surge of screams from the crowd, the same idea must click in his head because he follows through with it, deploying multiple attacks to Wesley's head. Wesley's arms fly up to deflect the blows, rendering him unable to counter.

I stare at my boyfriend in awe, swelling with unwavering pride. He continues to surprise me. The ruthlessness Jax wields in a fight is meticulous and fatal. He doesn't just throw and hope for the best; he aims with his fight IQ and fires with brute force and precision.

It makes me wonder if Perez is seeing all of this. I watched him fight earlier tonight. His reputation as a dangerous boxer precedes him, and he landed flush combinations against his opponents with controlled and methodical counter-striking. He turned the octagon into his own canvas, painting it red with every blow his fist struck. It was impressive, and I can see why he's held on to his title for so long.

But an underground buff would have to know he's well past his prime. Perez is prone to careless mistakes here and there, especially when his opponent gets him on the ground. With Jax's dynamism and unpredictability in the cage, it'll be difficult for Perez to get the upper hand unless he has something up his sleeve that we don't know about.

I scan the crowd for any sign of him in the bunker. He has to be watching. And sure enough, I spot him far behind me, hanging out with a couple of his friends: tan skin; shaved head; shoulders a mile wide; and shadows cutting through the hard edges of his scarred face. He's serious as he watches the fight unfold. I wonder what he's thinking about.

I follow his hardened gaze back to the fight. Jax and Wesley are exchanging kicks, both staying at bay for now. Wesley looks tired. Beaten. He's taken too many kicks to the body. His resolve has weakened. It's clear he won't last long now, and Jax knows it.

"Look at you." Dakota slides both her arms over my shoulders, hugging me tightly. "A few months ago, you swore you wouldn't be caught dead at one of these events."

I lean into her hug, unable to keep the smile off my face. "Can't a girl have a change of heart?"

It's funny just how much my feelings for Jax have changed from when he saved me from the clutches of Damien during my first-ever underground fight. Now, I still find myself so drawn to him. Back then, I promised myself I was going to do everything I could to avoid him, and yet somehow, I found myself falling into his arms anyway.

Mom was happy to hear that I'd listened to her advice and followed my heart when it came to Jax. And my heart *was* right about him. I brought Jax home a couple of times to meet her, and she thinks of him as "a fine and charming gentleman." It relieves me to know that she approves of him. Her opinion about Jax is the one in the house that matters most to me right now. The other two occupants, not so much.

The Lane family living situation hasn't been ideal lately. Since Jax and I started dating, Beth and I have been strangers to each other. We barely talk unless it's out of necessity. And our parents aren't doing so great either. For the past six months, Mom and Dad have been awkwardly navigating their singlehood in the same household. Dad wasted no time indulging in his new single status, going on dates nearly every day now.

Sometimes, I wonder what happened to the woman my dad cheated on Mom with. I didn't bother asking him that or anything else about her. There isn't any point. I gather she was more of a means to an end, which, if you ask me, is even more disgusting than if he left my mom for that woman.

Mom tried to jump into the dating scene too, but with little luck. She went on one date, said it was fine, and never went out again. She's clearly not over Dad yet, and the whole living situation probably makes it much harder for her to move on.

I wish one of them would move out. I hate that they're both too stubborn to do it. I think they want to pretend for my and Beth's sake so that we don't feel like they're abandoning us, but I'd rather be faced with the truth than keep pretending this works.

At least I have Jax as an escape now. He's been great in helping me deal with all of these family antics. Every time I feel overwhelmed, he's there to catch me and make me feel okay again.

"I wish we were back in the honeymoon phase," Dakota says to Trevor with a pout.

"Not me," Trevor says. "We were way too obsessed with each other."

Dakota cuts him a glare. "That's the point."

"Come on," he says, looping an arm around her and kissing her on the cheek. "What we have now is much better."

"I guess." She pouts unhappily.

A worried crease digs into my eyebrows. I shoot Dakota a look, but she shakes her head like she doesn't want to talk about it right now.

I draw my attention back to the fight. Wesley drops his guard and gets more aggressive in a desperate attempt to gain the upper hand. Big mistake. Wesley backs Jax into the perimeter, and just as he's about to strike, Jax fires a quick left jab before landing a booming right squarely on Wesley's chin, sending him to the ground.

There, Jax climbs on top of him and continues his barrage of hits to Wesley's face. Blood soaks the wooden platform, spurring on the crowd with excitement. I hold my breath in anticipation as Wesley's head knocks against the floor over and over again.

Too exhausted to fight back, Wesley taps out.

The audience detonates into hollers and cheers when Jax is announced the winner. I scream with joy, bouncing up and down on my feet.

Another win under Jax's belt. He's moving into the finals against Perez.

I look over to where Perez was last standing. He's gone now, and so are his friends.

Jax throws his arms up and lets out a beastly yell of victory. His happiness matches my own as I watch him scan the crowd with a wide grin until his gaze finally lands on me. He mouths, *Get over here, princess!*

Shivers rocket up my spine.

"Be right back," I say, my feet already moving toward the platform. I push my way into the crowd, but this time, it's easier to make it through as the crowd parts for me, with most spectators knowing who I am.

Jax hauls me up onto the makeshift platform, and I wind my arms and legs around him excitedly, smiling like I won that fight myself. He cups my butt swiftly with his huge hands, and I laugh, knowing how it looks to the audience. But I don't care. Let them stare. Let them see how fucking obsessed we are with each other.

"I never doubted you'd get this win, baby," I murmur against his lips.

Despite the sweat covering his body and the overpowering muskiness of his scent, I can't help but lean into him more. This is the body of a warrior. A king. A legend in the making.

He lowers his mouth so it's tight against my ear. "Did the fight turn you on?" There's no mistaking the smile present in his voice.

"Yes, because watching you get blood all over your face and hands sure gets my panties in a twist," I deadpan.

"Fine," he says, taking one of his hands and cupping my chin to angle it back toward him. "Then what about this?"

And he claims my mouth with a kiss.

I almost combust when his tongue sweeps across my bottom lip, opening me up to him. Just like the many other kisses we share, this is passionate. Fiery. Intense. Just like him. Just like how I want it to be.

The crowd's cheers are deafening as they respond to our kiss. I laugh and pull away from him, landing on both my feet, but he doesn't let me stray far. He traps me in his arms, and I rest my head against his torso. We gaze into the infinite sea of people worshipping and cheering for us, and I soak in the powerful feeling, realizing that this is exactly what Jax meant about claiming the world and it being ours to take.

And take it we shall.

TWELVE

"Jax, *oh my God*," I gasp out.

"Keep that pretty little mouth shut for me, princess. Or someone's gonna catch us." I clamp a hand around my mouth to stifle another breathy moan as he buries his face in between my thighs. My legs are propped up in the back seat, an ankle digging against the window while the other rests over Jax's shoulder. I feel him lifting my leg up so he can get a better angle.

Maybe I like the idea of getting caught, I can't help but think as his wicked tongue dashes across my swollen clit in tight little circles. I'm panting hard, losing breaths to every sweep of his tongue. *Holy shit.* Jax is giving me the best head of my life in the back of his sports car in an empty parking lot, and it feels deliciously sinful. I've been assured that the windows are tinted, but still, anyone close enough to our car can simply take a peek inside and gasp at the lewdness unfolding.

I should stop this. I really should. Dakota and Trevor are

waiting for us in the bar to celebrate Jax's win, and I can't leave them hanging like this.

Fuck 'em. You're so wet from his kisses that it won't be long now anyway.

I raise myself up on my elbows so I can look at him. He looks so good when he's in between my legs. One of the best sights I've ever seen. I initiated fooling around in the car, offering it as a reward for his win tonight, but he stopped me, pushing me down against the seat roughly so he could remove my skirt and underwear. *The only reward I need is the taste of you in my mouth*, he said, a rather devilish smile on his face before he descended on me.

"Do you like it when I fuck you with my tongue, baby?" His raspy breaths are hot against my clit.

"Yes," I somehow manage to stammer out.

"How about I fuck you with my fingers too?" He lifts his head long enough to demand my gaze as he watches me watch him slowly tease my opening with his index finger.

"Do you like that?" he purrs.

"Yes," I moan. "Please."

I don't know what I'm asking for; I just know I don't want him to stop. *Ever.* A groan shudders through his chest in response. He dips his head back down, tackling my clit with delicate force while matching the rhythm of his finger as it plunges straight into me. I nearly cry out with pleasure, arching my back greedily as my body responds to him like never before. My inner muscles clench as his finger moves in and out of me at a steady speed. I have to bite the inside of my arm to stop myself from moaning loudly and drawing any more attention to the car.

"Jax, I'm gonna come."

"Then come."

An orgasmic tidal wave crashes through me. I ride it out, my body trembling and shuddering with the full force of it until it subsides and I'm floating back down to earth. When my eyes flutter open this time, Jax's massive frame hovers over me. He looks so smug at the fact that he was able to make me come in a matter of minutes. The fastest it's ever happened.

"You're so fucking sexy." He leans down to nuzzle my neck. There's no mistaking the huge erection threatening to poke through his jeans as he presses his body flush against mine. "I want to be inside you so bad."

I bite my bottom lip contemplatively.

His proposition is tempting. And I want to feel him inside me. There's no doubt that sex with Jax would be phenomenal. It's not like we haven't tried before. But every time we've come close to it, my body clamps up like it's protecting me somehow. It's weird. I only hope that it'll go away eventually.

"Not tonight, baby. As much as I want to, there's no way I'm letting my first time be in the back of your car." I laugh, but he continues to latch on to the sensitive part of my neck. He always does it when he wants to get his way. And *oh God*, I fall for it every single time. My mouth makes an incoherent noise as soon as his nose grazes that sweet spot. "Come on, let's head back to the bar. You don't want to keep our friends waiting."

"All right," he grumbles. He arches a questioning brow at me. "Help me rub one out before we go?"

"Maybe later tonight?" I say while winding my arms around him and sweetly rubbing my nose over his. "I wanna take my sweet time with you. And I promise I'll make it good."

"Okay." He catches my lips with his in a swift kiss before helping me out of the back seat.

***

"Let's raise a glass to Jax 'Deadbeat' Deneris for being the absolutely unstoppable force that he is! Perez doesn't know what's coming to him!" Adam, one of Jax's tattooed friends, climbs on top of the bar, raising his beer glass toward the crowd of people under him.

"To Jax!" he roars, puffing out his massive chest, which looks like it may rip right through his shirt.

"To Jax!" everyone in the bar says in unison as they clink their glasses together.

The main room is jam-packed with people, most of them coming from the fight at the park to celebrate Jax's win. Jealousy gets me right in the gut when I notice that most of the fans here are girls, with their barely-even-a-top tops and miniskirts, practically eye-fucking my boyfriend as he hangs his legs off the bar and throws his head back, laughing. It takes everything in me not to punch their pretty faces.

Adam hoots with laughter as he jumps down from the bar. Jax lets out a loud chuckle as they walk away, drunk off the adrenaline from the crowd. His eyes are shining like stars, and my heart swells with happiness when I see him in his element.

I spot Dakota waving at me cheerfully from one of the booths, and I make my way through the sea of bodies. She moves over so I can sit next to her. Her dark hair is a little disheveled and greasy from watching the fight earlier, so she sweeps it away from her face and twists it so it lies neatly on her shoulder.

"So did you manage to get your hair tie from the car?" she asks.

"Huh?" I give her a perplexed look, only to suddenly remember what I texted her to explain my delay in getting to the bar. "Oh, right. Couldn't find it."

She makes a funny face like she *knows*, and I look down, too embarrassed to talk about it.

"He sure loves the attention," Dakota says, and I follow the direction of her gaze.

The men are all swarming around a standing table that's covered with dozens of shots. Jax's friends are downing the liquor like its water. Jax says something to them, and they rattle with rusty laughter, entranced by everything that comes out of his mouth. And Jax completely eats up their adoration. He's cockier when he's with them. More obnoxious as they egg him on. Sometimes I wonder if he only keeps them around for an ego boost, since he doesn't hang out with them unless it's at an event or to get wasted.

Dakota jerks her head. "Aren't you gonna go over there?"

I wave a dismissive hand. "I'll pass."

Most of Jax's friends are nice to be around . . . from a distance. They're the kind of guys that my mom would warn me against. The ones that brag about their lays and won't stop talking about how men have it worse than women. Slimy shit. It's mind-boggling to think Jax is friends with them.

"I get it," Dakota says, thinning her lips. "They don't seem like your crowd."

I place my glass on the table and snuggle closer to her, smiling sincerely. "I'm much better off with you, Dee."

"Good. Because I'm gonna need your support next week."

She sends a knowing grin my way, pulling a folded piece of paper from her tiny bag and handing it over to me. "Hot off the press."

When I peel the paper open, I gasp when I see Dakota's face printed on the poster, along with the floating heads of her co-stars. Below, it reads, *THE TAMING OF THE SHREW*, STARRING DAKOTA LEE JAMES AS KATHERINE MINOLA in a bright yellow font.

"Oh my God. Look at you!" I say with a squeal. "You look so good! You look so *mean*."

"I know! I love it! They're putting it up all over campus on Monday, but I wanted you to see it first," she says, giddy with glee. "You're coming, right? Cuz I already got you and Trevor free front-row tickets."

"Are you kidding? Of course I'm coming."

"Awesome. Let's drink up. To celebrate your boyfriend's first win of the season and my first college show ever!" Her arm shoots up from the booth, calling over one of the servers. "Excuse me, fifteen shots of tequila, please!"

"Jesus . . ." I don't realize I've said that out loud until I find Dakota smirking.

"That's right," she says in a self-assured tone. "We're going to get so fucked up we'll be seeing Jesus tonight." I roll my eyes. Dakota isn't ending her grand plan for tonight with just drinks, though. "I was also thinking about unleashing my horrible moves on the dance floor later. You know, bring all the boys to the yard with my milkshakes." She gives her chest a little jiggle, her breasts threatening to come out of her black tube top.

"If your milkshakes spill on that dance floor, your

boyfriend is gonna have to be fighting off some dudes. And have you *seen* your boyfriend? He's built like a stick. I don't think he'll make it past the first punch."

"He won't even notice anyway." Dakota waves her hand dismissively. "He's preoccupied with his blond."

My gaze veers over to Trevor, who appears to be having a rather flirty conversation with one of the female bartenders. She smiles shyly at something he says, flipping her hair to the side as she pours two glasses of beer then slides one to him and motions to cheers. The bartender's desire for Trevor is so obvious, and it makes me annoyed on Dakota's behalf that Trevor is reciprocating her flirtations. Usually, Dakota is all for Trevor getting a good lay, but this time, something just feels off.

I swing back in Dakota's direction. "Seriously, are you guys okay?" I say as I cover her hand with mine.

Dakota shrugs. Her shoulders are squared tightly together, and it's clear she'd rather talk about anything else. I love Dee, and opening up to her feels like the easiest thing in the world for me, but getting her to reciprocate is anything but.

"I'm fine," she squeaks out.

"You're not. I know because I make that exact same face when I'm not fine."

"It's just relationship drama. I don't feel like getting into it right now." She flips her hand over so it's clasped tightly around mine. "I think I'm more concerned about you and Jax."

My brows knit together. "What? Why?"

"Come on." When it's clear I'm oblivious, her expression grows more worried. "Si, this is the first time in the last month we've hung out together. And when we do, it's usually during or after one of these fights."

I uncross and cross my legs under the table uncomfortably. "I don't get what the problem is. I thought you liked the underground."

"I do," she assures me. "But sometimes I wanna see you when Jax isn't around. Don't get me wrong, I'm happy he makes you happy, but he has *all* your time. And it feels like I get none of it."

"He doesn't have all my time," I say defensively. "I've been busy with assignments. They've been kicking my ass."

That's only partially true. I'm struggling but coping fine. It's a shame the more interesting courses are in my junior year onward. At least doing a physiology degree is still a major step up from my original degree. I'm really looking at the bigger picture this time. I plan to use physiology as a stepping stone to a master's in athletic training, where I'd be able to help people suffering from sports-related injuries.

Dakota glares at me, unappreciative of me blaming my packed schedule on school. "I know for a fact that you don't study all the time."

"That's right. I also train at UFG."

She pouts. "But when you have time to spare, you're spending it all with him."

"Of course that's what I do, Dee. It's called being in a committed relationship."

"Are you really?" She looks at me warily. "In a committed relationship?"

A frown touches my mouth. "What's that supposed to mean?"

"It's just that . . ." Her plump lips curl inward. "I've never heard him call you his girlfriend."

I look away, not wanting her to see the embarrassment washing over my face.

"It just doesn't come naturally to him." I try to sound casual. Unaffected.

But Dakota knows it's a lie. She knows Jax isn't the type of guy to define the relationship first. I try my best to be comfortable with the pace we're going at, but the question of whether we're dating is always there, picking at my insecurities.

And every time I try to convince myself that there's no reason to be afraid, the fear of losing him makes the words die in my throat. Because I'm afraid I'm not going to like what I hear. And I'd rather have a little bit of him than none at all.

"You need to DTR," Dakota says urgently. "If neither of you knows what's going on, it's gonna be a problem."

I let out a defeated sigh.

"Fine. I will."

"He's coming over." Her gaze flickers over my shoulder for a brief second, then it's back on me, and now she's shoving me out of the booth. "Now's your chance. *Go.*"

I launch to my feet so fast that my hip hits the table. Jax finally makes it to the booth just as the waiter delivers our fifteen shots. He sends a friendly smile toward Dakota and then plants a kiss square on my lips. "Hi."

"Hi," I squeak out awkwardly, gripping the table with anxious claws behind my back.

His cheeks are slightly flushed, which means he's probably had more to drink than he's supposed to. When he spots the rows of tequila shots, his eyes flicker with wild excitement. He picks up a glass and chucks the liquid into his mouth eagerly, then grabs another two shots off the table to drink some more.

His eyes scroll up and down Dakota's body, admiring her dress. "Nice outfit, Dee."

"Thanks," she says, beaming.

He gestures to his friends at the back. "You want me to introduce you to some of the guys? They've been eyeing you all night."

Dakota shakes her head. "I'm good. I have a strict no-frat-boy rule. Maybe some other time when my standards hit the floor," she says, and Jax lets out a chuckle. Then, her gaze bounces over to me, and she mouths, *Talk to him now.*

I gulp nervously. I don't know why I'm having such trouble asking him. There aren't a lot of things that scare me, but somehow the phrase *So what are we?* is the most terrifying string of words to ever exist in the English language.

The thing is, Jax has never given me any reason to doubt his intentions. And we have fun. We have a lot of fun. We see each other nearly every day and text whenever we can. Things are going well. So I don't see why we should put a label on our relationship to complicate things.

"Hey," I say, smoothing a hand around Jax's shoulder. "Can we talk for a sec?"

"Hold on," he says, his attention already swinging elsewhere. The muscles in his body tighten up and his jaw tenses, brows pulling together as his eyes narrow toward the front door. "What the *fuck* are they doing here?"

I follow the direction of Jax's gaze. Swaggering into the bar like they own it are Damien and two of his cronies. The loud murmurings of the bar simmer to a low volume to accommodate their arrival, causing a smug grin to appear on Damien's face. He waves a hand at the bartender and points to a beer glass sitting by the bar, then curls his fingers into a four. I think about who the fourth glass is for when a taller, older man enters the bar, clad in a casual gray shirt and denim jeans.

Perez.

"Hey, this is a closed party," Jax thunders out to the unwanted newcomers as he charges toward them with determined, powerful strides.

The entire bar has fallen into an eerie silence. Sweat prickles along my neck. Tension sizzles in the air, making me feel uneasy.

Perez and Damien cut each other a look and laugh. It makes me uncomfortable that they're together. I've never once seen them hanging out, so their friendly appearance feels highly suspect.

"You're gonna make us leave?" Perez says impassively. "Come on, we just got here, man."

"Don't act like we're friends," Jax snaps. Adam and his friends have rallied behind him, already on standby if things escalate, which I fear they will. "I'm not the only one who sees through your game."

"What is my game?" Perez says innocently, stepping forward. Jax and Perez are now only a few dangerous feet away from each other. "Like I said, we're just here for a drink. I hardly think that's a reason to kick us out, is it?"

"Here's your drink," Jax snaps, then proceeds to tilt his glass forward, spilling the liquid all over the space between them. It splashes against Perez's shoes. When the glass has emptied, Jax lets it roll out of his grasp and drop to the floor, sending shards everywhere. The sharp noise prickles against my ear. "Now *leave*."

Perez rolls his shoulders back, rubbing his chin with a strong hand as he sizes Jax up.

"You newbies are all the same," he says, clicking his tongue. "Cop a few wins under your belt and you think you own the world. There's no respect anymore. There's a certain way things go around here, and if you're not careful, you'll be smoked out before you even throw your next punch."

"Come on, Perez. Everyone knows that your kind is dying. The underground demands new blood. New theatrics. You can only hope to cling on for a little while longer before you're forced into extinction. Which, I assure you, I'll be more than happy to do during our fight next month."

"Forced into extinction," Perez echoes with a laugh, a cold and heartless sound. "That your thing, huh? I wonder what your own stepdad has to say about it."

Jax's expression turns murderous.

"Shut your fucking mouth," he seethes.

I blink, confused. What the hell is Perez talking about?

"I'm just saying you're too eager to run your mouth, but it's you who hides in the shadows, too scared to take the blame for the shit that you did wrong," Perez says nonchalantly as he slowly paces around the pool table. "I mean, aren't you the one leading a double MMA life right now? Maybe it's a good thing your coach doesn't know. He won't want to see his prized fighter's head bouncing around in that cage like a pinball machine three weeks from now. So why don't you humble yourself before you do something you regret?"

Jax rubs a steady hand over his jaw, like he's trying to expel the tension that's formed in his body. "And who exactly am I humbling myself for? A well-past-his-prime fighter who's delusional enough to think that he still has what it takes to climb to the top? So full of himself that he thinks he can come into *my* bar and scare some sense into me?" The anger slips back under his skin, the harshness of his face and his words finally coming to light. "You're nothing, Perez. A soon-to-be-forgotten piece of history. A new age has arrived, and it has 'Deadbeat' written all over it in fucking gold. You say you're a king? Well, I'm a fucking *god*."

"Dead-beat! Dead-beat! Dead-beat!" Adam yells, stomping his foot against the hardwood floors.

Slowly, the entire bar ignites with the chant, rising in volume until it's loud enough that I can't even hear my own voice.

"Dead-beat! Dead-beat! Dead-beat!"

A new heaviness settles in my chest. I look at Dakota and find concern digging into her face too.

Perez produces a strained laugh. He snatches a beer mug from the bar and takes a huge swig of it, careful to draw out the time it takes to finish his drink as long as he can. When the chants simmer down, he gulps down the last of his beer and lowers the glass back onto the bar, releasing his grip.

And then he curls his fist and smashes it into Jax's face.

All hell breaks loose.

Fists start flying everywhere, from both sides of the bar. It takes a couple seconds for Jax to recover, but when he does, his eyes ignite with fury. With a yell, he returns Perez's punch by throwing a mean hook toward him. It hits Perez right in the nose, and his face and body slam onto the pool table, sending a half dozen billiards spilling onto the floor. A few girls scream in the distance. People scramble toward the door, desperate to get away.

Perez's hands are clutching his nose, trying to stop the bleeding. Jax doesn't waste any time; he picks up a pool cue from the floor and swings it like a bat, landing on Perez's back. Perez doubles over in pain. Jax swings the cue stick back a second time, but one of Damien's cronies attempts to yank the stick out of Jax's grasp. They wrestle with the stick for a few moments until Jax gets really frustrated and throws a front kick to get him off.

My gaze desperately cuts to the booth where I left Dakota, wondering if she escaped early on. But there she is, hiding under the table with Trevor shielding her, both of them too terrified to move an inch as the entire bar falls into a chaotic flurry of movement. A stool flies past me, and I whip my head to follow it as it crashes into one of Perez's goons. Adam slams past me and collides with another guy, while Jax and Perez continue to trade blows.

I need to get my friends out of there. I weave around all the men throwing punches, narrowly avoiding a weaponized pool cue. I can hear the roar of my heartbeat raging in my ears as I make it to the booth in one piece. I yank both my friends out from under the table and gesture to the other exit that leads to the back alley from the bathrooms. "Get out of here. *Now*. I'll cover you."

Both Dakota and Trevor nod wordlessly.

Their arms are around their heads as they make a beeline for the exit while I shield them with my arms and body. I pry the door open for them. Dakota chews on her lip worriedly.

"Are you sure you're gonna be okay?" she whispers.

"I'll be fine. I need to go get Jax, and then we'll be good," I say, and she nods. "Now go."

I push both of them out of the bar and shut the door behind them. When I turn back, I'm blocked by a threatening male presence.

"Well, look who we have here," Damien says, clicking his tongue. His arms are folded across his chest, and he leans a hip against the wall. "It's been a long time, Sienna."

"Not gonna lie, kinda wish it was longer."

We're alone in the hallway. The harsh bathroom lights catch the twisted smile ravaging Damien's face. Panic begins to set in, squeezing my rib cage. I don't like the way he's looking at me. Like he's finally found someone easy to prey on.

"No more feisty comebacks? It's a shame. I was very much looking forward to it," he slurs, inching closer to me. I inch back. He laughs. "You're all bark and no bite, aren't you? Nothing has changed since the last time I saw you."

"Funny, Damien. I guess I can't say the same about you, hanging out with Perez and all," I say casually. "Since when were you two all buddy-buddy?"

"Since we realized we have similar interests in the underground," he says.

"Maybe it's a good idea to be allies. You need someone protecting your honor since you've never been good at doing that on your own."

Damien grits his teeth. He straightens himself up, squaring his shoulders, puffing out his chest like he has something to prove. A little part of me feels bad for him. Really. He seems like the kind of guy who's been overshadowed by others his entire life. Even when he manages to wrangle the spotlight for himself, he still isn't taken seriously. Even right now, as I'm looking at him, it doesn't register to me that he's a threat.

"My honor? How about you worry about yours? We both know if I strike first, you're never getting back up," he says, grabbing my shirt and yanking me toward him aggressively, hauling me against the wall. He looks me up and down, proud of his showy display of force, and a slow smile begins to spread across his face. "Looks like your boyfriend isn't here to save you now."

"I'm perfectly fine to save myself, thanks."

Damien's eyes are bloodshot as he reaches for my neck. If there's anything that Jax has taught me over the months I've been training alongside him, it's that there's always an opening, even when you think there isn't. Before his hands can tighten fully around my neck, cutting off all air circulation, I bring both my hands into the space between his arms and shoot right up, breaking his grip on me. And then I push myself out and start running as fast as my legs can carry me.

I'm out of the hallway and into the bar in a matter of seconds. Damien catches up to me, this time reaching forward to grab a fistful of my hair and yanking me backward. I feel the numbing pain as my back hits the wooden floorboards, now sticky with alcohol and littered with glass shards. He climbs on top of me, and I get my elbows in, trying to keep him at bay in case he reaches for my neck again. If he gets a good grip on my throat and squeezes with full force, it'll get crushed by him.

I'm struggling against him. I go for a hip escape, using my right leg to turn me to my left side. I push his knee away so I can free mine, and, catching my shin on his thigh, I flip over to the other side and ram my leg into his torso to get him into an underhook. Damien is surprised by the catch. He struggles against me, and just as it's looking like I might be able to get out from under him, a barstool rams right onto Damien's head, knocking him completely off my body.

Jax lets the barstool clatter to the ground. He kneels down beside Damien, a murderous expression on his face. Even though Damien is likely unconscious, Jax doesn't fail to get in the last word.

"Touch her again," he hisses with a malice that makes my stomach twist into knots of dread, "and I'll rip your fucking throat out." When he sees me, he scrambles over, his huge hands going around to cup the sides of my face. "Are you okay?" he says, darkened eyes searching for any hint of bruising or wounds.

"Yeah, I'm fine," I say, a little annoyed that he had to come and rescue me when I was this close to getting out of the grapple myself.

"Let's go. They're not gonna be able to hold Perez off for much longer." My gaze travels to the bloodbath occurring by the pool table, where Perez continues to rain hit after hit on Adam and the rest of Jax's friends.

My gaze flickers to his friends, then back to him. "We can't leave them."

"They'll be fine," he assures me.

Before I can protest, Jax grabs my hand, propelling me out of the chaos with purposeful and careful strides. We slip out the doors and into the parking lot and jump into the sports car. We're already pulling out of the parking lot when Perez and his goons spill out of the doors, looking around frantically for us.

"This isn't over, Deadbeat," Perez yells as we speed past him.

Jax lets out a howling laugh, knowing he's already won

this round. I don't miss my opportunity to shove two middle fingers out the window as we race off into the night.

***

"You're staying here tonight," Jax tells me when we pull into the private parking lot under his complex. I don't protest the decision made for me. In fact, I've grown to love Jax's space a lot. Sometimes, I sleep over here during the weekdays when I can't be bothered with the long commute home from campus.

"That's fine with me," I say, biting my lip. "But don't you wanna go back to check up on your friends?"

Jax helps me out of the car, and we walk toward the elevator side by side. "They're fine. Adam just texted me that after we left, they got out too."

It bugs me how easily Jax abandoned them in the middle of a fight he helped create. Maybe at some point they agreed the priority was to get me out, but I don't like that we just left them there to finish the fight.

"How about the cops?"

Jax looks over at me. "Adam bribed the bar owner. It's like we were never there."

"Wow. Okay," I say breathlessly, slumping against the elevator wall. "I still can't believe that happened."

"I'm not surprised. Perez doesn't like it when someone new stirs things up in the underground. He's been around for a long time, and for good reason—he'll do anything to annihilate you if he sees you're a threat," Jax says quietly. He looks far worse off than me: his bottom lip is bruised, and he has a gnarly black eye from when Perez decked his face at the start. I make a mental note to grab the ice bag from the freezer to tend to the bruising. "At least I'm doing something right if he's scared."

The elevator pings, and the doors open. Jax slides his hand into mine and pulls me out and into the hallway.

My front teeth dig into my bottom lip. The whole confrontation with Perez and Jax doesn't sit right with me, especially after what Perez revealed about Jax and his past.

"What was Perez talking about when he mentioned your stepdad?" I say cautiously, a bad feeling tugging my heart.

"It's nothing. He's just trying to get under my skin," he says, not looking at me as he jams his key into the lock to open the front door.

"That doesn't sound like nothing, though," I press on. "It sounded like something bad happened between the both of you."

Jax rolls his eyes. "Perez is exaggerating."

"That's all you can say? After that bombshell?" I prod. "You know, come to think of it, I don't think I know anything about your parents. I didn't even know you *have* a stepdad."

Jax has always been unwilling to share much about his family, despite me asking. The only piece of information he continues to reiterate to me is that he and his family aren't close.

This time, he forces his gaze to meet mine. "My dad bolted when I was barely a teen, and my mom married my stepdad. I don't want to get into the details of it." He must notice that I look unsatisfied because he sighs and flattens his lips. "Look, Perez was just implying how estranged me and my stepdad are. That's all."

"I don't know. It's just weird that he brought it up."

He sighs again, wrenching the door open a little too hard. "Can we drop this? He's in the past, and I don't want to talk about him."

I step into the living room hesitantly. "Okay, then what do you wanna talk about?"

When he closes the door behind him, he turns over to look at me, eyes darkening with lust.

"I don't want to talk," he says as he strides over with fierce intent. His arms go around me to pull me into a hungry kiss.

I decide to let the stepdad topic go for now. Clearly he's not in the mood, and I don't want to push him in case he's not ready. Instead, I dive into his kiss, my mouth parting to let his tongue in, and he obliges me. I can taste the alcohol and the sweat on him. I wonder what I taste like. Probably not all that different from him.

Jax walks me toward his room and pushes me onto his bed. He wastes no time peeling the shirt off his ripped body and then fusing his lips together with mine again, with one knee wedged in between my legs. Every bone in my body rattles with anticipation.

His large hands snake their way up my body, sliding underneath my tank top. I love how they feel against my skin, drawing out goose bumps wherever they land.

I fit my lips over his, my entire body hot for him. I place a hand over his massive chest and push him over so I can climb on top of him and grind my hips against his, burning for relief. His fingers curve around my waist, holding me close to him.

"You looked so hot fighting Damien off like a champ," he whispers as he pulls himself up into a sitting position, head nuzzled against my neck.

"Yeah?" I whisper back. "You should've let me finish him off, though."

"I can't resist wanting to protect you, you know that. I'm far too obsessed with you." Jax doesn't stop kissing me when he talks. I try to ignore the ribbons of pleasure each of his kisses unfurls inside me, but they're impossible to disregard when they're coupled with his delicious-sounding words. "I'm obsessed with everything about you, princess. Your smile, your mouth, your body . . ." He pinches my skin with hands like rough paws, and I let out a whimper, pushing my hips down on him restlessly. A dangerously low growl escapes his mouth. "*Fuck*, I love that you're mine."

Mine. The word clings to my brain until it's the only thing that I can focus on.

I want to be his. I want to be claimed by him, to belong to him fully. But I need him to say the words. The words I've been afraid to ask him since I realized I didn't want to just mess around with him.

"Am I really?" I whisper.

Jax stops kissing me.

He looks up, confused. "What?"

"Am I really?" I whisper. "Am I yours? Like . . . as in, am I your girlfriend?" I say, already feeling the redness climbing up my cheeks. "It's embarrassing for me to ask you that, but I need to know. Dee said I should clear it up with you. She said that you might have other expectations with this relationship. Or whatever this is."

"Dee sure has a lot of opinions about me," he mutters.

His comment makes me frown. I don't like the way he

says it. Like Dee isn't trying to be the biggest supporter of our relationship.

"She's only looking out for me. She's one of the few people who ever do."

Jax lets out a sigh. "You know I do too, right?"

"That's why I'm asking."

He takes a couple of seconds to think. He releases his grip on my waist, and a hand sifts through his blond hair, mouth mashed together. After a while, his expression softens and his lips part as his eyes look at me with a newfound affection.

"You know what? We're whatever you want us to be," Jax tells me, planting a kiss on the square of my lips. "I just want to be with you. I want to kiss you every day. Touch you. Be the one you confide in. And the only one that ever gets to give you mind-blowing head."

I laugh. "That sounds like a relationship."

"Then, we're in a relationship."

My heart squeezes with emotion, and I mask the response by putting on a casual tone.

"Okay. Great."

"Great." He smiles.

It makes me smile too.

Holy fuck, I'm Jax's girlfriend.

I'm so happy I could scream.

"Now that that's settled . . ." Jax's voice trails off, his innocent smile now dissolving into a lewd one.

Grinning, I circle my arms around him and crush my lips against his again.

God, it feels so good to be in a relationship.

THIRTEEN

I wish I had a way to make the next few days fly by quickly, but they continue to stretch on as I crawl toward the finish line. I'm almost done with my exams—only one more left—which means more of barricading myself in the far end of the library, speed-reading through course materials I wish I'd kept up with during the semester. And while MMA training has contributed to my lack of preparation, it's really that my priorities have shifted over the course of these last few months. Time management has always been my worst enemy.

Amidst all the chaos of exam prep, I make sure to check up on Dakota and Trevor. I'm relieved to hear that they were just a bit shaken after the bar fight. There's no doubt in my mind that what happened with Perez and Jax at the bar was only a taste of what's to come in the underground. While getting into a fight with Damien was thrilling, I doubt I would have felt the same way had we not escaped in time. I can only hope that all this drama can be put to rest after the fight in three weeks.

I finally see the light at the end of the tunnel when the exam is done and dusted. I'm not sure how my GPA is going to look by the end of this, but I'm sure it'll be enough for me to come back next year. Hopefully by then I'll also be looking for somewhere to live in the city. I've finally got a good amount of money saved from doing odd jobs—my latest as a part-time security assistant on campus on the weekends, which is boring but easy since all I need to do is monitor the cameras and yell at students to stop smoking pot in the hallways. I've got those earnings saved for a deposit in the dorms. But eventually, I'll need to find a more sustainable way to pay rent.

I make sure to swing by UFG after my exam. It's late afternoon, which is reflected in the absence of people in the gym. Usually it gets busier right before dinner. Luckily, one of the few gym regulars, Sadie, is around, so I ask if she is willing to do a quick grappling session with me before either Jax or Julian arrives. I would say my strength comes from my striking, but I'm not the best when it comes to the ground stuff, and I want to get better at it so I won't get overpowered when I get taken to the floor.

I turn to face Sadie. She's gorgeous. With long dark hair put into a crown braid and a body of pure flesh and muscle, she's a force to be reckoned with in the cage. I aspire to be just as good as her one day. She's been fighting for five years now and recently revealed that she's going to transition from being part of an amateur MMA promotion to fighting for a big league. It's all super hush-hush at the moment, but she just signed a six-figure contract. Julian is really proud of her, but the downside is that she'll be moving to Las Vegas and turning to another training camp there to work her real good for her first fight, so he's sad to see her go.

"All right," she says as she gets on her knees, her hands padded up in a pair of black gloves. Since we're working on just grappling, we both start half kneeling instead of on our feet. "Show me what you got, Lane."

Immediately, I reach for her head, hooking my palm behind her neck while my other hand pushes against her arm in an attempt to dislodge her. Sadie pushes forward, suddenly tipping me onto my back. She mounts me and goes for a headlock, but I manage to escape the mount and get back into a guard position. I go for a Kimura, a type of armlock that painfully strains her shoulder, but I struggle to maintain control as Sadie works toward my back and, with a beautiful setup, rolls me straight into a triangle choke, my neck trapped between her thighs. I manage to escape the triangle and pass her guard. We struggle back and forth in a tangle of limbs until she manages to catch my head from side control and sink in a perfect Ezekiel submission. Trapped and exhausted, I finally tap out.

"Holy shit, you almost got me good," she says in awe when she climbs off me.

"Yeah, you think?"

"Yeah." She nods. "Can't wait to see you in full force."

"Thanks, Sadie," I say, giving her fist a bump. "Good luck in Vegas."

After I've cooled down, I decide to fill the time waiting for Julian by doing some solo grappling drills—the usual rockers, flat rolls, and roll outs to keep the momentum going. Halfway through my third drill, Julian bursts through the doors of the gym with his phone in his hand. I immediately drop my guard as a bad feeling travels down my spine.

Julian's gaze zips around the gym looking for someone, and when he spots me, his mouth tightens into a snarl.

"Where the fuck is he?" he demands.

"Jax? He should be here soon," I say, confused. "What's up?"

"What's up?" he echoes, like I just told him I'm part alien. "Seriously?"

I blink at him, confused. I've never seen Julian like this before. Usually he's hard on everyone, but he rarely gets this angry.

"What's going on?" I ask again, more urgently this time. "You're looking crazed right now."

Julian refuses to say anything. His whole body is trembling with rage, and it's clear he's trying hard to keep from completely exploding. I approach him slowly, unsure of how to calm him down. But I don't make it past the cage door because Jax arrives just then, and Julian beelines toward him with a death grip on his phone.

"'Sup, Jules." Jax gives him a casual wave.

"What the fuck is this?" Julian shoves the phone at Jax's face.

Jax's silence drags as he watches the phone. I can't see the screen, but as soon as I hear the sound of fists slamming into bones and the collective voices chanting Jax's name, my eyes squeeze shut in recognition. The underground fight.

Perez or someone in his gang must have sent a video of the fight to Julian. As soon as the thought enters my mind, the same conclusion seems to have surfaced in Jax as well.

"Who sent this to you?" Jax demands. "Was it Damien? Perez?"

"Doesn't fucking matter who sent it. You're with the underground?" Julian snatches the phone back. "Were you gonna tell me?"

"No. Because I knew you were going to act like this." Jax sighs, walking away from Julian and toward the lockers, but Julian isn't having any of it.

"Don't take another fucking step. Get back here!" Julian yells, yanking him by the shirt from behind so hard that Jax stumbles backward. "You know I have a strict no-underground policy, and you go and fight for them behind my back? You think I wouldn't find out?"

Jax turns to Julian, annoyed. "What is the big deal?"

"If word gets out that you're illegally brawling in greasy basements, no promotion's ever gonna want you," Julian says, anger rising in his throat. "You're destroying your own MMA career before it even begins!"

Jax scoffs, his arrogance taking root in his words. "Somehow, I doubt that."

"You don't believe me? Won't take the word of someone who's been in this business for over fifteen years?" Disbelief drips from Julian's voice. "I didn't peg you for being this dense."

"I'll gain your trust back. You have my word."

"Your word ain't *shit* around here no more! You've been switching up your strategy without consulting with me first. And you don't even talk about tryouts anymore. It's like you lost sight of the goal." He takes a step back from Jax like he doesn't need any more convincing as the realization sets on his face. "Now I know why."

The magnitude of Jax's silence makes it clear that Julian has him cornered. There's simply no way he can fight his way out of this, not when Julian has made the rules here very clear.

"I want you out," Julian says quietly.

My heart whacks fiercely in my ribs.

"You're not serious." Jax lets out a hoarse laugh. When he realizes Julian isn't budging, Jax's expression settles into shock, his entire world crumbling before his eyes. "Julian, you can't be serious—"

"Out. Of. My. Gym," Julian seethes, his voice scraping against his throat as he hurls his words at Jax. *"Now!"*

"This is bullshit!" Jax barks back. "You're seriously kicking me out? That video was an attempt at sabotage. If you do this, you're only going to prove them right!"

"I don't care about the stupid underground politics that you've gotten yourself into. You lied to me. You sabotaged *me*." There's a crack in his words, and for a second there, guilt flashes in Jax's eyes. "If you won't leave on your own, I'll have any of these guys help you to the door," Julian grumbles, gesturing to the few of us around the gym as he walks toward the doors. "And if you fight back, I'll call the fucking cops."

"Is this really how you treat your students? The ones that were loyal enough to stay with you for years?" Jax follows after him, the desperation beginning to show through the cracks in his steel-plated armor. "However will your shitshow of a gym stay afloat without someone like me representing you?"

"You seriously want to talk to me about loyalty?" Julian yanks the front door open hard and pushes Jax through with ease. "Get the fuck out of here. And don't come back. *Ever*."

Before Jax can utter anything else, Julian slams the door shut in his face.

"Julian," I say, immediately going over toward him. "Julian, wait—"

He stops me from coming a fraction closer with a strong hand. His eyes flutter closed, but there's no mistaking the betrayal lurking in them.

"You knew," he mutters to me. "You knew about him being in the underground, and you didn't even think to tell me about it." He shakes his head in disappointment. "Consider yourself lucky that I'm not kicking you out too, Sienna."

And with that, Julian shuffles back into his office and shuts the blinds.

Shame grips my entire body. He's right; I have been complicit in Jax's journey in the underground, and I should have flagged it to him when I found out it was against the rules. Instead, I got cold feet, knowing all too well that me telling Julian would threaten my relationship with Jax.

I can't deal with hurting Julian like this. He's hardheaded and mean most of the time, but I respect the hell out of him. He doesn't deserve this.

When I push through the front doors, I find Jax pacing back and forth in anger at the base of the steps.

"Jax," I say as I hop down the stairs. Relief washes over his expression. "Are you okay?" I ask urgently.

"Fuck Perez. He really wants to be this slimy? Fuck this shit!" Jax yells out angrily. "He's not going to throw me off my game. I'll find somewhere else to train. And when I do, that fucker isn't gonna know what's coming for him."

"Okay . . . but what about Jules?" I ask, maneuvering back to the real issue at hand. Is he not bothered about severing ties with his longtime trainer and friend? He broke a promise to Julian. He has a lot to answer for.

"If Julian wants me out, then he has nothing left to offer me," he snaps irrationally. "It's fine. It's about time I dropped him anyway. Julian is a good-for-nothing trainer who gave up on his own MMA career because it got too fucking hard."

I flinch because I know he doesn't really believe that. He's just too angry to see that he's wrong right now.

"He left because he wanted to leave a good legacy behind," I say defensively, cupping both his hands in mine. "Look, I'm so sorry that happened, but you were well aware of the consequences of pursuing an underground career."

"Well, it's not as big a deal as he's making it out to be," he mutters. "I don't need this, Sienna. We don't need him."

"What are you talking about?" I ask, hoping he isn't going to try to steer me away from Julian and UFG. "Just because you got kicked out doesn't mean I deserve the same fate, Jax."

"You're not being kicked out. You're leaving. With me." He tries to clamp his hand on my wrist, but my reflexes are faster, and I snatch it away from his grasp, stepping back from him confidently.

"I'm not leaving." I shake my head, planting my feet firmly on the ground.

Jax's eyebrows soar. "What?"

"I can't leave, Jax. You may have blown your chance here, but I've still got one. I like training with Julian. And maybe someday . . ." I let loose a long breath, preparing myself for what I'm about to say. "I want to work here."

Jax gives me a long look.

"You want to work here," he echoes in disbelief.

I bite back the annoyance rising to the surface. Why does he sound like me wanting a career here is such a ridiculous idea?

"You know I've been doing a degree in physiology," I explain to him. "And after that, I'm planning to pursue a master's in athletic training. I want to *help* people, Jax. And it'll be great if I can get paid for it too."

"There're other gyms around that will be glad to take you. You don't need to stay at UFG."

"But I want to," I say sharply. "I like training with Julian. And I like the place."

"I assure you, UFG isn't that special."

"I don't care. Julian is tough, but we get along, and he's a good trainer. And I know a relationship like that is hard to come by."

"I can't change your mind?" Jax asks, and I shake my head no. His frustration is clear in the way he steps away from me and pauses for a moment to ease the muscle pulsing in his jaw. "Sienna, seriously think about it. You're making a huge mistake. You're going to waste your MMA career if you stay here. Don't think for one second you're safe from his wrath. Julian isn't going to help you. He's only limiting your potential."

"You're making a big deal out of nothing," I say.

It's clear that Jax is so blinded by his anger toward Julian that he's projecting those insecurities toward me now. And it's fucking unfair of him. Just because he got found out doesn't negate the fact that Julian has been good to me so far.

Jax laughs in disbelief.

"You're seriously going to stick by him instead of me? Your *boyfriend*?" he lambasts.

I clench my teeth together. "You're really gonna pull that card on me? Really, Jax? What the fuck?"

My sympathy has run out now. I hate that he's made this a competition between him and Julian when that's not even the case to begin with.

"You're either on my side or you aren't, Sienna," he says dryly. "You know this shit's important to me."

"I *am* on your side," I insist. "I just can't do what you're asking me to do because it's *stupid*."

Jax throws his hands up in annoyance. "You know what? Fine. Do what you want. But don't come running back to me when you feel suffocated by Julian and realize that I was right about him all along."

"Jax," I protest when he turns his back toward me. "*Jax*. Seriously? Come on!"

He merely shakes his head, hauls his gym bag over his shoulder, and stalks away.

FOURTEEN

Jax and I haven't spoken in two days.

All of my attempts to call him have been useless as they immediately go straight to voicemail. He must have turned his phone off. Or blocked my number. I don't know how else to reach him.

Most days, he's more than eager to talk to me. I can't even go a few hours without him checking up on me, wondering what I'm doing and if I'm thinking of him.

Now the silence is deafening.

I check my phone again, as if my lock screen will look any different than it did the last hundred times I've checked it in the past hour. I watch the clock tick slowly, the hope that he'll realize he's wrong and reach out waning with every mocking minute.

"Entitled bastard," I mutter under my breath.

Why does he have to force me to choose like this? Why can't I stay with Julian *and* not have my loyalty to my relationship questioned?

I wonder how long I'm going to get the silent treatment for. The finals are in two weeks, so he's going to need all the emotional support he can get. Stress and overworking himself are his two greatest adversaries during this time, and I'm usually the one who soothes him and gets him back on track.

Maybe he doesn't need my support anymore.

Maybe he doesn't need *me*.

I know what I should do. I know it, but I'm unwilling to make the decision. Because making the decision means I might lose Jax forever. And I can't let him slip away from me like that. Not when we've only recently decided to make a deeper commitment to each other.

My mom taps her fist against the door hesitantly, asking me if I want to talk. She's worried about me because I haven't been okay since Jax and I stopped talking, and it's been hard for her to get me to share anything about it. It's been hard for her to get me to do anything, really. I haven't left my room since I first got back from our fight. My eating and sleeping schedule is all fucked up, and my hygiene is at an all-time low.

If I tell Mom about what went down with Jax, she'll probably tell me that I shouldn't let a man make me choose between him and a blossoming career, and I don't know if I'm ready to hear that. She already has a good impression of him; it feels counterproductive to strip all that away because of one argument.

Mom isn't the only one trying to get me to open up about the situation; Dakota has been trying to contact me, but I let her calls go straight to voicemail. I'm not in the mood to share what happened with her. It'll confirm her suspicions about Jax.

She's already wary enough about his intentions toward me; I don't want to give her another reason to doubt him.

This is so fucking stupid.

If Jax was actually a good boyfriend, I wouldn't feel the need to protect his image from my mom. If he was actually a good boyfriend, everyone wouldn't need convincing that he is good—his actions would already speak for themselves.

Frustration digs into my skin. All I want to do is to support Jax, but he makes it so hard for me. Whatever I choose, I'll have to sacrifice something that means a lot to me. I can only hope that Jax will snap out of it and realize what a jackass he's being. I don't know what I'm going to do if he doesn't.

I don't want to lose Jax.

Not when what I've dreamed of forever has only lasted a moment.

***

"Didn't think you'd be back." Julian doesn't even bother to look up from his desk when he senses my presence lurking by the door to his office this evening.

I peek at the shelf adjacent to his table when I walk in. Gone are the frames containing pictures of Jax and him together. And the broken shards of glass littering the base of the shelf help me form an idea of where they ended up.

"I didn't think you'd still want me here," I mutter, clicking my feet together awkwardly.

Visiting UFG is something I've debated doing since the blowout three days ago. If I still don't know where I stand with Jax, I at least need to know where I stand with Julian. At this point, it's looking like this is the only relationship that still has a fighting chance.

I decide to push the tension, shuffling into the office and standing in front of the seat opposite him. I've never been good with apologies. But unlike Jax, I'm willing to admit I'm wrong when the situation calls for it.

"I'm sorry I didn't tell you about Jax," I say remorsefully.

Julian sighs, takes off his reading glasses, and rests his arms over his desk.

"Sit down," he exhales, and I do what he says, sinking onto the chair. He drums his fingers against the desk's surface, leans forward, and curls his lips inward. "Look, I had some time to think about it. And while I wish you had told me, I get why you didn't. You're his girlfriend. It's an awkward position to be in."

I'm shocked. I thought he'd need more convincing than that. I prepared a whole monologue to go with my apology and everything.

But then again, Julian has always been a practical man. He's just uncompromising when it comes to his business affairs. It's a work ethic that I secretly admire, despite often being the prime target of his disapproval.

I exhale a sigh of relief. "Thanks, Jules."

"That wasn't an apology for being mad at you." He mashes his mouth together tightly, making him look like a tired, grumpy old man. "I'm still mad."

I try to hide my smile. It's funny how he's still clutching on to his anger so tightly despite it being slippery in his grasp.

"I know. I'd be kidding myself if I thought you were going

to let me off easy over this," I say, leaning forward and tapping my fingers against the table. "I'm curious, though, about who sent the video to you. Did you ever find out?"

"It was anonymous." Julian shrugs. "But if I followed the trail, I'm certain it'd lead me back to Perez. Or someone Perez-adjacent."

"Yeah. Jax has more than a few enemies in the underground."

"Has he put you on that target list yet?" he mutters. "You're either with him or against him. There's no in between with Jax. So where does that leave you?"

My eyelids flutter briefly. I say the words I feel defeated enough to say.

"If I choose him, will you be okay with that?"

Julian's gaze hardens, noticing my hesitation. "Do you want to choose him?"

"Feels like I have to if I want to save my relationship," I say defeatedly.

Julian blows out a strained breath as he shakes his head. It feels like I've disappointed him somehow. Other than my mom, Julian's the only adult figure in my life whom I have immense respect for, so this is soul-crushing to me.

He checks the time on his watch and looks back at me.

"What are you doing after this?" he asks.

"Nothing, why?"

"Get in your workout gear and follow me," he orders, pushing off his seat. "We're doing some ad hoc training today."

***

"Look what the cat finally dragged in this evening," a tall guy with a scruffy beard calls out as Julian and I walk onto the soccer field. Downes Field is a twenty-minute ride on the T from UFG. I've never been to this part of Brookline before. It's quieter, with lots of residential houses neatly tucked away from the rest of the city by trees.

"Hey, guys. Sorry I'm late." Julian gives an apologetic wave, the soccer ball wedged between his hip and his arm as he approaches his friends.

There are four of them, all looking like they're in their midforties, like Julian. Three of them are dressed in either red or blue shirts, denoting which team they'll be playing on, and the fourth member has a plain white shirt on with a whistle slung across his neck.

"We've got an extra player today. Everyone, this is Sienna. Sienna, everyone." I give a friendly nod, and I receive warm, eager smiles in return. Julian throws the ball at a beefy middle-aged man with jet-black hair and mousy features who I didn't realize was sitting on the sidelines. "Looks like you can finally play after all, Lloyd." Lloyd pumps a fist into the air and jogs over to the other guys. Julian turns to me. "Sienna, you're on the red team with me and Ward. You take left. I'll take right. Ward will be goalkeeper. Watch out for Pete over there." He jerks his head toward an olive-skinned man with a toupee wearing a blue shirt, who's looking a little too smug about a newbie joining the game today. "He likes to call foul when you try to steal the ball from him."

A dramatic gasp comes from Pete. "I do not," he says, holding both his hands up in reassurance. "I'll play fair, I promise."

"He also likes to lie," Julian mutters. It makes me laugh.

After a quick recap of the rules and a few minutes of warm-up, the ref whistles, and the game begins. I haven't played soccer since middle school, so I'm a bit rusty. But they're all nice enough to push their competitive edge aside for the first couple of rounds while I get my bearings.

"Take it easy, Sienna!" Pete offers an encouraging smile as he goes over to defend Lloyd, who currently has the ball. I push closer, unsure of how to get to Lloyd with Pete in the way. "You're in your head too much."

"Stop sabotaging our girl," Julian mutters, swerving from the other side to steal the ball from Lloyd. He makes it past Pete and launches the ball toward their goal. He scores, and Ward and I do a little high five.

At some point during the game, I get the ball. Our team gets pushed back by their offense, with Julian desperately defending their fierce attack as they come for me. I narrowly evade Pete as he tries to steal the ball from me, misleading him with an easy mouse trap. Pete's eyes flare with excitement as he watches me lose my footing. But the ball never leaves me. Instead, I use the distraction to shoot it in between his feet toward Julian. Julian throws his leg back and launches the ball straight into the goal. The whistle blows right on time.

Our team wins.

"Yes!" I holler.

"Nice work, Sienna." Ward gleams at me, giving me a congratulatory pat on the back.

"Thanks," I say, feeling relieved that I wasn't a liability to them. It's been a while since I've felt like that.

I head to the bench to towel myself off and squirt some

water into my mouth and over my face to wash off the coating of sweat clinging onto my skin. Julian approaches me, yanking his own towel off the bench and wiping his face with it. I drop down to the bench with an exhausted thud.

"You did good out there," Julian tells me.

I blink up at him, amused. "Did you just give me a compliment?"

"Don't get used to it."

A smile lifts the corners of my mouth. "I didn't know you play soccer."

"Yeah, I started playing in high school. Was even supposed to go pro before I discovered MMA," he says, plopping himself down onto the available space next to me. He rests both his arms over his thighs, staring at his friends as they do some practice shots. "I'm busy with the gym now, but I always try to find some time for soccer and to keep up with the guys whenever they get time off from their families."

"That's cool," I remark. "I always assumed you were a lone wolf kind of guy."

"I am," he says, his eyes skimming over the field. "I got divorced five years back. Both of my parents passed a long time ago, and my two older brothers moved away. One lives in Wyoming with his husband, and the other runs a potato farm in Idaho. It can be a lonely life here without family, but I'm never really alone."

I remain silent, parsing his words in my head. It must be nice to feel that there are people who have your back, even when they're not around all the time. I feel lonely, despite having friends and family who love me.

"Why did you bring me here, Jules?" I ask quietly.

He rests his arms on his knees, rubbing his forehead, like he's not sure if I'm going to like what he says next.

"I want to show you that there's a life outside of Jax." His attention is fully on me now. "When was the last time you hung out with anyone other than him?"

"Um, well, the other weekend—"

"*Without* him there?"

I clamp my mouth shut.

"That's what I thought." Julian gives a disappointed headshake. "I know this is not my place, but I'm going to say it anyway. Do not put everything into Jax. He's not the kind that'll stick around when the shit hits the fan. I learned that lesson a little too late," he says, hurt squeezing every syllable. "You're a good kid, Sienna. And I care about you because I see so much potential in you. I haven't had someone walk through the doors of my gym with the kind of swagger and confidence you have. It's annoying as hell, but your skill keeps up with your attitude, and I admire that. So whether or not you want to do MMA casually or professionally, there's always a place for you in UFG. But it's only there if you want it."

"I want it," I say without any form of hesitation. "I want to do MMA professionally. I don't want to fight in any big promotions or anything like that, but I want to be a trainer. And it's because of you that I want to be a trainer. I see the way you coach these people and build up their confidence through the sport. I can only hope I'll be half as good as you." They're the most earnest words I've said in a while, and I can tell he's touched by the way his expression softens. "And I know it takes years of honing technique and getting good at every type of combat sport. But you should know by now that I don't scare easily. I know I have what it takes."

Julian leans back slightly and nods, satisfied with my answer. "That's what I want to hear." He cuts me a serious look. "If you want to stick to this path, then Jax has no control over your professional decisions. Absolutely fucking none, you got me?"

"Fine."

It's the right thing to do. For myself.

"You'll need to ramp up your training sessions with me to get your MMA certification," Julian says. His elbows are digging into his thighs, his hands in a point against his chin when he adds, "I know you're tight with money right now, and you're all over the place with all the random part-time jobs you've been doing. So, let me make it easier for you: if you're looking for some extra income, you can always work at the gym. It'll be good for you to know how UFG operates from the ground up anyway."

I force my excitement inward and politely nod in understanding. Finally, a proper way to pay for rent on campus. A new purpose blooms in my stomach, creating a surge of energy in my body.

"Got it."

"Got it, as in, you'll listen to me and stay?"

"I'll stay," I say, and his mouth curls into a small smile. It's the first one that I've seen from him that is genuinely happy.

He picks himself up off the bench and extends a hand toward me. "Come on. I'll walk you to the station."

I nod again, letting him pull me up then moving to his side as we walk toward the center of the field. I can't resist smiling up at him. "Thanks, Jules."

"Least I can do for dragging you all the way here."

"No, I mean, for everything. This," I say, pausing as I look around the field. "I really needed this."

He loops me in for a side hug, looking down at me with pride. "I know you did."

"You think we can grab some food before we go?" I ask.

"Sure, what are you craving?"

"I heard there's a good doughnut shop nearby."

Julian makes a weird face. "Doughnuts? Not sure if I'm into that."

"Just try it." I pat him on the back, a smile radiating across my face. "You never know."

FIFTEEN

Last night was the first night I was able to get a good rest.

It's nice to have Julian not only as a mentor but as a friend I can rely on as well. And if I'm as serious about MMA as I want to be, I need to follow through with his advice and leave Jax out of my career. It's the right thing to do.

I wonder how Jax is going to take it. Probably not well, given his initial response. *Perhaps I shouldn't be with someone like that.* I used to think he wouldn't break up with me over something as trivial as this, but now I'm not sure.

As morning light filters through my window, I stare up at my bedroom ceiling, ruminating on the real possibility of having to break up with Jax. My heart clenches with hurt just thinking about it.

The past months with him have made me the happiest I've ever been. I don't know if I'd survive a heartbreak like that.

I don't allow the thought to take hold of my mind. Not when I've got a ton of things to do today. Right on cue, the alarm in my phone buzzes that it's 7:30 a.m., giving me a small window of time to commute into the city and report for work at the gym when it opens at 8:30. I hop out of bed and leap across the room for a change of clothes, not needing to worry about making a ruckus this early since Beth is away at cheer camp until tomorrow. I make my way to the bathroom, and as I wait for the shower to heat up, I check my phone for any messages to reply to. There are none from Jax, a couple from Julian running through my working hours for the week as well as my training schedule, and one from Dakota, which puts a smile on my face.

Remember my show is this Sat! Don't forget! I can practically hear her chirping with excitement through the message.

I'll be there! I shoot back, matching her tone.

After a quick shower, I get dressed with lightning speed. Stuffing all my MMA gear into my bag, I scramble down the stairs and leap into the living room to bid goodbye to my mom.

"Mom!" I yell, nearly tripping over the carpet. "I'm leaving now, don't wait up for me tonight!" But instead of finding my mother, I spot a woman I don't recognize sitting on the couch, clicking her feet together nervously. "Uh, who are you?" I ask uneasily.

Her body jolts with surprise. "Oh!" she says, looking like her soul has dropped out of her body. "Hello there." The slender figure rises from her seat awkwardly. With thick dark hair, a small round face, and a pair of naturally full lips, she's the complete opposite of my mom, yet equal in beauty. She looks like the kind of woman you'd find in *Architectural Digest*, with her sprayed-back hair, beige turtleneck, culottes, and leather boots. It's not cold out right now, so it strikes me as odd that she's dressed like that. Her nervous hands clutch the mint-green scarf on her lap as her humble gaze fixes onto me.

"I'm Alicia. Your dad's . . . girlfriend, I suppose," she says, like she's too mature to be called that. With a hesitant smile, she extends her hand toward me, flipping her hair aside with ease.

My stomach falls a little. Despite seeing it in fleeting moments around the house, I'm finally face-to-face with what my dad has been up to since the divorce.

I don't shake her hand. Instead, I shove my hands into the pockets of my joggers.

"What are you doing here?" I ask coldly.

"I'm waiting for your dad. We're headed to Vermont for the day." She drops her hand then retreats toward the couch, placing her scarf on the armrest while she waits. "He's in the bathroom."

My lips mash together with annoyance. Most of the time, he's careful not to bring women into the house since my mom's always around. But not only is one of them in our house—he had the audacity to bring her here without even arranging a proper meeting with us?

And to think I bothered with the courtesy of bringing Jax home to meet him once.

The toilet flushes in the bathroom, and my dad emerges from the creaking door. When he notices that I'm standing in the living room with his girlfriend, his face is stricken with surprise.

"Hey, Sienna." He tries to keep his expression vague. "Um, this is Alicia—"

"We've met," I snap, jerking my head toward his girlfriend. "Alicia, can you give us a second?"

Sensing the tension seeping into the room, Alicia gives a hard nod. "I'll be out at the front porch," she calls as she makes her way out of the living room.

When she slams the door shut behind her, I don't miss a second before I snap at my dad. "You're bringing women into the house now? While Mom's still living here? Were the shameless number of dates not enough, now you gotta rub it in all our faces?"

"I didn't think you were home," my dad says weakly. "Thought you were gonna be in class."

"It's spring break. I *have* no class," I say, rolling my eyes. "You would know that if you'd bothered to check in on me these past few weeks."

"I'm sorry. It slipped my mind," he tells me too casually.

He has officially lost touch with reality. The man standing in front of me is a complete stranger, void of any kind of empathy or compassion.

"God, you're such a disappointment to this family," I snap, swinging back toward the stairs, away from him. My dad relentlessly follows after me.

"Tell me what you want me to do, Sienna!" he yells, desperation edging his voice. "It's been over half a year now. I'm trying to move on!"

"Well, you're doing a splendid job so far!"

He gives his head a shake. "You know what? I'm tired of constantly having to defend myself. I'm trying to get better. I haven't touched a bottle in months. I'm starting a new job next week. I feel the best I've ever been. Why do you have to keep holding my happiness against me?"

"Because you don't deserve it. Because you should've done

all this shit when you had a family to take care of!" I shriek, practically spitting the words. "Instead, you only proved us right: that we were not enough for you to quit. And that a shitty affair and a parade of women were the two things that did it."

"Sienna, you have no idea how hard it has been for me. How hard your mom and I struggled. It was a bad situation to be in," he tries to explain, and I scoff at the selfishness of his answer. Like it wasn't him that caused the situation in the first place. "I'm not sorry for trying to find happiness again, Sienna. And for God's sake, your mom is going to be doing the exact same thing with her trip—" His mouth slams shut. Like he was going to blurt out something he wasn't supposed to say.

"What?" I step down from the stairs, curiosity propelling me toward him. If there's something about Mom I should know, he better spit it out. "What trip? What are you talking about?"

My dad swallows hard. The tone he takes afterward becomes thick with regret. "All I can say is Mom and I are ready for things to change now. We've held on as much as we can for you girls, but it's time. It's time for us to move on," he says cryptically, looking at me with sad eyes. "I love you, Sienna, and I wish all this wasn't happening, but it is, and neither she nor I can help it."

I look at him with a world of questions in my eyes. But he ignores them, like he always does, preferring that someone else take the responsibility of answering them for me.

"Honey." The front door pushes open, and Alicia's head pops through. Her smile is so forced that I want to scrub it off her stupid pretty face. "I'm sorry, I hate to interrupt this . . . moment, but we're gonna miss the train if we don't go now."

"I'll be right out," my dad says quickly, flashing her a warm smile. When his attention returns to me, his expression remains impassive. "Sienna—"

I wave a dismissive hand. "Go. You made your intentions clear. You say you want to move on, so go and do it. *Move on.* Erase everything bad you've ever done to this family and start a new one. I'm sure it'll be much better than the one you ruined."

He releases another headshake as the disappointment lurks in his eyes.

I turn around and head up the stairs. As I do, I hear him mutter something under his breath. It's so quiet, it's obvious I'm not supposed to hear it. But I do.

"Sometimes, I really wish you weren't my daughter," he whispers.

I don't stop walking up the stairs.

I don't stop the heavy flow of tears when I reach my room.

And I don't stop the sobbing after the distant sound of the front door closing reaches me.

Sometimes, I wish you didn't exist at all, Dad.

***

It's difficult to fully dive into my first day of work at the gym when there is so much going on in my head. Gym-goers dwindle in the afternoon, so Julian and I squeeze in a quick training session. But he and I both know that I'm not putting in my best effort. When Julian asks me why I'm distracted, I play it off as just another issue that Jax and I are having.

After closing up the gym, I take the train home, hoping that Mom will still be up. Thankfully, I catch her right as she's about to head to bed.

"Hey," my mom says, greeting me at the front door with a ridiculously pink fuzzy robe and slippers. I want to comment on how extremely huggable she looks tonight and tell her just how much I want to snuggle on the couch with her as we watch *Gilmore Girls*, but grimness overshadows my enthusiasm. The second she sees my face, her expression drops, like she already knows what I'm about to ask her.

"Can we talk?" I don't bother to shrug off my jacket or my bag before I spit out the question I've been meaning to ask. "This morning, Dad mentioned you were going on a trip. What's going on, Mom? Is there something I should know about?"

My mom's shoulders slump backward. She shuffles toward the staircase and sits herself at the foot of it, motioning for me to do the same.

"I was going to wait until Beth came home from cheer camp to tell you girls," she says, her voice soft and small. "I'm planning to take a long trip out of the country."

"Where? When?"

"I leave for Rio this Saturday."

I purse my lips inward. Okay, that's three days from now. It's weird that she didn't say anything about it until I pried it out of her, but it's not that big of a deal.

"Okay." I try to remain calm. "When are you coming back? After a week? Two?"

A breath pulls out of her, like she's trying to prolong the silence.

"I don't know," she says. "I bought a one-way ticket."

I squint at her, perplexed. "Are you not planning on coming back?"

"Of course I'm coming back. I just don't know when yet."

"Okay." I stare at her, puzzled. "Why Rio though?"

"I did an exchange program there for the summer while I was in college," she tells me, resting her arms over her knees. "A few of my friends are still around, so I figured I'd go pay them a visit."

"You have friends here too," I note unhelpfully.

"I know I do. But that's not the point." My heart compresses at the uncertainty of her answer. Her thumbs rub over my knuckles tenderly.

"You're leaving because of Dad," I say finally.

Slowly, she nods.

"How about me and Beth? Did we do something wrong too?"

"No, baby, *no*." My mom drags me toward her, her hands stroking my face. A tear leaks from her eye, and she makes no attempt to brush it away, still smiling through the pain. "Making the decision to leave has been difficult. I didn't want you to think I was abandoning you girls."

"But you are," I mumble, squeezing my eyes shut as if it'll help me brave the agony a little while longer. "And you sound like you're not coming back."

"I just . . . I need to do this. For myself." Her voice is firm, ringing with assurance. "I can't be around while he . . . you know." A lump forms in her throat as she's trying to get her words out. "I just need to get away and clear my head."

"I get it. But can't you just get your own place nearby or

something so we can still see you? I mean, Rio? That's so far away."

"Yeah, I know." Her lips make a flat, unhappy line. "But this would be a proper fresh start for me, you know? Away from this place, away from all the hurt that I've endured. And I figure if I want to live somewhere else, now's the time. I haven't stepped foot outside the country since I got pregnant with you. And besides, you guys all have your own lives now. You've got a boyfriend. And a sweet one at that." Her tone is tender as she gives my chin a little flick. I let out a laugh despite my awfully low spirits. "Money-wise, you guys should be okay now that Dad's starting his new job soon. And I'll still be working remotely from Rio, anyway, so I can still support you two financially if you guys ever need the extra money. But with Beth finishing high school next year and you being off at college, I'm just not needed around here as much as I used to be."

My heart clenches hard. I can't believe she would feel abandoned by us growing up. Just because I'm not around as much in the house doesn't mean I don't need her in my life.

"That's not true. I always need you." A helpless chord wobbles my voice.

"Oh, baby." My mom draws me into a side hug, a strong arm wrapped around me. I want to bury myself in her embrace as long as I can. "Could you still need me while I try to figure things out on my own?" she asks me, kissing the top of my head.

"Well, I don't have a choice, do I?" I say miserably, staring straight ahead.

"I know it's hard, and you don't have to be okay with it, but your support would mean a lot to me."

A rush of wariness wreaks havoc in my chest. As much as it kills me to let her go, I have to. The least I can do is to trust what she feels is right for her.

"I think I'll be fine. You go do what you need to do," I murmur, leaning into her warmth.

So many things are changing, and way too quickly. I wish I could just slow it all down so I could better prepare for each heartbreak. Because right now, my heart is being held together by a thread.

"But you need to call Beth," I tell her urgently. "Now."

"I know. I will."

I help my mom off the stairs, pulling her up to her feet. When she walks into the living room, she looks around like she senses something off about the space and purses her mouth unhappily.

"Was another woman here?"

"No," I lie.

She walks over to pick up the mint-green scarf that was abandoned on the couch. *Oh, right.*

"Okay, fine," I backtrack. "A woman was here."

Her fingers smooth over the soft cashmere fabric, staring at the scarf for a couple of beats. "What does she look like?"

I figured Mom was strict with not wanting to involve herself in Dad's new life, but I guess the curiosity must have been eating her alive.

I wind my arms around her from the back and rub my chin over her shoulder. "She's nothing compared to you."

"That's sweet." I can barely make out her features as she angles her head to the side, but enough that I catch a strained smile. "I wish I could believe you."

I don't say anything. I just hug her again, taking in all of her motherly warmth since this might be one of the last times I can for a while.

SIXTEEN

Beth cries nonstop the morning of Mom's flight. Out of everyone in the family, she's taking it the hardest. I try my best not to break down, but it's impossible to hide my tears when Mom collects her boarding pass from the check-in counter and I know her leaving is imminent.

We spent our last day together having a picnic. Mom insisted that she make the food, and Beth and I helped her prep. The two of us were civil with each other as we prepared the ingredients, but it was clear we were there for Mom, not each other. The three of us wore our best clothes and spent the afternoon at a nearby park, eating pie. The park was crowded with people soaking up the sun. Later that evening, we went to the movies and then ended up spending the rest of the night holed up in my and Beth's room while Mom talked about her plans in Rio.

Her face glowed with excitement as she rambled about the places she wanted to visit and the food she was dying to eat.

It was hard not to get emotional, but I forced my own feelings aside because I didn't want to make this about me. I want to be happy and excited for her so she knows she has my blessing. Mom has always been the backbone of this family, and it's about time we gave her a proper break.

Now it feels like a weird fever dream, watching my mom as she wheels her luggage in the direction of the departures gate. My heart breaks all over again when I think about the fact that she might be leaving long-term or that she might not wish to come back at all.

I hate that this family keeps on shrinking.

"Take care of your sister while I'm gone, okay?" Mom whispers to me as she draws me into one last hug. "I know you guys are in a weird place right now, but try to get to a better one, all right? I don't want her to be a stranger to you."

"Okay. I'll try." I give a hard nod, my eyes brimming with tears. "Call me when you get to Carol's."

"I will." She plants an affectionate kiss on my forehead.

I watch her as she disappears up the escalator, her figure growing smaller and smaller until she disappears completely.

The numbness slips into my skin and stays.

***

I try to ignore the oppressive torment of missing my mom, but it's difficult.

She's been the only thing I look forward to when I get home, and now that she's not there, the mood in the house feels sad. Empty. Hopeless.

I wish I could spend every spare moment burying myself

in the comfort of Jax, but it's been more than a week since I last saw him. He finally texted yesterday asking if we could talk, but with everything that's been going on, I haven't texted back yet.

I figure the only way to combat missing my mom is to respect the last thing she told me to do before she left. I don't like that I've allowed Beth and I to drift apart for this long, but my mom gave me the push I needed to finally hash things out with her. Perhaps now is as good a time as any to start.

I told Julian I could only work the morning shift today, so I can make it back in time to pick Beth up from school—something I haven't done in months.

I arrive just as the final bell rings and spot Beth as she emerges from the building. She's wearing her cheer uniform as usual—I don't think there's been an occasion when she hasn't been wearing it—but unlike the rest of her peers who chatter in crowds as they wait for their rides home, she emerges alone, awkward and sullen-faced. I watch as a few cheerleaders nudge her aside as they hop into their rides, like they don't know who she is. A frown drags her face down as she watches them zoom off.

"Hey," I say, pushing myself off the trunk of the tree I was leaning against and sauntering over toward Beth as she jogs down the school entrance steps.

"Sienna?" She narrows her eyes at me. "What are you doing here?" Her backpack is slung off one shoulder, and her hands are trying to straighten the crooked bow sitting on top of her ponytail.

I place a hand behind her bag to guide her across the parking lot. "Thought I'd pick you up from school today."

"Okay." It does nothing to dissolve her surprise. "Why?"

I bite back my ego for two seconds, allowing my vulnerability to flow through me.

"I just really miss you," I say earnestly.

She doesn't say anything back. She just sighs and starts walking. I fall into step beside her, not wanting to lose her to the distance. When we reach the end of the parking lot, we take our usual route through the gleaming bungalows with their pristine lawns and backyard pools.

"We haven't walked together since you started seeing Jax," she mutters quietly.

"Yeah. A lot of things have changed since then," I say to Beth with a frown, noting our estrangement. "Look, I know when I got with Jax, I hurt you. A lot. But I still love you, Beth. And I know things have been awkward between us for a while because of what happened with him, but I really want to try to make it work again."

She nods silently, but my words don't quite reach her. She stops in front of the intersection and turns to face me. I can feel my heart jackhammering at a million miles an hour as I wait for her to speak.

"Sienna . . . I forgive you for what you did," she starts off, sympathy lacing her tone. "I know how hard you tried to stay away from him in the beginning. And the last thing I want is for you to set aside your feelings for Jax for my sake. So I'm okay with you being together." A spark of relief flits through my core, but Beth shakes her head, and I realize she's not done. "But how do you think it makes me feel when I see you two? Laughing and kissing and being happy in front of me? It's just not easy for me to be around you when you're with him. That's all." She looks at her feet uneasily, hurt tugging her beautiful features down.

"I'm so sorry," I say, stepping toward her, but she steps back. "But can't we just try to fight through the awkwardness? There has to be a way that all of us can be in the same room together."

"I don't know if there is," Beth murmurs. "I'm just not ready yet."

"Beth, we only have each other. I don't want us to drift apart like this," I plead desperately.

With Mom gone, I'm only a fraction of a soul. I don't know what will be left of me if I can't get things back to the way they were with Beth.

But my pleas don't affect her decision. Her mind is already made up, and her heart is a world away from me.

"We'll still be sisters. I'll always be there when you need me," she tells me. "We just . . . can't be close like we used to be. I'm sorry."

I force my dissatisfaction inward, my lips pressed tightly together so I won't say anything more. At the end of the day, I need to respect her decision.

Beth offers me a sympathetic smile. I smile back, but it's a sad one.

We spend the rest of the walk home in silence.

***

Misery has never had better company than me this evening.

I feel like I'm supposed to be doing something tonight, with it being a Saturday and all, but instead, I've been sitting in the shower for forty minutes, my knees pulled tight against my chest, letting the water catapult down my back. Despite the harshness, the water is soothing. It drowns out all the noise in my head that's telling me I'm just a useless instrument of chaos that can't seem to do anything right: by my mom, my boyfriend, or even myself.

There's a reason why I don't allow more than a moment to myself every day. I don't want to think or feel like this. Because as soon as a tiny seed of doubt plants itself inside my brain, it festers into a whole ecosystem of insecurities I'm not mentally equipped to handle.

I used to think that I could survive anything, but this . . . this is something entirely different. People won't stop leaving me, no matter how much I beg them to stay.

Maybe it's me.

Maybe I'm the problem after all.

Sometimes, I wish you weren't my daughter, my dad said. He might as well have said, *Sometimes, I wish you were dead.* Both would hurt the same.

I don't know how long I can keep holding myself together like this. I'm tired. I'm numb. I'm worn down.

I'm not strong enough.

The statement clangs in my head, nullifying every other thought I've ever had. I let the harrowing thought echo again, this time coming to the realization that the statement might be true.

I'm not strong enough *at all.* I try to search for the strength that's supposedly there, burrowed somewhere in my body, but it's absent, and I feel sad all over again.

Maybe I wasn't strong to begin with. Maybe I got all my

strength from Jax, and when he left, he took all of it with him.

I don't know how to function without him.

Look at what's happened since he stopped talking to me. My mom left. My dad wants nothing to do with me. My sister is practically a stranger to me. *And I will be a stranger to myself.*

My palms are flat against the shower floor as they push me off and get me on my feet. I wobble when I stand, my body feeling like it's too weak to carry me and the weight of my depressive thoughts. I towel myself off and grab my phone from the edge of the sink. My mind catches up to what I'm about to do and screams at me to stop, but I'm desperate, and I can't think of any other option.

Where r u? I text Jax before I can think twice about it.

Not even ten seconds later, I get a reply.

In my apartment. Just got off training.

I need him. It feels impossible to breathe.

I want to see you, I send. My heart thunders wildly against my chest when I read his text back.

Me too. I miss you so much. Come over.

Five minutes later, I call a cab to his place.

I don't think about the stupid argument we had with the stupid ultimatum. I don't think about him icing me out afterward and not bothering to text me even once to see if I was okay. I don't think at all when I ride up the elevator to his floor and stride into the apartment when he opens the door for me.

"Princess," Jax breathes.

"Kiss first. Talk later," I say, my mind emptying itself out.

And then my lips are crashing into his.

Every cell, every atom immediately gravitates toward his

presence. If I could fuse into him, I would. His tongue slips into the seam of my mouth, warm and wet and skilled as it tangles with mine. I'm helpless against him as he backs me up against the door, lifts both my hands up, and, with a steady arm, traps them on top of my head while he continues to consume me with his lips.

Jax kisses me like he wants to destroy me from the inside out.

He doesn't even have to ask. I'll just let him.

Hell, I'll even hand him the detonator myself.

We don't stop kissing each other. His lips have latched on to my neck, worshipping the skin there, and I'm sighing against him, my hands reaching down to cling to his shoulders. I need to tether myself to something, otherwise I'll fly off into space.

"You have no idea how much I've missed you," he whispers as he comes back up, burying his fingers in my hair. Searching for forgiveness in my gaze. "I'm so sorry, baby. For what I said to you."

"I'm sorry. I shouldn't have let our argument get this far," I murmur back.

Our lips meet again, and Jax sweeps his tongue across my bottom lip. His large hands snake their way down my body and lift up my shirt. When my bare skin is exposed for him, his eyes flare, and he sucks in a tortured breath.

Jax grabs me by the waist and hauls me up, bringing me to the couch. After he lays me down, he climbs on top of me and dips down to kiss me again on the lips, then continues down my collarbone. And he doesn't stop. He goes lower and lower until he's kissing the valley between my breasts. Skillfully, he unclasps my bra and frees my chest. The coldness circulating in his apartment causes my nipples to harden immediately.

"Let me make you feel good," Jax murmurs, kissing a circle around my nipple. I squirm under him as he kisses me mercilessly. "Let me show you how much I've missed you. Ached for you. Dreamed of tasting you again."

And when his tongue flicks over the peak, I forget every bad thought I've ever had about him.

***

I can't believe I thought for one second that it would be better if Jax and I broke up.

We're so fucking perfect together.

Every kiss is electric. Every touch sends me into a different reality. One second I'm sinking into the depths of hell with him and the next I'm soaring to heaven and swimming in the clouds.

After his tongue has its way with me on the couch, I go down on him to return the favor. It's been a while since I had him in my mouth, and I can't deny I've missed his taste. I miss everything about him.

Now we're both lying on the couch under a blanket Jax pulled over us, my head resting in the crook of his arm, my hair splayed across his chest. His hand strokes my hip lazily. He stares at me, and his lips purse into a frown when he notices how quiet I am. Usually, I'm chatty afterward, but there's a hollowness inside me that I can't seem to get rid of, no matter how good the oral sex was.

"Hey," he says, concern bending his voice. "You okay?"

"Yeah. I'm just . . . taking it all in."

"The head?" he asks. "Or the stuff that's happening with your mom?"

I lay a kiss on the corner of his mouth, smiling. "No, the head was great," I say. "But yeah, it's about my mom."

Among other things, I want to add, but I don't want to lay it all on him this soon. Talking to him about my mom was news enough for him. Plus, Jax and I have just gotten back together after more than a week apart, so I'm hesitant to do or say anything that'll overwhelm him.

"I'm sure she'll be back soon," he tries to reassure me, but the words don't quite reach me.

"I don't know," I say, staring straight ahead. "Everything just feels different."

Jax's body tenses up, and I have a feeling he's going to say something I won't like.

"Aren't you a little angry that your mom decided to up and leave the country and didn't even have the courtesy to tell you until a few days before she's supposed to fly off?" he asks. "No offense, but that's kind of asshole behavior."

I lift my head up from his chest and shoot him a pointed look.

"Don't say that."

"But isn't it true?" He shrugs. "Don't get me wrong, I love your mom, but that's a major dick move. Doesn't seem like she's any different than your scumbag of a dad."

"There's a difference, okay? My mom is a good person. She wouldn't do it unless she felt like she had no choice."

"Goodness doesn't get you anywhere. It only gets you hurt. Look how she turned out."

I flinch. I don't know why he's saying all this. All I want

right now is to receive some comfort from my boyfriend, and here he is attacking my mother's character.

"Why are you saying this?" I demand. "Do you want to hurt me?"

"No, of course not. I'm just telling you the truth." Jax's hand smooths delicately over my face. "I think you need to stop putting her on a pedestal and see her for who she really is. An incredibly flawed person. Just like your dad."

I shake my head, refusing to let his words get to me. I'm not going to sit here and take this kind of slander toward my mom. She's been nothing but selfless her whole life, and I'm not going to let her one selfish decision to leave the country define her as a person.

"You know what? Fuck you, Jax. You know nothing about my mom. You don't have the right to make that kind of judgment," I say simply, pushing off the couch to grab my clothes. "I don't go around making judgments about your family. Not that I would be able to anyway, because I don't even know a single thing about them."

His jaw tenses. "That's not true. You know enough," he says like he just expects me to be okay with that. But at the same time, I don't know how to keep prodding about it without sounding demanding. He sighs as he watches me loop my top over my head and arms. "Look, I'm only looking out for you, Sienna. And your mom is hurting you more than you realize."

"I don't wanna talk about this anymore, Jax," I snap back. "Just leave it alone."

"Fine. I'm sorry if I went too far."

You always do.

I say nothing, slipping back into my pants and shoes. Jax

gets up from the couch and slips a hand around my waist from the back, leaning down to kiss my shoulder.

"I didn't mean to make you mad. Don't leave," he mumbles against my skin.

I hate it when he does this. One minute he's pissing me off and the next he makes that anger go away with his sweet words and featherlight kisses.

I sigh against him, deciding to let it go for now. I don't think I have enough space in my body for more anger.

"Okay. Fine," I say, and I let him guide me back to the couch.

"How's Julian lately?" he asks, desperate for a change of subject.

"He's fine. He offered me a job."

"Oh yeah?"

"I don't earn much, but it could lead to a training job once I get my certification."

"Mmm," Jax hums, tilting his body so he can face me fully. "Did he say it was Perez who sent him the video?"

"No. He said it was anonymous. But it's probably him. Or Damien," I say. "You think they're planning something for the finals?" I throw the question into the air. It's no secret now that Perez will do anything it takes to win. I wonder what other tricks he has up his sleeve that we don't know about yet.

"It's possible," Jax says, but he doesn't sound that fazed.

"Doesn't it get tiring? With all these rivalries?" I question. "Have you ever thought about quitting underground fighting?"

"Once," he says cryptically.

"And?" I prod.

"I came back anyway."

I frown at the vague answer, expecting more. It annoys me that he doesn't like to indulge in anything other than the present. It gets me curious about what other things he hasn't told me yet. I have to keep reminding myself to be patient—that we're only six months into dating and we just became official two weeks ago.

And almost broke up a few days later.

I shove the mocking thought out of my mind.

"You should meet my new trainer, Si," he tells me, gently caressing the skin on my arm. "We train at this gym called Lean Machines. He's better than Jules. A real MMA powerhouse. And at least he listens to whatever I have to say."

"Building your army of yes-men, I see."

"Can't seem to recruit you, though," he says, flicking my chin with his finger. "Maybe that's why you piss me off so much."

"Maybe that's also why you like me so much."

"Mmm, I do like a woman with a fiery mouth." His satin voice wraps around my body as his lip graze mine.

"Any chance you can feed it?" I whisper back, feeling my tummy rumble from not having any food today.

"With my dick or with some food?" he whispers back.

"With *food*," I say, smiling at how ridiculous it is that he still wants to have another go.

"All right." He drops a kiss on my mouth before hopping off me. "I'll place an order. You're cool to eat in, right? I don't know if you have any Saturday-night plans, but I'm free for the night. We can just stay in and watch a movie if you want."

Saturday night.

A bad feeling triggers in my stomach. Details feel fuzzy, but I'm certain I had today blocked off for something important. I sift through the fog in my brain for anything I'm supposed to remember, any event that I'm supposed to be at . . .

Oh.

My.

God.

Dakota's play.

Fuck. Fuck, fuck, fuck, *fuck*—

Panic seizes me in full force, propelling me to lurch across the coffee table to snatch my phone. My entire body is on high alert when I check all the notifications of missed calls and text messages from Trevor, time-stamped from two hours ago.

Hey, I'm already here. Got us some popcorn.

Yo, you good? Show's starting in 10 minutes.

Where are you??? Dee's gonna be pissed if you're not here.

Show's starting NOW! Pick up your phone, Sienna!

And the last haunting message from Trevor:

The show just ended. Dee knows you didn't make it.

SEVENTEEN

It's a two hour ride out to Holyoke from the city for the championship finals. The phantom park's entrance is unmarked, so it's easy to miss except for the hordes of people heading in that direction. It's an uphill climb through the woods to get to the Scott Tower. It's hard to miss once you know what you're looking for, given how it pokes out above the tree line. The massive fifty-foot stone tower used to be a spectacular vista; now it's mostly run-down and littered with graffiti, a perfect place for squatters.

There are two levels to the tower. The first one is raised on a walled dais made from river stones. On top of that, there's a circular archway of pillars supporting the balcony on top of the tower, which is about ten feet above the ground. Erected on top of the balcony is a lookout post from which to take in the sweeping views of the lower valley. Tonight's fight is at the first level, which will form the cage, with the audience watching from the ground.

We're in a closed-off section at the back of the tower. While Jax is fixated on the cage, analyzing any potential obstacles in his plan to take down Perez, my attention is planted on my phone, waiting anxiously for Dakota to pick up my call.

It's been a week, and she still refuses to talk to me. I don't know how she's managed to avoid talking to me on campus since I have her schedule memorized, but she has. Which means I really pissed her off this time.

I can't say I blame her. She has every right to be mad at me. She needed my support, and I wasn't there to give it to her. I just wish she knew how awful I feel about breaking my promise. But every time I've tried to call, it always goes straight to voicemail. And when I try to intercept her on campus, she just says she's busy and hurries away. I can't even recall the number of times I've Grubhubbed Caffeinated coffee to her dorm room only to have her send it back or give it to the driver.

You know it's bad when she rejects a Caffeinated coffee.

I can't let my relationship with my best friend crash and burn over this. There has to be a way I can salvage it.

Jax drops his water bottle from his lips and cuts me an annoyed look. "Sienna, can you put the phone down?"

I ignore him as I continue to pace. Trying to get a good signal here is almost as impossible as getting out of an anaconda choke. Luckily, I've stumbled on a tiny pocket of cell reception and am redialing Dakota's number, hoping to get through.

I don't stray far from the area since Perez and his men have staked their territory on the opposite end. They look like they're deep in conversation, probably going through Perez's strategy for tonight. I glance at the top of my phone screen.

Fifteen minutes left until the fight starts. Good. I've got fifteen minutes to get through to my best friend.

"Come on, come on, come on," I mumble to myself, pressing my phone harder against my ear, like that'll somehow get her to pick up.

I notice that Jax has stopped shadowboxing, failing to reel in his annoyance at me. "Seriously. Hang up. I need to focus, and you're throwing me off my game."

"I need a minute. This is important," I snap back. It's hard to hide the resentment in my voice when my unwavering attention to him is the reason I've been screwing up with the other important people in my life.

He rolls his eyes and continues shadowboxing. I turn away from him and focus on the phone, every silent beat between rings stretching on for what feels like minutes. Just when I anticipate the last ring giving way to her voicemail, Dakota's voice stabs at my ear.

"What do you want?" she snaps.

I'm so surprised to hear her voice that the phone almost slips from my grasp.

"Dee. Oh my God," I gasp. "Wow, I didn't expect you to pick up."

She's silent for a beat, like she isn't sure how to respond to my shock. "Would you like me to send you to voicemail again?"

"No," I say quickly. My hand smooths through my hair; I'm careful with what I say next. "Look, I'm sorry I didn't make it to your play. Things have been so hectic lately, and I lost track of time. It's my fault."

"You lost track of time," she echoes with a laugh, mocking

me. "Come on, Si. We both know the real reason why you didn't come."

A heavy breath drops from my mouth. "Dee . . ."

"Were you with Jax? Yes or no."

My gaze pivots to Jax. His attention is somewhere else completely, on the cage in front of him. It's being engulfed by a huge crowd.

"Yes," I whisper.

I hear Dakota suck in a long breath.

"Goodbye, Sienna."

"Wait, please," I say desperately. "It's not like that."

She huffs. "Oh, really? Then what is it like?"

"Jax and I, we've been having some problems, okay? And my mom left recently, and I just couldn't handle it. I went to him for comfort, that's all."

"At what point did you think that I wasn't an option for comfort too, Sienna?"

"What?"

"I've been there for you since the beginning. I've tried so hard to reach out to you because I really fucking miss you, and I'm gutted I don't see you as often as I'd like. But I get it. He's your first boyfriend, and you're crazy about him, so I was willing to let it slide as long as you were there for the important stuff. But the one time I wanted you to make the effort . . ." She pauses, swallowing hard.

"I know, Dee," I croak out. "I'm sorry. I don't know what else you want me to say."

"I want you to admit that you're blinded by this man, Si."

"I'm not!" I raise my voice, prompting both Jax and a few of Perez's men from the other corner to look my way.

Embarrassment washes across my face. I press my hand to my forehead to calm myself down. "Dee, you're not being fair."

"*I'm* not being fair? I'm more levelheaded than you are right now."

"I don't get it. I thought you liked him."

"That was before . . . all of this." She sighs. "Can't you see that you've molded your entire life around him, but he hasn't made any effort to mold his around yours? He's sucking the life out of you, Sienna, and you aren't even aware of it," she tells me determinedly. My mouth flies open to deny all her claims, but she beats me to it. "And *please* no more excuses defending him. I know you, Sienna. If you could make the effort to see me, you would. You just don't see me as one of your priorities anymore. You don't see me as anything but an inconvenience. All that you see is him."

I clamp my mouth shut, hurt squeezing my throat. My grip on my phone is shaky at best.

Dakota lets out a sigh, like she knows she's being harsh. "Jax has you under some kind of spell, and it isn't good for you. *You* know it isn't. Whatever this is, it's just . . . toxic. I can only hope that one day you see it too," she says, sounding regretful. "Goodbye, Sienna. Please don't call me again."

"Wait, please—" I say frantically, but I get cut off before I can utter another word. "Fuck!"

I attempt to hit Redial when a hand clamps around my wrist.

"*Stop,*" Jax commands.

"Don't fucking tell me to stop!" I warn.

He snatches the phone from my grasp easily and kills the call. I release a groan.

"It's not worth it. Fuck her," he tells me. "If she can't see that she's being unreasonable, then she doesn't deserve to be in your life."

"You don't understand," I protest. "Dee is my *best friend*. I need to make things right—"

"No, you don't," he interjects. "Look at you, you've been a mess for a week now trying to get her to talk to you. You've done your part. If she can't see that, she's not worth keeping around. Stop putting effort into someone who's not going to return the favor. All right?"

I purse my lips unhappily.

Maybe Jax has a point. Dakota has made it clear she no longer wants anything to do with me. And even though I don't want to be done with her, there's no use hounding her for another chance.

Besides, if it's this easy for her to cut ties with me, perhaps letting go of her wouldn't be the worst thing to happen. It will sting, sure, but maybe that's exactly what I need to grow. Jax has helped me realize the truth about most people in our lives—they're temporary residents who don't stick around once we've served our purpose to them.

At this point, he's the only person I can count on who'd fight to stay.

"Here, have some water," he says, thrusting his bottle toward me.

I take a swig of it and scrunch my face up when the unexpected burning of liquor flows in a fiery path down my throat. I thrust the bottle back at him. "That is *not* water."

He smiles. "Either way, it'll help."

My eyebrows pinch together. "I thought no alcohol before a fight."

"That was a Julian rule," he whispers, setting the bottle down beside his left foot. "Did that help to soothe your nerves?"

"I guess."

"Good," Jax says, smoothing his thumb over my chin. "You're my anchor, princess. And I need you to be present. Now more than ever."

I give a firm nod. He claims me with a swift kiss, like he's trying to draw the courage out of me and into himself. I part my lips wide open for him, allowing easy access. Tonight, I have a purpose, and it's to support him any way I can. He shifts his body and tightens his arms around me, knocking over his bottle in the process. It rolls in the opposite direction, away from us.

Damien kneels down to pick up the bottle from the ground. His short dark hair is combed to the side under an excess of hair product, and he wears a black collared shirt, the buttons straining to stay closed across his massive chest. He's lucky his height draws more attention than his poor sense of fashion. He stares at the bottle with avid interest, his eyes tracing the faded "UFG" on it with amusement. "Still got this, huh? Though you stopped training there."

"No thanks to him," Jax bites back, glancing behind Damien, and I follow his gaze, meeting the cold, crinkled eyes of Perez from the other side of the closed-off area a few yards away.

Damien's expression remains nonchalant. "I have no idea what you're talking about."

"Sure, you don't."

A ghost of a smile. "Well, I'm sorry to hear that you're no longer working with Julian. If you feel off your game tonight, there is a way we can both benefit from this."

Jax gives Damien a suspicious look. "What are you talking about?"

"Let's just say Perez would be open to a different kind of arrangement."

He lets out an incredulous laugh. "What? Like throwing the fight?"

He waits for Damien to dispute the suggestion, but Damien merely smiles, dangling Jax's bottle from his index finger like it's a corpse hanging on a noose.

A flicker of anger flashes in Jax's eyes.

"Are you fucking serious?"

"Just name your price."

Jax scoffs. It's loud enough to draw the attention of several of Perez's goons. They exchange shoulder nudges, grinning, and then they begin to sidle up to us, slowly caging us in. Jax doesn't let an ounce of fear show in his face. His attention remains glued to Damien. But a bad feeling festers in my chest at how close all of them are.

"I can't be bought. I will never be bought," my boyfriend sneers, unfazed by the intimidation tactics. "There's no figure you or Perez can throw out that will get me to concede."

"Come on," Damien coos. He tosses the bottle over to one of the goons before pulling out a thick wad of cash from his back pocket and holding it up in front of Jax's face. "If you're going to lose, you might as well do it with a fat stack in your pocket. And there's more where this came from. You can live comfortably off the money for the next two seasons."

"Yeah, I don't give a shit about that," Jax insists. "I want a fair fight."

"Oh, don't give me that honorable bullshit. We all know it

ain't your thing." Damien lets out a sardonic chuckle, hinting at something that I'm clearly not privy to. My gaze swings to Jax, pleading with him to clear my confusion. He refuses to look at me.

"Fuck off, Wells." There's a thread of anger in Jax's voice now.

"Or what? You're going to waste your time fighting me too?" Damien says with a cold shrug. "The recovery's gonna be tough, you know."

"With you, I doubt I'll need more than a couple punches."

Damien chuckles, unable to contain his excitement at getting Jax riled up like this.

"Don't," I warn Jax, my hand immediately clamping around his shoulder, pulling him back. "Don't let him get under your skin. It's not worth it."

"Last chance, Deadbeat," Damien says, slipping the cash back into his pocket. "Perez is waiting. Once I leave, the offer's leaving with me."

"Then I should start warming up," he says through his teeth. He snatches the bottle back from one of the goons and gives Damien a hard shove as he stalks toward the cage, passing Perez on the other side of the closed-off area. Instead of acknowledging them, Jax turns away and stares straight ahead. With one final swig from his bottle, he prepares for his entrance, determination spanning his muscled body.

***

A cacophony of cheers erupts as Jax explodes into the cage, knocking his fists together. He rolls his shoulders back and dances from side to side, a mixture of anticipation and loathing on his face. Perez stands at the ready and grins back at him maliciously.

When the announcer yells, "Fight!" Perez is immediately on the move. He strikes first, an unexpected move given he usually prefers to hang back and assess his opponent before throwing a punch. Perez's fists hammer down as Jax throws up a high guard. Perez reels back, surprised, and spins into a kick, catching Jax in his side. Jax grunts, taking the blow, but then manages to clip Perez with a right hook.

They disengage and step back to size each other up. Jax stalks circles around Perez as Perez spins to keep Jax in his sight line, showing equal parts ferocity and confidence.

Jax suddenly darts forward, coming in with a flurry of blows. Perez ducks and weaves the first few punches and throws in some counters of his own, but Jax is on his A game tonight. Fists meet forearms, knees get blocked, and kicks meet empty air as Jax slips through Perez's defense and lands a solid uppercut, smashing Perez's jaw with an audible crack.

A series of gasps reverberates through the crowd.

Perez shakes off the blow, and just as Jax is feeling cocky, Perez gives him no rest as he digs two body shots into Jax's ribs followed by a massive kick to his sternum.

Jax loses his footing and stumbles backward. He recovers, and with a sudden yell he throws a wild haymaker at Perez, but Perez blocks it easily. He then slips around Jax, grabs his arm, and, using the momentum, flips Jax over his shoulder, smashing him to the ground. *Hard.* Jax manages to get to his feet again before Perez can force a grapple. I furrow my brows, confused. Jax should have stayed down; he'd have the upper hand on Perez since Jax is a better ground fighter. In fact, Jax should never have thrown such a sloppy punch in the first place. Both fighters continue to trade blows, but Jax is fumbling; he keeps squinting hard and blinking, and he's visibly fighting the urge to wipe his face from the streams of sweat pouring all over his skin.

Something's wrong, I realize, frantically searching for help. I'm close enough to the action that I spot the ref on the opposite end of the cage. He's not even looking up at the fight but rather is engaged in conversation with the beefy man next to him. Damien.

A bad feeling prickles at my skin.

My gaze pivots back to the fight. Jax is taking a serious beating. His back clashes against the ground, and Perez overpowers him easily by getting on top of Jax and raining blow after blow on him. Jax shakes his head, looking disoriented. He's not even looking at Perez anymore. He's blinking too much now. He looks like he's fighting an invisible enemy inside his mind. He looks like—

He's been drugged.

The thought cuts through all the white noise in my head, the moment hitting me like a sucker punch in the gut.

Damien. The water bottle.

Jax taking a swig of it before the fight started.

No. That can't be right. The bottle was in my peripheral the entire time Damien was holding it—

Except when he threw it toward one of Perez's goons.

That's why Perez sought out Damien: he knew Damien had access to all kinds of drugs because of his mother and needed a sure way to incapacitate Jax. And that was the real reason Damien came over to negotiate Jax throwing the fight. He already knew Jax wasn't going to be tempted by the offer. He and the offer were just distractions so they could slip in the drug.

Panic and dread start to set in.

"Stop the fight!" I yell out as loud as I possibly can. *"Jax has been drugged! Stop the fiiiight!"*

My pleas go unheard amidst all the yelling for blood and gore from the mob. I push my way around to the other side of the cage, ignoring the curse words and angry stares as I elbow my way through, desperately waving my arms above me to catch the attention of the announcer or the referee. But neither of them so much as glances in my direction.

As their faces morph into a mixture of shock and excitement, a sinking feeling descends into my stomach.

I look over to see Jax slumped near the side of the cage, eyes barely open, shoulders hunched forward in defeat.

My heart shatters into a million pieces.

"Looks like we have a winner!" the announcer blasts out, and the referee climbs into the cage, lifting up Perez's arm. The crowd explodes into cheers. "Ladies and gentlemen, the champion of the underground title goes to the undefeated, untamed Perez 'The King' Mills!"

***

Fifteen minutes later, they drag Jax back to the closed-off area we were in earlier, and I rush toward him, ignoring the horde of concerned fans eager to catch a glimpse of their fallen fighter. Jax is completely out of it: his eyes flutter open and closed, and his mouth mumbles gibberish. He's confused and nauseated. Littered with bruises and a split bottom lip, this is the most beaten up I've seen him.

I spend the next hour helping him as he pukes his guts out and slowly gets back to a fully conscious state. It's gnarly. People watch us, horrified by the sight of the once-invincible Deadbeat hurling nasties on the ground. There's so much of it. My heart sinks, wishing I trusted my instincts to keep a lookout back when we were with Damien. How the hell did I not catch it? It's my job to support Jax, to take care of him, and it's my responsibility to be looking closer for signs of sabotage. I failed him.

After Jax has nothing more left in him to heave out, he just lies there, one hand clutching his stomach, trying to catch his breath. There's nothing the medics nor I can do to help him. If we want more help, we'd have to take him to the hospital, a decision that Jax is vehemently against when I ask him about it.

"I'm fine." He swats my hand away. I'm surprised by the strength in his arm given that he was nearly unconscious on the cage floor barely an hour ago.

"You're not," I assure him. "You need to go to the hospital."

"No. There's no point." He pulls himself into a sitting position on the ground, then confirms what I already deduced. "The effects are already wearing off."

"But the drug is still in your system," I tell him urgently, propping myself beside him. "We need to know what it is, because it could get worse. I think it's K, but I'm not sure. We need to get you an ambulance."

"I don't want an ambulance. I want a rematch," Jax seethes

as he watches Perez show off his gleaming new belt to his fans. He's smug as hell, drunk off the victory. Damien has joined him, one hand on the golden belt like it was his win to share. The sight of them sharing it—after knowing what they did to secure it—is despicable.

"No, don't look at him." I tip Jax's chin toward mine. But his gaze is elsewhere. "We'll get the rematch. We'll prove that you've been drugged. You still have that bottle, right? That's evidence. And you'll need to take a urine test to show that you ingested the drug. There's a way to fight this, Jax. We just need to get you to the hospital."

"None of that will make any difference," he snaps. "'The only rule that exists here is that there are no rules.'" He quotes the announcer's standard speech back to me.

"There has to be a way," I say desperately. "They'll have to strip Perez of his title once we prove to them that he did nothing to deserve it. It'll threaten the integrity of what they've built here if he gets away with it."

Jax doesn't answer. He doesn't even look at me. He just watches silently as Perez lifts the belt above his head, spurring on the enthusiasm of the small crowd that hasn't left yet, desperate for a glimpse of the shiny, gleaming prize. I wonder, if they knew what he did, would they turn on him? Or would they not care? Like Jax, Perez has his loyalists wrapped around his finger; it wouldn't surprise me how much they're willing to forgive.

The look Jax gives Perez from here is bone-chillingly deadly. The one thing he craved most in the entire world has been stolen by his greatest adversary. It's humiliating. He bares his teeth like a beast, his body shaking with pure rage. I don't realize something in him has snapped until he's already launched out of my grasp and is charging straight toward Perez.

"Jax," I say in a panicked tone. I'm already on my feet, desperately trying to catch up to him. "Where the hell are you going? Jax!"

Perez doesn't see Jax barreling toward him in time. Jax pushes through the crowd with punishing force, swings his fist back, and—

Bam!

He lands a mean right hook straight to Perez's face. Perez tumbles to the ground, blood streaming out of his nostrils. Damien loses his footing from the momentum and falls backward into the crowd in both shock and horror. The fans who were surrounding him shriek and scramble away.

"Get up," Jax growls as he hovers over Perez, hauling him off the ground with a hard tug. "*Get up*, you fucking piece of shit."

"What the hell?" Perez yells with a mixture of surprise and fear.

"You think you can just *drug* me and *win*?" Jax lets out a roar that rips through the air before striking Perez with a hard uppercut to the ribs. Perez struggles with his footing, absorbing the deft blow with gritted teeth. "Fucking piece of shit coward. Fight me like a real man. *Come on!*" Through the blood caking his face, Perez scowls, which further fuels Jax's excitement. He swipes his tongue over his teeth, wearing a callous smile. "That's it. There's that look. Come on, Perez. Give me an actual fight worth winning."

Jax pounces on Perez again. Perez tries to block, but Jax

is on the offensive, spurred on by rage, and Perez struggles to keep up. The crowd surrounding us thickens as Jax continues to torment him with his fists, his elbows, his legs. The sickening sound of ribs cracking stabs the air. At some point, Perez lands back on the ground again, and Jax pounces on him, bracketing him with his knees, and lands another two solid shots to Perez's face. It's a goddamned bloodbath. Red sprays on my clothes, and my eyes sting from the stench of it.

This isn't like the fight in the cage, where the spirit is kept light for the sake of entertainment.

This feels real.

Animalistic. Brutal.

Damien reaches for Jax, trying to pry him off Perez. "Hey. *Hey.* That's enough."

Jax elbows Damien hard in the face, slamming him backward again. "Stay the fuck out of this. After I'm done with him, I'm coming for your ass too," he says with icy venom.

Damien shoots him a murderous look. A few hands haul Damien to his feet and pull him back, worried about him getting caught in the cross fire again as Jax leaves Perez no time to recover.

Every single blow Jax delivers, Perez takes, already too exhausted to fight back. His teeth clench together from the pain, and he clutches his ribs as his body absorbs the weight of Jax's hits. Perez wheezes as another one of Jax's punches lands, his voice barely audible now. His eyes flutter, and I can see the whites of his eyeballs as they roll backward into his head.

My heart is in my throat.

Jax is many things. Arrogant. Dangerous. Relentless.

But there's a limit. There *has* to be.

"Jax, stop," I say carefully, pushing out of the crowd and into the clearing so I can get to him. "It's done. He gets it. Now stop, or you're going to kill him!"

"*No mercy.*" He rams another fist into Perez's chest. It's littered with ugly red splotches now. I think he might even have broken a rib. He's no longer moving. His eyes are closed, his body lying limp on the cold concrete floor, and I'm scared he's not breathing. "*Give everything, take nothing—*"

I try to pull Jax up off the ground, but he's too strong for me. He shrugs me off and continues his barrage. I look around desperately, hoping someone will help me, but no one wants to meet my gaze. They're all too terrified to get caught up in Jax's wrath. My panicked heart is slamming so hard against my chest I can hear the loud pounding in my head. I don't know what to do. *I don't know what to do.* All I know is that I can't let Jax kill him, I can't—

"*No mercy, give everything, take nothing—*"

"Jax, stop!" My hands grab at his shirt to tug him back again, but he doesn't budge. "Please!"

He continues to dominate Perez as if in a trance as he repeats the words, "*No mercy, give everything, take nothing—*"

"Jax—"

"*No mercy—*"

"Jax, please," I cry out, hot tears of frustration burning my eyes. "Please, *for the love of God, stop it!*"

Finally, *finally*, Jax stops his assault.

It's like the fog in his brain clears. His eyes widen, and his fists unclench. He looks down at the unconscious body. Then at the crowd. He swallows hard, like he expected adoration in their gazes but is surprised to be confronted with newfound fear in them instead.

He turns to me.

The world stops.

Everything is quiet. Still.

"Sienna," he chokes out.

He meets my disbelieving stare, his face crestfallen.

I step away from him, numb. My legs feel untethered, as if separate from my body. My mind whirls, and yet my tongue is frozen, my mouth refusing to form words. Not that it matters. There are no words I could string together to ease the shock of what I've just witnessed.

I should leave.

This is beyond what I thought I was capable of dealing with. This kind of violence should send me running the other way. There's no other option left but to leave him and never return.

But . . . I can't.

EIGHTEEN

We ride home in silence.

I stare straight ahead, unable to meet Jax's eyes. I know that if I do, my heart may not be capable of holding the weight of all my emotions.

I'm surprised Jax is able to drive at all with what he just put his body through. He's tense, the veins in his arms bulging as he grips the steering wheel. His knuckles are bleeding red, and a strange question creeps into my mind as I stare at them. How many people have been on the receiving end of those fists? I wonder if anyone has died by those hands before.

I've seen Jax fight countless times in that cage. I've seen him spar with Julian. Hell, *I've* sparred with him. Never have I seen him look the way he did tonight when he went after Perez. It was like a switch flipped inside him and he became a different person. Scratch that. Not a person. A vicious, barbaric animal.

"Stop the car," I command.

Jax turns his head briefly and casts a puzzled look in my direction. "What?"

"I said stop the fucking car."

"We're in the middle of the goddamned road—"

"Pull over now!" I scream, panicked and crippled with fear. The car feels claustrophobic, like the walls are closing in and constricting my airflow.

Jax clenches his teeth together but obliges me. He pulls over to the side of the road and kills the engine. We're in the middle of nowhere. He appears to have come to the same realization as he pivots toward me, probably about to tell me that we should just have this conversation at home. But I'm too wired up right now to let this slide for a moment longer.

"Sienna—" he starts.

"Why didn't you stop hitting Perez when I told you to let up?" I blurt out, allowing my confusion and anger to spill into the cabin of the car. I turn toward him, my face full of recrimination. "You almost killed him. You almost *killed* a guy, Jax."

"I know."

"And all for what, some stupid win?" I ask, baffled.

"You think I was gonna let what Perez did to me slide?" Jax clenches his jaw hard, like he's holding back his own anger. "All you have in this game is your pride, Sienna. That's it and that's all. And let's not forget the fact that he *drugged* me. He doesn't deserve to live, much less hold the title."

"Yes, Perez is a piece of shit, and of course he deserves to be punished for what he did. But when we fight, we fight the right way. Did you forget that?"

"This is the underground! There is no right way. The sooner you realize that, the better."

"How many times has this happened before, Jax? Have you ever . . . I mean, have you *killed* anyone before?" I ask with trepidation, horrified at what the answer might be.

His light eyebrows hit the ceiling. "What? *No*. Of course not."

"But you've hurt people enough to kill them?" I press him further.

"In that cage? Probably."

"No, I mean outside it."

He blinks at me hard. "What difference does it make?"

"What difference does it make?" I echo, my voice going shrill. I'm so aggravated that my arm accidentally hits the dashboard. The sting doesn't even register given my shock that Jax doesn't recognize a distinction between violence in his sport and violence in his life. To him, the cage isn't the exception for violence. It's just one of many places for him to inflict it. I shake my head, unwilling to accept it as true. "I don't understand, Jax. *How* can you not see that there's a difference?"

"Because there isn't, Sienna. What I did to Perez after he cheated is probably exactly what I'd have done to him in that cage if he hadn't." My eyes must betray my anxiety and fear because he shakes his head as if he doesn't like what he sees. "No. Don't you dare look at me like that. You knew this about me when you first saw me in that cage last year. You *knew* it, and deep down, it's what you wanted, what you signed up for. So don't go looking at me like I'm some monster you're disgusted by just because you've seen some twisted, dark side of me you don't like."

"I'm looking at you like that because what you did was

wrong," I say, a crack wobbling my voice. "And the fact that you can't see that is beyond fucked up!"

"How is it fucked up that I wanted a fair fight?" Jax demands. "After months of preparation and hard work? After he sabotaged my working relationship with Julian? All so he can incapacitate me with a drug to get a win he didn't deserve?"

"Why is it so important to you that you win, no matter the cost?" I fire back. "Why do you always have to *win*?"

"Because it's what I do, Sienna!" he blasts out, punching the steering wheel. "I *win*. I win because I'm good at it. And if I don't have that . . ." His voice trails off, not allowing his thoughts to stray.

I inhale a ragged breath. I wish I could feel pity for him, but his self-assurance has turned into delusion, and I'm done egging him on.

"You once told me you tried to leave the underground. But you couldn't stay away, could you? You like the violence. You crave it. Why?" His silence emboldens me. I feel compelled to ask, my brain trying to work out what little I know about his life, just the nuggets of information fed to me when he talks to Perez. "Why don't you ever tell me anything about your stepdad, Jax? Perez seems to know more than me." I lift my gaze, meeting his fearlessly. "Is your family connected to the underground? Did you hurt them too?"

He huffs out an incredulous breath, rubbing a hand over his mouth. "I can't believe you just asked me that."

I tip my nose upward with an air of self-assurance, though we're crossing into dangerous territory. "Can you blame me, after what I just witnessed? What if I do something to really piss you off, huh? Would you make sure I pay the price too? It's all about strategy with you, finding your opponent's weaknesses and using them to your advantage. Would you manipulate me like that? How can I trust you to know that difference? How can I trust you when you've told me nothing about your family, about your past?"

He shakes his head vehemently. "I would never hurt you like that, Sienna. I swear it. I swear on my fucking life."

"Why should I believe you?"

"Because!" Jax raises his voice, annoyed. "Because you have a hold on me I can't explain. It's cosmic. My whole world spun when I met you. You are the exception, Sienna. You are *always* the exception."

"So you draw the line at me? But not everybody else?"

"Fuck everybody else! All that matters to me is *you*," he asserts. "What I need to know is whether you can accept that or not."

I slump against my seat, staring straight ahead through the windshield. The headlights are on full blast, eating up the darkness laid in front of us. And in this moment, a similar kind of clarity arrives, clearing up my mind.

"You need to quit the underground," I whisper. "You're losing yourself to the fight, and I don't know how else to help you."

He drags a hand down his face, his shoulders dropping with a sigh. "Quitting is not an option, Sienna."

"Why not?"

Jax remains quiet.

"Does Breaking Point have something on you?" I prod.

He shakes his head. "It's not like that."

"Then what is it?"

Again, silence.

"You need to *quit*, Jax," I say, exasperated. "Because this . . . you . . . it's too overwhelming. I can't keep fighting for you when you don't let me in. And with you being so unpredictable . . . I'm wondering if I can even trust you at all."

Hurt flashes in Jax's eyes. It takes everything in me not to take back what I said just so that he won't look like that.

"Don't do this, Sienna," he says with a shake of his head, already knowing where this is headed. "Please."

I can't bear to look anymore.

"I'm sorry. I need time to think about all of this," I say, taking the opportunity to yank the door open and get out of the car.

I hear him calling out to me, but I ignore him.

And minutes later, when I hear the soft rumble of the engine and see the car speeding down the road away from me, I feel the tears slide down my cheeks in salty, unending waves.

NINETEEN

There is no chance for sleep, not when my eyes are constantly oozing tears onto my pillow.

My crying wakes Beth up. She asks me what happened, but I shrug her off, not really in a sharing mood. Plus, I doubt she wants to hear about me and Jax. She made it very clear that she wanted to be kept out of our dating life.

No matter how uncertain things between Jax and me get, I also don't wish for Beth's perception of him to be colored. She doesn't deserve it. Even though it would probably bring us closer together if she knew what an ass he is. Maybe a little part of me believes that it'll still work out between me and Jax, that Beth will come around and we'll all be this little perfect trio.

But how can I feel that hope when I just told him I couldn't trust him anymore?

When I met Jax, I thought he was the most honest man I've ever known. In a way, I suppose he still is. He has always made it clear that he enjoys the violence in the cage. I was a fool to assume that violence was limited to his Deadbeat persona.

Violence is just second nature to him. I should've known better.

But can I accept it? Can I accept him as he is, even the darkest parts of him that he isn't willing to share?

I don't know. Fuck, *I don't know.*

All I've wanted is to be on Jax's side. But the more of him that gets revealed to me, the harder it is to do so. And if he keeps closing me off like this, what am I fighting for, really?

My heart squeezes with hurt. It's hard to breathe with so much tightness in my chest. How can I feel so much pain and still crave the man causing it?

Maybe that's just how love is. It's supposed to make you feel like the pain is worth the pleasure of being loved.

Love.

My God, I'm in love with him.

The revelation hits me like a ton of bricks.

Holy shit.

I'm in love with this stupid, troubled man.

I've been rolling these words across my tongue for hours now, and somehow it still feels strange. It's foreign but familiar all at the same time, like my body is meant to carry this feeling toward him but is also fighting hard against it. *Love* seems like the simplest word in the world until the feeling consumes you, and then it becomes so loaded—heavy and explosive and intense—that it's the only thing you can think about.

I love him.

I love Jax.

My heart doesn't have space for anything or anyone else.

And that could very well mean that I'm heading down the path to my own destruction.

But maybe . . . I don't care.

Maybe love doesn't have to make any sense. After all, it's a feeling created by the heart, not the brain. Unlike in an MMA fight, I can't logic my way out of it. And whether I like it or not, it's here to stay. Everything else comes second.

Love.

That's what I'm fighting for.

I love Jax beyond reason.

And that's enough for me.

I can't give up on this. Not now. Not when there's so much yet to uncover. Six months ago, he took me in when I was at my lowest. Accepted me when there was no one else in the world willing to. Embraced every stubborn flaw and wicked part of me. And this Perez thing is going to be what scares me away from Jax? I can't let that happen.

I won't abandon him just because things are getting a little tough. I won't fail just because I'm scared of the unknown.

Funny how I used to think that my mom was weak for staying with my dad until the end. For not turning against him, even after he admitted to his affair. But now I realize she possesses the kind of strength I aspire to have.

She fought hard for her marriage. So I will do the same for my relationship until there's nothing more left for me to give.

If Jax and I work together, the world can be ours. We won't need anyone else—just each other.

By 4:00 a.m. the words are nestled in my chest: *I love you,* ready to rise up into my throat and fly out of my mouth as soon as the time is right. I wonder if Jax will call me. He's never been good at making the first move when it comes to apologies. That's fine with me. I decide to be the bigger person and dial his phone number. Before I can utter a word, Jax beats me to the punch.

"Hey. Can we talk?" he asks desperately.

***

It's too early to take the T to the city, and I'm too broke to take a cab, so Jax quietly picks me up from my house. We don't go to his house this time. It's too far.

It's a little past five in the morning by the time we check into the nearest motel. The sky is still dark, but the first rays of morning are not far away. I close the curtains, relieved to be able to sort this out with Jax on neutral territory. Neither of us has spoken since he picked me up. There is so much to say. The weight of the words feels heavy on my shoulders.

Jax sits down at the edge of the bed and rubs his hands together. He looks like he hasn't gone home since our argument: he's still wearing the same clothes as he was before, and his blond hair is still slick with grease from the fight. I sit beside him, my hands falling awkwardly on either side of me. My arm grazes his ever so slightly. I want to reach out to hug him, but I want to hear what he has to say before I show him more affection.

Despite being knocked down from the fight and looking like he also got no sleep, Jax is still the most hauntingly beautiful man I've ever seen.

I'm in love with you, Jax.
I'm so crazy in love with you.

"I'm sorry," Jax says after a while. When his gaze meets mine, his eyes are sad and filled with longing. "I want you to trust me. And I know you expect a lot of me. I want to try, okay? For you. I'll do it all for you. I just don't want to go through it alone."

I nod because I feel exactly the same way. I want to endure it all with him.

"I'm sorry too," I say. "I want to trust you too. And I shouldn't have kept pushing you if you weren't ready to talk about your stepdad."

Jax's eyes flutter closed, like those words somehow released him.

"Thank you," he breathes.

I rest my chin on his shoulder, and he reaches a hand around me to stroke my hair. Everything softens under the power of his touch.

Jax clears his throat. "I have some news. Breaking Point just called. Said that the outcome of the fight with Perez during the finals is going to be voided, and as compensation, the belt is going to be awarded to me." He takes a pause before announcing, "I'm a title holder now."

"That's great news," I murmur, and he nods, but the excitement doesn't reach his eyes. I guess it's hard to stomach a win with a fight like that. It's not like he didn't deserve it. The championship was as good as in his pocket until Perez cheated.

"How did they find out about Perez?" I ask.

"After you left, I went and got tested at the hospital, then got the report sent to them," he tells me. That explains why he's still in the same clothes as he was before. He's just gotten back from the hospital. "I told Point what they wanted to do with the report was up to them, but if the report got leaked to my fans, they'd likely start a riot. Point came back to me later and told me the belt was mine if I still wanted it and they were going to make the announcement."

"What about Perez and Damien?" I probe.

"A lifetime ban from ever fighting again. Their reputations are done for."

"That's good. They deserve it."

"Yeah," he says, rubbing his knuckles over his jaw as he stares at me. "When we fight, we fight the right way, right?"

"Yeah," I say, mouth curving toward a smile. "We do."

"I don't wanna lose you, Sienna," he whispers, moving his hands toward my hair. "If quitting the underground is what it takes to keep you, then I'll do it."

"Really?" I breathe.

"Really. It's not good for me, I know that. I've always known that. I just never had a reason big enough to quit. Now I do." His lips twitch into a smile. "We belong together, Sienna. Nobody understands me the way you do. And you . . . *fuck*, baby, you . . ." His nose grazes my cheek as he inhales my scent, and my self-control finds itself on the brink of extinction. A string of curse words falls out of him when he drags his face down to my neck, fingers dancing over my collarbone. God, his touch is intoxicating. A pheromonal love potion in the form of his wicked fingertips. "Don't tell me you don't feel it too," he murmurs.

I do feel it. And I want him to know I feel it.

But I refuse to give any more of myself unless I get my answer for the one question that really matters.

"You say you want me and you want to be better for me," I say softly. "But do you love me? You should already know if you do."

It doesn't feel right putting him on the spot like this, but I need to know that he's committed to this as much as I am. I *need* it.

"Yes," he says without a pause. "I love you, Sienna."

I kiss him.

Jax is surprised by my response but doesn't complain, moving his lips over mine just as eagerly. He devours my mouth like he can't get enough of my taste. He yanks me into his embrace when he deepens the kiss, clinging to me like he wants to permanently fuse our bodies together. I climb on top of him and wrap my legs around his hips. He hisses out a breath when I tighten my arms behind his neck and bite on his bottom lip, making sure to drag out the action for as long as I can before slowly releasing. I'm starving to get as close as humanly possible to this man.

The inside of my thigh rubs along the zipper of Jax's jeans, making him hard. He groans, hands going down to squeeze my ass as he grinds his hips mercilessly against mine. Despite the clothing separating us, it feels exquisite, the friction causing my clit to throb and ache. I want him desperately. As if he can hear my thoughts, Jax pushes me down onto the bed and removes his pants, leaving him in only his underwear. My body writhes with anticipation when his huge bulge comes into view, his erection poking the fabric and pleading for release.

Jax climbs on top of me and wastes no time putting his lips on mine. I moan against him when his hand slips underneath my top, snaking under my bra. He closes his palm over my breast, and I love that it fits so perfectly. I want him to touch me everywhere. I pause his kiss long enough to free myself of my clothes so he can reach the most sensitive parts of me. A pleased rumble rises from his throat, and he buries his face in my neck while both of his hands run over my nipples, sending shot after shot of pleasure coursing through my body.

Meanwhile, I reach into Jax's boxers so I can feel his erection, closing my fingers over the base of his length and moving over it with long, hard strokes. Jax's head falls down to the crook of my neck as he lets out a low grunt. I hum in response. I never seem to get over how big it is in my hand. I wonder how it's going to feel inside me for the first time.

The thought jerks my yearning awake.

We've explored each other's bodies to death these past few months, but this time, it feels different. This time, it's leading up to something that's only been living in my imagination.

Heat begins to rise in my body. I break apart our kiss and look deeply into Jax's eyes.

"I'm ready. I want this," I say with conviction. "I want you."

His brow dips low on his face. "You sure?"

"Yes."

He smiles and leans down to brush his lips against mine in such a soft and tender manner, I dissolve. It's a rare moment, making me feel even more confident in my decision.

I help him discard his underwear and kick our clothes away. Jax reaches down to his jeans, pulls out his wallet, and digs around for a condom. I wonder if he knew we'd be needing it tonight or if he just stayed ready for when I said yes. He rips the condom wrapper open with his teeth and expertly rolls the rubber onto himself. He settles himself in between my thighs, rubbing the length of his shaft with his hand like he's preparing it for me. The sight of it alone feels so sinfully erotic that I lose a thousand breaths.

"This might hurt a little, okay?" Jax tells me, his eyes oozing with concern.

I nod. "Okay."

I'm dizzy with anticipation. *This is it*, I tell myself. *This is who you've been saving yourself for. You are going to remember this, remember* him, *for the rest of your life.*

Jax leans forward to press a gentle kiss on my forehead before pressing up against me. I lift my hips higher so he can slide himself inside me, watching him as he does because I don't want to miss a single thing. He does it slowly, making sure I'm adjusting to his length with every inch that he feeds in. I wince in pain at the first two inches, trying to relax my inner muscles so the pain gives way to pleasure, and soon enough, it does. When he's all the way in, we both breathe a sigh of relief.

"Wrap your legs around me," he whispers.

I do what he says, and the switch in angle gives Jax the perfect opportunity to push in and out of me, hitting that sweet spot I didn't even know I had. Oh God, sex is great. I didn't think I was going to enjoy it this much the first time, but I do, and it's because Jax makes it so fucking perfect. He shows me how he feels for me with every skillful thrust and tender kiss he lays on my sweat-glistened body.

"Baby, you feel so good," he says as he rocks himself inside me.

"Oh, Jax," I moan out. "Oh *God*."

I hold on tight, digging my fingers into his strong, muscled back as he pushes in and out of my body. Jax's elbows dig hard into the mattress on either side of me as he increases the pace, using the new position to get better leverage with his hips as he slams into me, hard and fast. I feel my own orgasm forming, building in between my thighs until the tension snaps and suddenly I'm no longer in bed with Jax but swimming with the stars and shimmering in space. Jax convulses against me, joining me in his own release. I shudder watching him lose control like this. I love that it's because of me.

Minutes pass, and neither of us says a word. We just stare at each other, smiling like idiots. I want him to know that I'll be by his side no matter what. Us against the world. Forever.

"I love you too, Jax," I breathe.

PART THREE
The Ruin

TWENTY

One Year Later

I hate you, Jax.

My anger is so visceral it coats my throat and makes my hands tremble as the cab pulls up in front of the abandoned warehouse. It's the same one I visited with Dakota and Beth during my first underground fight almost two years ago, except tonight, I'm here alone. And up until twenty minutes ago, I had no intention of ever coming back.

I hate you, Jax.

I hate what you keep doing to me.

Wrenching the cab door open, I hand a twenty to the driver, collecting the change out of his hand before he speeds away. I head to the back of the warehouse, where I know Jax will be hanging out before the fight. Most likely with Adam and a few other goons.

I expertly weave through the mass of fighters in the hallway and push through the back door. The memory of Jax and me passing through this same hallway, escaping through the fence and into the woods, pierces my mind, but I shove the memory away just as quickly. I'm not here to be sentimental.

I'm here to stoke a fire.

When I step outside, I'm confronted with exactly what I expected. There he is, my supposed boyfriend, draped in his black MMA robe, a beer resting casually in one hand. He tips his head back and chuckles, joining in the laughter of his friends surrounding him. His side is toward me, and it takes a couple of seconds for him to realize that I'm at the door. Adam, who's standing beside him, is the first to notice and nudges him with a shoulder. Jax looks at him, then follows his gaze toward me.

His entire face collapses.

His free hand goes to smooth over his jaw. I can feel everyone's eyes lasering in on me, but I don't meet any of their gazes. I look only at Jax, cold and seething, allowing my anger to speak for me when my mouth cannot.

Jax walks over to me, a frown pulling down his mouth. He appears embarrassed that I'm here right now and that I'm upset I wasn't invited when all of his other friends were. But that's only part of the reason, and he knows it.

"Let's talk somewhere else," he mutters.

I say nothing as I walk toward the fence, jerking my head for Jax to follow me through the opening.

***

We're in the woods, far from the loud techno music and the curious glances of his friends. Far from anyone else who would recognize us and think, *God, what a dysfunctional couple they are.* It's not like I don't agree with them. I'm aware that we are. I'd be blind not to realize how bad it's gotten between us. I'm just not in the mood to prove them right yet again by having a screaming match in front of an audience.

We're standing in front of each other in the small clearing in the woods. It's awkward and tense, like the past few weeks have been. My eyes scroll from his face to his huge body, taking in the familiar contours of his arms, shoulders, and chest. He looks good, as usual. I don't know why that bothers me so much. At least if he looked miserable, I'd know he's been beating himself up over the way he's treated me these past six weeks. Even now, he appears indifferent to my presence.

My heart deflates.

I miss him just as much as I hate him right now. I haven't kissed him in weeks. I haven't felt close to him in months. I don't even recall the last time he said that he loves me. And the last time we had sex, it was rough and distant and lacked feeling. We both just wanted to get it over with. I didn't mind; it's the only way for me to feel like I'm close to him.

Nowadays, there's this weird tension between us. It's a permanent presence now. It's hard to recall a time when we were just enjoying each other's company without turning it into a fight.

I watch Jax as he leans against the bark of the tree and takes a huge swig of beer. It irritates me how casual he's being with me. Like the past few weeks never happened.

I snatch the beer can from him. It feels unsurprisingly light in my hand.

"You're drinking again?" I arch a brow at Jax.

My question doesn't sit well with him because he reaches forward to snatch the can back. "It's just a beer. It's how I keep calm before a fight. You know I don't drink more than that. I need to stay sharp."

"Right. But other times, it's okay to overindulge?" I say dryly, recalling the number of times he's stormed off after an argument in my apartment only to return in a wildly drunken state. He promised he was going to stop after I had to fish him out of a dumpster one morning, prompting a tough reprimand from Julian after I failed to open the gym on time.

"Are you really here to talk about my drinking?" Jax says with a tilt of his head, almost like he's goading me. Challenging me to lay all my anger out on him.

He always used to tell me he was tired of fighting with me, but I think he secretly enjoys it. It's a way for him to exert a different kind of power, one he can't find in the cage. Not that he's successful at wielding it since I push back twice as hard. But the challenge of trying to one-up me entices him, just like the challenge of getting me to date him did.

"I'm here because you told me you weren't fighting in the underground anymore," I say, gesturing to him all decked out in his black robe, matching wraps secured around his hands. "So what the hell is all this?"

Jax sighs, like it's an inconvenience for him to explain.

"It is what it is."

"It is what it is? *That's* the best excuse you can come up with?"

"Then what do you want me to say?"

"I want you to explain why you lied to me. You said you

weren't gonna fight this season, Jax. After what happened with Perez last year, I thought you wanted to quit," I say, stepping forward to ease the animosity, which is amplified by the unfriendly space between our bodies. "Why couldn't you just tell me that this is what you've been doing these last six weeks?"

Jax rolls his head, placing his hands on either side of his hips. "Because I knew you'd give me shit about it, Sienna."

"Of course I was gonna give you shit about it." I match his tone, making my displeasure known. "Why promise me you weren't gonna touch the underground if you knew you were gonna come back?"

"Because I didn't really plan on coming back," he tells me, his eyes growing distant and murky. "You know I've been good so far. I haven't fought in any of Point's one-off fights since last season. But . . . circumstances have changed."

"What the hell does that mean?"

He pauses, lip curling inward.

"I don't expect you to understand."

"Right. I never understand anything." I let out a humorless laugh. "I'm just a stupid fucking airhead to you, right?"

"Seriously?" He glares at me. "You're gonna be a brat about it?"

"Yes! If you're gonna keep acting like you don't have a girlfriend to answer to!" I blast out, exasperated. "You know, this is the first time I've seen you in a long time. You don't call, you don't visit, you don't text. And when I try to reach out, you go radio silent on me. It's like you're a fucking ghost."

Jax's gaze is pinned back on me. "You don't know the shit I'm going through, the fucking situation I'm in right now—"

I roll my eyes. "Right. There's always a situation."

"This one's different," he insists.

"And let me guess: you're not going to tell me anything about it?"

Jax slams his mouth shut. His head gives a thorough shake.

My heart clenches with pain. It hurts because we've gone around this topic so many times, and we end up going nowhere. I'm not sure how much more of this I can take.

"I'm sorry. I can't let the underground go," Jax mutters. "It's my last chance to claim my pride back. I'm not going to let what happened with Perez happen again. You think I wanna be the laughingstock of this place? The guy who won by *default*? That's not me. I win because I'm good, not because I got a fucking handout."

"Oh. My. God. Who the fuck *cares*?" I blast out. I'm surprised by how uncontained and bratty it sounds as it echoes through the clearing. "Seriously. Beyond this small community of bums and lowlives, who the fuck cares?"

"*I do!*" Red flares in Jax's eyes. "I care. Just because you don't give a fuck about it doesn't mean you get to trivialize it, okay?" He smooths a hand along his forehead and sucks in a long breath to quell the anger bellowing in his chest. "Look, I don't need this back-and-forth right now. I have a fight in ten minutes. I promise it'll all be over soon." When his eyes connect with mine, they soften, and I'm reminded of how empathetic he can look when he wants to wrap an argument up as quickly as he can without really admitting responsibility. He comes over to me and slides his hands up my shoulders, murmuring, "I'm sorry I've been pushing you to the side, princess. You know I don't like being away from you for this long, but this is important to me. If something was important to you, you bet I'd be supporting you all the way, cheering for you on the sidelines."

I scoff. He's so easy with his words, but he usually forgets to back them up with action.

"You missed my last training session," I make sure to mention. "It was the second-last one before my grading exam. I wanted you to be there, and you weren't."

"I didn't get the memo."

"Because you *blocked my fucking number*," I hiss between my teeth.

Jax drops his hands from my body and steps back. "I only did it because you wouldn't stop with the hounding."

"I'm your girlfriend. That's what girlfriends do when they find out they've been lied to!"

He gives his head a tough shake. "Withholding information does not count as a lie—"

"That's bullshit, and you know it, Jax!" I seethe. "It's just another excuse for your shitty behavior."

I'm a fool to have come here expecting answers from him when all he's given me is more questions. That's all our relationship has been reduced to—me chasing him and him dodging me.

I tilt my head up and blow out a heavy breath, shifting my gaze to the murky ink-black sky. I wonder what it'd be like to feel so weightless that I could float up there, away from all the problems, away from *Jax*. I used to think that's what love is supposed to feel like. Like there's nothing tying you down. Your chest would feel airy and your heart light, and your soul would glow so brightly it could blind everyone else.

But no. This love is different. This love is difficult. It tests me every single day. I'm well aware that making a relationship work requires effort, but does it really require *this* much?

Maybe that's what love really is: a lot of hard work for little to no reward. My parents' failed marriage is certainly a prime example of that. If I have to keep fighting, I'll have to pick my battles. Because if I try to win all of them, there will be nothing left of me.

"You know what, Jax? Good luck with your fight. I'm sure you'll kill it," I mutter. It hurts to even look into his eyes now that I've confirmed where his priorities lie. "I'm leaving."

"Don't be ridiculous," Jax says, approaching me again. "You just got here."

"I don't care," I snap, already turning on my heel toward the fence.

The last thing I want to do is get lost in these woods with him. If we start going at it again, there's a strong chance only one of us will make it out alive.

Jax isn't having any of my attitude tonight. He grabs hold of my wrist to spin me around back to him. "Sienna, wait. Just wait. Stay with me. Just stay for the fight, and then I'll take you home after I win. I want you here. I want you on the sidelines."

I jerk my hand away from his grasp, feeling the anger wend its way around my chest again. "Oh, *now* you want me here. As soon as you want me to play the part of the loving, supportive girlfriend, suddenly I'm useful to you." My voice becomes higher pitched, more demure as I bat my eyelashes at him sweetly. "Oh, Jax, do you need some water? Do you want to go over your strategy again? Do you want to bend me over and fuck my brains out until you get rid of your nerves?" I drop my act and spit at him, "Go fuck yourself, Jax."

I spin around and trudge back toward the fence, far too wired up to think straight anymore.

"Seriously?" I hear him yell. "Sienna? *Sienna!*"

As I keep walking, his voice shrinks until I barely hear him at all.

TWENTY-ONE

"Out of my way," I say as I head back into the warehouse, moving through the swath of spectators and fighters crowding the hallway. There's more of them than I expect, coming from either direction. Some of them are trying to squeeze a last-minute smoke break in before the fight starts, but most of them are making their way toward the cage. At least there's enough space for me to move around and avoid crashing into people . . .

Someone on my left bumps my shoulder a little too hard, forcing me to lose my balance and hit my side against someone else coming from the opposite direction.

"Hey, watch where you're going. Or you won't be so lucky next time," a distinctive male voice hisses at me.

"Mind your damn business—" I blast out as I recoil from him, pulling my gaze up to meet his.

The first thing I notice is that his eyes are a startling shade of gray, like a storm cloud—murky and angry and wistful.

His facial features are distinct and dark, with messy dark hair sweeping across his head and stubble dusting his jaw. Just like the intensity of his eyes, his size is striking as well: he looks well over six feet, with corded muscles spanning his broad shoulders and his back, tucked into a plain white T-shirt. It's weird for me to be so affected by a stranger's presence, but I am, causing me to stumble backward in surprise.

The scowl disappears off the man's face just as quickly, like he recognized the same thing.

"I'm sorry," he says, and surprise flickers in his face, like he's shocked that the apology even came out of his mouth. He gets a good look at my face, seeming to notice my frantic nature, my disheveled hair, and my sad, anxious eyes. "Are you okay?"

He looks like he's about to reach out to me, but my instincts are screaming at me to protect my personal space.

"Don't touch me," I snap. His eyes widen, and I realize that I shouldn't have snapped at someone who hasn't done me any wrong. "Sorry. I just need . . ." I begin to back away.

The man doesn't let me pass. He's taking up so much space with his lean frame, it interferes with the flow of the hallway. When someone brushes past him and sends a nasty look his way, he mumbles out an apology and backs me up against the wall, all the while making sure to put a respectable amount of distance between us. His hands are planted on either side of me, like he's trying to shield me from everyone else. He lowers his voice so only I can hear him, but his gaze remains on me, worry amplifying in his face.

"Did someone hurt you?" he asks, his voice dangerously low.

I open my mouth to answer, but not before a piercing "Sienna!" shoots through the crowd.

The man's attention snaps toward the direction of the voice. Jax's head bobs in the distance, getting closer. The man returns his gaze to me; this time, his expression is fierce. "Did he hurt you?"

"I . . . I gotta go," I rush out, quickly ducking under his left arm and scurrying off.

I make it out of the warehouse, pushing through the last of the crowd. Outside, there's barely anyone around anymore. My body slackens with relief, not only at successfully getting away from Jax but also pulling myself away from that stranger. Despite not knowing him, there was a small part of me that didn't want to leave him. I felt safe trapped in his arms. I haven't felt that way with Jax in a while . . .

In front of me, there's a stretch of cars a mile long disappearing to the main road. The relief fizzles away. It took my cab thirty minutes to get here, and it looks like it's going to take me much longer to get out.

"Lovers' spat?"

I whip my head around and find Perez lingering beside the entrance, casually taking a drag of a cigarette in a leather jacket and jeans. He has one foot kicked up against the wall and one hand slipped into his jacket pocket. He looks different than when I last saw him. Older, perhaps. Though that's a given, since the last time I saw him was a year ago. He's also gained quite a bit of weight now.

"I'm not in the mood, Perez," I say with a bored stare before resuming scrolling through my phone to get to the Uber app.

I feel him come up beside me, so I lower my phone and

shoot an annoyed glare his way. *Take the hint, asshole.* But he doesn't. He stays put.

"Hey, I'm just observing," he points out, holding his hands up in surrender, the cigarette still dangling between his fingers. "I was right, wasn't I? You look agitated. Did you blow your top off at Jax?"

"Yes, but I don't feel like talking about it. Especially with you," I say, eyeing him with suspicion. "What the hell are you doing here anyway? I thought you were banned."

"From ever fighting again, yes," he says, casually taking another drag of his cigarette. "Doesn't mean I can't watch."

I purse my lips unhappily. With that stunt he pulled on Jax last year, I'm surprised he wasn't permanently kicked off the premises too. I heard Damien was, since he was the one who secured the drugs and gave them to Perez in the first place, and they didn't want to risk him starting a big doping movement in Breaking Point. Perhaps Perez has some pull with Breaking Point, which could explain why he's still here. I wouldn't be surprised, since he was their prized champion for years before Jax came along.

I wonder if Perez thinks his actions were worth condemning himself to this life of spectating rather than participating. If he hadn't been so blinded by ambition, perhaps he could have had a proper fighting chance against Jax. Now he's lost everything he's ever worked for, and it's nobody's fault but his own.

"I know what you're thinking. I did it for a reason, you know," Perez says, his voice gruff from the smoke choking up his throat. "Well, I did it for many reasons—"

"I don't care."

Perez grins at my rude response. When he reaches the end

of his cigarette, he walks over to a nearby pole and jams the butt against it before chucking it to the ground.

"It probably wasn't the best decision to cheat, but Jax has done worse things than me, so I figure we're even," Perez says dryly. "In fact, I was doing a huge favor to those he's screwed over."

That piques my attention. "What are you talking about?"

"You still don't know?" My blank stare causes him to chuckle hard, a hand clutching his broad chest. "Shit, he really keeps you in the dark, doesn't he? What else do you let him get away with?"

My cheeks flush pink with embarrassment.

"I can tell you everything, if you want. No holds barred," Perez says with a slimy grin on his face as he lights another cigarette. "I'll show you what a selfish bastard he really is."

I mash my lips together tightly. The prospect of Perez telling me what I still haven't managed to get out of Jax is tempting. *Really* tempting. And for a moment, I consider it. It's exhausting being the one person that Jax is supposedly the closest to even though his enemies seem to know more about him than I do.

But then again, this is Perez we're talking about. Perez, who would do anything to sabotage Jax—including turning his own girlfriend against him. Even if I were delusional enough to entertain him, who's to say the information he's offering me isn't just some scheme to break us up as some sort of final payback for what Jax did to him after the fight last year?

"Forget it," I grumble, turning away from him. "I know better than to trust a single thing that you say."

Perez makes a funny sound. "I consider myself more trustworthy than your boyfriend."

I choke on a laugh. "Forgive me if I find that hard to believe, given your reputation of being a saboteur."

In my hand, my phone buzzes with a notification from the Uber app. However, it doesn't come with good news.

Perez takes a peek at my screen and shrugs. "Tough luck. Even if you manage to get a car to pick you up, you're not going to get it in here."

"Why not?"

"Cops," he says, pointing his cigarette to the far end of the road, where the exit to the main road lies. Sure enough, some guys in blue uniforms have just pulled up.

"They'll go away. They always do," I say dryly.

"Yeah, but they're looking for some easy catches before they'll be on their way. Gotta look like they're doing their job, right?" Perez brings the cigarette back to his mouth. "So you definitely don't want your name showing up on that Uber guy's phone when the car gets here."

"Why are you being nice to me?" I side-eye him.

"Because if you're not on Jax's side, that makes you better than anyone else here."

"Who says I'm not on Jax's side?"

"You're sitting here waiting for a ride instead of watching him fight. You could not be any less on his side."

Inside the warehouse, the cheers grow in momentum. I hear the announcer riling up the crowd and getting them warmed up for the imminent fight. Beside me, Perez shrugs, rolling the smoke up his nostrils and releasing it through his teeth.

I look back toward the entrance, biting my lip. This will be Jax's first fight since we've been dating that I won't be around to witness. Guilt tramples over my skin at the thought of it.

Jax always counted on me to be there on the sidelines, cheering him on. He told me once that it was the cherry on top for him whenever he'd look around at the hundreds of faces after he won and find mine smiling up at him with pride. It made him feel good. And making him feel good made *me* feel good. I wonder how he feels knowing that's not going to happen tonight.

What if he fights terribly tonight because I'm not there? Or worse, what if he loses and can't handle it again like last time? Win or lose, he always has hordes of women flocking to his aid, wanting to steal a night of good fun from him. They're usually careful not to overstep when I'm around. If I'm not there this time, would they be tempted? Would *he*?

No. I shake the paranoia away, but the feeling clamps firmer around my chest, taking root. No way. Jax wouldn't do that . . . right?

It's hard to say. He's been impossible to predict lately.

I can't lose him. I can't.

"Well, looks like I was wrong," Perez observes with a disappointed shake of his head. He must think I'm so pathetic. I *am*. I can't seem to stay away from Jax, just like how he can't stay away from that fight.

"Fuck," I say to myself, shoving my phone back into my pocket. This body, this heart, keeps winning over my common sense. *Fuck.*

I sprint back toward the warehouse, ignoring Perez's hearty laugh as he watches me from outside.

***

Tonight, the announcer is all dressed up like a Viking, with the horned helmet and red paint slathered sloppily all across his cheeks and body. I hang back at the edge of the crowd, watching silently as Jax beats his fists together in the cage.

At the other end stands the other fighter. He has his hood up, a dark shadow casting over most of his features.

"And on the other side, we've got a fighter who's been the talk of the town all season! Last time we got a newbie this good, it didn't end so well, did it?" The announcer tsks as he alludes to Jax, and the crowd lambasts him with boos. "He's a force to be reckoned with. He aims to kill with his brooding charm and a deadly skill set. Ladies and gentlemen, give it up for Kayden 'Killer' Williams!"

The fighter pulls his hood down and acknowledges the audience with a closed fist.

My stomach bottoms out when I realize who he is.

He's the guy I bumped into in the hallway a few minutes ago.

He's far enough away that I can't make out most of his facial features, but there's no mistaking the dark hair and sharp jaw and that tall, lean, muscular body.

When Kayden climbs into the cage, I gulp with worry. The size discrepancy is noticeable, with Jax carrying at least twenty pounds more than Kayden. It's no question who has the advantage here.

When the referee yells, "Fight," Jax is already on the move, throwing all of his effort into rapid, overwhelming force. A flurry of punches catch Kayden on the cheek and jaw, and he momentarily loses balance, but he straightens up before Jax can take him to the floor.

Kayden picks his punches even in his weakened position, throwing accurate body shots and precise hooks to Jax's side. He's unpolished and significantly smaller than Jax, but this opponent is not going down in the swift, crippling defeat I expected. Kayden fights hard. I watch both of them, captivated, as they engage in a serious war of attrition, exchanging skillful punches, kicks, and tackles that I've rarely seen employed in an amateur underground fight.

Kayden dances in, coming up inside Jax's guard, attempting to land a classic jab-cross-hook combo, but Jax sees it coming, deftly stepping back. He swings a knee up to disrupt the punches and in the same instant explodes into a heavy front push kick, sending Kayden reeling backward. Kayden stumbles, losing his balance, but manages to slam his heel back just in time to catch himself from falling. The flow of the fight shifts, with Kayden now hanging back, his guard up, threatening Jax with knees and uppercuts. He knows if he ends up on the ground, Jax will swoop in and try for a takedown.

The fight goes on for a long while. Longer than most fights in the underground, which is surprising. At the tenth minute, both fighters seem antsy. They're tired, understandably so. Jax's power is a lot to absorb, and as such, Kayden seems more tired than Jax. Jax gets another surge of energy and catches Kayden in another front kick, followed by the same jab-cross-hook combo that Kayden attempted just a short while before. Kayden's head clashes against the cage, which is the opening Jax needs to unleash the full force of his skill and show Kayden exactly why he's here to stay in the underground.

I hold my breath, my attention firmly planted on Kayden rather than my boyfriend. I didn't realize that I've been rooting for him the entire fight. It should feel wrong, but for some reason, it doesn't.

No. I'm on Jax's side.

I *should* be on Jax's side.

Jax now has Kayden locked against the cage. They struggle with each other for a while, both of them trying to grasp at each other. Jax has a hold of Kayden's neck, while Kayden desperately tries to pry his way out of it by grabbing his arms. Jax plows into him with a series of body shots, forcing Kayden to stumble. It gives Jax a golden opportunity to sweep Kayden's legs out from under him, planting him on the ground. Jax switches positions, hooking his legs around Kayden's neck and crushing his shoulder into Kayden's arm, pinning it to the floor. The lethal Jax triangle armbar.

Kayden gets flushed, the blood rushing to his head, slowly turning it purple as Jax applies pressure onto Kayden's neck. I hear the crowd surge in volume, as if everyone in that warehouse already knows what's coming.

Come on, I pray silently. *Come on, you can get out of the chokehold. Just hold on a little longer, just a little more—*

Kayden, too exhausted to fight back, taps out.

The crowd goes nuclear with cheers.

My eyes flutter closed, unable to stop the disappointment flooding my body.

Jax's power and size won at the end of the day. But a little part of me feels for Kayden, whose toughness and determination made this a much closer fight than anyone anticipated. Jax had to push back hard to get him to submit.

Someone from the crowd spots me and gestures for me to meet Jax up in the cage. The gesture slowly picks up attention until the whole warehouse is cheering me on and rooting for me.

"Sienna!" Jax yells, just as the announcer comes over with the shiny golden belt. "Get in here."

I gulp, moving through the crowd as it parts for me. The last time I went into that cage, I was so excited to be there.

Now I just feel empty.

"Congratulations, baby," I say to him.

"Thanks, princess." He smiles back.

"I love you," I whisper, a little desperately. My frantic gaze searches for any sign of the same love I believe he's had for me.

His smile wanes.

He doesn't say he loves me back.

Instead, he just kisses me, showing everyone that we're okay, even though we're anything but. I lean into the kiss anyway, because despite what's going on between us, it feels nice to belong to him again. To feel wanted. My heart balloons with happiness for him that he finally gets to claim a win that's deservedly his, and for a moment, it makes me think that things might finally be normal between us again. But I know the feeling will not stay. I know that as soon as he lets me go, the emptiness will slide right back.

From the corner of my eye, I spot a defeated Kayden slump against the cage. His eyes are trained on us—or, to be specific, on me. I can feel the tension rolling off of him. The magnitude of his stare makes me feel so exposed, as if I'm transparent in front of him and he sees exactly how miserable I am.

Something tells me that he understands exactly how I'm feeling, which is deeply intriguing and unsettling at the same time.

TWENTY-TWO

Jax and I barely talked after he won the fight.

Following our cage kiss, he's immediately whisked away by his buddies. I keep close for a while so his groupies know they need to behave. As soon as it's clear Jax is only interested in hanging with his friends, I choose not to stick around. I do see a couple of missed calls from him when I get home, so I guess I'm officially unblocked from his phone now. How kind of him. I must send him a fruit basket to show my eternal gratitude.

I'm well aware most girls would break it off with a guy if he'd been ghosting them for several weeks. It's sad that I have a higher capacity for tolerating bullshit. At first, I thought that meant I had more perseverance than most, but now I know it just makes me sad.

The next morning, I'm itching for a shower before leaving for work at UFG, but one of my roommates, Lori, decides that hogging the bathroom with her latest one-night stand is in everyone's best interests today. After I tell her to hurry up, her annoyed "In a minute" turns into ten minutes, then twenty-five, and by then, I'm already late to open up the gym, so I say fuck it and leave.

Living with roommates in this tiny apartment has truly been a perverted version of hell. I live with two other girls and a guy—all sophomores like me. I'm not close to them, but the three have been friends since freshman year. Well, *friends* is a loose term for what they are to each other. They bitch about one another more than they're nice to one another. And sometimes I get dragged into their drama by association. When one of them gets banished from the friend group, that person usually goes out of their way to be nice to me so that they don't feel lonely, and once they're all good with each other again, he or she is back to pretending I don't exist.

You'd think that this kind of drama would happen only in high school—that college kids would be too mature to handle friendship in such a trivial way—but you'd be surprised by how many people don't grow out of that pettiness.

Jax hates my roommates. No surprise there. Even when things were still good between us, he refused to come over. I ended up spending more than half of my nights at his place. I didn't mind. It's not like I missed my roommates anyway.

Despite the roommate politics, I am glad to be living in the city. I needed to put some long-overdue distance between me and my family. There isn't much tying me to the family home anyway. Dad had the same sentiment and finally made the decision to sell the house and move into a bigger place with his third wife and Beth. He finally got everything he ever wanted after his divorce settlement from wife number two—poor Alicia; she won't be missed—including a bungalow in Newton with a decent-size pool. I've only visited the place a couple of times, and even I have to admit that it's a nice home. Lorraine does the upkeep, and she does it well.

I would call her a trophy wife, but it's my dad who's been sucking her dry of her five-million-dollar inheritance. Lorraine's posh and loves to rant about the trailer homes outside her second home ruining the view from her bedroom, which just shows how out of touch she is with real problems in the world, but I like that she doesn't try to form a relationship with me. Maybe it's because I don't visit enough for her to care. That's fine with me; I'm not looking for another stepmom anyway. But I know that Lorraine's been trying with Beth because she's still living with them. I wonder if Beth is thinking about moving out as soon as she graduates. She's dead set on BU as her first choice, but if she gets in, Dad will likely want to keep her close by making her stay at home.

I hope she doesn't make the same mistake I made.

When I finally make it to UFG, ten minutes late, I'm relieved to find that no one's waiting to get in. I immediately get to work oiling the machines and making sure all the weights are in their proper spots. Then I get started on cleaning: first the lockers, then the MMA cage and gym equipment, and lastly the front desk. Julian is very particular when it comes to cleanliness, so I've learned how to keep the gym organized in the way that he likes. He's adamant about not using a cleaning spray on the equipment but using wipes instead, since he doesn't want to take the slightest risk of damaging any of their electronic components. He never lets me leave cleaning supplies around for gym-goers to use, preferring me or anyone on duty to clean the equipment for them, which means more work for us, but I understand why. When Julian invests in a piece of equipment, he dedicates himself wholly to the maintenance of it. It's why most of his gym pieces are relics from the early 2000s but are all still in top-notch condition.

By the time I'm done setting up, a few gym members have already breezed through the doors, ready to get started with their workouts. I wave a friendly hello at them and get started on preparing the petty cash. When I finish up with the coins, Julian is strolling through the doors.

"Morning," I say, trying to sound enthusiastic.

Julian says nothing, merely acknowledging me with a slight tilt of his head. Then he scans the gym like he always does, making sure that everything is up to his standards. Immediately, he goes over to the mats to pick up a pair of abandoned MMA gloves and lifts them up for me to see. I send him a sheepish smile, internally screaming at myself for missing them. He goes over to the lost and found shelf and shoves the gloves there.

"How was the fight last night?" Julian makes sure to ask when he walks over toward me. He hovers over the counter, looking down at me interrogatively.

My brows sink down on my face. "How did you know there was one?"

"Come on. Jax and I may not be on speaking terms, but I have eyes and ears everywhere."

"Then you must know how it ended."

"Yeah, I do," he says with a slight pause. "He was good."

"Jax is always on top of his game—"

"No. I mean the new guy. He was good."

Julian has never been free with compliments—he rarely even uses them when he's training with me—so the fact that he just casually gave Kayden a decent compliment is really something. I'm surprised and, quite frankly, a little jealous. I wonder if it's a genuine compliment or if he's just rooting for someone who isn't Jax.

"It was a tough fight, wasn't it?" he asks me, and I nod. He gives his fingers a little drum across the desk, pursing his mouth unhappily when he adds, "Bet Jax didn't like that."

"You know he doesn't."

Julian notices how quiet I'm being as he keeps talking about Jax, so he clears his throat and tenderly asks, "Did you guys get a chance to talk? You've been upset about the fact that you guys aren't talking."

"Yeah, we talked," I say, rubbing my cheeks with my hands. Whenever I think about Jax, I can always feel my face flaring with annoyance. "It didn't go as well as I'd hoped."

"Really?" Julian arches a brow. "If my sources are right, there was a rather gratuitous public display of affection after he was declared the winner."

I look down, embarrassed. "I had to."

"Come on. You never do anything unless you want to. It's what's been infuriating about training you."

"I missed him, all right? So sue me," I confess. "But that doesn't mean we're on good terms."

I find a pen hooked on the logbook to my right and pick it up, clicking it anxiously. Since we're on the topic of Jax, I might as well let Julian in on what else happened that night.

"I bumped into Perez yesterday," I blurt out. "He said something interesting to me."

Julian flashes me a suspicious look. "What did he say?"

"He said that Jax has 'done worse things' than him. I think it has something to do with his stepdad," I say, looking down briefly before catching Julian's gaze again. "Do you know anything about that? He's only told me bits and pieces."

Julian's forehead scrunches. "No, but it's concerning that you don't."

"He doesn't like to talk about any of those things. He always says it shouldn't concern me," I say, resuming my pen clicking. "I just want to understand why he feels like he needs the underground to survive."

Julian snatches the pen from me, grimacing. "Or maybe you just want someone else to blame for his shitty behavior."

"He's not a shitty person." Even as I say it, it astounds me that I'm so quick to defend Jax when I'm the one who complains about him the most.

"You're right. He's worse. Shitty people don't realize how rotten they are. Jax knows exactly how rotten he is and is proud of it," Julian mutters, a little irritated.

"I can't let him go, Jules," I mumble pathetically. "I love him."

"You can love someone. Doesn't mean it's right for you to be with them."

Julian's statement gets me right in the gut.

It's unfair that I've found myself in love with someone who brings me equal parts joy and pain. And it's not like I have a choice. Loving Jax is not a choice. It's servitude, I realize. Whether I like it or not, I'm shackled to him. And there's no way out without destroying myself completely.

"You know it's not that simple, Jules," I say quietly.

Julian releases a frustrated breath. I can tell he's at his wit's end with me, and I feel bad laying it all down on him in the first place.

"You know what? You do what you want, Sienna. Just make sure Jax doesn't take all your focus again. You still got school," he reminds me sternly. "Plus, your kickboxing grading exam is coming up soon. And if you botch that, I'll have to stop sponsoring you."

"I'll ace it, I promise."

"You better." He gives me a steady look. "I will not see you fail."

I watch soundlessly as he disappears into his office.

I won't fail.

I'll have nothing left to look forward to if I do.

***

I get a couple of messages from Jax throughout the day. There were a couple of *I miss you*s and *I want to see you*s followed by an invitation for me to come over after my training session with Julian in the evening. At first, I consider giving him the silent treatment, just so he can have a taste of his own medicine, but my willpower crumples in on itself when I find myself on the train to his place rather than mine.

I'm not even surprised by myself anymore.

What I am surprised by is the loud pounding of music coming out of Jax's apartment when I knock on his door.

Nobody answers, prompting me to knock again. After about twenty seconds and some shuffling noises, the front door wrenches open and a casual-looking Jax greets me in a fluffy black robe and matching fluffy slippers. There's a huge gash above his brow, and it looks like it's been stitched up quite poorly. A paper crown is resting a little crookedly on his blond hair, and his underground belt is slung around his waist, the gold catching the harsh beams of disco lights.

Behind him, partygoers crowd the living room, some pouring themselves drinks and others grinding against one another to whatever song the DJ put on. Most of the furniture has been cleared out to make way for two beer pong tables and a large dance floor.

Annoyance pinches at my skin.

"Hey, princess," Jax says sweetly. He reaches an arm toward my waist, but I sidestep. His smile falters a bit at my rejection before steadying.

"I thought we were gonna talk," I say irritably.

"We are talking."

"In *private*. What the hell is this?"

"It's my victory party," he says, seemingly proud of it.

"Did you not have one yesterday?"

"I did. I decided to have another one."

I roll my eyes. "You could've mentioned that to me before inviting me over. I'm not in the mood to celebrate. I want to talk."

"Fine." The smile disappears from his perfectly chiseled face. "Let's go in there."

Jax offers his hand again, but I ignore him, pushing past him and the many others taking up space in the living room. I pry open the door to his room and walk in. His sheets are messy, and there's an empty bottle of gin lying at the base of the bed. Jax follows me in, shutting the door behind him.

As soon as we're alone, he walks over to me and brackets me in his arms. The first thing that hits me is the smell of liquor on his breath as he leans in to whisper against my lips, "I missed you."

Blocking my number was his way of missing me.

Not telling me he had a fight last night was his way of missing me.

I place a hand on his chest, making sure to keep distance so he can't kiss me. Not unless I hear an apology come out of his mouth first.

"You still haven't said you're sorry for giving me the silent treatment," I tell him.

"You're right. I'm sorry. I meant to say sorry," Jax says, a hand crawling up the length of my spine to cup the back of my neck. His head dips down to press what's supposed to be a comforting kiss to the sweet spot on my skin. "That's why I called you over."

"Maybe for once you can come to me instead of me coming to you."

He releases his hold on me, the tenderness in his face subsiding. "I told you I hate coming to your place. Lori's a piece of shit. And Cassie keeps giving me the side-eye, like I'm the scum of the earth for fighting in the underground."

"Maybe Cassie has a point."

He rolls his eyes. "At least with Dakota, all I had to worry about was her saying I wasn't good enough for you."

At the mention of my former best friend, an unexpected wave of sadness washes over me. I haven't allowed myself to think about her ever since our falling-out last year. There's a lot of sorrow and guilt attached to the fact that I let our friendship wither away like this.

"Well, right now, you're proving her right," I say, prompting Jax's face to twist with displeasure. What looked so pristine and perfect last night is puffy and bruised now, fresh blood trickling down from the gash on his brow. My fingers drift to his face to touch the wound, my annoyance slipping away momentarily. "You're bleeding. Who the hell stitched this up for you?"

"Adam."

"He can't even hold his beer, what makes you think he could hold a needle?" My face pinches in horror. "I think it might be infected. You may need to go get it checked."

"No, I'm fine," Jax insists, pushing my arm away from his face. "Don't worry about it."

Even when I point out that he's bleeding, he refuses to touch that spot on his face. It's like he refuses to acknowledge the wound's existence. Like doing so would be detrimental to his whole spiel about being invincible.

"Was it worth it?" I dare to ask. "It was a close fight. Was that what you wanted?"

My words hang in the air like smoke. Jax freezes in his stance.

"I *won*," he insists, his voice hoarse like it's scratching its way up his throat. "I won that fight."

"You could've lost," I insist, because a part of me wants to hurt him for hurting me.

"I know you're just saying that to get back at me for not talking to you," he says, his voice careful. "Look, I'm sorry, Sienna. I was too focused on the game. Now that it's over, you have my undivided attention. Now and always." He engulfs my face in his big calloused hands. Our mouths are so close I can feel his hot breath caressing my lips.

"It's over. Really?"

"Let me show you," he whispers, sweeping his lips over mine. He kisses me like he wants to erase the past few weeks. I don't kiss him back. My mouth stays unmoving as he slowly works his magic on me.

I can hear my heart thrumming loudly. It doesn't beat like a normal heart does; it beats a name.

Jax. Jax. Jax.

I want so badly to continue where we left off in that cage after the finals before we were interrupted by his friends. I hate him for what he's done to me. The weeks of no contact. But I miss him. *God*, I miss him. Every day that we don't speak is absolute torture.

I think he's telling the truth this time.

He's going to focus on me now. He's going to focus on us.

It's over, I will myself to believe. *The stuff with the underground . . . it's over.*

It's my turn now.

I cave in, returning his kiss.

Jax groans, relief pouring out of his mouth and into me.

He crushes me against his body, and I cling to his shoulders desperately. It doesn't take long until we are peeling each other's clothes off. We're frantic, like if we wait a second longer to do this, we'll lose the feeling.

In a matter of minutes, we're both fully naked.

Jax flips me around and crushes me against the door, my back pressed up against his chest. He leaves me for a bit to sheathe himself with a condom and then returns, gripping my hips. I watch his face go slack as he eases into me from behind. There is a collective gasp of relief. His delicious weight pushes me up against the door so hard my face is squished against the wooden surface as he pumps into me hard and fast. Rough hands grab at my hips, steadying me, forcing me to match his rhythm. A moan escapes my mouth when he deepens his thrusts.

There are still people outside. Anyone could hear us. I don't care.

I shut everything out.

I shut everything out but Jax.

I angle my face so I can see his face. I don't think I enjoy the actual sex as much as I enjoy watching him get off inside me. His eyes shut in bliss and his hips thrust hungrily into me; he looks satiated in a way I haven't seen in a long time.

"Oh, *fuck*," Jax groans. "Fuck, princess."

I arch my back against him restlessly with every frantic movement, moving my body back just as he slides in, intensifying the exquisite feeling. We're both chasing the high, but it's not enough. He flips me around so we're face-to-face and grabs me. I wind my legs around him, my arms going around his neck, just as he presses my back against the door and eases into me again. I catch the door stopper above me with an arm, using it as leverage to move against him greedily. I want to fuck him just as much as he's fucking me.

"Oh God, Jax," I moan out. "Please. *Harder*."

He answers me, pushing into me so hard that my legs buckle with the movement.

We were loud before.

We're deafening now.

Our heavy breathing connects in the air. His loud groans are like heaven singing in my ears. We ride against each other like we've been starved for each other for years.

"I'm coming," Jax grunts.

I brace myself, pulling him in with my legs so we'll be as close as we can possibly be when he comes.

Jax trembles against me, driving into me one final time. I'm too distracted to join him in the release. I want to see him come inside me. Satisfaction rolls in my stomach when his eyes flutter and his bottom lip curls under his teeth as he spills everything into the condom.

I savor the moment, because I don't know when the next time will be that he'll need me like this.

***

"I'm thinking about quitting the underground eventually. And starting a gym," Jax says, stroking the side of my hip lazily as we lie together. I'm curled up against him naked, too tired to get dressed.

Meanwhile, sometime after our second session of the night, he managed to slip back into his boxers. It was only to leave the room for a couple minutes to clear his apartment of all the guests still taking up space. I didn't ask him to do that, but I'm happy he did so I can have him all to myself tonight. Now he glances down at me. I'm nuzzled against the crook of his shoulder.

"What do you think?" he asks, hope shining in his eyes. "We could do it together. I'll train clients, you run the business."

I laugh. "How about I train clients, you run the business."

"How about we both train clients and run the business."

"We'll run the business into the ground, that's for sure."

Jax smiles. I like it when I'm the reason he smiles.

"Fuck fear, right?" He kisses me on the top of my head, and I melt into him. It's been a while since he's said that.

"Fuck fear," I say back.

He hums when I adjust myself so I'm lying on his chest instead of his shoulder. I feel safe in his arms, like he'd burn the whole world down for me and shield me from the flames.

"I know it doesn't seem like it, Sienna, but I really did miss you," he admits. "I . . ." I ready myself for the three words I haven't heard him say to me in a long time, needing the comfort of those words, but tragically, they don't arrive. Instead, he braces himself and sighs. "I just really wish you would let me do what I need to do."

My heart deflates.

Things are still a little rocky between you and him, Si. You can't expect him to give up those words easily again.

"I *do* let you do what you need to do," I insist. "You just can't seem to make up your mind about what you want."

"I know I want you. Isn't that enough?" he whispers, looking deeply into my eyes.

I stay quiet. Sometimes I think that's enough. Sometimes I think that all that really matters is the two of us and the fact we care for each other, that that alone should feel right and full.

He still hasn't said he loves me.

"Maybe," I say after a while. "If you tell me why you changed your mind about the underground and hid it from me in the first place."

"I told you, I wasn't planning to."

"And yet you did it anyway. Something's bothering you, and I wish you would tell me what it is."

"It's nothing." He shrugs.

I frown, disappointment settling in the pit of my stomach. I'm tired of feeling like this every time he shuts me out.

"You know . . . I bumped into Perez before your fight yesterday," I say. "He had a bit to say about you."

The familiar scowl arrives on his face when I mention Perez's name. "He doesn't know shit, Sienna. Don't believe a single word he says."

"Funny, that's kind of what he said about you too."

Jax's jaw hardens. He pulls himself up into a sitting position, and I lift my body, angling it toward his. The tension in his jaw remains as he asks me, with an edge to his voice, "What did he tell you?"

I swallow heavily before speaking up. "He said that you're a selfish bastard. And that you've screwed people over in the past."

"And you believe him?"

"I wouldn't put it past you."

A muscle pulses in Jax's jaw. I knew he wouldn't like that answer, but I wanted to say it anyway to gauge what kind of reaction I got. Would it confirm what Perez said about him? Or would he be angry that Perez is spreading lies about him?

He gives me nothing as he slides a hand over his mouth, his thumb and index finger pressing against his chin.

"What else did he say?"

"Nothing. That's all."

"Good," he says, even though he doesn't seem pleased. "Don't entertain him anymore. He'll do anything it takes to get one last dig at me, and I don't want you getting hurt because of his lies." When I don't answer, his frown deepens. "Promise me."

I hesitate. I should be honest and tell him that I can't make that promise. Because as much as I love him, I trust him less than I trust even Perez. But I don't tell him any of that because it'll turn into a whole argument, and for once, I just want things to go back to normal between us.

"Sienna?" he says pleadingly. *"Please."*

"Okay. Okay . . . fine," I say eventually. "I promise."

I can't tell if my answer is the truth or a lie.

TWENTY-THREE

For my kickboxing grading exam, Julian recommended a friend of his, an instructor, Deana Jones, who runs a retreat not far from the city. She has over twenty years of experience in the field and will be the one grading me today.

It would be much easier for Julian to grade me, but he's expressed concern about the conflict of interest since I'm gunning for a job in his gym and it would call into question his own biases. So Deana, Julian, and I worked out a plan to do the training sessions at UFG, and, along with Deana popping in once every two weeks to check my progress, I would eventually be graded by her as well.

Getting the black belt is only half the work done, unfortunately. I still have a written theory exam to get through after this, but that should be easy since it's multiple choice, and I've been going through my textbooks cover to cover nearly every night. There's a reason Julian's requirements for being a trainer in his gym are high. Although MMA as a sport is strictly regulated, the coaching aspect of it often isn't, which means there are many inexperienced trainers and coaches out there. Julian wants every trainer he hires to go through the certification process to legitimize their skills. It's why UFG's reputation is the gold standard for MMA.

I'm nervous when I enter Deana's gym. I don't get nervous about a lot of things, but I have a lot riding on this exam. I'm surprised to find the gym is a much smaller space than UFG. Instead of MMA cages, there are kickboxing rings as well as heavy and speed bags hanging on every available corner. There are a dozen or so people sitting around the red floor mats, all looking anxious, all waiting to be graded. I opt to stand since I'm not acquainted with anyone here, and I lean against a pillar as I watch Deana begin the sparring session with her first student.

It doesn't take long until my name is called. I put on a mouth guard, strap on my headgear and boxing gloves, and get onto the mats where Deana is waiting for me in the same gear.

You can do this, princess. Jax's voice slides into my mind, erasing all my nerves. *Fuck fear.*

I take a deep breath and focus up, then propel forward.

***

April rolls around, and classes begin to pick up their pace. It's hard to pay attention to anything since I feel like I'm on top of the world right now, having passed both my theory and physical certification exams. Jax was ecstatic for my newly awarded status as an MMA trainer. He took me out for a fancy dinner to celebrate, and then we had sex, where he made me come, like, five times. It was one of the best nights of my life.

Afterward, it was time to get back to business. Julian made me interview for the trainer position, scrutinizing every aspect of my résumé. But even he had to admit that no other candidates came close. In less than two years, I've mastered kickboxing—earning myself a black belt—and I'm about a third of the way there with Muay Thai. I was practically squealing in my seat when he handed me my employment letter. I am officially an MMA trainer now, and I start next month. My cleaning and administrative days are finally over.

The urge to just quit school and do MMA full-time entices me now that I've officially secured my dream career. But Mom always told me I should have a backup plan if things go south, and I owe it to her to finish college since she worked so hard to make sure I have a place here.

My class finishes at lunchtime today, and I am the first one out of the lecture hall, hoping to find a good spot in the quad to get some much-needed sunshine. After speed walking down the hallway to the exit, I swing the door open to find an easily recognizable dark-haired woman standing on the other side.

I hold the door for her, sidestepping to let her through, but she does the same on her side. We stare at each other for a while and laugh when we realize neither of us is going to walk through first. Since she isn't going to budge, I decide to make the first move, only to crash right into her when she makes the same decision.

"Oh my God," Dakota says, steadying herself.

"I'm sorry," we say in unison.

"It's cool," we each reply.

Dakota and I let out another laugh.

When the laughter dies down, an awkward silence hangs between us. Dakota scratches her head, her gaze trained on the ground. I purse my lips together nervously. It's been so long since I last saw her face-to-face. She looks different now. Her hair is much shorter—the medium-length cut frames her round face so well—and there's less shine in her eyes.

"How . . . um," she says uncomfortably. "How are you?"

"I'm doing okay." I shrug.

A student behind me clears her throat, and I realize we're blocking the doorway. I join Dakota and move to the side.

Dakota looks at me, offering me a sympathetic smile, but it's clear she can't think of a damn thing to say to me.

I point to the poster taped to the door. It's not the first time I've come across this poster on campus recently, so I recognize it easily. It's promoting an original play. Dakota's name is printed on the third row, small enough that it'd be easy to miss if you were just passing by. But I notice it. I always do.

"I saw that you're in a play. Congratulations," I say.

"Yeah. Thanks," she replies a little shyly. "It's a small role this time, though."

"It's still a great achievement."

"Thanks," she says appreciatively.

"How're you and Trevor?" I feel compelled to ask. I haven't seen him around in a while, so naturally, I'm curious.

"We're okay," she tells me. Then a pause. "Actually, no. We're in a rough patch right now." Her response earns a frown from me. She brushes the topic off quickly with another question. "How about you? You still with Jax?"

I almost don't want to say it because I know how she'll react, but since we're not exactly friends anymore, I don't see why I should hide it.

"Yeah." I nod.

"Cool, cool," she says, mashing her lips together tightly.

The conversation feels like it's coming to a close, so I get ready to walk away with a *See you around* ready to shoot out from my throat, but she opens her mouth first.

"I don't know if you're doing anything right now, but would you like to have coffee?" Dakota blurts out. She sounds sad but hopeful.

She doesn't know I've been waiting to hear those words for a year now.

"Yeah. Coffee sounds good," I say, unable to keep the grin from breaking onto my face. "Coffee sounds great."

***

"She did *what*?" A gasp blasts out of Dakota.

We're sitting at a table outside Caffeinated, soaking up the sun with our lattes. Dakota offered to get the drinks this round. I'm surprised that she still remembers my order—a dirty matcha latte with an extra shot, no whipped cream.

It takes us a while to get rid of the awkwardness as we find our bearings with each other again. After she asked me how I'm doing with my roommates, I couldn't stop myself from divulging every piece of drama that has occurred so far, ending with Lori's recent escapade with some eggs and a microwave.

"I know," I say through half a mouthful of latte as I set my steaming cup down on the table. "And now she refuses to buy us a new microwave because she thinks it's a genuine accident and we should all chip in. Like it's our fault she's a dumbass."

"Jeez," Dakota groans.

"Well, Cassie's way worse. One time, she secretly dosed Mike with sleeping pills because she 'couldn't be bothered with him anymore,'" I tell her, flipping my hair so it rests on one side of my shoulder. "Mike was so close to pressing charges, but Cassie has some shit against him, so he had to drop the case. I keep my door locked at all times now for this specific reason."

"Okay, *please* tell me you're moving out," she begs, her hand moving to close over mine in urgency.

"Yeah. I might do it soon."

Now that I'm gonna be jumping into my training job in a few weeks, getting a place of my own is something that's always on my mind.

Dakota smiles at me, and it inspires a warm feeling in my chest. God, I haven't felt that way in a long time.

"I missed you," she admits, giving my hand a tight squeeze.

"I missed you too," I murmur.

To be honest, it's been a shitty year without Dakota. She was the only friend I had for a long time, and when I lost her, I had no one else to fall back on but Jax. I love him so much, but there are some things that I just can't talk to him about, things I can only say to Dee.

I take another long sip of my latte and ask Dakota all the burning questions I've been dying to ask. I ask how she's really doing, apart from the casual "I'm doing okay." She tells me that she and Trevor are still together but it's complicated between them, which makes me sad. She doesn't go into much detail, but I get the impression that it's worse than she's letting on, and it makes me wonder if I'd still been in her life, would I have helped her through it all?

A lot of things would've been different if we'd remained friends.

"Have you, um, have you talked to Beth lately?" I say, finger circling the rim of my coffee cup. Beth and I haven't kept in touch as much as I'd like since I moved out. The only time we talk is when I'm over at Dad's, and our conversations there have always been surface-level. I miss my little sister. I miss what we used to share.

"Yeah." Dakota's hands go around her steaming cup. She stares at the liquid for a while before saying, rather hesitantly, "I think she really misses you."

It's weird that my ex–best friend is closer to my sister than I am. The jealousy that rolls through me is almost audible.

"Yeah? She has a weird way of showing she misses me."

"I don't think she's doing very well. Lorraine and your dad have been giving her a hard time," she replies with a shrug. "Maybe you should reach out."

"I *have* reached out. Many times." I frown deeply. "She doesn't wanna talk to me. I don't know if she's still mad at me for Jax or if she's just used to keeping me at arm's length now."

Her eyes are sad when she glances at me. "Sometimes people don't like to admit that they're wrong."

I can sense a double meaning to her words, which gets me a little excited. Maybe we can finally address what happened between us last year and put all that drama to rest.

"Yeah, maybe," I say, shifting in my seat. "How about you? Are you one of those people too?"

"What do you mean?"

I let out a long sigh, wrapping my hands around my cup and staring straight at her. "Come on, Dee. I was really hurt when you stopped talking to me. And now you're here . . . I just want to know: What changed your mind? Do you feel bad about what happened?"

Dakota looks at me all confused.

"Okay. Wait a minute." She puts a hand up to stop me. "You think I'm here because I felt *guilty* for cutting you off?"

"I don't get it." I look at her, puzzled. "Then why are you here?"

Dakota looks at me. *Really* looks at me.

Then she releases a hoarse laugh, like she can't quite believe I had the nerve to even ask that.

"Holy shit," she breathes, covering her mouth. "I can't believe it. You think I'm in the wrong here."

"Well, yes, I think so. I did my part in apologizing. You chose to shut me out because of the play."

Dakota rolls her eyes. "For the last time, it's not just about the play."

I purse my lips unhappily. I hate that every time we talk, we somehow always manage to circle back to Jax.

"I don't know what you want me to say, Dee," I mumble. "He's my boyfriend."

"But he's not everything," Dakota insists.

"What does it matter? Trevor's *your* everything."

"He's a big part of my life, yes, but he doesn't consume me. But you . . . it's like you have no free will when it comes to Jax." There is spitefulness in her voice. "I heard about what happened with Perez last year. The fact that you're still with him doesn't make any sense."

"What happened with Perez was a fluke," I correct her, sounding aggrieved.

"What happened with Perez shows that he's a narcissistic prick who only cares about himself and what he can get from hurting people," Dakota says. "And one day, he's going to hurt you too, if he hasn't done so already."

I shake my head. She doesn't get it. She doesn't understand him the same way I do. If she thinks what happened with Perez is going to scare me away, she's wrong. I've been through so much with Jax since. We've fought so hard to be where we are now.

"You're wrong," I say, a little too defensively. "You just don't know him like I do."

"Oh yeah? What do you know about him? Really?" she presses on. "Do you know what he does outside of fighting? What was his life like before joining the underground? His life before you?"

I slam my cup on the table a little too hard. "Why does everyone keep bringing this up?" My hands bury deep into my hair. "I'm so tired of hearing it! 'Sienna, you don't know this. Sienna, you don't know that. Sienna, you're letting him get away with so much.' It's infuriating!"

"But it's the truth!" Dakota counters.

"Don't you think I *know* that?" I say, my voice breaking. "If you knew how *hard* I tried . . ." I loosen a breath, trying to calm myself down. I refuse to get worked up about Jax again. I just can't. My lungs burn and my skin gets all hot, and I lose my whole day just trying to seize my sanity back.

Dakota scoots her chair so she's beside me rather than in front of me. She pulls me to her side, and my head rests on her shoulder, her hand caressing my arm to alleviate some of the stress.

"Maybe . . . a part of you wants to give up because it's better to not know. It's better to be kept in the dark because it's easier to love him that way," she says, her voice softening. "But you can't live like this forever, Si. What you're doing is only slapping a bandage over a gunshot wound. What if . . . what if what happened with Perez wasn't the first time he lost control? What if he did terrible things before you came along? Do you really not want to know? You've been dating for a year and a half now. Isn't it about time that you got some answers?"

I force myself to look up at Dakota. She appears sick with worry. Even back then, she always gave me that look when I was with Jax. And now that it's back again, it means nothing has changed between me and Jax in the span of a year. Absolutely nothing. We've been arguing and fixing things only to have the same argument again and repeat the whole damn cycle.

I'm *so* tired of existing in that cycle.

Dakota is right about this.

It has to end.

"You already know what to do, Si," Dakota soothes. I lift my head from her shoulder enough to peer at her through my lashes. "You just need to have the same courage to face Jax as you'd have to face someone in that cage."

I nod wordlessly, collecting those words of courage and keeping them in my heart.

I have a feeling I'm going to need them soon.

"Yeah." I exhale. "Okay."

"Okay?"

I nod. Her expression softens with relief.

"I've really missed you, Dee," I whisper. "And I'm so sorry for everything."

Dakota tightens her arm around me, squeezing hard.

"I'm sorry for everything too."

And with that, the strain between us dissolves.

With that, our friendship finally begins to heal.

TWENTY-FOUR

This is a terrible fucking idea, I say to myself as the smell of alcohol and sweat and instant regret hits my nostrils.

Although this isn't the same bar that Jax frequents with his friends, it's just as dingy. The lighting is dim, the décor is shabby, and neon beer signs are propped on the walls. As I approach the bar, I eye the half-empty glass of beer that Perez is silently nursing. I wonder how long he's been here. I do a little survey around the place to see if he's gone against his word and brought his men tonight. None of the other faces in the bar look familiar, and they all seem to be minding their own business, so I figure I should be safe. For now.

Tracking Perez down was difficult, mostly because I wasn't sure how to go about it without raising suspicion from Jax or his friends. Perez is also a notoriously paranoid person, only giving his contact information to people in his inner circle. But I managed to squeeze a tip from someone who knows which gym he trains at, so I just waited around until he showed up.

I admit, this isn't my finest moment. I'm crossing a clear line with Jax meeting Perez here tonight since he made me promise not to go near him. But I swallow down my doubts. It's justified . . . I think. What other choice do I have when he goes out of his way to hide things from me? I've already let it go on for far too long.

It's time to break the cycle.

"Hey," I say, sliding onto the barstool beside him, refusing to meet his eyes.

Perez laughs dryly at my nervousness. "Relax, sweetheart. This isn't an interrogation. If anything, you're interrogating me, so . . ."

I'm afraid. I'm afraid of what I might find out about Jax tonight.

Come on, Si. Fuck fear.

The irony that Jax has always been the one to remind me of that isn't lost on me. A pang of guilt hits me hard in the stomach.

"Just have a beer, all right?" Perez is already gesturing at the bartender.

"I'm good." I shake my head, putting my guard up even higher. "Don't think I've forgotten your drugging history."

"And you think I'm gonna drug you?" He lifts an amused brow. "Don't flatter yourself. I have nothing to gain from doing that." He notices that I'm still hesitant. "Fine, suit yourself." He shrugs, plucking his beer glass from the bar and taking a long, hard sip. I don't know what else to do other than watch as he turns the glass up and empties it out, alcohol dripping from the sides of his mouth. He's barely finished before he gestures to the bartender to get him another. Then he turns to face me. "So, what do you want to know?"

"Everything."

He lifts a finger up to give him a moment, slipping a hand into the pocket of his jeans and revealing a crumpled piece of paper. He lays it on the bar and smooths it out before sliding it over to me. Upon closer inspection, I realize it's a copy of some newspaper article.

He taps on the picture. "Recognize this man?"

I squint at the picture attached to the article. It's so dark in here that it's difficult to make out anything on the paper, but from what I can tell, the man in question looks like he's in his fifties. His size is massive, his square face grim with a tuft of graying hair on his head and a pair of haunted-looking black eyes. My mind draws a blank.

"No, I don't."

"His name is Charles. He's Jax's stepdad," he explains.

My eyes squint at the article again. "It says he was sentenced to six years in prison."

"Yep. Guess who put him there?"

"No," I breathe, bracing myself for what's next.

"Yes," Perez says, leaning back in his seat. "Like I said, Jax's lack of loyalty is a pattern of behavior."

So that was what Perez was referencing when we bumped into each other outside the warehouse.

Perez releases a deep sigh. "There used to be this fight club called Heavyweight. Years ago. Charles and a few other partners co-owned the place. The operation wasn't running on a big scale like Point, but the fights were just as savage, maybe more so. It was grimy, unsanctioned, bare-knuckle kinda bullshit, held at some cheap basement in Roxbury," he explains. "I'd been there once, but it wasn't my thing. But the one time I was there, I was watching, And I saw Jax."

"He fought there?" I prod.

"All the time."

I force the lump in my throat down.

It doesn't surprise me that Jax used to have a history with underground fighting before he joined up with Breaking Point. Someone like him doesn't just come out of nowhere and suddenly have the skills to take down a reigning champ.

"But back then, he didn't go by Jax," he explains. "He went by Jackson."

My heart sinks in my chest. *First I learn he put his stepdad in prison, and now I find out Jax isn't even his real name?*

"Heavyweight was where Jax got his start with underground fighting," Perez continues. "He was a kid then, and he wasn't half as good as he is now, but he had heart when he fought, and the guys in the club liked that. I don't think he ever missed a fight. And Charles always had a lot of money riding on him. Jax was his prime ticket to getting the big bucks. But after a while, I guess Jax got tired of Charles taking a cut of his earnings. He wanted more," he outlines, his mouth a grim line. "That got Charles pissed, because Charles felt like he made him, you know? Him and Jax got into a huge argument about it. Next fight comes around and surprise, surprise. Jax dips. Nobody knows where he's gone. And next thing you know, cops are flooding the joint and making arrests."

"So Jax sold everyone out?" I say with an audible gasp. I've been in the underground long enough to know that there may not be any rules, but there's still a code.

He shrugs coldly. "A rat's a rat. Some managed to escape. Others were held in lockup for the night. Can't hold the fighters on anything if it's mutual combat," he says with a pause. "The rest of the partners got off easy too. They had some connections in the BPD. So Charles became the scapegoat. He had piles of charges laid against him that night. Someone had tipped them off to drug possession and trafficking and battery and assault against a minor. I can only assume who that was. And those weren't Charles's first offenses, so the cops pulled out all the stops."

Christ. This is what I feared all along about Jax—that his ego and self-interest would follow him out of that cage and into the real world, where there are consequences.

I always pegged Jax as someone who is ruthless but still has integrity. If he could do something like this to his own stepfather . . .

I can't believe I'm in love with a man who would do such despicable things to the people he loves.

The thought sends an electric current of agitation and panic through me.

Perez takes a sip of his beer. "After what happened with Charles, Jackson stayed low for a couple years, then changed his name to Jax so nobody in the underground would make the connection. He was barely an adult anyway, so most people don't recognize him. The ones that do keep quiet because they are afraid of what he might do to them."

I purse my lips unhappily. "And what about Point?"

"What about them?"

"Do they know about Jax's history?"

A laugh shudders out of him, making a mockery of my question. "Do you think they *care*? He's too good of a fighter for them to throw away. You've seen the crowds he draws. He's too good for business." He rubs his thumb across the inside of his fingertips, the universal sign for *money talks.*

I thought the underground had strict rules when it came to vetting both fighters and spectators.

"I don't understand. I thought—"

"You think they have some moral code, that they stick to the integrity of MMA?" Perez barks out a laugh. "If I got paid each time some fucked-up shit went down in the underground, I wouldn't need to fight for a living anymore. Point may seem self-regulated, but they always bend their own rules as they see fit. That's why Damien's banned from the premises but I still get to see the fights. And if I play my cards right, I'll be back in that cage in no time."

I swallow hard, pressing my hands to my face to give myself a moment.

Holy shit.

Jax really is invincible in the underground. Maybe that's why he's never taken a real interest in MMA promotions and why he keeps going back to Point. In a real MMA cage, your odds are entirely up to you. In the underground, your odds can change based on what connections you have and whether you're good for business. It's fucked up.

The whole thing is fucked up.

"I fight real dirty in that cage. Everybody knows that," Perez says, looking me dead in the eye. "I took it too far last season. I get that. But I don't regret it. Jax deserved what he got. And I don't respect people who have no allegiance to anyone but themselves, especially when it comes at the expense of my brothers."

My whole body is trembling. I don't have any reason to

trust what Perez says, but deep down, I recognize some truth in the story that he's told. Jax's odd behavior comes into clearer focus now. Why he never likes to talk about his family. Why he keeps me at arm's length. Why he never really lets me in . . .

"This is a lot to take in," I breathe as I rest my elbows on the bar, pushing my hair back with my hands.

Perez nods, finishing the last of his beer. When he does, he wipes his mouth with the back of his arm and pushes himself off the stool. His gaze meets mine again, and there is a flash of sympathy in his eyes.

"A little advice, Sienna? Don't be so willing to stick around for him. If this is the kind of shit he'll go out of his way for you to never find out, I can only imagine what other things he'll be willing to hide from you," he says brutally, giving me a hard tap on the shoulder. "Thanks for the beer."

Perez grins then shoves his hands into his pockets and walks out of the bar without another word.

Goddammit.

I hear someone clearing their throat, and I whip around to find the bartender glaring after Perez. His arm then shoots toward me, palm up, demanding payment.

Swearing under my breath, I chuck him a ten, making sure to grab the article that Perez left on the bar, and head out.

TWENTY-FIVE

What. The. Fuck. Did. I. Just. Do?

It takes me over half an hour to calm down. I don't know where I'm going. I've walked past my apartment block three times now, working hard to get my anxiety levels down so I can be levelheaded about what I should do next.

Should I tell Jax what I know? But that would mean I'd have to explain *how* I know. And it'll turn into an argument about me breaking my word.

But I deserve to confront Jax. He broke his word first. He lied to me. He iced me out.

His real name isn't even Jax.

I squeeze my eyes shut, wishing all of this weren't true.

There were so many instances when he could have at least fessed up about his real name, but he didn't. So many instances when he could have come clean about Charles. *It's none of your concern*, he'd say. *It doesn't have anything to do with us.*

The fuck it doesn't.

I'm pissed off now. And hurt. I chose to love him after what he did to Perez because I thought deep down he was a good person. A good person who just has their bad days.

But that's not the case. He's greedy. He's selfish. He only thinks about how he can help himself and no one else.

I should feel bad about going behind his back. I should. But damn if I don't feel justified in doing it.

The article balled up in my hand is heavy with consequence. It's the physical proof of me breaking Jax's trust. I stop walking and open the crumpled paper again. I don't know why I expect something different every time I stare at this article. The title says, UNDERGROUND RING IN ROXBURY: 7 ARRESTED, 1 CHARGED. My eyes skim over the big picture on the side, accompanying the text. It's a close-up shot of Jax's stepdad's face, cold and flat as he gets handcuffed by the police.

I do a little digging into Charles on my phone. He gets out of prison next month. *Next month.* Surely Jax must know about that. Is that why he entered the underground this year after telling me he was going to quit? Was it all a twisted way of trying to exert some kind of power in his own life, knowing full well that there's a chance his stepdad might come looking for him?

I came to Perez looking to have my questions answered, but I left with a dozen more pinging in my head.

Should I wait it out before confronting Jax? I doubt I can. But I don't know what I want to do about it all yet. I should probably break up with him. Everyone seems to think I should, even before they knew how rotten he really is.

But I don't know if I'm brave enough to do it. A desperate part of me still clings to the hope that none of this is true, that this is just some elaborate ploy by Perez to get back at Jax and rip our relationship apart. And I'd be falling right into the trap.

I don't know I don't know I don't know.

My frantic pacing is interrupted by my phone buzzing with an incoming call. Panic sets in. Is it Jax? Does he know I met up with Perez? Is he calling to break up with me? I'm not ready to let go yet. I'm not—

I glance at my screen.

It's my sister.

Temporary relief flows through me. But the feeling evaporates when I remember that Beth doesn't usually call me anymore. Either she's suddenly in the mood to make up or something's wrong.

I pick up her call.

"Beth?" I whisper.

There's a long pause on her end.

"Beth—"

"Can we talk?" she blurts out.

"Uh, now's seriously not a good time."

"We really need to talk."

I press my lips together tightly. Dakota's voice drifts into my mind.

She misses you. Sometimes people don't like to admit that they're wrong.

"Please," Beth croaks out.

"Okay. Okay, fine." I yield. "What's going on?"

"Are you going to be home soon?" There's uneasiness in her voice.

"I'm downstairs right now. Why?"

"Hurry."

And then she hangs up.

I rush toward the lobby, taking the stairs two at a time until I reach the third floor. My heart goes into overdrive, fearing the absolute worst. Is she hurt? Did someone hurt her? Did *Perez*? I don't know if that would be possible, but I wouldn't put it past him to do something like that. If that dickwad lays a hand on my sister, I swear to God he'll never know peace again.

When I make it to my apartment door, I find Beth on the floor, her knees pulled up to her chest. It takes a moment for her to realize that I'm here. When she does, she slowly rises to her feet. Her eyes are puffy and her cheeks are red, dried tears staining her face.

My heart splits wide open.

"Beth . . ." I say, looking a little stumped. "What are you doing here? And why do you have your bags with you?"

"I had nowhere else to go. I had to get out of the house," she says. She appears anxious but in an exasperated way. The last time I saw her like this, we'd just found out Mom and Dad were getting divorced.

My eyes flutter closed briefly, fearing a similar situation has come up.

"Dad and Lorraine are separating, aren't they?" I whisper.

Slowly, she nods.

I suck in a breath. What my dad does no longer shocks me, but it still sucks every time something like this happens.

"Come on. Let's get you inside," I say, helping her with her bags. After some fiddling with the doorknob, I push the door open for her, letting her go in first. "First door on the left," I tell Beth. She nods again and walks in the direction of my room, and I follow behind her. I don't bring up the fact that we've barely talked in a year. It doesn't matter anymore.

All that matters is that my sister is back where she belongs. By my side.

***

"I shouldn't have left you with him. I should've taken you with me when I had the chance," I mutter when I bring Beth a steaming cup of tea to soothe her nerves. I pour myself a cup too to dispel some of my guilt about abandoning my little sister, but the feeling stays put even after a few sips of the chamomile blend.

We're both cooped up in my room for some privacy. My roommates all know that my sister's staying in the apartment, but they don't know why, and the last thing I want is for them to walk in on us in the living room while we're talking.

Beth's still a little shaken but insists she's fine. She grabs the cup with both hands and sits cross-legged on my bed. Her hair is still damp from the shower she took, falling past her shoulders in thick, curly blond strands, droplets of water sinking into her seaweed-green tank top.

"Si, it's okay," she says, waving me off. "It's not your fault."

"But it's my responsibility to take care of you. I shouldn't have left it up to Dad," I insist, too agitated to sit down on the bed with her. I pace back and forth, the mug still in my hands. "He's always been a scumbag. You'd think he'd have mellowed out by now with his third marriage. But *nooooo*," I stretch the last syllable out. "Honestly, I don't know why you keep giving him so many chances."

Dad has already made it clear he's not the type to stick around when things go south. Sometimes, I do pity these women when this happens because they all end up so madly in love with him. I wonder if they get into these crazy, whirlwind relationships with him despite knowing about his shitty behavior and just choosing to ignore it. I doubt all of them are that naive, given the massive state of their finances and their interest in protecting them.

I just feel bad that Beth always has to get caught in the midst of these separations. I've learned from my mom and dad's divorce to stay far away when shit hits the fan. It's too emotionally draining for me, and the heartache is never worth it.

"I don't exactly have a choice, Si. I'm not financially independent like you," she mumbles, staring down at her lap.

"But you're graduating soon. Which means you'll be free to do whatever you want. So you can stay with me."

"In this room?" Her voice is wary.

"It's big enough for us," I say, my hands gesturing around the space. "I have a double bed, a decent-size closet, and a window—we'll be able to make do. It's only temporary anyway. My lease is ending soon, and I don't think I'm gonna renew it."

"You're moving out? Why?"

"Roommate drama. Among other things." I decide to keep the friendship politics vague because if I start talking about it, we'll be up for hours. There are far more important things to worry about.

Beth purses her lips, looking at me with concern. "Have you talked to Mom about you moving out?"

"No," I say, pushing my hair back with a hand and staring

at my feet. "I don't have any concrete plans yet, and I don't want her to worry."

"Still . . ." Beth lets her voice trail off. "She told me you haven't talked in a while. She feels like you don't need her anymore."

"I feel like she doesn't need me anymore," I say miserably.

It's true that I haven't been keeping in contact with my mom. I'm well aware it's my fault. I love my mom fiercely, and I enjoy talking to her, but getting glimpses of her new life always makes me sad about her leaving her old one.

"Of course she needs you. You are needed much more than you think." Beth frowns, tugging on my arm, forcing me to sit beside her. There's a long pause before she adds, more quietly, "I need you, even when I don't like to admit it."

My heart lurches in my chest. I didn't know that was what I needed to hear from my sister until I heard it, and now my insides feel all warm and fuzzy.

"I thought you said before you didn't wanna talk anymore," I say, fiddling with the edge of my top.

"I said I didn't want to be as close as we used to be. I didn't say I never wanted to talk again." Beth leans forward, away from the pillows, and pulls her knees toward her chest, hugging them. "But I was stupid. I let my crush on Jax get in the way of us. And now I'm mad that I wasn't there for you."

"I'm mad I wasn't there for you," I reply back.

She laughs. It's a sound that I thought I'd never get to hear again.

"Can we please be okay again?" I say. "Please?"

Beth breaks into a smile. "Yeah, of course we can."

I rope her into a hug, longing for a physical reminder

that things between us are finally okay again. She clings to my shoulders, her cheek pressed against my chest. I miss her warmth. She's a ray of sunshine melting away the gloominess inside me.

When Beth pulls away, she looks at me with a world of questions.

"So, if you're not staying here anymore, where are you staying?" she probes. "At Jax's?"

At the mention of my boyfriend, I can feel myself sinking deeper into the bed.

"No. I'm not gonna be staying there."

"Why not? He already has a place."

"It's . . . complicated." I feel my chest tightening at the words.

Beth senses something is wrong because her next question is, "You guys are still together, right?"

"Yeah. We are," I say, and I decide to leave it at that. The last thing I want to do right now is to pull her into my relationship drama. It's too messy and complicated, and I still haven't made a decision about whether to confront him about his stepdad yet. I throw out the first excuse that comes to mind. "We're just not in a place to move in together yet." Technically, not a lie. "But I was thinking of getting a studio," I add on, scooting closer so my shoulder bumps against one of her knees. "You got accepted into BU, right? Maybe you prefer the dorms, for that full college experience, but if you wanna move in with me, we can look for a bigger place."

Beth hums in contemplation. "I don't know. I'll have to ask Dad about moving out."

She's worried about the money. It's not like Dad can't afford any kind of housing she wants. It's a matter of whether he wants to. With me constantly being in and out of the picture, he'd do anything to keep his favorite daughter in close proximity.

"No. You don't. You don't have to ask for his permission anymore. Or his money," I say. "I'll pay for rent and utilities."

"For both of us? Can you afford that?"

"Yeah, I can. I have money saved up," I explain to her. "I also just got a job as an MMA trainer, so that's going to pay well."

"I don't know, Si. I can't let you take care of everything." Beth chews on her cheek, and for a moment, a kernel of fear settles into my stomach, thinking I'm going to lose her again. She takes a couple of seconds to think, and then eventually she says, "I guess I can look for a part-time job once I graduate. That'll probably help ease the burden on our expenses."

"So is that a yes? You're moving in with me?" I ask, my voice hopeful.

"Yeah," she says, smiling, "I guess I am."

"Oh my God," I say, not quite believing it myself. "That's awesome!"

We hug and squeal and smile and hug some more until we're both giddy with excitement. Beth lets out a wonderful, dizzying laugh and falls back onto the pillows, looking up at the ceiling. I join her, plopping my head down and staring at her with anticipation.

"I can't believe this is happening. Holy shit," Beth says, covering her mouth with a gasp. "We'll finally have a place to ourselves."

"Yeah. It's kind of perfect," I say, my happiness mirroring hers. With all the craziness that's been going on in my life, it's nice to finally have something to look forward to.

Beth turns to me, and her face is painted with gratitude.

"Thanks, Si," she says with the biggest smile on her face. "I'll be the best roommate ever. I promise. You won't regret this."

TWENTY-SIX

As expected, Dad isn't too happy about Beth wanting to move out, but there isn't much he can do to talk her out of it. He calls me up and basically accuses me of being a bad influence on her, to which I counter that he's the one pushing Beth away in the first place. And when he says that there is no way he's going to pay for our rent, I proudly assert that one way or another, we are going to make our own way without him. He has nothing much to say after that, and I hang up, too worked up to say anything else.

I decide to put all my remaining energy into apartment hunting. During my spare time over the next week, Beth and I tour some apartments in various neighborhoods, hoping to find a place that's within our budget. We manage to find a cheap unit; it's a forty-minute walk from campus, which is further than I would have liked, but it is the best option for affordability and safety in the city.

The next two weeks are spent settling our paperwork and getting everything ready for the big move. Between putting in my hours at UFG, wrapping up the semester, and moving, I barely have time to think about Jax. We haven't talked since I met up with Perez. I decided it was better to ignore his messages while I figure out what to do about what I know. But really, there hasn't been any figuring out at all. When thoughts of him begin to trickle into my mind, I shove them as far away as I can, not wanting to go down that rabbit hole of anger and hurt. Everything about Jax is messy and tumultuous. And after patching things up with Beth and getting ready for the move, for the first time, things are starting to look up.

My phone buzzes with yet another incoming message. I groan, moving the box so it balances on my hip, and then use my free hand to swipe my phone from my pocket. So far, I've tallied Jax's attempts to contact me up to twenty-nine missed calls and seventeen messages.

Where are you now?

Are you mad at me for something?

You tryna get back at me for what happened during the finals?

Come on. This is unfair.

I thought we were over that. I apologized.

Fine. Let's talk it out.

Call me, please. I miss you.

I miss him, I really do. And I could very well see him if I wanted to.

But I'm scared shitless of seeing him. Because if I do, there's a big chance that I'll ignore all the red flags that Perez rightfully pointed out; I might just fall back into his arms and never leave. The power Jax has over me is so potent that sometimes I don't know how to function without being all wrapped up in it.

"God, it's so hot in here. Can you turn up the AC?" Beth moans as she pushes a box through the doorway of our new apartment. The early signs of summer are beginning to wear us down, coating our skin with sweat as we haul boxes into the living room.

"Temperature's already at its lowest, Beth," I say, stacking the box I'm holding on top of another one labeled, ALL SHOES... EXCEPT FOR ONE. LITERALLY ONE SHOE. Definitely Beth's box. She's got way too many pairs to keep track of.

Beth pushes another box into the living room and makes a frustrated noise. She stands up, placing her hands on her hips, breathing heavily through her mouth to catch her breath. "There's way too many boxes."

I cock my head sideways. "And whose fault is that?"

Of the boxes that we have, two-thirds of them belong to Beth. I specifically told her there was no way her entire wardrobe would fit in her new closet, but she insisted on bringing all of her clothes from Dad's place. I've accepted the fact that she'll be taking up most of my closet space too.

"I'm gonna start bringing stuff into my room," Beth declares, shoving her hands under the box she laid on the floor and waddling in the direction of her room.

"If you need help with the bigger boxes, call me," I yell down the hallway before I start cutting into the boxes in the living room with a pair of scissors. There's a lot of them to get through, so I might as well start now.

"How rude of you girls to have a moving-in day and not

invite me." A deep voice travels from the front door of the apartment. I whip around, surprised to find Jax sauntering into the living room in a casual manner, hands shoved deep into his pockets. He frowns when he inspects the place, disapproving of the rental choice. I drop the scissors on the floor and let out a big sigh, annoyance climbing up my body.

"What are you doing here?" I demand.

"Visiting my girlfriend at her new place," Jax says as he walks over toward me, then gives me a look, like he's daring me to voice if I have a problem with that.

"How did you get the address?"

"I went over to your old apartment, and Lori gave it to me. I gotta say, she's starting to warm up to me."

"You could've just texted."

"Like you would've replied?"

My lips press together tightly. He's waiting for me to say something, but the last thing I want to do right now is to get into an argument with him while we're in the midst of a big move. That's the whole reason I didn't want to invite him here in the first place.

"Sienna, have you seen my bed frame—" Beth emerges from the hallway and stops in her tracks when she realizes I'm not alone in the living room. Her eyes light up in recognition. "Oh, hey, Jax." She immediately straightens herself up, her mouth pulling into a sweet, demure smile. "I, uh, didn't know you were joining us today."

"Hey," Jax says, giving her a glance. His gaze roams her from head to toe. He returns to her face, and they lock eyes for a moment longer than they should. "You look . . . really good today, Beth."

"I do? Really?" Beth peers down at her outfit: a baby pink tank top and a pair of cycling shorts paired with retro sneakers. Her blond hair is swept into a rather unkempt braid, with strands of hair poking out from the plait. She looks back up at him, smiling sheepishly. "I look like a sweaty mess."

"You're fine." The corners of Jax's lips lift. He leans a casual hand on the wall, flipping his attention to her. "I heard you're going to BU in the fall. What're you studying?"

"Costume production," she says shyly, like she's embarrassed at the choice, even though she's got no reason to be. "I like fashion, so I figured why not."

"It suits you," he remarks, strolling over toward her. I don't know why it bothers me so much that he didn't stay beside me. "Maybe you can make me a new robe one day," he suggests. "Been thinking of upgrading my gear."

Beth's expression lights up. "Yeah. I can definitely help you with that."

"Great," Jax says, pleased. "Bed frame, you said?" She nods, and he goes out to the hallway outside the apartment, brushing past me in an unbothered way. He hauls the huge rectangular block into the apartment with minimal effort, corded muscles flexing in his arms and neck as he does. "You want it in your room, right?"

"Yeah," Beth says, playing with her hair. "I'll need some help installing the whole thing. You think you can lend me a hand?"

"Sure. I'd love to," he chirps brightly.

What the hell are you playing at, Jax?

"*Jax*," I say warningly instead.

"What?" He pretends to look innocent. "You'll be fine on your own, I'm sure."

He quirks a challenging brow then turns his back on me, tailing my sister to her room.

***

By the time we're done unpacking all the boxes, it's past dinner. Jax gets us some takeout, and the three of us end up eating around the tiny coffee table since our dining table is still cluttered with ripped-up packing materials and miscellaneous items that we haven't sorted out yet.

I let Jax and Beth take charge of the conversation. As soon as Jax mentions something about MMA, Beth chimes in with an opinion about the latest UFC fight, which catches me off guard, since I wasn't aware she's become a fan of the sport. I stay quiet throughout, my gaze ping-ponging between them, worried that their common interest might turn into something more. The thought continues to stab at my brain as Jax offers to help Beth with dishwashing duty, his hip bumping against hers every time he reaches over to her side to place the freshly cleaned dishes on the drying rack.

Later that night, while I'm arranging the towels in the bathroom, Jax appears. He crosses his arms over his massive chest and leans against the doorframe, watching me slide the folded towels underneath the sink and shut the cabinet door with my foot. I pick up my dirty clothes that I wore in the afternoon and turn in his direction. I purse my lips into a low frown, waiting for him to say something. His Adam's apple bobs in his throat.

"You look nice today," Jax says.

I huff. "Come on, I'm sure you can do better than that. If I recall, your words to my sister were more complimentary."

"It was an innocent compliment," he deadpans.

"Nothing about you is innocent, Jax." I push past him to get into my room.

"What's that supposed to mean?"

"It means . . ." I shove the pile of clothes into the laundry bag a little too hard and swing back in his direction. "You were hitting on my sister, you fucking asshole, to get back at me for not texting you back."

He shakes his head in disagreement. "I was not hitting on your sister."

"Really?" I rest a hand on my hip. "Because it looked a lot like you were trying to get a reaction out of me."

"I don't know what you're on about. I was just being nice to her."

"Can't you be nice in a *friendly* way?" I snap. "What the fuck is wrong with you?"

Jax's jaw sets into a hard line. "What's it to you, anyway? It's not like you've been acting like a girlfriend recently."

"Wow. Okay. So just because I haven't been a good girlfriend, you want to *punish* me by seducing Beth instead?"

"I wasn't trying to seduce her. *Fuck!*" Jax slams a fist against the bedroom door, and I flinch. He hisses out a breath between his teeth, his chest heaving out the anger he's clearly been holding in ever since he stepped foot into the apartment. His head tilts toward me questioningly. "Why haven't we been talking, Sienna? I said I was sorry for what happened in the underground. And now you're giving me the cold shoulder?

Why are you trying to be spiteful now when things are back on track with us?"

"I've been busy," I mumble.

"Cut the bullshit. What's this really about?"

I rip my gaze away from Jax. My heart is beating so wildly, exacerbated by the guilt I've been carrying for the past three weeks. Maybe now's the time to tell him. I can't keep pretending everything's fine between us.

"I talked to Perez," I say softly. "And he told me everything about your stepdad."

Shock slams into Jax.

"You talked to Perez?" he echoes, baffled. "After I told you not to?"

"Yes." I'm surprised I say it with so much courage.

A muscle twitches in his jaw as he allows the one word to sink into his brain. He doesn't speak for a moment as he paces around my room, the silence slowly choking me as I wait for him to say something. *Anything*.

"What did he tell you?" he asks quietly. Carefully.

"He talked about Charles. How you fought for him in a fight club. And how you sold him out, along with everyone in that club, just so you could carve your own path in the underground," I say, gripping the edge of my vanity table with my hands behind me. "It's true, isn't it? What he said?"

Jax shakes his head.

"It's not true."

"Which part? All of it? None of it?" I demand. He doesn't answer. It aggravates me further, so I keep pushing his buttons. "You know what he said to me, Jax? He said your name isn't even your real name. Your name is *Jackson*. That's ridiculous, right?" I probe, hoping to God that Perez was wrong about that at least. Because if I don't even know my boyfriend's name, then what the hell am I doing with him?

But upon hearing that name, Jax's eyes spark. In anger, but also in recognition.

"Don't call me that."

The acknowledgment of his name stops my breath.

Oh my God. It's true.

My entire relationship is a lie.

The man I've been dating for nearly two years is a liar.

I must seem destroyed because the next thing I know, Jax is shuffling toward me carefully, pleading at me with his eyes to give him a chance to explain.

"Sienna," he says carefully, "wait—"

"Oh my God, who *are* you?" I retreat from him, tone dripping with disgust. He comes at me again, but I shove my hands against his chest, pushing him backward. He nearly collides with the side of my dresser. "You're a fucking *liar*, Jax! You *lied* to me!"

"Stop it!" Jax grabs my wrists, holding me captive. I refuse to look at him. I'm crying now, fat tears clouding my vision and rolling down my cheeks. "I didn't lie to you. Jax is my real name. I changed it legally. I saw no reason to tell you that because Jackson no longer exists. He is a long-forgotten piece of the past, and I want it to stay that way."

"He's in the past? Really?" I want to scoff at the absurdity of his statement. "Because I heard that your past is going to catch up to you real soon, with your stepdad getting out of prison now. And I don't know what's going to happen, but I doubt he took lightly the fact that you put him in there in the first place."

Again, Jax doesn't answer. His jaw is clamped so tight that if he holds on a little longer, it will likely shatter. Well, I fucking hope it does.

"How could I have been so stupid?" I rasp. "Everything everyone has ever said about you is right. Julian. Dakota. Damien. Perez. You truly have no loyalty to anyone but yourself."

"Are you kidding? I've stayed by your side for almost two years now, and *I'm still here*. Still fighting for you. So don't tell me I have no loyalty."

"Your loyalty is conditional. It doesn't come with anything good. The second I ask you for more, you run the other fucking way," I retort. "If you really loved me, I wouldn't have needed to jump through hoops to find out what I now know about you."

"*If* I loved you?" He gapes.

"Yes, *if*. Because you don't love me. I don't think you ever did to begin with," I say, my words cracking in the same way my heart does. "You shut me out when things get hard or uncomfortable. You don't call or visit unless you're craving attention. You don't even *tell* me that you love me anymore. Or if you do, it's completely half-assed. And I always make excuses for you in my head, you know. *Oh, maybe he's not in the mood to say it. Maybe he's tired. Maybe he's just winded from training.* But I know better now. Those excuses are only there to make me feel better," I croak out. Jax just stares at me, mouth hanging open like he doesn't know what to say. "You went after me because I was the only girl who rejected all your advances, and you were all for the chase. Now that you've finally had your hands on me, you don't want any of the hard stuff that comes with a relationship. And not only have you consistently kept me out of nearly every aspect of your life, but you *lied* to me about it!"

"For the last time: I didn't lie!"

"You *lied*. And I had to pry the truth out of Perez, of all people!"

"And you think Perez is such a reliable source? Perez, who would do anything to get one final jab at me? You really believe him over me?"

"He was right about your real name, so it wouldn't be too far of a stretch to think that he's telling the truth about everything else."

"His perspective is skewed."

"So is yours! And I'm more inclined to believe him than *you*!"

"Wow," Jax breathes. "You're not even gonna let me explain myself?"

"Why should I?" I bite back, my mind already made up. "You're just going to feed me even more bullshit."

He grits his teeth, seething. I wish I wasn't accustomed to his anger by now, but sadly, I am.

"Fine," he snarls. "If that's what you want, then go ahead. *Make me a villain.* I don't care. But don't think for one second your hands are clean. You crossed a line when you went to Perez."

"Only because *you made me!*" I yell out, my body trembling hard with anger. I don't care if that was loud enough for Beth to hear. I don't care if the entire apartment block hears me. I'm done trying to contain my emotions. "I didn't have a choice, Jax. Don't stand there and say I didn't try with you. I did, but you chose to shut me out. I didn't know what else to do."

"*No*," he says through clenched teeth, "you don't get to blame this all on me. Take some goddamned responsibility, Sienna. Ever since I met you, you've been blaming other people for your own problems. Your parents, Dakota, your sister. All of them. You think they each have a vendetta against you and that you're an innocent victim in your own life. Guess what? It's all in your fucking head. You're just as bad as the rest of them. You just don't want to admit it because dodging responsibility is second nature to you."

"Says the guy who taught me how to dodge responsibility in the first place," I scoff. "When have you taken responsibility for the hurt you put me through, huh? When have you ever taken responsibility for what you did to your stepdad all those years ago? There was never a time in your life when you ever admitted you were wrong. Fighters fight for a cause, you know. You only fight to serve your own ego."

"Oh? And your cause is so innocent?" He marches up to me, making his displeasure known. His body is threatening as he makes his way over to me. "Fighting because you think it'll solve everything in your life? Admit it: you do it to fill some huge, empty hole in your heart, to distract yourself from the fact *you* are the one who pushes people away, not the other way around. And now you're doing the exact same thing with me."

"At least with you, I know that there's a chance my life will be better without you in it." My voice is firm, ringing with reassurance.

I don't know where I've found the bravery to say that. Must have been the little voice in my head that goes, *Fuck fear.* That phrase used to convince me to jump into something scary and new with Jax, but now it's telling me to step away from him. For good.

And I do, when I find my feet moving my body away from his massive, controlling presence.

"I'm done making excuses for you," I proclaim. "You lied to me. And you will continue to lie to me. One day, I'll be drowning in so many lies that I won't be able to recognize myself anymore."

Jax inhales a sharp breath. It's clear he didn't anticipate things going south the way they have. And to be honest, neither did I.

But the point of moving day was supposed to be a fresh start—away from my dad, my old roommates, anyone that was holding me back.

Perhaps Jax belongs with them.

"I want you to leave," I say quietly.

Jax's eyebrows shoot up.

"What?"

"I want you to *leave*, Jax." Tears prickle in my eyes again, but I hold them at bay because I don't want to cry in front of him a second time. He doesn't deserve to see me fall apart for him again.

Jax clenches his teeth together, contemplating. He retreats toward the door and grabs a hold of the doorknob, then turns to me again.

"Is this really what you want?" he whispers.

No, I don't, my heart screams. *I love you. I don't care who you are, Jax, I love you, please don't go—*

"Yes. Leave. Now."

He swallows hard then looks at me one last time and breaks my fucking heart.

"Have it your way, then," he says with finality.

And when he wrenches the door open and slams it shut behind him, I fall apart.

***

Half an hour after Jax leaves, Beth appears at my doorway in her pajamas. Her lips are closed into a thin, grim line as her eyes gaze over at me in pity. I've lost count of the number of times I've been given that look by someone because of how Jax has hurt me.

"I heard," Beth whispers.

My stomach plunges into a new wave of misery.

"Everything?" I sniff.

"Most things," she whispers. "Are you guys broken up?"

"I don't know. It feels like it," I choke out, and she rushes to my side, sliding her arms around me and pulling me in for a tight hug. I'm sobbing so hard that my tears drench her shirt, but she holds me tighter anyway, allowing the tears to consume us both.

I've never felt this much pain before. Every time I feel like I've hit my pain threshold, I get flooded with another wave of misery.

I'm living my worst fucking nightmare.

"I think you should call Mom," Beth says after a while.

I shake my head. I'm crying so hard that I doubt I'd even be able to form a proper sentence.

"Not . . . tonight." My chest heaves, and I wonder if she knows what I'm saying. "But . . . I will."

Beth doesn't say anything. She just nods and holds me in her arms until the daylight arrives and my body is limp and dried out from all the tears I've cried.

TWENTY-SEVEN

I haven't heard from Jax since the day he left our apartment.

I should feel relieved. It has been difficult enough holding myself together lately. I'm not sure how I'll react if I see his name light up my phone screen. At the same time, I can't help but wonder if the reason he's not texting me is not because he respects my decision but because it's that easy for him to let go of me.

There is a constant ache in my chest that is impossible to get rid of. No amount of sleep or work or distractions makes it go away. Even Julian is starting to get worried. My first week on the job as an MMA trainer and I was already blowing it. I couldn't seem to do anything right. I'd last thirty seconds coaching before my thoughts wandered to Jax and I'd get emotional about him all over again. Eventually, I had to get another trainer to take over some of my sessions for the week because there was no way I could function in a professional setting. It was humiliating.

I don't understand why I'm feeling so broken when I was the one who told Jax to leave. I was the one who made it clear that he had no more space in my life after he lied about everything.

And yet, *I'm* the one who's left an absolute wreck.

I should at least feel at peace with my decision. Telling him to go was the most logical, clearheaded decision I've made since getting together with him.

But I'm not sure if I'm really at peace. When I told him to leave, I just wanted the pain of loving him to be gone. But if anything, the pain has intensified.

Was that night just a setback, or does it mean we're broken up forever? Which one do I even want it to be?

After work today, I decide not to return to the apartment. I was so excited about the place before, but now that my room is tainted with the scars of my biggest argument with Jax to date, I don't want to relive it again by being in there. It's a shame because I've only been living there for two weeks.

And as much as I love Beth, I can't see her right now because she'll look at me like I'm some wounded puppy in desperate need of Mommy's love, and I'm not in the mood to be coddled right now.

I need some tough love.

Somehow, I find myself back on campus. It's a Friday night, so there are students mingling about, carrying six-packs and chattering loudly amongst themselves. I somehow wind up on the west side of campus at Sleeper Hall, banging on Dakota's door to let me in.

"In a minute!" she yells, her voice muffled by the door as she shuffles around her room. When she peels open the door, she takes one good look at my face and sighs deeply, like she already knows why I'm here.

"You were right about Jax, Dee. All of it," I whisper.

I don't know why I expect an *I told you so* to come out of her then, even though Dakota is the last person to rub it in my face like that, unless she knew I was capable of handling it.

She just holds the door open wider for me.

"Come in. You want a beer? Or five?" she offers.

"As many as you can give me until I forget," I say.

"You got it."

***

Seven beers later, I'm hammered as fuck, but I've never felt more alive.

"I'm never dating an underground fighter again!" I blast out drunkenly, the bottle of Corona swinging violently in my hand, making a few splashes over Dakota's desk. She lives in a suite, which means privacy, but it also means that drunk me thinks that I have a license to be as loud and annoying as I want, prancing around like it's a private room in a nightclub.

I'm not usually a heavy drinker. I don't like what alcohol did to my dad when I was younger, so I don't feel drawn to it in the way that most other college students are. But tonight is an exception. Tonight, I'm determined to throw all my rules out the window.

Dakota laughs, reaching up to snatch the Corona from my hand and setting it down on the desk. "Are you sure about that?"

"Yep. Fighters are too much drama. So not worth the

pain," I groan, hopping off her bed and plopping down beside her on the floor, bouncing hard upon impact. I sling an arm around her to pull her close, mushing her face beside mine. "Promise me if you ever break up with Trevor, you're never gonna date a fighter, Dee. I'll make that promise with you."

She laughs, peeling herself off me. "That's a tall order. You work as an MMA trainer. I'm not gonna make that promise with you because you're definitely gonna break it."

"You're being ridiculous. I never break my promises. My promise is gonna start *now*," I say, going over to her fridge and picking out another Corona, despite there still being a half-full bottle sitting on the desk. I bump the cap open against the corner of the desk and take a huge swig of it.

Dakota's eyes trace every drunken movement of mine. She swipes her beer off the desk and brings it to her lips, watching me with worry.

I don't want her to worry. I'm fine.

"So it's really over with you and Jax, then?" she asks, frowning.

"I don't know. Maybe . . . it feels like it," I say miserably. Despite the fuzziness in my brain, I can feel the pain as it wends its way through my chest again. I set the Corona down and grip the desk with both hands, taking in deep breaths to manage the sharpness.

She smooths a hand over my back. "Are you okay?"

The pain in my chest doesn't ease. I inhale and exhale again.

"God, Dee. It hurts," I choke out. "It really fucking *hurts*."

"I know, Si. I'm sorry."

"I wanna bawl my eyes out again, but I don't think there's any tears left in me to cry out."

"Good. Cuz he's so not worth crying over," she tells me, her expression sparking with anger. "He spent nearly two years lying his ass off to you, Si. That's two years of your life you're never gonna get back. Hell, I'm pissed off for you."

"Thank you!" I slur, my hands flying toward her in an exaggerated manner. "I'm pissed off for me too!"

Dakota has a hard time fighting a smile. I realize it's been far too long since we've hung out like this—just me and her. Usually, there's some kind of drama that gets in the way of our fun.

"You know what? The hell with this. We're not gonna spend our Friday night holed up in my room, drinking in mourning," she says with finality, snatching her keys and her purse. Then she grabs my hand, pulling me in the direction of the door. "We're gonna get shit-faced and tear this fucking city up until you forget about Jax. Now, you can say no, but—"

"Fine, you've convinced me!" I shriek.

She laughs, and I willingly let her pull me along, making sure to grab another two Coronas on the way out.

***

By midnight, we've already been in and out of two dive bars, and we're on our way to a third one in the north end, which Dakota convinced me is going to be a good one since it's a hot spot for some of the hockey guys. Dakota is so hammered after downing four Jäger bombs at the last bar that when she ordered us our Uber, she accidentally got us a limousine rather than a regular five-seater. I'm not complaining: there's a nice sunroof at the back and enough room to dance around in. I make Dakota plug her Spotify into the car speaker and play Lily Allen's "Fuck You" on repeat. Dakota suggests we tweak the chorus lyrics and sing the new version out loud to all of Boston.

"Fuck Jax, fuck him *very, very muchhhh*!" Dakota screams drunkenly as she sticks her head out of the sunroof. I laugh so hard that beer comes out of my nostrils. She ducks down and sends me a deathly glare. "I *swear to God*, Sienna, if you don't do this with me, I will *whack you across your stupid, stubborn little head*!"

"All right, all right!" I say, getting to my feet and squeezing into the tiny space at the top. The wind whips at my blond hair, scratching my face with the loose strands, and I push them away laughingly, enjoying the feeling of tearing through the streets.

"Fuck you, Jax!" Dakota yells, cupping her mouth with her hands to amplify her voice.

"Fuck you, Jax!" I scream until my voice comes out all thin and scratchy. *"Fuck you!"*

"Fuck you!" Dakota yells, shoving two middle fingers in the air. Both of us roar with laughter.

We float in the wind as the limo breezes us through the city, our hands flying high and our voices belting out every pop song of the early 2000s like we're the main characters of a rom-com. I missed feeling high and free like this, like nothing could ever weigh me down. When I was with Jax, he was my anchor. But not only did he ground me, he made sure I could never fly without him.

I proved him wrong. Because here I am. Soaring like never before.

Fuck him.

Fuck him for wasting my *goddamned time.*

I invested so much into this relationship. *So* much. Nearly two years of my life I've lived and breathed for this man. I gave him everything. I gave him my whole life. And he dares to throw all that effort back in my face? Who does he think I am? Does he think I'll just sit quietly and take it?

He called me a hurricane once. A swirling, raging storm that's going to reset the whole world.

Well, I'm going to show him.

Every bone in my body burns with wild, barely contained anger. The limo races through familiar streets, the ones I used to walk to get to Jax's apartment, and I clench my fists, allowing my spine to straighten up.

"Stop the car," I order the driver.

Dakota's hair whips back in a frenzy. "Why?"

"We're not far from his place. Just a couple blocks, probably."

"What? Whose place?"

"Stop the car!" I yell, ducking down from the sunroof and moving up to the front of the limo. The driver pulls over at the curbside, and I wrench the door open, hopping out.

And then I just start running.

"Sienna! Wait!" Dakota screams.

I cross the street while the light's still on red, narrowly avoiding a truck as it barrels past me at full speed. The driver pops his head out of his window and yells a flurry of insults, honking at me with rage. He doesn't stop until I've reached the other side of the street. I don't look back to see if Dakota is following me. She probably is, most likely confused and terrified for me. But she shouldn't be. The anger and the alcohol may still be fizzing in my body, but I've never felt more clearheaded in my life.

I'm full-on sprinting now, a little surprised at how fast I can run with so much beer speeding through my veins. Jax's building grows closer and closer in my peripheral vision until I can see his apartment block from here. I count floors until I spot his unit. The light is on; the curtains are closed, but they're translucent enough for me to see some fleeting movement.

"Hey, Jackson! Jax! Whoever the *hell* you are!" I wave my hands above my head like a maniac, as if he can see me so far below him. *"Fuck you!"*

Like an idiot, I wait to see if he hears me.

He doesn't, and it spurs my anger even more.

"Look what you've done to me!" I yell at him some more. The couple walking past me on the sidewalk give me a dirty look, but I ignore them. My gaze fixates itself on Jax's window, my neck straining so hard it's starting to hurt. My hands cup the sides of my mouth, hoping it'll amplify my voice. "Come down and face me, you fucking coward! *Come on!*"

"Sienna!" Dakota screams from the opposite side of the street, nearly breathless. "What in God's name are you *doing*?"

"You told me to get angry." I grit my teeth, turning to face her. "Well, this is me going nuclear."

"Sienna, don't you dare—"

I tune her out. I tune out everything but the devilish little voice in my head that orders me to get inside that building and wreak some havoc on Jax. I slip inside the building, walking past the concierge as I trail a resident into the elevator and punch in Jax's floor. My mind is buzzing from all the words I'm dying to say.

Look at how you've ruined me, I want to tell him. *I was fine before you came along. I was thriving. And now look at me! You did this! You and your selfishness and your lies!*

We're really over this time, I imagine myself screaming straight to his face. *We're over, and it's ALL YOUR FAULT!*

The words are all bottled up, ready to launch from my throat the second I reach his door. My heart leaps in anticipation when the elevator opens onto Jax's floor, and I step out. My legs wobble a little when I do, nearly giving out, but I grab a hold of the walls in the nick of time to steady myself.

Whoa. I guess I'm really not as sober as I think.

Doesn't matter. This is still what I want, I think to myself, puffing my chest out, gaining confidence with every step as I approach his apartment. *This is payback for what he's done to me. This is how I want it to end. On my terms. This is—*

Wrong.

A terrible feeling plunges deep into my stomach, forcing the wind out of my lungs, when my gaze zeroes in on the door that's been left ajar.

Something's wrong.

I stop a few feet away, holding in a nervous shudder. I squint again. Yep, I'm seeing it right. The metal door handle appears to have been bent in a rather awkward way, like somebody has broken into the place.

My body immediately spurs into action. I keep my guard up as I slowly inch closer to the door, ready to fight off an intruder if it comes down to it. Maybe Jax isn't at home right now, so he's unaware that he's been robbed. Besides, what are the odds that the thieves are still around?

A crashing sound escaping through the open door causes my body to flinch.

Pretty damn high.

What sounds like a person crashing hard against a table, followed by the sound of ribs cracking, fills the air, forcing me to reevaluate my theory. I brace myself against the wall beside the doorway, ears straining to catch any sign of who's inside. And then I hear it. Two voices—one belonging to Jax, the other a deeper, older voice that I don't recognize.

"I'm a little disappointed, Jackson. I thought you were going to put up more of a fight. Looks like all those years of being in the underground did jack shit for you," the unknown man says in a drawl that makes it hard to tell if he is drunk or not. "I told you when I got out, I was coming for your ass. And *this* is the fight you give me? You owe me better than that."

"The only thing I owe you is a fucking beatdown for the shit you put me through," I hear Jax retort.

My thoughts muddle together, absorbing what is happening. I brave a peek through the gap, pushing the door open a little more.

That's when I see them. Jax is bracing himself against the sofa as he struggles to push himself onto his feet. A much older, graying man watches him with amusement. His back is toward me, but his face turns ever so slightly to the right, and a flash of two sharp slits, yellow staining the whites of his eyes, stuns me into recognition.

His size is what strikes me the most. I thought Jax was big, but this man towers over him, the large muscles of his back straining against the fabric of his white shirt. It appears that he put his prison time to good use.

My heart leaps into my mouth in fear.

"The shit *I* put you through?" Charles's shock manifests in a sharp laugh. "You had it easy, boy, you have no idea. You didn't have to spend six years behind bars after being ratted out by your own *son*."

"*Stepson*," Jax corrects, holding his ground. "I've never been a son of yours."

"Well, in that case, this will be easy for me to do." He cracks his knuckles like he's preparing to throw down again.

Jax's fists clench on either side of him. "I am *not* scared of you."

Charles's head cocks to the side in amusement. "Then why are your hands trembling?"

Jax gulps hard. For the first time, bone-chilling fear penetrates his expression.

I feel the elation of the alcohol in my bloodstream fizzling out.

With a yell, Charles charges recklessly at Jax. Jax is on the defensive, deftly blocking Charles's throws. He narrowly evades a right elbow to the temple, sneering as he comes up to face his stepdad again, only to be met with a mean left hook that causes him to lose his footing and stumble back.

Fists collide in the air, with Jax's once-strong defense crumbling before my eyes at the sheer strength behind Charles's punches. Another hook to the face later and Jax stumbles to the ground, which is all Charles needs to get on top of Jax and trap him underneath him. I've never seen Jax struggle like this before. Usually, with Jax's size, it's easy for him to overpower an opponent on the ground, but Charles is *massive*, crushing the wind out of Jax without breaking a damn sweat.

I need to do something to help. Anything.

With trembling hands, I grab my phone from my pocket and punch 911 in as quietly and quickly as I can.

As I wait to get through to the operator, I watch as Jax braces himself for the incoming flurry of blows, his arms locked tight over his face. But it does little to break Charles's unshaken resolve to get that vicious ground and pound in.

"Come on, come on, come on," I whisper nervously to myself.

"Looks like deep down you're still that same little boy who ran away after a beatdown because it got a little too hard, a little too painful," Charles sneers.

Bam!

"I'll whip you into shape, I thought. To get you strong, to get you good for that cage."

Bam! Bam! Bam!

"Oh, you yelled and screamed and hollered like the devil's very own."

"Nine-one-one, what's your emergency?" I hear a woman on the line say.

I swing my gaze away from the fight, too terrified to look, but I flinch anyway from the deafening sound of the hits.

Bam! Bam! Bam!

"Hello? Is anyone on the line?" the woman repeats.

I struggle to even get out a breath.

"The world is cruel, just like me. You have to be strong to survive." Charles sneers as his knuckles crash against Jax's already injured nose. I hear the horrible crunching sound from all the way over here. "You show them that real men know no pain. They take what they want by the strength of their own two hands. They won't show us any mercy, so we don't show them any back."

Jax grabs his broken nose with both hands, crying out in pain.

I wheeze out the last of my air. My throat burns with tears.

I can't look. God, I *can't look.*

"No mercy," his stepdad growls. "No mercy. Take everything. Give nothing. No mercy—"

"Stop!"

"No mercy. Take everything. Give nothing. No mercy—"

I hear Jax coughing up blood. "Fuck off! Fuck off—"

"No mercy. Take everything. Give nothing—"

"Get the fuck away from me!" Jax screams, his voice already hoarse.

"I repeat: Is anyone on the line?" the woman on the phone blares.

"Yes!" I say in a wildly panicked tone.

Shit.

Instant regret slams hard into me, pushing the air out of my chest.

Shit shit shit—

Jax's eyes immediately snap to the doorway. When he sees me there, his skin pales.

"Sienna," Jax gasps, pained.

I turn away swiftly, tightening my grip over my phone.

"Yes," I say shakily, fear possessing every inch of my body, "I'd like to report a crime."

Charles climbs off Jax, wiping his stepson's blood off his own face. He's looking at me with such unnerving calm that my blood stops.

"Well, who's this pretty little thing?" He clicks his tongue as he strides toward the door. Toward me.

"Talk me through what's going on, ma'am." The woman on the line tugs my attention back.

Charles glances at the phone then back at me. The intrigue on his smug face evaporates. Annoyance climbs up the span of his body, slithering through his fisted hands. "You ratting me out, sweetheart?"

"Sienna, *hang up the phone!*" Jax shouts.

"Listen to him, *Sienna.*" Charles rolls each syllable over his tongue with careful precision. "You don't want to send me back there, do you?"

"Yeah, I do," I snarl, a death grip on my phone. "Because it's pretty damn clear you belong there."

Charles nostrils flare wide with rage. He steps forward toward me, ready to pounce.

"Stay the fuck away from her," Jax grabs a fistful of Charles's shirt, pulling him back, and slams a hard fist into his face. "Sienna, *run!*"

I twist around and sprint as fast as I can toward the elevator. I slam my finger over the Down button as many times as possible, like that'll somehow get the elevator to climb up the floors faster.

"There's a physical altercation between my boyfriend and his stepdad," I say quickly, my phone pressed up against my ear as I leap into the open elevator. "The address is 110 Beverly Street," I add. *"Please hurry!"*

The elevator doors slam shut right before Charles's fist collides with my face.

TWENTY-EIGHT

When I spill out of the elevator into the lobby, the relief of the narrow escape buckles my knees, sending my body crashing to the floor. The young woman behind the reception desk gasps, a hand flying over her mouth.

Holy shit. My mind spins, unable to process what's just happened. *Holy fucking shit.* I swallow hard, trying my best to push down the fist-size ball of puke threatening to projectile out of my mouth.

"Sienna!" A slender pair of arms reach around my waist, hauling me back up to my feet. Worry attacks Dakota's features. "Sienna, my God! What the hell happened?"

"I shouldn't have left him up there," I choke out, regret seizing my throat. "I think . . . I think I need to go back—"

Dakota shakes her head firmly. "You're *not* going anywhere until you tell me what's going on! Who's 'him'? Is Jax hurt?"

I nod. "I left him there, Dee. I just *left him there.* Charles—

he was chasing after me, and I had to leave because Jax was telling me to run—" I shudder, squeezing both of Dakota's arms so hard my nails dig into her skin. "They're both still up there, and it could get worse . . ."

"Which floor are they on?"

"Tenth."

"Okay. I'll deal with it," Dakota says calmly. She snaps her attention toward the concierge, who doesn't look like she has any clue what to do here. "There's been an altercation between two men on the tenth floor. Call security. Now!"

The concierge nods, picking up a walkie-talkie to make contact with building security and hurrying away.

"I'll wait here for the cops to come," I say, tugging on the sleeve of Dakota's shirt. "You should go. It'll be a while until we can go home."

"If you're staying, I'm staying," Dakota says with determination, gritting her teeth.

Less than a minute later, the concierge gives us an update. "Security has been called. They're on their way up now. Do you need me to call you an ambulance?"

I shake my head. My body is shaken but not hurt. Jax is the one in need of an ambulance. I shudder, remembering the awful sound of his nose cracking against Charles's fist . . .

"Come, sit," Dakota urges, tugging me toward the gray couch. "You're shivering." I snatch my wrist from her grasp.

"I can't sit while my boyfriend is up there being beaten to near death, Dee!" I wail in desperation.

"*Ex*-boyfriend," she corrects sternly. "And you heard the woman. Security is taking care of it. Now, *please* sit down. And tell me what is happening before I lose my mind."

I nod wordlessly and sit down, my mind feeling too disconnected from my body to disobey her orders.

By the time I'm done relaying to Dakota what I witnessed, the midnight sky bleeds red and blue from the lights of two police cars that come to a screeching stop outside the building's entrance. The concierge provides us with some blankets. I'm grateful for the warmth as I pull the blanket tight around my shoulder. Dakota slumps against the sofa, far from the realm of intoxication that she was in just minutes before as she tries to take in all the drama.

I wonder what she's thinking right now. Does it reinforce what she's thought of Jax all along—that he's dangerous, that I should stay far away from him? I wonder if she's worried at all about his safety like I am.

"Excuse me, miss." A female cop approaches me, tipping her head. "Were you the one who called nine-one-one?"

I nod, shrugging the blanket off as I launch to my feet. "Yeah. Are you heading up there? I'll go with you."

She holds up a hand to stop me as she waves two officers waiting outside into the building. "No, you stay put."

"But—"

"Stay put, ma'am," she orders again in a no-nonsense voice. "It's for your own good."

The cops file into the elevator, and the doors shut in front of them as I look on.

***

Almost an hour passes before the elevator doors ping and the cops emerge into the lobby. They're not alone; Jax and Charles are with them. But only one of them has been restrained. Jax tips his head at the cops, bidding them goodbye, as Charles gets whisked off to a waiting squad car in a pair of metal handcuffs.

Relief oozes from every pore in my body.

Jax is safe.

Beaten and bruised, but safe.

He looks terrible. His bottom lip is swelling purple, his nose is mashed and bloody, and his eyes are red and puffy from the assault to his face. He doesn't need to lift his shirt for me to know that he's probably cracked a rib or two. It's the gnarliest I've ever seen him, and my heart is heavy knowing that a family member did this to him.

I rise from the couch and approach him slowly. When he sees me, relief momentarily washes across his face. But it disappears just as quickly, replaced with disappointment and quiet, seething anger.

"They took your statement?" I prod. "Are you pressing charges?"

"Seems like I have no choice," Jax says, his mouth making a flat, unhappy line. I'm confused as to why he doesn't look more relieved about it.

"You're hurt, Jax," I say, gingerly placing a hand on his large shoulder. "You should go to the hospital . . ." My voice trails off. I already know what he'll say.

He shrugs me off coldly. "I told the cops I was fine. Nothing I haven't handled before."

I drop my hands to my sides, the humiliation at having been shrugged off overpowered by my concern. "Jax, this is *nothing* like what you've handled before. You might have broken a rib. Not to mention your nose. You need to get yourself checked out."

"I said I'm fine. Just a few scrapes," Jax mutters pridefully. "Just drop it."

He tears his eyes from my face, his gaze landing on Dakota. He doesn't bother to conceal his displeasure that she's here and has witnessed everything.

"Hey," Dakota mumbles sorrowfully.

A strain hardens his jaw. "Come on. I'll take you girls home."

I want to ask him if he's even okay to do that, given the condition he's in, but I sense that if I keep hounding him about his health, he might snap again. I simply nod, grabbing Dakota's hand and following Jax out to the parking lot.

The drive back is quiet. Too quiet. Jax has the radio off, and an eerie, tense silence fills the car. Discomfort twists in my stomach, along with a wave of self-consciousness. From the passenger seat, I catch Dakota's eyes in the rearview mirror. Neither of us dares utter a word.

We drop Dakota off first. As she exits the car, she throws me a desperate, questioning look and puts her hand on my shoulder, as if to ask if I'm okay to be alone with him. I give a small nod, squeezing her hand comfortingly.

"Text me when you're home," she murmurs before she's out of the car.

Jax nods at her curtly and watches her walk into her building before he pulls away from the curb and out onto the street. When we reach my apartment building, he pulls into a quiet alleyway opposite. My heart squeezes in fear and anticipation, and I steady myself. Better to get it all out in the open here rather than in my apartment, where Beth can hear everything.

Jax kills the engine. He shoves the door open and climbs out of the car. His fingers lace behind his neck as he paces the width of the narrow, grimy street, blowing out a long, heavy breath.

I step out of the car too, anxiousness rolling down my back.

"You had no right to interfere, Sienna." Jax's head gives a tough shake, his body trembling with quiet anger. "You had *no right*."

I feel my nostrils flaring in frustration.

"Excuse me? I had no right? I just saved your life, Jax. Charles could've killed you—"

"It wasn't your call to make, Sienna!" Jax slams his hand against the hood of the car, causing me to flinch. The vein in his forehead strains as he glares at me. "Why were you at my apartment, Sienna? You just couldn't stay out of it, could you?"

I feel the flush of anger burn my cheeks. "I didn't go to your apartment to get in the way of you and Charles. I was there because I was drunk and heartbroken and angry at you. And I wanted to end our relationship, properly this time. I didn't know what the hell I was walking into until it was too late."

"Then you should've turned back around and left."

"You expect me to not stick up for you? If I hadn't called the cops, you would've been dead!"

"I would've been able to get out of it if you hadn't interrupted me with your call!"

"Are you fucking serious?" A strained breath falls out of me, my hands pulling my hair back in frustration. "I didn't peg you for being this delusional, Jax. I know you don't like admitting defeat in that cage, but this is *real life* we're talking about. And Charles was going to kill you. And just because you sold him out—"

"I *told* you, Sienna. That was only half the truth," Jax cuts in, his tone laced with spite.

"Half the truth?" I echo, stepping around to the front of the car where he's standing. "What's the other half?"

"Oh, *now* you wanna know?" He lets out a dry laugh. "You were so quick to believe Perez before."

"Well, can you blame me for not believing you? After the lies you told me?"

"*I didn't lie!*" He erupts. He takes a few deep breaths, soldiering on as he forcefully meets my gaze again. "You know, I thought you were better than that, Sienna. I thought you were better than to pass such quick fucking judgment on me. Especially when I've never once done the same to you."

Guilt kicks into gear, followed by its loyal companion, remorse. Dammit, He's right. I haven't exactly been fair to him. Whenever I went through something, he was always there to listen patiently while I said my piece. At the very least, he deserves the same courtesy to be extended to him.

"Okay. Then, tell me." I sigh, losing steam. "What is the real truth? Tell me what really happened with you and Charles. No holds barred. *Please*. I'm done losing my mind trying to figure it all out."

Jax shudders, fingers from one hand rubbing his temple while the other braces him against the hood. Eventually, he lets loose a defeated sigh.

"Fine," he whispers, meeting my gaze. "Here's the truth: after my mom and dad got divorced and my dad moved away, my mom got married to Charles." He sucks in a sharp breath before continuing. "He was a decent enough guy . . . at least, that's what my mom thought. I didn't really care. My mom didn't have the best track record with men, so I was immune to shitty behavior from them. Charles tended to ignore me anyway, so I just stayed out of his way." Jax's whole body is leaning against the hood of the car now, arm muscles straining beneath him. "It wasn't until I turned sixteen that he started to take notice. I was getting into a lot of fights at school, you know, typical teen bullshit. And instead of cursing me out for being a problematic delinquent like a normal dad, Charles taught me how to refine my fighting skills. I thought he was trying to bond with me. Turns out, he was preparing me."

"For the underground?" I whisper softly, beginning to connect the dots.

"Yeah. The first time he brought me into his club . . . it felt like a whole new world. And for an angsty teen, it was fucking nirvana. I loved it. When I stepped into that cage for the first time, it was like I finally found my purpose," Jax explains, his eyes taking on a faraway gaze. There's an air of sarcasm in his voice as he continues. "I was good at fighting, thanks to Charles, so he kept me around. It was a win-win situation for the both of us: I got my share of adrenaline and violence, and he got to reap the rewards of my victories. I got better, and as I did, I brought the crowds in. It was great for business." Jax's mouth pulls into a low frown. "But Charles got too greedy. And when the club grew in popularity, so did the pool of fighters. The ones that were good were bigger, stronger, and out for my blood. I was still a kid then, you know? Still making mistakes. Still learning. But Charles didn't see me as a kid. He saw me as a moneymaking machine. And when I didn't give him the wins, there were always . . . consequences."

A shudder runs through my body when I think back to what I witnessed a few hours ago, Charles's fists ramming into Jax with precision, as if he already knew his tells—exactly where to hit to hurt him the most.

"Surely your mother knew what was going on," I say.

"She did. But she caught on too late, and when she found out what Charles and I were up to, I guess she decided the money I was raking in was worth it." *Jesus*. My heart aches for Jax, contemplating how his own mother could throw him to the wolves like that. "When he hit me, it made me fight shittier, and I started to lose my confidence, along with the fights. Then I'd lose, and he'd do the same thing. It began a vicious cycle. Sometimes, Charles would even have other fighters join in, just for his amusement. Nothing was off-limits in that club, so I just had to take it, like some fucking wounded animal. I was *humiliated*.

"And when I heard he'd been going around blackballing me from other circuits, that was the last straw for me. He wanted to trap me in his fight club forever, and there was no way I was gonna let that happen. Decided then and there that I'd had enough, that no one would ever get to dictate my life again. I still wanted to fight. Still loved it. But I wanted to do it on my own terms. Away from Charles and from those fighters who'd been complicit in delivering his cruel punishments. I was done having him take all that power from me. So I took it back," he huffs out, a gleeful twitch on his lips. "Drug charges, battery, assault . . . Charles got slapped with everything the cops could possibly get him on. When he got sent away, I was finally free."

"So when you sold him out, it wasn't because you got greedy and wanted more from his club . . ." I whisper.

"More?" Jax says incredulously. "I was trying to escape it, Sienna."

The wounded look on his face guts me like a rusty hook in a fish.

I brace myself against the wall of the alleyway, dropping my face in shame.

"Does Julian know?" I ask softly. I recall all the times that I asked him to clue me in about Jax's past, but he was never willing to divulge.

"No, he doesn't. When he found me, I'd changed my name and was trying to stay low. But he immediately saw my potential. I never told him I fought in a circuit before, but I think he always had his suspicions. There was no way he couldn't have known, seeing that I was miles ahead of any amateur fighter. But Julian never asked me about my past; he only cared that I gave him my present. I had massive respect for him, so I agreed. I kept training with Jules to get better and stronger. It was hard and rigorous, but I enjoyed it. For once, there was a sense of normalcy to what I was doing. But . . . after a while, he wanted more out of me. He started pushing me to do professional MMA. To represent the gym. I felt pressured. And after the shit that happened with Charles . . . it felt like I was being controlled again, taken advantage of, and I swore I wasn't going to let anyone shove me into that box again." He says the last part with indignation, a muscle pulsing along his neck.

"So that was when you joined Breaking Point's underground?"

Jax nods. "By then, nobody knew who I was. I had a different name anyway, and I looked different than when I was sixteen, so it was easy to get a fresh start. But I should've known that Perez would recognize me. He's been in the underground long enough to have remembered what happened. Hell, he probably even had friends fighting in Charles's club that took part in my weekly beatings. But I doubt he knew about any of that. Or if he did, he chose to spin the story the worst way he could."

"But you were going to quit the underground this year. You promised."

"Contrary to what you think of me, I had every intention of fulfilling that promise. I was actually trying my best to change. For you," he says in all seriousness. "But as hard as I tried, I just couldn't stay away from it, all right? I was weak. I admit that. I couldn't ignore the voices in my head, pulling me back. The underground was my *whole life*, Sienna. All I ever really knew. I have power there, I'm a *winner*. I felt guilty for letting you down, which was why I stayed away from you all those weeks leading up to the finals."

Shame wends its way through my chest, tight and constricting. I kick off the wall and stride toward him, my boots clicking against the pavement, feeling the overwhelming need to show him how sorry I am for having judged him so harshly. And for going behind his back and taking the word of Perez, his nemesis, a man who would hurt him at any cost . . .

What have I done? Is this what Perez was after? To deal Jax the most hurtful blow of all by having the woman he loves betray his trust? And I knew I was falling into his trap, but I didn't care . . .

"Shit, I'm sorry, Jax," I say sorrowfully. "I'm so, so sorry, for all of it. And for what Charles did to you."

Jax laughs again, his jaw as tight and tense as his words. "There it is."

"What?"

"*Pity.*" His voice drips with ice, his narrowed gaze swinging toward me. "That's exactly why I didn't want to tell you, Sienna. I don't need your pity."

"But if I'd known what happened, I wouldn't have—"

"What? You wouldn't have gone out of your way to pry the distorted truth out of Perez? And when I tried to explain, you refused to even give me a chance? Now you finally have the sob story you always wanted from me. Poor little Jax and his fucked-up childhood trauma. Now you have someone who's worse off than you to make you feel better about your own shitty life."

"That's a low blow, Jax," I mutter. His words sting more than they hurt. I know that he's only trying to deflect his own pain. "I only wanted to understand you because I love you and I wanted to help you."

"I don't need your help, Sienna. The shit that happened with Charles is in the past, and I want to leave it that way."

"You're wrong," I find the courage to say. "Even if he's behind bars now, he's still got such a hold over you. For fuck's sake, Jax, you still fight in the underground. You walked right out of one prison cell into another. He still controls you. He controls everything you do, even if you don't realize it." His fingers rub his temple, and his tongue licks over his teeth, not quite believing me. "He abused you for years, but that's not your fault. I'm so sorry that happened to you, that you had to experience all of that, you have no idea. But because of it . . . because you never got the help you needed, you're trapped—"

"Trapped?" Jax laughs hoarsely. "Can't you see I'm completely *free*? I own myself. Not Charles, not Julian, not you."

"Oh yeah?" I scoff. "Then tell me why you don't give up the underground and fight the bigger fight? Why not join the UFC or any of the other big promotions? I'll tell you why: you fight in the underground because you'd rather fight the easier fight than challenge yourself with the big leagues. That's your stepdad, Jax. That's why he tormented you when you were a kid. Not because it was fair, but because the fight was *easy*."

He drops his arms and glances at me, looking as pained as he was on the floor of his apartment when Charles rained blows down on him.

"That's not true," Jax croaks out.

I'm too wired up to listen to him now, so I keep pushing. "'Take everything. Give nothing. Show no mercy.' That's his motto, isn't it? Those are the exact words you said when you beat down Perez. Don't you see? The violence has *become* you." With trembling hands, I reach for his shoulders, feeling the contours of his skin. "You need help, Jax. Please, let me help you—"

"Help me," he echoes, his voice tight and clipped as if he's holding in the full might of his anger. "Sienna, do you think after crossing the lines that you did that I would ever let you into my life again? Much less let you *help* me?"

My heart rips out of my chest and splatters against the road.

"Don't say that," I croak out, shaking my head. "You know I wouldn't have done all that unless I felt like I had no other choice."

"You want to talk to me about choices?" He scowls at me. "You practically jumped at the opportunity to wrangle anything you could from Perez. So quick to betray me at the first sign of temptation!"

"You made your choice to not tell me about Charles!" I snap back defensively. "How do you think that made me feel, Jax? A sleaze like Perez knowing more about you than your own girlfriend? It's humiliating. It's degrading." My hands rest on either side of my hips as I look up at the night sky, trying to keep the tears from spilling down my cheeks as the revelation hits. "I can't believe it. You just don't trust me, do you?"

"And you don't trust me." Jax looks at me with over-whelming sadness.

My eyelids squeeze shut.

The last time we approached the subject of trust, it was after Jax and Perez's fight. We promised we'd do better for each other. It worked for a while. And then it didn't. How did it go so wrong again? Why didn't we learn then?

"Tell me what happens now, Jax," I say pleadingly. "Tell me."

His gaze falls to the road. He stares and stares as if he's searching for an answer that might contradict the conclusion he's already come to.

"When you came to my apartment tonight, you were looking for a breakup," he whispers, glancing back at me with a bitter sadness in his eyes. It rips my soul apart to be the object of that look. "Well, now you got it."

Time stops.

My insides lurch. I exhale, trying to wrap my head around the words coming out of his mouth.

No. *No.*

This can't be the end. Not yet. There *must* be a way to salvage this. There must be. We can't just give up now—not when everything is finally out in the open, when tonight bled us dry with such brutal but much-needed honesty—

"No, Jax, please." I try to pull his body close to mine, desperate to hold on to the last tiny scrap of our love. My forehead clings to his, sticky with anxious sweat. "Please. We can fix this. I know we can. I'm—*so* sorry. *Please*, Jax. I love you . . ."

Jax shakes his head, rejecting my pleas. He merely kisses my forehead and steps away from me.

"Wait. Just wait, Jax!" A sob warbles out of me. "Please! Don't do this!"

He doesn't say a word. He climbs back into his car and peels out of the alleyway, his tires screeching as if he can't get away from me fast enough. I follow the trail of his lights until they disappear, two red dots fading into the night, and then he is gone. My body slumps to the ground, and I'm frozen there in the alley, my back against the cold brick wall, unable to move.

TWENTY-NINE

I don't know how much time passes, an hour maybe. The sensation of being in some kind of lucid dream makes every part of my body numb and fuzzy. I must have figured out how to move my legs because I manage to scrape myself off the ground and stagger down the street toward my apartment building.

I'm still sobbing when I climb the stairs to my floor.

I'm still sobbing when I undress and climb into my bed.

I'm still sobbing when the sun finally pokes over the horizon and soaks me in its early-morning rays.

I sob until all the water in my body has dried up and my bed is a swamp that could swallow me whole.

The tears won't stop. They leak out of me like blood from an open wound, until they mix with the snot coming out of my nostrils. I grab the box of tissues beside me and stuff them up my nostrils so that I can sob some more. My body is curled up against the pillow, my mouth swallowing salty streams of snot. I feel disgusted with myself. I feel like a hysterical child.

I feel *weak*.

That's what I really am.

I've shown the world I'm tough as nails, but deep down, I'm not. I allowed myself to be complicit in Jax's withholding of the truth; I refused to listen to Jax after what Perez told me; I didn't dare step in between Charles and Jax—all of those were cowardly acts.

I am weak.

This is the real me. Fragile. Vulnerable. Useless.

I don't know when I lost my strength. Perhaps I didn't have any to begin with, and I was just pretending I had it together because I couldn't face myself for what I truly am.

But I know I certainly didn't feel this way when things were good between me and Jax.

I already feel mangled by his absence. Mutilated. Jax pulled apart every limb, every bone, every selfish chunk of flesh he could get his hands on and left me to bleed out on my own.

I'm not sure if I can keep going on like this. I close my eyes and wonder if the pain will hurt so much that it'll actually stop my heart. It's possible to die of heartbreak. It's extremely unlikely, but possible.

Maybe I'll be the exception.

I keep my eyes shut, daring my heart to stop beating. Daring it to put an end to me. They say nothing hurts quite like your first heartbreak. Which implies you eventually get over it. I don't think I ever want to.

I'd rather let the pain kill me.

At least I'll still be all wrapped up in Jax when I go.

The door creaks open, and my heart lurches. I want it to

be Jax so badly, and my mind is convinced that he's come to get me back.

"Sienna?" Beth's voice is small, barely audible.

Disappointment inflates in my chest. My eyes flutter open.

"Hey," I whisper.

I face away from her, wiping my tears with the back of my hand. My head feels like it's made of lead as I drag it off the pillow and pull myself into a sitting position. My brow furrows in confusion, expecting her to be in her PJs since it's so early in the morning. Instead, she's all dressed up as if for a date in a dainty floral dress and a pair of heels.

"What . . . um . . ." The crease between my brows deepens. "Did you go out?"

"Uh, yeah. Last night, for a bit." She looks uncomfortable admitting it.

"That's weird. I didn't hear you go out."

"I was trying to be quiet."

"Why were you out?"

"Um . . . Kinley wanted to talk."

"Okay," I say with a cautious tone. "Until . . ." I peek at my phone's lock screen. "Until seven in the morning?"

"Yeah," she says, like that's not weird at all. Her gaze roams my face, noticing the puffy eyes, tired expression, and red-stained cheeks. Concern writes itself across her delicate features. "Are you okay? What happened?"

I brave a steady breath.

"It's over," I say tiredly. "Jax and I are done. For real this time."

There it is. The words I've held trapped in my head the past few hours, not wanting them to be real, are out in the open.

I'll never again feel Jax breathing desire and love and passion into me. I'll never hear his beautiful laugh again. I'll never feel his warm body as it slides next to mine, clutching me so close like he needs me to breathe. I'll never get to taste him in the early mornings before he's sweaty and greasy from training. Or watch his eyes light up when he spots me in the crowd, attributing all of his wins to me.

These revelations paralyze me as I sit there, stunned, heat reaching my face. And then I'm bawling again, burying my face in my hands while I cry ugly tears.

"Oh, Si," Beth whispers.

I hear my sister rushing toward me, her warm hands pulling me into an embrace. I feel the cold, wrinkled solitude of my bed as the blanket gets pulled up over me, nestling me in a warmth that isn't Jax's. I feel my eyelids give out. I'm too tired and spent to keep my eyes open, and the pain dwindles to a low frequency—barely there, almost bearable.

And then, as I sink into sleep, I finally feel nothing at all.

***

Like a boat with no anchor, I drift into and out of my own life aimlessly.

My days start to blend together. I think it's been five days since Jax and I broke up, but I'm not sure. Maybe six. Or eight. It doesn't matter.

Nothing I do has any meaning anymore.

I've been falling behind on my classes. Definitely not a good way of ending the semester. Dakota has been coming to my apartment every day just so she can drag me out of bed. We don't talk about Jax when she picks me up. It's too exhausting for either of us. She tries to cheer me up with other things, catching me up on the latest drama from the drama club—how fitting—and how her and Trevor's relationship is still shaky, but they're trying to make it work. I listen intently, trying my best to give advice, but it somehow comes out all generic and one-note, like I'm reciting quotes off someone's Facebook wall. It's hard giving relationship advice while you're going through a breakup of your own because it makes you see relationships in such a cynical, pessimistic light.

I hate what my life has been reduced to these days.

I used to be a woman on a mission. Now I can barely keep my focus. At this point, I'm so untethered from my own body that I don't realize I'm doing something until I'm halfway through it, and I barely register when someone's talking to me.

"What?" I whisper, looking straight at Julian.

He's at the doorway to his office, a disapproving look on his face. I haven't seen that look in a while now. More often than not, it spells trouble.

"I said *get in here.*" The last of his patience snaps like a brittle bone.

I hurry into his office, realizing as I do that my last client for the day, Sheila, has already gone home. Funny how I don't even remember dismissing her tonight.

"Sit," Julian orders.

I obey and sink into the seat in front of him. Julian paces back and forth behind his desk, hand on his mouth as he contemplates what to do with me. Eventually, he stops and rests both hands on his desk, letting out a long breath. Before he can ask what the hell is going on with me, I beat him to it.

"I know I'm distracted. And it's not good for business," I acknowledge earnestly, painfully.

A sigh pulls out of him. "At least you're aware of it. But why are you distracted?"

"I think you already know why."

Remorse paints Julian's features. I haven't told anyone other than Beth and Dakota that Jax and I are over. Perhaps, in a way, I figured the less people I told, the less real it would be.

Julian walks over to me and lays a comforting hand on my shoulder. This is the most affection he has ever displayed toward me, so I must look broken enough for him to feel the need to express it.

"I'm sorry about you and Jax. I really am. He was a big part of your life, and I understand how it feels." His throat bobs, like what he's about to say next is going to be uncomfortable. "But I can't have you working in my gym like this."

The floor completely drops out from underneath me. Is he implying what I think he's implying?

"Are you . . . firing me?" I croak out in a barely audible whisper since there's no air left in my lungs.

This is my dream job. One that I've been working toward for nearly two years. And now, having just landed it and only a month in, I'm being let go?

I will have nothing left now. The horror settles deep into my stomach. *Nothing left to cling to. Nothing that'll keep me going, that'll bring me any form of happiness or fulfillment. I'll no longer have any purpose in life, and it's all my fault—*

"What? No. I'm not going to fire you. You just started here." Julian dismisses my ludicrous suggestion. "I'm only suggesting that you take a week or two off to work out your stuff."

Oh, thank God.

All my muscles unclench, and my body relaxes against the seat.

"I appreciate the offer," I say. "But I can't take a break. I'm fully booked for the next few weeks."

"Don't worry about it. I'll handle it myself."

I blink twice, a little dumbfounded.

"I thought you said you didn't want to train anymore," I whisper, recalling that after Jax left the gym, Julian told me that I was going to be his last MMA student. He doesn't like to admit it, but I think he found Jax's betrayal too hard to process and therefore prefers to maintain a bigger distance between himself and the students that train here.

"Yeah, I know," he says, his gaze softening a little when he glances at me. "But I'll do this for you. At least until you get better."

My face mellows with affection. I can't believe he would do that for me. It's clear I haven't been the easiest person to deal with lately, so it's nice to know that he hasn't given up on me.

"Thank you," I breathe.

"Now go before I change my mind." Julian's voice gets gruff again. He holds the door open for me as I lift myself from the seat.

"I am sorry about Jax," he adds as I walk toward the door. "I know how hard you tried to make it work with him."

"Thanks," I mumble.

Julian's lips fold together. "Take care of yourself, Sienna."

I nod.

I owe it to him to get better. Today, I still have my job, but if I keep spiraling, I may lose it for real.

I'm barely surviving without Jax; it'll most certainly be the end of me if I lose the gym too.

***

I turn twenty today.

I'm now the same age Jax was when he first met me in that warehouse. It's a weird age to be. I'm supposed to suddenly be an adult, but I feel like I've only just barely begun to grasp what adulthood is. Funny how I thought Jax was so mature when I met him. In hindsight, he was probably just fumbling around the way I am now.

At least the crying has stopped now. I was getting tired of being a soggy mess all the time. The gutting pain has given way to numbness, which isn't that big of an upgrade, but it's an upgrade, nonetheless. Beth prefers me feeling sad instead of empty. At least I'm feeling something, she says.

Like my birthday today. I'm usually not eager to celebrate special occasions, but I always try to show some excitement for Beth, who loves to go all out for me—birthday party, gifts, the whole nine yards. Today, Beth has been hell-bent on not letting me celebrate my birthday in unfeeling solitude. She drags me out to the mall, where she treats me to a Caffeinated coffee and picks out a gift for me—a cute pair of gold-plated earrings. We have dinner at the Korean place near our apartment. The food is good as usual, but it would probably be easier to swallow if I weren't slapped with a view of the alleyway where Jax unceremoniously dumped me.

After dinner, we head back to the apartment, and Beth

drags me out of my room again to end the night with a *Gilmore Girls* marathon. It's the only show lately that forces any kind of emotional response from me. It's mostly a byproduct of me being frustrated with Rory for making the stupidest decisions. But at least I'm feeling something.

Beth tugs me toward her, allowing me to rest my head on her shoulder. I really do wish I could give Beth more enthusiasm, but tonight, I'm feeling emptier than usual because as much as I love my sister, there's only one person I want to be ending my birthday night with.

"Sienna," Beth says, smoothing my hair with a hand, "I think it's time."

"Time for what?"

"Time to call Mom."

I lift my head up, giving her a blank look. Beth leans over the coffee table and picks up my phone, offering it to me.

"No." I shake my head. "I can't."

"Why? She wants you to call her today. You've been dodging her for weeks now. She thinks you hate her."

I bite my lip, frowning. "I don't hate her."

"Then why won't you talk to her?"

I shake my head again. Beth won't understand.

Beth places the phone on my hand and closes my fingers over the screen. "Call her. *Please.* I love you, Si, but you're slipping away, and I don't know how else to pull you back."

I glance up at her. There's agony on her face, and I feel awful that it's there because of me. Because I'm not strong enough to pick up the broken pieces of my heart by myself.

I nod wordlessly, and Beth's shoulders slump with relief. She kisses me on the cheek and pushes herself off the couch.

"I'll give you two some privacy," she whispers before disappearing into her room.

As the FaceTime screen appears, I pray that she doesn't pick up. I'm not sure I'll be able to hold in all these feelings if she does.

"Hey, happy birthday, baby!" my mom hoots. She tells me to hold on and puts the phone down for a minute or two. She returns with a paper birthday hat on her head, a party blower dangling from her mouth, and a large banner with tacky gold letters hanging behind her that spells out, "Cheers to twenty!" It's clear she planned this on the off chance we might talk today, and I'm so raw with emotion that I start to choke up.

When she takes in my crestfallen expression, she plucks the party blower out of her mouth and peers closely at me through the screen. "Oh, sweetie." She sighs knowingly. "You're not doing so good, are you?"

I mash my mouth together tightly.

"I take it Beth told you about the breakup?"

"She might have mentioned it," my mom admits. "She's not the only one worried about you, you know. Do you want to talk about it? It might make you feel better."

"Oh, Mom," I croak out.

And then I let everything out. The arguments Jax and I had recently. Him icing me out. Me icing him out. Discovering his abuse after stumbling upon him with his stepdad, culminating in what went down between us that night in the alley.

"I was in the wrong, wasn't I?" I say, hugging my knees close to my chest.

She puckers her lips into a frown. At some point during

my ramblings, she removed the party hat from her head and went into her bedroom—a more neutral space.

"Yes and no," she says after a while. "I understand why you did what you did. You felt like you were backed into a corner. But it was up to Jax to share those details about his past with you. Going behind his back to get that information was a breach of trust."

"Yeah, I know," I murmur, my palms pressing against my face. "I feel awful. I never thought I was that kind of girl, you know? I never thought I would cross that line. I mean, look at you and Dad. The way he hurt you, especially with the affair. And still you stayed with him, supported him, until the end. If that's not strength, then I don't know what is. You showed me that love means standing by someone, even when they hurt you or disappoint you. Not just throwing in the towel when things get tough."

Mom's inner strength is a quality I've always strived to emulate. Jax often wondered why I put Mom on such a pedestal. He never understood that I put her there because she deserves to be there.

"Sienna, that's not true at all," my mom says, looking puzzled. "What gave you that idea?"

"You forgave Dad even when he betrayed your trust with the affair. You sat by him on the couch that day when he broke the news to us. You never said a word against him. *That's* holding it together."

My mom tears her gaze away from her phone, clearly distressed.

"What's wrong?" I whisper.

"Okay, this is gonna be hard for me to say, but I think it's time you know the truth." Mom looks ashamed. "Your father didn't cheat, Sienna . . . I did."

"Wh-what?" I stammer out, shell-shocked.

"I was the one who cheated," Mom repeats, a bit more conviction in her voice.

"I don't get it," I say, unable to comprehend how this can even be a possibility. I feel my world turning upside down, the pedestal upon which Mom sits knocked over as she tumbles to the ground.

She inhales a ragged breath. "You know your dad and I were fighting constantly. It was getting hard to even be in the same room with each other. I felt like I wasn't being heard at all. He didn't seem to care about what I needed from him, what I needed from the marriage. He just wanted me to stop nagging him. And I wanted him to step up. No matter how much we fought about it, nothing was working. It was as if he had just given up, and I felt so shut out and alone . . ." she explains, her voice taking on a faraway quality. "One night, it all just got to be too much, and I left the house. I was so angry and desperate to do something, anything, that would shake your dad into caring again, about me, and you and Beth, about this family. I made a mistake, Sienna."

I vaguely recall the night that she's talking about. It occurred about two weeks before she and Dad announced their divorce to us. I found it strange that she never came home that night; I always assumed she'd just needed the time away and had spent the night with one of her girlfriends.

"So, you slept with another man," I say, the revelation forcing my back against the couch.

Mom nods quietly, tears springing into her eyes as she

continues. "I went to the nearest bar and drank the night away, trying to numb the pain I was feeling. It didn't take long for a man to notice me. It felt nice to be noticed, Sienna. And heard. He listened to me rant about your father for hours," she says with an easy smile. It's clear she remembers the moment with fondness. "And later, when I went home with him, I'm ashamed to admit it, but I didn't feel guilty. At all. In fact, I felt like the shackles on my feet had finally cracked open."

"Did you tell Dad?"

"Yes. I came clean the next day," Mom says, looking away briefly. "I expected your dad to feel rage. But he didn't. He just sat there, quietly, while I told him what had happened. And when I was done, he began to cry. It wasn't just that I had cheated on him with another man that got to him, though. It was because he felt responsible for me feeling like it was the only option left." Her voice is sad as she recalls the events.

"We talked about how we could move forward after all that had happened. We wanted to make it work for you and Beth, but all of the yelling and hurt was causing you girls a pain that we felt was worse than if we made the hard decision to part ways. At least then we might find some peace."

I squeeze my eyes shut, and an unfamiliar mixture of guilt and sympathy squeezes my heart as I consider how awful I've been to my dad. All this time I've blamed him for breaking our family apart, for breaking my mom's heart, and it turns out my mom was the one who dealt the fatal blow.

"If you were the one who cheated, then why did Dad take responsibility for the affair?" I ask, trying to make sense of why they'd go to such lengths to hide the truth from me and Beth.

She ponders the question for a beat. "I think he felt like

it wasn't my burden to carry," she says. "I told him that if you ever asked me about it, I would be honest. But he begged me not to. He thought it was better for you both to think you just had one bad parent, rather than two."

My cheeks are wet with tears before I even realize I'm crying.

I can't believe my dad would make that sacrifice, deciding it would be better that I hate him and continuing to play the role I so narrowly boxed him into rather than forcing me to turn my hatred toward my mom.

I lower the phone onto my lap, giving my arms a rest from holding it up so long. I use my hand to wipe away the tears coating my face.

"You should have told me sooner, Mom," I mutter. "You let me go on for so long hating him for an affair he didn't even have. How *could* you?"

"I'm so sorry, baby. I was just so ashamed of what I'd done," my mom tells me earnestly. "I'm your mom, and it's my job to be your touchstone for right and wrong. I didn't know how to face disappointing you so badly. I loved your father, Sienna. And I did a lot of things right by him. But I also betrayed him. And I cannot take that back," she whispers. "You have to know that love made me a lot of things. Kind. Passionate. Selfless. But it also made me ugly. *Really* ugly."

I set the phone on the sofa, burying my face in my hands. I don't know what's worse, that my mom was the one who had the affair in the first place or that she let my father take the blame for it. I should despise her for what she's done. It's how I treated my dad when I thought he was the one to cheat, so doesn't she deserve the same treatment from me?

But . . . I can't seem to bring myself to hate her, at least not entirely.

Because it makes sense. All of it.

Dad felt suffocated, pushing him to escape into a cycle of alcohol abuse, and because of it, Mom felt unwanted and alone, leading her to break the boundaries of their relationship. They pushed each other away and hurt each other even more in the process.

I can't hate her for that. In fact, I sympathize with her.

Because Jax and I were in the same position for nearly two years.

"It's funny, isn't it?" she says, looking straight through my eyes as if into some deeper part of me. "Women . . . we're taught to just sit there and do nothing while we watch our partners screw up time and time again. And we're supposed to take it like a champ because it's the right thing to do. But the second we step a toe out of line, we're the bad guy in the relationship." Mom slowly shakes her head in resignation.

I nod quietly. I wonder if Jax will ever see me as anything but an irrational girlfriend who wasn't satisfied with what she'd been given. Throughout our entire relationship, I gave him so many chances to be better. All I wanted was the same courtesy in return.

"I don't blame you, Mom. You and Dad both made your mistakes," I say after a while, a peaceful clarity arriving and settling in my core. Suddenly, I'm able to see my relationship with Jax more clearly. And now my heart hurts just a little bit less.

It took everything we had to make it work, but we were too stubborn to admit fault. Perhaps if we'd spent more time fighting for each other rather than with each other, we wouldn't have broken under the pressure of it all, just like my mom and dad.

"Thanks for telling me the truth," I say, my tone infused with gratitude. "And . . . I'm sorry I haven't called in a while."

Her eyes brighten at my words. "I know you've been busy. Just don't push the people you love away, okay? You have a bad habit of doing that."

"Okay." I promise to try.

She blows me an air kiss, and I catch it, smiling, smacking it on my cheek. After we bid goodbye to each other, I shuffle back to my room, climb into bed, and shut off the lights.

For the first time in weeks, it's easy to fall asleep.

THIRTY

There is a renewed sense of hope having talked to Mom, and the heaviness that set up camp in my heart has begun to ebb slowly. It feels like I'm standing at the edge of the ocean, and as the tide rushes away, it settles me deeper into the sand, anchoring me.

I want to be happy again.

And if happiness is a tall order, then I at least want to be okay.

There is a life worth living after heartbreak; I realize that now. My mom is proof of it. I just need to keep looking forward.

Today is gonna be a good day without Jax. I repeat this phrase like a mantra as I get ready. *Today is gonna be a good day without Jax.*

As usual, I hear shuffling in the living room, followed by Dakota's voice echoing indistinctly down the hallway toward me. My shoulders sag with relief. She can't possibly comprehend how appreciative I am of her company lately. She lives on campus, and yet she comes over to my apartment every day to pick me up so I won't be alone with my thoughts. It sickens me that I let my friendship with her deteriorate because of Jax. I don't ever want to let that happen again. I'm not sure she'd forgive me if I did.

As I get ready, I pick out a colorful top, putting on a baby blue camisole with a pair of beige jeans. I'm usually so comfortable in black. But today, my outfit needs to match my mantra.

I slip into my sneakers and am prying my bedroom door open while stuffing my laptop into my bag when I hear Dakota again. I'm about to holler an apology for keeping her longer than usual when I realize she's talking to someone in the living room. Her tone is exasperated and hostile.

"You need to tell her!" Dakota whisper-shouts. "I don't care what it takes."

I inch my way into the hall so I can hear better.

"Now is not the time," Beth squeaks out nervously.

"Then *when*?" Dakota demands in utter disbelief.

"I need time to gather my thoughts," Beth whispers back, urgency in her tone. "And you can't tell either."

"Why the fuck not?"

"Because if anyone is going to tell her, it should be me."

"*If?* Beth, you *need* to do it. This is—"

Looping my bag over my shoulder, I shuffle into the living room, my gaze zigzagging between the two of them. They're standing by the door. Beth is in nothing but a flimsy robe. Dakota looks like she's ready to deck her across the face.

"What's going on, guys?" I interrogate.

Their heads snap toward me. Dakota squeezes her eyes shut, her bottom lip trembling. Beth looks away, a shadow of guilt across her face.

"Um," Dakota starts off. "Listen . . ."

"We were just talking about my friend Kinley." Beth intercepts, forcing a brave face as her eyes meet mine.

"Right . . ." I say, my voice trailing off. "Is she okay?"

"She's just going through a lot right now." Beth sounds uncertain. "She just, um, she found out that she's pregnant."

"Oh, God. Wow. She's barely eighteen." I shift my weight between my legs. "That must be hard."

"Right." Dakota swings her gaze toward Beth, her eyes narrowing. "And I'm just telling Beth here that even though Kinley's no longer with her partner, he still deserves to know."

"And I'm trying to convince Dakota that it's really none of her ex-partner's business. After all, they're already broken up," Beth challenges, her expression defiant.

I bite my lip, contemplating what's been said. A funny feeling rises from my gut, but I can't quite put my finger on what it's trying to tell me.

"I think I'm with Dee on this one," I venture. "I get that what Kinley's going through is really difficult, but he still deserves to know."

Dakota tilts her head sideways knowingly. *See?*

Beth frowns, worry creasing her brow. "I'll think about it. I'm . . . gonna go change. See you later when you get home, Si."

I lift a brow at her. "You don't wanna walk with us?"

"I'm good."

"Okay, see you later," I say, watching as she disappears into her room. When her door shuts, I whip toward Dakota.

"Okay, that was weird. Do you know something I don't?"

Dakota rubs a hand over her mouth in frustration. "Look, um . . . let's not do this now."

"Why not?"

"You seem like you're in a better mood today, and I don't wanna ruin it," she says, sizing me up with an approving look as she takes in the brighter colors of my outfit. "You're usually dressed like you're going to a funeral, so this is a nice change," she jibes, poking me in the ribs. "How about dinner tonight? At Basil Kitchen? We can talk more about it then."

"Okay. Should I be worried?" I ask, looping an arm through hers. "You don't usually take me out to fancy dinners. Not that I'm complaining. I'm just warning you: if you expect me to put out tonight, it better be a minimum five-course meal."

I expect her to smile, but instead, she bites down on her bottom lip with worry. "Well, after I'm done telling you what I know, you might not have an appetite at all."

"Jeez. That bad, huh?" I say, my stomach dropping as I fear the worst.

No. I school myself. *Today is going to be a good day without Jax.*

Nothing—not even Dakota's news—is going to get in the way of that.

"Well, it's a good thing I have you, then . . . to soften the blow." I smile at her and give my best friend's arm an affectionate squeeze.

Dakota smiles back.

"It's the best thing."

***

Since Julian has forced me to take an unofficial sabbatical from the gym, my afternoons are suddenly wide open. After class, I stay on campus and catch up on all my missed work. There's a lot to go through, and I hang out in the library for hours, combing through my notes and hustling to complete assignments.

Later, on the way home, I put my earphones in and catch up on some correspondence. I schedule a follow-up meeting with Julian to talk about resuming work starting next week. Then I shoot a message to Mom that I'd be down for a FaceTime call this weekend to catch up on what's been going on with her. I even reply to my dad, accepting an invitation to have dinner with him on the weekend. I owe it to him to try to mend our relationship. There's still a lot of hostility between us, and I'd be a fool to think it'll get resolved overnight. At the very least, I want us to put this cheating thing to rest and find a way forward.

When I get back to the apartment, I pull my keys out of my bag, only to find the front door unlocked. I'm immediately reminded of that night at Jax's apartment. What if it's Charles again, and he somehow escaped police custody to get back at me for calling the cops on him? My instincts go on instant high alert, and I brace my fists in front of me, ready to tussle. But as soon as I turn the door handle and peek in, my hand loosens and drops to my side.

The scent of the room hits me first. Roses and candles sit on every available surface in the living room, infusing the air with a heavy aroma that gives me a head rush. And there, standing in the middle of it all, is Jax, wearing a white long-sleeved button-down and black slacks. Just like our first date.

"Happy belated birthday," Jax whispers.

Damn, I nearly forgot how breathtaking he is. The mane of golden-blond hair, his sharp features, and that signature winning smile . . . my heartbeat skitters.

And just like that, all my resentment toward him seems to dissolve, like the wax in those scented candles.

My mind loops back through the mantra in my head.

Today is going to be a good day without Jax.

"What are you doing here?" I squint at him. "How the hell did you get in?"

Jax's hands dig into his pockets as he shrugs. "I asked Beth for her keys."

I shake my head. "You have to go. I have somewhere to be tonight," I point out, crossing the living room toward my bedroom.

Jax steps in front of me, blocking my way. "What? You got a date or something?"

I reel back, amused by his jealousy. Of course that's the first place his mind would go.

"What's it to you, anyway?" I say, playing into it. "You broke up with me, remember?"

As soon as the words leave my mouth, regret grips my chest. I thought I was moving past him . . . *us* . . . so why does he still have this strong hold on me? Like a vise grip on my heart that I can't shake loose.

"I just want to talk," Jax says pleadingly.

A sigh pulls out of me. I click my phone on and check the time. If I give him time to explain himself, I know I'm going to be late to meet Dakota.

"*Please*, Sienna," he croaks, an unfamiliar desperation in his voice. The plea squeezes the vise tighter.

Today is going to be a good day without Jax . . .

I slide my phone back into my pocket and lean my body against the dining table, sighing in resignation as I wait for him to speak. "Fine. What do you want?"

Jax takes the cue. "Look, I would've come sooner, but I had to deal with this whole Charles situation. They've set his court date for next week, and it looks like I'll have to testify."

"So he'll go back to prison?"

"Probably." He shrugs. "Assaulting his stepson a week after being released from prison is a violation of his parole, not to mention an indication that he's not exactly rehabilitated."

I should just leave it at that, but when it strikes me how uncomfortable he looks talking about this recent development with Charles, I whisper, "How do you feel about all of it?"

Jax bites down on his bottom lip, like he'd rather not go there. But after a few moments, he relents.

"Relieved. For the most part."

"But you also feel sad," I add softly, noting the somber tone in his voice.

Jax gives a slow shrug and looks down, as if the floor has suddenly captured his attention. "It's funny, I spent so much time hating his guts . . . but now a part of me wishes we could start over." He looks embarrassed to admit it out loud.

"I know how that feels," I say with genuine empathy.

Jax's expression turns serious when he glances back up at me. "Look, after that night with Charles, I had some time to think about us. About how terrible we've been to each other. And I realize a lot of it was my fault. As much as I didn't want to go back there, into the past, I'm actually happy that you know, Sienna. I'm sorry I wasn't the one to come clean to you about Charles and the rest of it," he says, repenting. It's hard to believe this is the same Jax standing in front of me, the one whose arrogance and outsize ego would never allow him to make such an admission.

Today is going to be a good day without Jax . . .

He steps toward me, our feet bumping against each other.

"I love you, Sienna. We're so alike sometimes, it's scary. And I know the crazy capacity we have to hurt each other. But I also know that what we have is just too fucking special to let go of. And I want to be better. For you."

I can't help the humorless laugh that spills out of me. "That's what you said last time, Jax. That you were gonna change and be better and all that bullshit. Why should I trust that this time will be any different?"

"Because I've never been okay with being vulnerable. And it scared me, because if there was anyone who could get in, it was you," he says with a candor that's refreshing. "I'm sorry, princess," he murmurs, sweeping me into his arms and burying his face in the crook of my neck. "I'm so sorry for everything."

I sigh into him, letting myself dissolve into his embrace. This is all I ever wanted, for him to be honest about how he was feeling, to apologize for what he put me through. My dad refused to change for my mom. And he ruined her.

Jax is standing here, ready to change. For me. For us.

We'll be better than my parents. We'll do better than they ever could.

We'll fight hard for this. Especially when everything is dark and grim and all hope seems lost. That's when we'll fight the hardest.

My body slackens against Jax. "I'm sorry too," I murmur into Jax's shoulder. "For breaking your trust."

"Can we start over?" Jax whispers into my hair.

I nod slowly.

When Jax's lips move over mine, I part them for him. A bit at first, then eagerly as my body remembers the taste of him. He groans into my mouth when our tongues meet.

Today was going to be a good day without Jax . . .

But it's better day with him.

"I've missed you so fucking much, princess, you have no idea," he says huskily, dragging his lips to my ear.

"Tell me you love me," I say as Jax peppers my face with kisses.

"I love you," he rasps against my lips. The weight lifts from my shoulders as he repeats the words over and over again.

"Tell me you'll never lie to me."

"I won't."

"Promise me we won't fight again."

"We won't," he says, claiming my lips again. "From now on, we'll be perfect."

And as he carries me into my room and lays me down on my bed, peeling off my clothes and covering my body with his, I truly believe we will be. I believe every kiss, every touch, every stroke as he maneuvers himself inside me, fusing our bodies together as one.

ACKNOWLEDGMENTS

This book wouldn't have been possible without the entire Wattpad Books team. Rebecca Sands, my editor—thank you for being so patient with me while I brainstormed the craziest ideas with you. This was a difficult book to adapt from the Wattpad version, and I'm glad we did it! Also a huge thanks to Prakriti Tandon. You have been such a force in shaping this manuscript into what I'd truly envisioned it to be. Thanks for taking on this project at the last minute. Thank you to Deanna McFadden, as well, for believing in the Perfect series.

To my parents, thank you for supporting my dreams to become an author. Without you guys cheering me on, I don't think I'd be on this journey that I am on today. To Nicole, you are my OG. My day one. My very first commenter on Wattpad. I love you, and I cannot imagine life without you and your constant support. To Irwin, you already know how much I love you. Thanks for being an incredibly patient and loving boyfriend who soothes me when I get panicky about getting stuck on a chapter, and for helping me edit the fight scenes. FS Cheng, thank you for always helping me fact-check my MMA. You are an incredible Muay Thai trainer.

And of course, last but never least, my lovely Wattpad readers. You guys are the reason I keep going! Thank you for keeping the Perfect series in your hearts. The publication of the series would not be possible without you. I love each and every single one of you.

Now, onto Jax's story . . . The best is yet to come.

ABOUT THE AUTHOR

Claudia Tan is a new adult romance writer. She graduated from Lancaster University with a BA in English literature and history. Her massively popular Perfect series is a two-time Watty Award winner and has accumulated over 160 million reads on Wattpad. The series has also been published in French by Hachette Romans. *Perfect Addiction* was released by W by Wattpad Books in 2022 and is now being adapted into a major motion picture with Wattpad WEBTOON Studios and Constantin Film.

Are you ready for the final installment of
THE PERFECT SERIES?

PERFECT REDEMPTION

The **PERFECT** *Series*

CLAUDIA TAN

w

COMING JULY 2024